# Candy Coated
# CHAOS

*Sweet Treats*
Book One

*Jamie,
Thank you so
much for all your
support I love you
and I hope you enjoy
the journey Stay
Sweet!
- Charity B.*

# CHARITY B.

Editor: Joanne LaRe Thompson
Cover Design: Murphy Hopkins
Formatting: Champagne Book Design

# Author's Note

First of all, thank you so much for reading my debut novel. Please be aware that this is the first book in a three part series and does end in a cliffhanger. As the story goes on, it gets very dark and contains most triggers, so if you are a sensitive reader, know what you are getting into.

I hope you enjoy this story as much as I loved writing it.

**Trigger Warning**
This novel contains drug use, explicit sexual content, violence, and sensitive subject matter which may be triggering to some readers.

# Dedication

To Mom and sister, Kristin: I know you would have been my biggest fans. If you could see me now, I know you would be proud that I followed my dreams. You both believed in me and I will never forget it. I love you and I miss you both every single day. I understand more than ever, how lucky I truly was.

She was delightfully chaotic; a beautiful mess.
—*Steve Maraboli*

# CHAPTER ONE
## *Lollipop*

*Monday, April 20th*

*Alexander*

D AMN. THE BOTTLE-BLONDE THAT JUST GOT IN THE elevator is hot as hell. She presses the button for her floor and I lean back to properly check out her ass. Oh yes, very nice. Moving my suit sleeve, I look at the time… ten thirty. As I glance up, I see large, possibly fake breasts fighting to be contained in what can hardly be called a shirt. Her pencil skirt shows nice calves and I can't keep myself from picturing those black pumps wrapped around my neck.

"Hi." The word rumbles from my throat deeper than I intend in the small space.

Looking up at me, she smiles. "Hello." Her attention shifts to the light tan Burberry bag hanging from her shoulder as she pulls out some papers and sighs. "I need to have this report to my boss by lunch and it's nowhere near finished."

I flash her a quick smile and point to my name next to *CEO* and the Vulture Theaters logo at the top of the page. "Make sure to put a line through the *O* in my last name."

Her eyes bug out a bit as she gasps, "You're Alexander Sørensen? It's so nice to meet you!"

I take the papers from her hand. "How about this? Come to my office and we'll go over these? And don't worry about your boss. I'll talk to him if you have any issues."

She bats her eyelashes and smiles. "Thank you. That would be wonderful."

Her finished report and our empty bourbon glasses are moving across my desk with every one of my thrusts. I hold her wrist so she doesn't knock anything off and I'm fighting the urge to reach around and cover her mouth with my free hand.

I press my chest to her back and murmur in her ear, "You really need to keep it down."

"Then you really need to ease up." She moans, "You're not exactly packin' light ya know."

The corner of my mouth lifts into a smirk as I flip her over to her back. The indentations from where my desk dug into her skin are marking her pelvis and I trace my thumb across the red lines, when a knock causes my head to jerk up to the door.

I completely stop, hold my finger to my lips, and slide out. The girl nods with a pout as I pull my pants back on. Combing my fingers through my hair, I smooth out the pale strands and try to straighten myself up as much as possible before I open my office door.

It's barely cracked open enough to allow me to stand in the space and hide the naked woman in my office. Immediately, I'm required to look down, and when I do, I'm staring at the top of a girl's head with chocolate hair that falls halfway down her back. Her fingers are wrapped around a lollipop that she's clearly been working on for a while because there's barely any left. When her head leans back and she looks up at me, all I see is bright violet eyes under wispy bangs.

Her stare sucks the air from my lungs and I have to consciously remember to breathe until her eyes shift to the nameplate by my door.

She's short and skinny. I love the small ones and she's fucking tiny. However, it's her face I can't take my eyes from. Her cheeks look so soft, I have to fight the urge to reach out and rub my fingers over them.

Her eyes widen before she squeezes them shut. She jerks her head as she whispers, "Shit."

Looking in every direction other than at me, she's clearly not sure of what to do. She's so cute in her confusion, I can't stop myself from grinning in amusement.

"Can I help you?"

Her eyes flip to mine and the hollowness in them takes me aback. She's the living definition of a tragic beauty.

Stepping away, she holds up her hands as if I pulled a gun on her. "Oh no, uh… I'm sorry."

Her voice is soft and raspy and seriously the sexiest thing I have ever heard. If I wasn't hard before, I sure as hell am now. She spins on her heel and snaps her eyes to the slate-gray floor as she speed-walks to the next door. Being in an office building, she stands out in her flip-flops, skinny jeans, and sheer bohemian shirt.

After pausing to read Silas' nameplate, she shakes her head and continues walking to Eric's office. She looks back to the receptionist as she throws away the sucker and lifts a balled fist to knock on his door.

I fight the urge to laugh. What exactly is she doing?

The girl on my desk whispers behind me, "Is everything alright?"

Shit. I somehow forgot about her. Closing the door, I

don't even make it back to my desk before there's another knock.

Silas' mop of jet black hair pops in. "Oh damn. I didn't realize you were with someone." He winks at her and grins at me.

Nodding my head, I gesture for him to get out. He chuckles and closes the door as I turn to the blonde.

"Hey, I need to get back to work, but if Mr. Walt has any issues with these," I hand the papers back to her, "send him to me."

She cocks her head to the side and takes them. "Oh, yeah, uh thanks."

I wait for her to be completely clothed before I open the door. "Have a good rest of your day."

Pausing for a moment on my threshold, she nods. "Yeah sure, you too Mr. Sørensen."

Silas stares at her ass while she waits for the elevator. "You done with that?"

I shrug as he follows me back into my office and I straighten up my desk. "So what's up?"

Plopping down in the leather chair in front of me, he crosses his arms. "I was wrong about the cotton candy bar." I glare at him as he props his shiny black shoes on my desk. "It's surprisingly lucrative. The top selling flavor is, get this shit: bacon." He shudders. "God that's disgusting."

I shove his feet off as I get up to go to the minibar.

The glasses clank when I pull them off the bar and grab a bottle. "Hey, did you ever get the chance to read over my proposal for V sports?"

He grins and nods. "I love it. Other than the fact that Jefferson might need some convincing, and there will be some insurance issues we'll need to work out, I think it's the perfect next step."

I look to the clock above the yellow Vulture Theaters

logo on my screen and ask him, "So are we going out tonight or what?"

I hand him his scotch, down mine, and grab my keys while he's tearing off his tie.

"Hell yes we are."

Dinner smells incredible as I walk through the sunlit entryway to my kitchen.

Cara Jo shakes some spices into a pan and adjusts the knobs on the stove. "Hello, Alex. Did you have a good day?"

"I did, thanks." My keys jangle as I toss them into the bowl on the side table. "How much longer until dinner is ready?"

"How much longer until you stop letting your little lady friends leave their underclothes for me to clean up?" She whips her silver haired head around, points the spatula at me, and stares me down with narrowed blue eyes. "I found another thong."

I laugh as I give her a side hug and a kiss on the temple.

"Sorry about that." Scrunching my nose and holding up two fingers, I add, "Though to be fair, it was two lady friends, so I at least got one of them to grab their shit."

"Uh huh."

Growing up, Cara Jo was mine and my twin sister's nanny until we were thirteen and then stayed on as help until we graduated high school. She was present at every award ceremony, every game, and every graduation. Four years ago, I bought this house and asked her to work for me. She's too good to me. I know it and I love her like a mother.

I smirk at her. "I have some work to do in my office. Will you come get me when the food is done?"

She nods and I head upstairs to look through the newest reports. Let's just hope they are as great as last month's.

Staring at a computer screen all day makes my eyes tired. I keep spinning my pen in my hand and I try to concentrate on the benefits of a new location in Reno, as my mind keeps wandering to the little thing with the candy, from this morning. She looked so heartbroken and so breathtaking at the same time. I'm kicking myself for not asking for her number. Though to be fair, I had been a bit preoccupied at the time.

Who knows, maybe I'll see her again

### Sunday, April 26th

On my way home from Benny's Boxing Gym, I stop by my parents' estate. Bridget, one of the maids, informs me that my dad is away on business, and my mother is in the garden. I walk outside through the lush green archway peppered in purple flowers and see my mother next to her prized tulips. She looks just as she always has in an expensive dress, a large sun hat, and the ever present drink in her hand.

"Alexander, I wasn't expecting you."

The irritation in her voice from my failure to call doesn't go unnoticed, just ignored. She stands, and her long blonde hair drapes over her shoulders. Her slender figure and taut features are made more severe with age, and regardless, I still think she's beautiful.

"Hey, Mom." She allows me a small kiss to her cheek before she leads me to the round iron table where she holds her tea times and brunches.

She sighs, "Well, since you are here, you might as well eat lunch."

"It's so good to see you too."

The sarcasm is lost on her as she sips her drink. "Hmm." My mother has always been somewhat cold. While I have grown accustomed to her lack of affection, there have been times when I really needed it from her.

*Eleven years ago...*

*Her soft taps on the door automatically make my eyes roll. I can't believe Cara Jo sent my mother after me.*

*"Alexander? Cara Jo said you won't come down and dinner is in twenty minutes." She slowly walks into my room. "Our guests will arrive at any moment."*

*Why can't they leave me alone? I just want everyone to leave me alone.*

*"Mom, seriously, let me skip it. Please?"*

*She sits on my bed and her eyes look like she cares, however the fact that she can't force herself to give me a hug, even now, makes it impossible for me not to question it.*

*"I know you are struggling dear, but you have been in here for days."*

*Struggling? Yeah you could say that. Every time I think about it, it feels as if it's choking me. I want to yell and hit something. I want to hurt Carrie like she hurt me. I want to weep at everything I've lost. I'm just so... sad.*

*The need to cry climbs up my throat.*

*"How could she do it? How could she do that to me?"*

*The tears have too much force and they burst from my eyes. This hurts so much.*

*She stands and smooths her skirt with the hand not holding her glass. "I need you downstairs and presentable in twenty minutes."*

*I'm angry. I'm angry at Carrie for being so selfish. I hate her for lying to me and I hate her for making me feel this way. How am I ever supposed to be able to trust anyone again? I loved her and trusted her more than anyone, besides Sasha. I told her everything, and she threw it all in my face. I'm angry at my mother for never understanding or backing up Sasha and I. And I'm angry that she won't just let me skip this stupid dinner!*

*I jump off the bed to face her.* "Jesus, why can't you be my mother for just one second? Cara Jo has done it for you our entire lives. Put the fucking drink down and listen to me for once!"

*I hear it before I feel it. The hot sting begins to blossom across my face.*

"Skjerp deg! You are not a child any longer so do not throw a tantrum like one. It's time to pull yourself together, clean yourself up, get dressed, and get your ass downstairs. Adult decisions have adult consequences, Alexander."

*Nobody understands. Nobody really gets it. As much as Cara Jo and Sasha try, they don't feel this.*

*She wants me to man-up and pretend everything is okay when I'm heartbroken? Pretend that I'm not a shattered mess inside? Fine. She just lost any chance of me ever trying to open up to her again.*

"Yes ma'am."

*She walks away and I allow myself to fall to my bed and drop my face in my hands. Sorrow is exhausting.*

"Carrie handled the situation poorly. I am sorry for that." *I look up to see her standing in the doorway with her back to me.* "I love you, Alexander, and it does hurt me to see you in pain."

*She disappears from my threshold and I take a deep breath to mentally prepare for my performance.*

"I love you too, Mom."

My mother's favorite servant serves us lunch as she asks the same question she has every time I've come over the last few months.

"Have you talked to your sister recently?"

Her thick Norwegian accent is dripping with accusation.

"Christ. No, Mom, you know that I haven't."

"You really need to let all that go, dear." She waves it off as she takes a drink.

"Let it go? Are you serious? She stole Aslaug's tiara and sold it for drug money. That isn't something I'm just going to 'let go.'"

"I do wish you wouldn't have named her," she dabs her perfectly painted lips with a handkerchief, "especially after your *Mormor*."

I still don't see how she doesn't understand. She's a mother for Christ's sake.

"Yeah I know, you've made that clear."

"Oh darling, it was nearly three years ago and she has been clean for almost two now. Don't you think it's time to take the hatchet to the grave yard?"

My parents moved to the States from Norway, before my sister and I were born, and for some reason she still confuses some common phrases.

I laugh, "You mean bury the hatchet, Mom. It's bury the hatchet, and I tried to help. You know that. I'm the one who paid for her rehab when you guys cut her off, remember?"

Our trust funds were supposed to be given to us on our twenty-fifth birthday. Mine was, however Sasha was so strung out, there was no way my parents were giving her that kind of cash. They still haven't relinquished it to her.

"Oh don't be so melodramatic. I know for a fact your father was giving her money the whole time, and it all went into her arm. So she was hardly 'cut off.'"

"Regardless, I said some cruel things to her when she tried to reconcile. She doesn't want to talk to me either."

"You came into this world together, Alexander. Most people have to do that alone. I know you two sometimes clash, as well as you mesh, nevertheless I am leaving it up to you to fix this."

I roll my eyes. "Yeah, okay, Mom."


### Friday, May 1st

I've come to the conclusion that the lollipop girl was probably interviewing for Eric's assistant position. He goes through them at an alarmingly fast rate. Considering I haven't seen her again and it's been almost two weeks, I can safely assume she didn't get the job. I look at my alarm and it's about to go off.

The girl from last night, whose name evades me, mumbles in her sleep.

"Hey," I smack her ass to wake her up. "You need to go. I have to get ready for work."

She props herself on her elbow and rubs her fingers down my arm. "What about breakfast?"

"No breakfast."

Pulling back, she kind of huffs. "Well, do you want my number?"

"Not really."

"Wow. Seriously?"

They always want to make me out to be this huge dick, but watch this:

"I'll make you a deal. Tell me what my name is within three tries and we'll go out again. Oh, and I'll even give you a hint: it isn't God, despite what you kept screaming last night."

"Andrew?"

She sits up and her tits bounce with the action. I'm pretty impressed she got the *A* right.

"Nope."

"Adam?"

"No."

"Um…Kevin?"

"Kevin? Where the hell did that one come from?"

She sighs and without another word, dresses and walks out the door. Yeah, that's what I thought.

As I leave my room to go run in my gym, I pass Cara Jo smiling at me in the hall. "Good morning, Alex. Is there anything special you want me to make you for breakfast?"

"No thank you. I'm just going to have some Mateys."

Marshmallow Mateys is the off brand version of Lucky Charms. I think it tastes so much better, and the industrial sized bag it comes in lasts me weeks.

"Alright," She shuffles past with a basket full of towels. "Is your guest staying for breakfast?"

I snort, "Uh, no."

Shaking her head, she keeps walking. "That's the third one this week Alexander."

I can't retort without yelling because she's already half-way down the stairs. Yeah sure, she's nice and fucking speedy when she wants to be.

I drink my bourbon as I look through the V Bar's sales reports. We have been nearly doubling last year's revenue for the past three months. The V Bar and Grill is the restaurant inside a large portion of our theaters. All the food names are corny, such as The 'Breakfast Club' sandwich, and the waitresses dress as slutty versions of popular movie characters. Just last month at the east side location, I had a threesome with Hermione Granger and Mary Poppins. True story.

My eyes shift to the clock at the bottom of the screen and it's already after one. I shut down my computer and grab my jacket as I leave. Turning the key to lock my door, I glance up and I can't believe my breath actually hitches.

It's the lollipop girl.

Her hair is down in brown waves. The short vintage dress she wears has a peter pan collar and God freaking help me. She's wearing gray wool knee highs.

Oh yeah, I have a major hard on for stockings.

Eric's hands are gripping his office door frame as his brows pinch together and he murmurs through clenched teeth. She has her hands tucked in her dress pockets as she nods at whatever he's saying. Is he yelling at her? He takes a sucker from his pocket and when he holds it out in front of her, she snatches it from his hand. His door slams in her face and she doesn't look at me when she tosses the candy wrapper in the trash. She pulls down a pair of huge sunglasses, sticks the lollipop in her mouth, and bee-lines for the elevator.

This is the ideal opportunity to talk to her.

I slide in after her and she lifts her head as she takes the candy from her mouth. The doors close, and when I look down, I try not to smile at the fact her head barely comes to my chest. I bet she isn't even five feet tall.

"Hi."

"Oh…uh, hi." She speaks softly.

God she smells good. It's subtle and reminds me of almond oil. I'm going to need this one back in my office immediately.

Just as I open my mouth, I realize I don't really want her to be a quick in-out. She makes me curious and I kind of want to hear that voice telling me things before it begs for my cock.

"I'm on my way to grab a coffee. Would you like to join me?"

Her eyebrows rise above her sunglasses and she smiles

while a dark laugh creeps from her lips.

"Oh no, no, no, you don't want that." She's shaking her head and crossing her arms.

Jesus, her voice is an aphrodisiac, though her response isn't what I expected.

I let out a half chuckle, "How could you possibly know that?"

She sniffs and her head makes a little jerk as she holds out her hand to emphasize her point.

"Just trust me."

I do laugh then. She is trying so hard to be deterring only to achieve the opposite effect.

"Well now I'm intrigued." Turning my body, I face her. "Go out with me tonight. At least let me decide for myself."

She looks away, but not enough for me to miss the smile she's trying to hide. My eye catches something. Is that... blood? Her forehead is cut above her right eyebrow, so I reach my finger out to wipe away the crimson.

"Are you alright? You're bleeding."

As soon as my touch makes contact with her skin she flinches away from me. Putting her hand to her head, she sees the blood when she wipes it. Did Eric do this to her?

I ask her again, "Are you okay?"

"Oh yeah, I'm fine, um...thanks though."

The elevator dings. My window of time is coming to an end. She's fidgety and keeps almost putting the lollipop back in her mouth before deciding against it.

"Do you know where The Necco Room is? Say... ten o'clock tonight?" I ask.

I'm having to rush this and she won't even look at me.

She shakes her head and sighs, "The Necco Room, ten o'clock."

Is that a yes? She steps out of the elevator and is on her way out without a backward glance.

My hands hold open the door. "Wait! What's your name?"

She turns back and smirks. "I'm Tavin, Tavin Winters."

Tavin. I definitely don't hate her name, and it's cute she told me all of it.

"It's nice to meet you, Tavin. My name is Alexander. I look forward to tonight..." I nod my head toward her legs, "and wear the knee highs."

She slides the candy in between her lips and spins around to leave.

# CHAPTER TWO
## *Carnival*

I ARRIVE AT THE NECCO ROOM AT 9:51 P.M. AND SIT AT the bar. Ordering a shot of bourbon, I kill time on my phone while I wait for her. When I look at the clock again, it shows fifteen after ten.

Holy shit. Am I being stood up?

This has never happened to me before and I'm not at all impressed. Still, I can't bring myself to lift my ass off the seat. Maybe she's just running late or got lost. We never exchanged numbers so she has no way of getting a hold of me. Another five minutes pass before I cut my losses and salvage my remaining pride. I hand the bartender his tip and slide off the leather bar stool as I slip my phone into my pocket. Just as I turn around to leave, I see her.

She's here, and it relieves me more than it should.

The cream sweater she's wearing is loosely knit, just not quite enough to see through. I think she's crazy for sporting a sweater in May, regardless, she's paired it with a flowy, short, ivory skirt that is trimmed in lace and has a slit up her right thigh. Doing as I requested, she's wearing the gray knee highs and her hair is down in long, loose curls. She looks incredible.

As she passes an empty table, she reaches for a shot glass

and throws it back…She seriously just drank some random person's drink. Who does that? Our eyes make contact seconds later, and we don't break it as she makes her way to me.

"Hi," she murmurs as she tucks her hair behind her ear with one hand and waves awkwardly with the other.

I know I'm not being subtle about looking her up and down, but Jesus.

"Hi."

She seems shy. I'm not used to that. Not that I'm not into the innocent thing, I most definitely am, however the girls I usually seem to end up with are… how do I say this nicely? Well, they're experienced and they're anything other than shy.

"Do you want a drink?"

Her eyes meet mine. "Yes, Alexander."

Whoa. Okay, two things. First, the way she said that was mechanical as hell, and honestly, a little weird. Second, hearing her voice around my name is so much sexier than I imagined.

"What do you want?" I ask.

Her big eyes widen and her head kind of moves.

"What?!"

I'm having to put some actual effort into not laughing. The poor girl is a bit deer-in-the-headlights.

"To drink?"

She relaxes for just a moment before she begins to fidget with her sleeves and looks over her shoulder.

"Oh yeah, um, whatever will fuck me up."

Her cheeks flush and my laugh breaks free. Definitely not the answer I thought I'd hear. The word 'fuck' has never sounded so damn cute.

"Well okay then." She's clearly anxious the way she keeps looking around the bar. "Why don't you pick a seat and I'll bring over our drinks."

"Yes Ale- uh… okay."

Her face brightens again before she spins around to pick a table. This one is definitely going to be entertaining.

After ordering, I bring our drinks to the secluded table she picks and place hers in front of her.

"Bourbon. One-thirty proof. Guaranteed to fuck you up."

Hopefully it does too, she's too tense. I smile at her as I slide into the booth.

Both hands wrap around her glass before she takes a drink. "That's great… thank you."

Not that it really matters, still, part of me wants them to be real so I ask, "Are those your natural eyes or are they contacts?"

Tucking her hair behind an ear, she sort of smiles. "They're natural." She takes another drink of her bourbon and rubs her nose. She reminds me of Audrey Hepburn in some ways. She would make a killer Holly Golightly at the V Bar downtown.

"What do you do for a living?"

She momentarily stills before looking around again as if she's waiting for someone. "Oh you know, a little of this, some of that." She waves her hand without looking at me. What kind of answer is that? Vague responses are a little too close to lies for my liking. Finally, she turns to me. "So do you come to bars like this a lot?"

I laugh. Cheesy pick-up lines always make me think of the summer I turned twenty-two. I made a bet with Silas that I could still get girls by using only bad one-liners, for an entire month no less. My personal favorite? When you pretend to lick your finger, touch a girl's shirt and say: *Let's get you out of those wet clothes.* You would be shocked at how often it actually worked. It was still a dry month though.

"Are you asking me if I come here often?" I tease her. If

her facial expression is any indication, she has no idea what I'm talking about so I clear my throat, "Yeah, a few times a week." Her eyes make their way to my half sleeve tattoo, curiosity blooming across her features making her look even softer.

Shifting around, she tugs on her sleeve again. She looks like she's about to jump from her seat. Christ, I wonder if she'll relax when I put my tongue between her legs.

Once again, she is staring around the bar, and it's kind of starting to drive me up the damn wall.

"Tavin." She snaps her head in my direction and I gesture to her bourbon. "Do you want another?"

"Yes…" Again with the looking around. "Um, where are the restrooms?"

Exhaling away my irritation at her lack of attention, I point to show her. "There's a hallway behind the bar, right back there."

She nods. "I'll be right back."

My cheeks puff out with my sigh as she walks away. How do I get this chick to chill?

I get us more drinks and place them on the table when I turn to see her determined face as she tramps back. She marches right by me and climbs up to stand on the booth seat. Before I know what's happening, she takes my face in-between her little hands and kisses me. This isn't a sweet, gentle kiss either, oh no. Her tongue is caressing mine, fingers tangle in my hair, and her soft lips press fiercely against me. My body is simultaneously hot and cold as I bring my hands around her tiny ribs. She tastes of honey with a hint of the bourbon and I almost wish we weren't drinking so I could taste only her. The room is somehow silent, the only sound is my heart beating. When she pulls back, her eyes are wild and her fingers softly touch her lips with pale purple painted fingernails.

The noise around us begins again as she climbs down to pick up her drink. The tumbler is empty when she places it back on the table.

"Why don't you finish that," she points to my still full glass, "and then we can dance."

Okay... that's a complete one-eighty.

I barely finish my drink before her hand wraps around mine and pulls me to the dance floor. She dances as if she's alone and I love it, losing herself in whatever song is playing.

She's can't be more than ninety pounds soaking wet, and I swear to God, after four shots she isn't even tipsy. I on the other hand, am starting to feel pretty damn buzzed. During this glorious moment, my hands are on her little hips trying desperately to not move them to touch her ass. She really could use one of Cara Jo's steaks. She's a skinny little thing.

"Do you want to take a break?"

I'm right next to her ear to make sure she can hear me. The place has gotten packed in the last couple of hours. She leans her head back so her lips are close enough for me to hear.

"Whatever you want, Alexander."

My heart punches my chest. I thought hearing her say my name before was hot. Something about hearing it inside of that sentence makes me so hard I have to adjust my body so she doesn't feel it.

She says she needs to stop at the bathroom, and as I'm waiting on her to get back, I check the time. When I look up, I see her walking back and our eyes meet again, forcing smiles from each other. There have been more than a few of those little moments tonight.

"What do you say we hit another bar? There are a ton of them on this street." I don't know why I suggest it. All I really want to do is go home and hear that voice moaning my name.

She smiles and nods. "Let's go."

I hold her hand as we walk down the street and look for a promising bar. Flashing lights in my peripheral make me turn, and I see a street carnival. When I look down at her, she's gawking. Her eyes are all lit up and it's painfully obvious that she is dying to go.

"What do you say we go check that out?" I offer.

For the first time she smiles a genuine, full on smile. She clasps her hands together and I swear her eyes get bigger.

"Really?!"

Her comical enthusiasm forces me to chuckle. "Of course."

After nearly getting my arm yanked from its socket, she pulls me to the ticket counter while her eyes scan feverishly.

I gesture to our many choices. "Where to?"

Even as I ask, I know she has no idea. You would think she's never seen a carnival in her life. She's about to burst. As she starts to head in one direction, something else will catch her eye, changing her trajectory.

"I- uh. Well, um…"

I take her hand to lace my fingers between hers. "We'll get to all of it, I promise. How about we start with the tilt-a-whirl?" I point next to the fresh squeezed lemonade stand. "That was always my favorite as a kid."

She has the sweetest little dimple on her right cheek that appears with her grin and she nods. I don't know her well enough to tease her when she walks past the '*You must be this tall to ride this ride*' sign, but I chuckle at the fact she is passable by less than two inches.

She picks the pink cart and we climb inside. Bouncing with anticipation, she grips my hand while the technician locks the bar. Once the ride begins to really get going, our cart makes its first fast spin and she throws her head back and laughs. It is such a pretty sound, a true laugh filled with abandon. She giggles the entire time, squealing at every spin. Her excitement is contagious and after it's over, I run right along with her, hand in hand to the big slide.

We race down a few times, although the word 'race' is a bit of a stretch. She is too light and can't gain enough speed. She wants to beat me so bad, it's just never going to happen.

"Will you ride with me?" I think she's talking to me, until I see she is looking up at the idiot in line with her. My initial reaction is to get pissed and immediately I chastise myself because that's absolutely ridiculous. She grins at me. "I want to win."

Well of course I can't deny her that, even if the asshole she asks is a bit too happy to oblige.

Once she finally gets her wish, I take her to the carousel. She's been staring at it since we got here.

We choose a decorative carriage seat, slowly moving up and down next to intricately carved horses as the ride circles. I look down and her thighs are so sexy, barely parted, with the hems of her stockings peeking over her knees. "It's been so long since I've been to one of these places," I tell her as I take the initiative and place my hand on her thigh. She doesn't flinch or acknowledge that I'm touching her at all.

"I've never been." Her eyes are still absorbing the scene around us, apparently for the first time.

"Never?" She shakes her head and I move my hand a little higher. "So how do you know Eric?"

Her face pales before she blinks a few times and chews on her lip. "Oh… um, he's just… an acquaintance."

Another blanket response. I don't want to push the subject because tonight is going so well, incredible, actually. Nevertheless, at some point I'm going to need to find out what she's doing with him in my building.

I tuck a curled piece of hair behind her ear to see her

stunning profile. The ride begins to slow so I change the subject.

"Do you like cotton candy?"

She snaps her head up to look at me as her entire face brightens. "*Cotton* candy? I've never tried it."

What a deprived life to have never had cotton candy. "Do you want to?"

Not that I need to ask, she clearly does.

"Very much."

We watch as the carnie turns the sugary strings into a fluffy pink ball. When it's finished, he hands it to her and she tilts her head as she pokes at it.

"Take a bite," I urge her.

She pulls off a piece and the moment the flavor hits her tongue, her face is hilarious. Her eyes go wide and she rips away another large piece and shoves it into her open mouth. I laugh at her enthusiasm as I order a lemonade from the carnie. When I turn around to offer her a drink, the paper handle is bare and she is licking the cotton candy remnants off her fingers.

Good thing I didn't want any.

"Good huh?" I laugh at her as I lead her to the scramblers.

We ride every single ride and a few of them twice. I'm literally having more fun than I think I have ever had on a date. In fact, I don't remember having fun, real honest to God fun, in a long time.

We pass by a line of game booths. Isn't it a rule or something that if you take a girl to a carnival you have to win her a cheap toy?

I gesture to the wall of stuffed monstrosities. "Which one do you want?"

She immediately points to a pink and purple dragon. "That one."

"One girly-ass dragon coming up."

It takes me three tries. When I hand it to her, her lips lift at the corners, yet when she looks up at me, her eyes are sad, making them sparkle as the lights shine against her unfallen tears. "Thank you, Alexander."

I want to kiss away her sorrow. As I lean in, the little girl next to us begins to cry.

Looking over to them, I see her mother is red with embarrassment. "I'm sorry, Annabel. I wish I could let you play all day, I just can't afford any more games."

"Mommy, please? I tried so hard, I know I can do it! Please?"

When I look down at Tavin, she's staring at the girl, clearly feeling sorry for her as she glances at her dragon then back at the child. Awe, that's sweet. She wants to give her the toy.

Tucking her hair behind her ear I whisper, "I swear I'll win you another one."

When she looks up at me all traces of melancholy are gone. She smiles as she hands the dragon to the girl. "Do you want this one?"

The little girl immediately stops crying and takes the toy and smiles with missing teeth. "Thank you."

The mother nods her thanks and as they leave, I turn back to the game to get another toy.

After the fifth lost game, I'm actually starting to get a little pissed. It should not be this difficult to knock over clay bottles with a stupid wooden ball.

I turn to the carnie and whisper, "Just let me buy the fucking dragon."

"But you said you would win me another one, not buy it," she pipes up with a grin.

Damn it.

Apparently my struggle with this dumb game is hilarious because she's laughing so hard she is holding her stomach.

Finally, she grabs my hand. "I honestly don't care about the dragon, let's go ride more rides."

She is amazing. Her anxiety from earlier is a distant memory as she pulls me around the carnival. In fact, she seems completely at ease. Her smile is constantly gracing her angelic face and I've had the pleasure of hearing her cute little laugh all night.

Holding hands as we look for our next adventure, she points, "Let's go to the Wacky House!"

She hauls us inside and as soon as we cross the threshold, she tumbles into me. I catch her so she doesn't fall to the floor as she laughs and covers her mouth.

"You got it?" I chuckle at her.

Her cheeks are pink when she nods in response. The floor is slanted, designed to throw off your equilibrium and the furniture is glued to the walls and ceiling, adding to the effect. I take her hand to lead her down a hallway with an array of tricks and illusions decorating the walls.

She's staring at a box that appears to have a diamond inside. The glass is broken on the box, so it looks as though you can just put a hand inside and grab the jewel. I nod for her to try. She reaches in and her eyebrows scrunch together in the most adorable way when she realizes there isn't a diamond at all, merely a reflection of one. When the fake alarm goes off, she jumps backwards and laughs. She is still smiling when she turns her head to look at me.

Then she winks.

I know she is just trying to be cute and flirty, but she might as well have taken her shirt off. It's that sexy. I grab her wrist, pull her to the door at the end of the hall, and push her through. My intentions are sidetracked for a moment when I see we are in a room of mirrors. Everywhere I look, there she is.

"Whoa, this is trippy!" She turns to look at me, her curls

bouncing, eyes sparkling, and her mouth seducing me.

I pounce on the poor girl. I have her up against the mirrored wall kissing her with barely contained aggression. She gasps in surprise as her hands tangle in my hair once again, tugging gently. I move one hand to the nape of her neck and the other against the inside of her thigh. Her smell fuels my lust while my fingers slowly trail up her skirt. When I feel the lace of her panties, I see our reflection in the wall and we look incredible together. I apply extremely soft touches over what I believe are boy shorts, until she begins a subtle rock toward me. I pull them to the side, and when my finger barely touches her slit, her body goes rigid.

"No," she whispers against my lips.

Fuck. Seriously?

I guess I am kind of an asshole for assuming every girl is going to take it on the first date. I remove my hand from beneath her skirt and back off. "Shit, I'm sorry—"

When I meet her eyes, she looks all confused. "No, don't stop...I... that wasn't a no..."

What is that supposed to mean?

"That most definitely was a fucking no."

"I...I didn't mean it."

Her shoulders sag and she rubs her arm as she looks at me with pleading eyes. The sadness is back in her demeanor as if she seriously doesn't want this to stop. Maybe that's a red flag and I'm probably a dick for still planning on tearing her up and I don't care. I want to destroy this girl. Bad. She just has to want it too.

I place a hand against the mirror on either side of her head to make sure she is looking at me and lean closer.

"I don't take pussy that isn't offered. If you want this to continue, you're going to have to make the next move."

Her cheeks flush and her breathing picks up when she barely nods and removes my hand from the mirror. It feels huge when she places it on her small thigh. I stay perfectly still, watching her bright eyes as she moves her panties. She holds on to my pointer finger and uses it to spread apart her lips allowing me to instantly feel how soaking wet she is.

That's all I need to know.

I smile as I take control of my own hand and she welcomes my touch with a clench. Leaning forward to press my forehead against hers, I slowly slide my drenched finger in and out. She never breaks eye contact until I slip in a second and give her clit some attention. God, I'm so hard, it's actually a little uncomfortable in these jeans. She's rocking onto my fingers and her eyelids start to drop a bit when she lets out a soft sound that's too quiet to be a moan. I want to taste her so bad and I'm fighting doing just that when the door at the end of the mirrored hall opens.

"Shit," I groan.

People are coming in so I grab her hand, pulling her to the opposite end and through the exit. Once we are outside, I can't stop my laugh as I run my hand through my hair. I feel like we just got busted making out like teenagers. Catching me by surprise, she pushes me up against the building, stands up on her tippy toes and tries to get to my mouth. I laugh to myself and help her out by lowering the rest of the way. Eventually, I pick her up so her legs wrap around my waist and flip our bodies so that she's the one against the wall. We kiss right there for at least ten minutes. It's becoming nearly impossible to not shove myself inside her and I don't want to do it here.

My hand covers her entire cheek as I rub the pad of my thumb over her soft flesh. "Come home with me."

She bites her lip and responds with nothing more than a nod and a slow release of breath. I take her hand as we walk to the valet at The Necco Room. My car gets pulled around and I keep waiting for her to make a big deal out of how nice the Alfa is. Apparently, I'll be waiting a while. Truth be told, that bruises my ego a smidge.

I get in after her and *Come as you are* is blaring out of the speakers so I quickly turn it down.

She is gaping at me. "You like Nirvana?"

"Oh yeah. You?"

She smiles and nods. "My best friend got so sick of this album."

I laugh at the coincidence. Silas is much more of a rap kind of guy.

"That's actually pretty funny, so did mine. He threatened breaking it on more than one occasion."

I pull out of the parking lot and into the street when she reaches across the console and presses her hand against my cock through my jeans.

Whoa! Well look at little Miss Initiative.

My erection moves in my jeans and by the time I realize what she's doing, she has my belt and fly undone. She begins to stroke me and I want to watch her. This is one of the few times I actually consider getting a driver. Her tiny hand doesn't reach all the way around and I can't help myself, I thrust up, fighting the urge to close my eyes. Without warning, her warm mouth is wrapped around me, sucking with force and nearly causing me to crash.

"Jesus!"

I would laugh if this didn't feel so damn good. I have no idea what to expect with this chick. She is incredible at this and honestly not at it that long before I feel my release build. I don't want to come yet, nevertheless I'm not going to be able to stop myself. I take my hand from the steering wheel and push her head down a little further, properly fucking her mouth. The street lights are shining in the car, giving me little glimpses of her lips, her bangs, and her eyelashes. She's so quiet, I don't think she gags once, and she's taking quite a bit.

"Okay, I'm gonna come."

I expect her to push against my hand to lift her head, instead she just goes further down. I groan as my skin crackles with my orgasm.

Sitting here in shock that she actually just did that, I watch her sit up and lick her bottom lip clean. Good God, you got to love a girl who swallows.

Her hands are folded in her lap until I reach across the car and up her skirt. She grasps my forearm as she rocks her pelvis against my hand and she's soaking wet, so I slide a couple fingers in. Soft, husky whimpers are the only sound as she moves her hand down my arm, grabs hold of my wrist, and pushes me in deeper.

The remainder of the drive seems to take forever and I practically drag her inside when we get to my house. Tossing my keys somewhere in the vicinity of the bowl, I press her up against the wall. With one hand bracing next to her head, I kiss up her neck as the fingers on my other hand find their way back inside her.

"Those raspy little moans of yours have me hard as fuck," I murmur against her skin as her broken breathing shudders in my ear.

I lace our fingers together and pull her up the stairs to my room. Flipping on the light, I turn on some music and tell myself to relax. I have no desire to rush through anything with this one.

Apparently, she has different plans. She releases my hand before feverishly ripping off her boots and is about to do the same with her skirt.

No and hell no. That pleasure is all mine.

"Whoa, slow down. There's no need to rush."

She completely stills as I comb my fingers through her hair. While I want to grab her face and crash my mouth against hers, I keep it sweet. Wrapping my arm around her waist, I lift her up and flush her short body against mine. She keeps her hands on my biceps as our lips meet and I savor the taste of her mouth. I let my fingers lightly fondle the lace hem of her skirt before gliding beneath it to gently squeeze and set her back down.

Her hands go straight to my zipper. God she's ready to get this going isn't she? I shake my head as I hold her wrists and bring them to my waist.

"No. Be patient."

She tilts her head, perplexed. "Yes, Alexan-...okay." Her eyes close in embarrassment.

I bite back the urge to ask her why she keeps saying that and focus on wanting her lips back against mine. Bringing my finger beneath her chin, I softly kiss her while my other hand presses to the small of her back. My fingers lift the sweater hem to unzip her skirt. I take my time. Savor it. The skirt slithers over her ass as I slide it down her body to the floor.

Well look at that, I was right: lace boy shorts. White ones.

I'm actually excited. I have been with more women than I can begin to count, and this little wisp of a girl is making it feel like my first time.

Goosebumps pop beneath my fingertips as I trail them down her arms to her narrow hips. I want so badly to bite her neck, and yet I kiss it before dropping to my knees. Being at eye level with her lingerie allows me to deeply breathe in her aroma as I kiss her over the top of the panties. She smells good enough to eat and that's exactly what I intend to do. My fingers grip into her hips before I pull the lace panties down over her thighs and knees, allowing her to step out as she uses my head to balance. She is bare and I cannot wait to spread those adorable lips apart with my tongue.

"You have got the cutest little pussy I've ever seen."

I softly press my mouth against her mound before I look up at her. Her cheeks are pink and the tip of her tongue is swiping her lip.

My eye catches something on her left thigh. Trailing my kisses across her stomach for a closer look, I see it's a band of little dotted scars that wrap high around her leg. They are about an inch below her panty line and each roughly the size of a mustard seed. Some of the dots are white and old while others are red and still healing. That's weird. What the hell could have caused that? Regardless, her legs look so damn sexy in these knee socks that I softly press my lips to the skin at the hem. As I stand, I cup her cheek and kiss her. I can't help it, I need my mouth on her. When I pull back, she bends over to take off her stockings.

Um. No.

"No. Keep them on." I shake my head and move her hand away from the knee high.

She is trying to contain a smile and it's so damn adorable that I pick her up by the waist to look directly into those big eyes. She leans forward, giving me the sweetest peck on my nose.

This is different. She is different. I grin at her before throwing her on my bed. A quiet squeal escapes her lips and she's softly giggling when I basically attack her. She brings her hands around my waist, lifts my shirt over my head and tosses it to the side. I'm struggling here. Half of me wants to ram into her so hard she feels me for a week, while the other half wants to touch, taste, and smell as much of her as I can. Make it last.

I lean back and her eyebrows raise. Those swollen lips are in that dick-throbbing half smile. I put a hand above each knee and slowly spread her legs while her eyes stalk me as I lower down. I kiss inside her thigh, feeling small ridges beneath my lips. As I pull back to look, I see that there are multiple white raised scars. Again, some are fresher than others. I kiss the other side and discover more.

Huh… Well that's a bit disturbing.

Temporarily forgetting the scars, and continuing what I came down here to do, I show extreme self-control by taking my time. She is spread open before me and all I want to do is devour her. Instead, I slowly kiss along her panty line as I watch her little body rising and falling with her quiet, shattered breathing. Her little bud is swollen and more than ready for some attention when I press my nose against it. The sexiest whimper falls from her lips and I'll be damned if I don't get even harder. The tip of my tongue traces up her slit as a little gasp falls from her mouth and she grabs a fistful of my white duvet.

I love to eat pussy. Something about the taste, feeling the pulse under my tongue, the way they pull my hair, and scream my name is such a Goddamn turn on.

"You taste even better than I imagined."

She squirms and tightens around my fingers. I think little Tavin here likes knowing I made myself come while thinking of her.

She's making sexy, frustrated noises and I have to say I'm getting a little frustrated myself. She still hasn't gotten off. I look up at her and she is watching me intently as I pump my finger back in, pulling back her hood to flick her button quickly with the tip of my tongue. She arches her back and her increased breathing has a major hitch. I add the other finger, twisting them in and out. I keep at it for a while and Jesus Christ, still nothing.

I am literally trying every trick I know here. I am searching my mental vault for what seemed to get the best results in the past, and she still won't come. This doesn't happen to me. I excel at most things I do and sex, oral sex included, is no exception. It isn't unheard of for a girl not to be able to get off from cunnilingus, I simply have never encountered it before. My pride has been bruised for the second time tonight.

When I'm positive I'm not going to lick an orgasm out of her, I run my hand along the top of her knee high and I kiss her pubic bone. Her sweater is in my way and it needs to be off anyway, so I slide my fingers under the fabric to push it up. She immediately tenses and shoves her arms down to keep me from lifting it further.

She shakes her head. "Leave it on."

Seriously? I don't get to see? Yeah, it definitely sucks. On the other hand though, I don't want to make her uncomfortable, so I just make a mental promise to myself to break her down next time.

Next time?

I guess I've known I don't want this to be a one night stand. It's been a decade since I've felt anything more than a boner for someone. Hell, it's been almost a year since I've had sex with the same girl twice.

I kiss her mouth hard and move to her jawline. Every part of her, I want to kiss every single part of her. She lets out an erotic groan as I lightly bite the lobe of her ear and lean up to retrieve a condom from the bedside table. Her fingers start to fumble with my belt again, and this time I let her. She wastes no time pushing my pants and boxer briefs over my ass before jerking me off. My cock looks so much bigger with her little hand around it. I allow her to stroke me until I can't wait a second longer. Backing up off the bed, I remove the rest of my clothes and when I lift my eyes to look at her, she's checking me out.

"God," she chokes out. Her eyebrows are raised and her gaze keeps going up and down, "You sure do have a body to go with that face, don't you?"

I laugh as I slide on the condom. She's a charming little

thing. She looks so gorgeous lying there, propped up on her elbows watching me, making my dick jump in excitement. I climb over her body, kissing her neck as I rock against her wetness. She's perfectly still as the tip finds her entrance, and I push inside.

Jesus Christ she's tight. She inhales a sharp breath when her hands fly to my hips as I ram back into her. After a moment, she rocks herself against me as we begin to get our rhythm. I reach under her left leg and push it toward her chest so I can see those knee highs, as well as feel deeper. That pulls a moan out of her sexy-ass mouth. I reach in between her legs to press my hand against her clit, and God, she feels amazing. She keeps tightening around me in a death grip and I have to intently focus so I don't come too early.

"Jesus, that clenching thing you're doing feels insane."

I bite the crook of her neck, feeling more goose bumps under my lips as her breathing becomes erratic and she shudders.

Oh, she likes that.

Leaning back, I pull her on my lap to straddle me. Damn it. I want this stupid sweater off. I get a handful of that little bitty ass as she rides me as if her life depends on it. Sitting up so that we are face-to-face, I move my hands to the impeccable curves of her hips as I push her body harder onto me. I am so close to her eyes. They're mostly violet with little blue lines in her irises and I'm lost in them. I kiss her slowly, her soft lips against mine, and I earn another moan. She moves her ass, hips, and waist in a rolling motion that almost does me in.

This little thing can fuck.

"Damn you're good at this."

She pulls back, and softly places a hand to my face, while a beautiful yet odd expression graces hers. "So are you."

Oh really? I can't fucking tell because she still hasn't come yet.

I lay her onto her back once again as I lace our fingers, hold her hands over her head, and pound the hell out of her. Her whimpers are drowning in pleasure and she's probably going to leave a spot she's so wet, so I know she is enjoying herself.

Not one girl has ever left this room without getting off at least once…ever, and I'm definitely not changing that tonight. I will figure this shit out one way or another. I pull out of her quickly, causing her to lift her head and gasp when I move down her body, to try my luck with my tongue again.

She leans up on an elbow and watches me as I suck, flick, and lick. She's biting her lip and rocking ever so slightly. I'm nothing if not persistent. I try everything sans a NASA launch, and although she moans and rolls into me, I still get zilch.

What. The. Ever-loving. Hell.

"Shit," I grumble before giving up on my tongue doing its fucking job. I hook her legs over my forearms as I sit up and slam back inside. Hard. She lets out a gasp and pushes herself further onto me. I'm frustrated with her lack of climax, so I may be taking it out on her a bit, while she's taking it like a champ.

This is getting ridiculous. It's getting to the point I'm going to have to ask her for direction. I haven't had to ask a girl how to give an orgasm since my freshman year of college.

"Tell me what I need to do to make you come."

Her eyelashes flutter just before she murmurs, "Uh… I already did."

My eyebrows scrunch together as I continue thrusting into her body. She just outright lied to me.

"That's bullshit. Tell me. Now."

Her eyelashes flutter again and she blurts, "I can't come

when I've been drinking."

"Are you kidding me?"

I wish I would have known that before I bought her shots the entire Goddamn night.

"I'm sorry, Alexander," she whispers.

My nostrils flare as my name dipped in her raspy voice sends me over the edge. My orgasm jolts out of me in pulses as I groan and fill the condom.

I look down at her and she keeps averting her eyes as if she isn't sure what to expect. I softly trail a finger under her chin, lifting it so she will stop looking around.

"You have to give me another try."

Her expressions are difficult to read. Her eyebrows are barely knit together and the corner of her mouth has an ever so slight lift to it, though she says nothing. I slide out of her and she inhales a small, sharp breath. Climbing off the bed, I remove the condom and throw it into the trash. When I return to her, I run my hand over her un-climaxed pussy, sliding a couple fingers in and out.

"I'm going to take a shower. You are welcome to join or you can go downstairs and have a glass of wine…actually, no wine." No more alcohol for this girl. Ever. "Coffee. You can have coffee."

She still doesn't say anything, she just nods as she goes to the edge of the bed to reach for her skirt and underwear. I pull out a t-shirt and a pair of boxer briefs from my dresser and hand them to her.

"These will be much more comfortable for the night."

I haven't given a girl a piece of my clothing since college. She takes them, however makes no move to put them on. Why isn't she talking? I lean down and kiss her again. It's meant to be sweet and tender, but she wraps her arms around my neck, pulls my body against hers, and presses her lips firmly to mine. Her fingers are in my hair as her little tongue darts out. She stops for a second, breathing against my lips and I think the kiss is over, then she melds into me again as if I'm her life support. Her breathing is soft and erratic while mine is nonexistent. She tightens her arms around me, kisses my cheek, and releases me.

I pick up a strand of her soft hair and tell her, "I'll be right out."

Disappearing behind my bathroom, I glare at myself in the mirror before I slip into the shower. The hot water rolls down my back and I rub it over my face. I can't believe she didn't get off, and then the little tart lied about it.

Wrapping a towel around my waist, I walk back into my room to find it empty. She must have gone to get the coffee. I go to my drawer to pull out a pair of basketball shorts and notice the shirt and boxer briefs I gave her are sitting on the bed. I circle around, see her clothes aren't there, and I know even before going downstairs to check... she left.

# CHAPTER THREE
## *Tickets*

S HE LEFT? WHY? BECAUSE I DIDN'T MAKE HER COME? Well it wasn't from the lack of motherfucking trying I'll tell you that.

I can't have been the only one to feel a connection to-night, though my empty house says otherwise. I open the kitchen cabinet to get a glass and pour a drink. The irony isn't escaping me, I finally find a girl who seems worth the time to date, and all she wants is my dick.

Then there's the thing with the scars. The peculiar thing is that they were all clearly inflicted at different times. I would be willing to bet there are more scars under that sweater and I think I felt some ridges on her ass as well. Of course I wonder if she's in some kind of trouble, except she never really came across as scared. Other than being skit-tish in the beginning, most of the time she was having as much fun as I was. There were moments of forlornness though, scattered throughout the night, when she didn't know I was watching.

There's something unique about her. I don't want to use the word eccentric exactly, though she's definitely not what I'm used to. She is just so... *whimsical*. That's it. That de-scribes her perfectly. Unpredictable and fanciful.

One of my favorite moments of the night was when we were dancing. She wasn't trying to be seductive or slutty, she wasn't trying to be anything. It was as though whatever emotion that particular song made her feel was guiding her movements. I'm pretty sure she's into me, and I don't actually believe her failure to come had anything to do with why she left. That kiss she gave me at The Necco Room was award winning, and the one she gave me just moments ago was raw and impassioned.

The sound that floats out of those pretty lips is as alluring as a siren song and my mind keeps picturing violet irises highlighted by ivory skin. Long, warm brown curls are the frame to that perfect picture...Damn it. Obviously nailing her to the bed didn't cure my craving, and that's just fantastic because I have no idea if I will ever see her again. All I know about her is that she's a Nirvana fan, can devour cotton candy in nearly one bite, is sprinkled in scars, and is hands down the best lay of my life. I know she's an 'acquaintance' of Eric, whatever that's supposed to mean. He and I have no relationship outside of Vulture, so it would be extremely unprofessional to ask him about his personal life. On the other hand, he is bringing her into my building for whatever reason. I kind of wish I would have pushed that question a bit further. Regardless, I had fun tonight. Her enthusiasm at the carnival was just so sweet, and the memory of her laugh makes my pulse quicken.

I need to stop thinking about this. She's gone. It's done and over with.

Climbing the steps back to my room, I slip into the bed she was just in. I close my eyes and memories of tonight are the lullaby sending me into sleep. Reality fades as my thoughts distort into dreams of gray knee highs and violet eyes.

*Saturday, May 2nd*

Last night I was tipsy and post orgasmic, today however, I'm pissed and taking out my aggression on the bag. My mood even has Benny keeping his distance. I still can't believe I couldn't get her off and I'm irritated as hell because we had such an incredible time together, yet she didn't have the basic courtesy to explain why she was leaving. Whatever. I'm over it. It's done. The girl that gets to come home with me tonight is going to get off so many times she won't be able to see straight.

I'm on edge all day and it doesn't subside until Silas and I are taking our first shots of the night. I do what I set out to do. Find a girl, make her come, and send her on her way.

It doesn't help. If anything it makes it worse. I don't know why I'm driving myself so crazy, I obviously know what I'm doing.

It was her problem, not mine.

*Tuesday, May 5th*

Even shaving makes me think of her. The way the pads of her fingers felt when she rubbed them over my stubble. No matter what I do, I can't seem to shake her. She had such an innocence about her, a wonder that was so bright it had shown through her eyes. While she clearly isn't a virgin, not the way she fucked, she had been hesitant; part of her had held back.

I scoff at myself and rinse my razor. This is ridiculous. I need to stop. So what if I think I felt something for her? What I 'felt' was my cock in her beautiful cunt- nothing more. My pride's just wounded because the sex was so incredible for me and obviously less than stellar for her.

On my way out the door to go to work, Cara Jo hollers after me, "I found these tickets in your pants. You didn't want to save them did you?"

She holds up the tickets from the carnival. I shake my head. I was ditched. I'm not about to keep some sentimental shit over one incredible date. I'm not completely pathetic.

"No, just toss 'em."

I'm gonna walk out the door, just turn the knob and... damn it.

Spinning on my heel, I stomp back over to Cara Jo and snatch the tickets from her hand as I scowl in response to the annoying smirk she has on her face. I don't know why I fucking want them.

⟋

I need to stop by the South side Vulture location to check on the new V Bar. Pulling into the parking garage, I turn my radio down as my phone starts ringing. When I see the name across the screen, I groan and slam my head against the headrest.

I pound the answer key and sigh. "Hey, Dad."

"Alexander. I'll make this quick. I would appreciate if you would attend a small dinner at the country club this evening. Mr. James has been wanting to meet you, and it wouldn't hurt for you to make some of those connections."

Jesus, this again. My father's business methods differ drastically from my own. Basically, I like to do things legally. He and his associates at the country club...not so much.

"Yeah, I don't think—"

"Is that a yes or a no? I don't have time for this, Son."

I flip him off through the phone, "I'll have to check my schedule."

"You do that."

*Click.*

Great.

I walk inside to find the bar fairly busy for this early in the day. The yellow tables are like polka dots against the gray slate floor and the colorful wait-staff energizes the space. I greet a few patrons and...what do we have here? When did we hire Jessica Rabbit?

I introduce myself because I believe it's important to know your employees. Especially ones with an ass like that.

After my encounter with Miss Rabbit, I finish up around the bar and drive back to the office. Silas is walking into the lobby just as I am.

He points to my shirt and smirks. "You've obviously had a good day."

I look down at what he's talking about and there's a lip-stick stain. "Shit. Can I borrow a shirt? I keep forgetting to bring extras."                                    •

I tell him all about the limberness and flexibility of Miss Rabbit as I get dressed. Truth be told I'm over selling it, though if it's to convince him or myself I'm not sure.

"No shit? I get the next one. You have Winchester Bay on your schedule next week. I'm taking it."

I pull my jacket on over his shirt and chuckle when there's a rap on his door.

My assistant Lauren peeks in, "Mr. Sørensen, the meeting is about to start." She holds up a folder, "Would you like these with you or in the board room?"

"The board room is fine."

She nods and shuts the door as Silas' phone buzzes.

"Damn," he groans.

"What?"

"There was some damage to the West Sheraton location from a storm. I have no idea how extensive. I'll have to send someone out there."

"Don't worry about it. I'll take care of it. I'll drive down after the meeting."

He laughs, "Uh okay…why?"

"Because it gets me out of a dinner."


### Saturday, May 9th


The bar is getting close to last call and Silas and I have been hanging out with the same two hot blondes all night. They are best friends and roommates and I swear to God, both named Sarah.

They invite us over and we follow them to their modest, albeit, clean apartment to continue the night. After loading up their coffee table with bottles of vodka and whiskey, Sarah #1 sways over to pick up a little box on a bookshelf. When she comes back, she holds up a rainbow striped pipe.

"You guys wanna smoke a bowl?"

I shrug and rest my arm across the couch. "Sure."

Silas grins and nods his enthusiasm as she lights up. It's been awhile since I've smoked weed. The taste is rich and earthy, the smell is pungent, and I've always enjoyed it.

"What kind of music are you guys into?" Sarah #2 asks.

"Whatever your fine ass wants to listen to is great, Angel."

I roll my eyes and grin. Silas is so damn cheesy.

Sarah #1 is sitting cross legged on the couch. "So are you guys roommates too?"

I scoff at her. "Uh, no. I'm nearly thirty."

Wow, I just sounded like a dick. I really don't mean to come across that way, so I smile at her to soften my comment.

Eminem blares from the speakers as I hit the pipe. I don't mind rap except I need to be in the mood for it and at the moment, I'm not. I catch myself wondering what Tavin could be doing…Shit. It doesn't matter what she's doing.

I need another shot.

Sarah #1, no wait, Sarah #2 asks, "What kind of business do you do?"

"Have you ever been to any of the Vulture theaters?" Silas responds with so much pride I think his chest puffs out. She nods and he points his thumb toward me. "He owns them."

Her mouth drops open. "All of them?"

Wow, she can really open her mouth wide...

I chuckle, "Yes, all of them." Pouring more shots, I add, "It was just as much his idea as mine, and the asshole owns nearly as much stock as I do, so don't let him bullshit you."

I don't know how many more drinks we have or how many bowls we smoke, I just know I'm nice and stoned. I have no idea which Sarah I'm supposed to be with and I don't really give a damn to be completely honest. They are the exact same to me. I pick one and jerk my head to summon her over to the couch. She plops down next to me and I lean over to kiss her. Her tongue slides into my mouth as she climbs up to straddle across my lap.

After a few minutes of making out, I pull off her shirt and notice Silas and the other one pretty much doing the same thing we are. My Sarah is grinding against me through our jeans and my intoxication allows her to slowly transform into Tavin.

God, she had moved with so much heart and passion it was enthralling. It hadn't been just sex to her, I could see her put her whole heart, her whole self into each of her thrusts. Sometimes it feels as if I imagined her.

The Sarah I'm with breaks me away from my fantasy when she unzips my jeans. She crawls to the floor to take me in her mouth and it feels good; she just looks so absurd. How someone can suck dick with grace, I have no idea, but Tavin had done it. From the glimpses I saw, she looked so sultry with her wispy bangs and pink lips. She used her tongue to caress as she sucked the life out of me, all while being as quiet as a church mouse. Every time I get into my car I imagine that blow job.

I need to think about something else. I grip her blonde hair and slide her mouth off of me. "Get up here and lie down."

She climbs onto the couch and rests her head on the arm. I look up at Silas and he and the other Sarah are both completely naked and they're already going at it. How did they get undressed so fast? Popping the button on this Sarah's blue jeans, I pull them down along with her orange panties, before spreading her legs and leaning down in-between them.

Memories of my night with Tavin force their way into my mind no matter how hard I try to focus. I loved the way she watched me devour her, she kept her eyes locked on mine constantly and it made me feel indestructible. She's the perfectly balanced line between innocent and erotic. For the hundredth time I wonder why she left.

I am lost in my thoughts, so it's good to know that I can eat pussy on autopilot because Sarah is currently coming in my mouth. Pulling the condom out of my pocket to put it on, I watch Silas and the other Sarah come over to us, holding hands. His Sarah bends over and kisses my Sarah as Silas runs his hand down her back. He grips his erection as he wets the tip with her juices and shoves into her.

So we are actually doing this? While we've tag teamed plenty of times, three or foursomes are new.

I can't focus and I'm not even sure which girl I'm inside of half the time. I'm high, drunk, and at some point I stop fighting the flashes of Tavin's lips, thighs, scars, and eyes... the way she felt, tasted, smelt, the sound of her laugh and her graceful face, her skin...so soft...she feels so good...

"God, Tavin."

"Who the hell is Tavin?" Sarah who-really-knows-at-this-point asks.

I'm slung back to the present. Shit, did I say that out loud? All three of them are looking at me as though I've lost my mind and maybe I have. I slide out from the girl I'm inside of and stand to pull on my jeans.

"I need to go."

Silas mouths, *What the fuck?* as I walk out.

Once I leave their building and step onto the sidewalk, the fresh air blows against my face and feels amazing. I take a huge breath, trying to clear my head.

What am I doing? Driving myself insane by the looks of it. I just need to talk to her again. Maybe then I will see I have just built her up in my head. It's clear she has secrets and the more I think about the scars, the more they eat at me. I don't know, I'm blitzed and I feel like I'm going in circles. I need to go to bed.

### Sunday, May 10th

Since it's such a beautiful day, I decide to take out the yacht. As I pack the beers and burgers in the cooler, Silas barrels into my kitchen. He has a key so he never actually knocks anymore, he just storms in as if he owns the damn place.

"They were both named Sarah, you tool. How do you fuck that up?" He walks over to my fridge and pulls out a beer. "You've been off all week, what's up with you?"

"Nothing, I guess I've just been sidetracked." Closing the cooler, I appeal to his obsession with my boat. "I'm taking out the yacht. Do you want to come?"

He sighs. "You know I do."

We finish packing and load everything into the car

before we head to the docks.

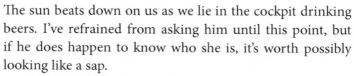

The sun beats down on us as we lie in the cockpit drinking beers. I've refrained from asking him until this point, but if he does happen to know who she is, it's worth possibly looking like a sap.

"How well do you know Eric?"

He shrugs as he brings the bottle to his lips. "I don't know, why?"

I have never had any problem talking about my sexual conquests with him before, so I can't explain why I don't want to now.

"There was a girl that came to see him the other day. I'm just curious how he knows her."

He arches an eyebrow and grins. "Hot huh?"

I nod at his understatement. "Gorgeous."

The seagulls squawking and the water lapping are the only sounds for a few moments before he clears his throat.

"My application to the Shadoebox Country Club got accepted." He rolls the beer in his hands and my jaw falls open. I cannot believe I'm hearing this.

I scoff, "So you're really doing it, huh? Going to the dark side?"

"Come on, it's the country club, Alex, not the Sith."

"At least the Sith has The Force," I mumble at him before taking a swig.

He rolls his eyes. "You know, this is exactly like when I joined that fraternity."

"You're not making the point you're trying to. You were a royal dick that entire time."

He narrows his eyes because he knows I'm right. "Tons of connections are floating around that place and you know it."

I laugh and get up for more beer. "Yeah, dirty ones. There are plenty of ways to make connections Silas. This wouldn't have anything to do with the golf course would it?"

He throws his head back and groans, "Oh come on! Have you seen the green? I'm getting hard thinking about it."

"Go ahead, Silas. Sell your soul for eighteen holes."

He snickers, "How many holes would it take to sell yours?"

# CHAPTER FOUR
## Morningstar Ave.

*Monday, May 11th*

IT'S BEEN OVER A WEEK SINCE MY DATE WITH TAVIN. IT'S driving me crazy not knowing why she left. I honestly don't know why it's bugging me so much. I just need an explanation and I'll be fine. It's how to get one, that's the question.

I've had a busy morning and am just now leaving for lunch. I happen to look toward the elevator, and I'm shocked frozen. She's standing right inside. Her eyes go wide for the fraction of a second that they lock with mine, before the doors close. I run to the elevator and pound the buttons as if it will bring her back to me. I'm stupid for even wasting time. I turn around and yank open the stairwell door before flying down the steps.

Shit. Why do we need to have so many damn floors? I refrain from stopping to catch my breath as the door to the main floor bangs open. I burst through the lobby and people are already getting into the elevator car she was in. She can't have gotten that far. Running outside, I scan the sidewalk before I see her slide into the back of a cab across the street.

Cab four fifty-seven.

Thirty seconds earlier and I would have caught up to her.

Fuck it, I'm asking Eric about her. Spinning on my heel, I walk back into the lobby and get back into the elevator. I don't know what I'm going to ask him, I just know anything he tells me at this point will be beneficial.

Our floor receptionist gives me a questioning expression at my immediate return, so I nod to her before my fist raps against Eric's door.

"It's open!"

I peek my head inside to see him typing away. "Hi Eric, I'm sorry to bother you, I have an un-work related question for you.

He gestures me inside and leans back in his seat. "Yeah of course. How can I help you?"

"I need to ask you about Tavin."

I swear his face loses about six shades of color. "I'm sorry, I can't talk about her." He turns back to his computer as if it's the end of the conversation. His hands shake as he clicks the mouse and looks as if he is staring at a dead body instead of a computer screen, while I try not to laugh at the fact that he's afraid of a ninety pound pixie.

"Are you dating her?"

Repulsion covers his face when he scoffs, "Hell no."

Why is it 'hell' no?

"Can you tell me how to reach her?"

He's all twitchy. "I'm sorry…I-I can't. I swear she won't be around here anymore though."

Why is he freaking out? He isn't going to tell me anything and he's about to have a nervous breakdown so I let him be.

"Alright Eric, thank you for your time."

He nods in relief and I close the door behind me. It's time to try plan B: bribery.

I go back to my office and call the cab company, specifically requesting the driver that was in cab four fifty-seven, at the time I saw her.

Fifteen minutes later, I stop at the ATM outside Vulture and I take out what I hope is a sufficient amount of money before I meet the cabbie.

I see the four fifty-seven on the side of the bright green car and slip into the back seat. Gross. I wish there was a way I could stand up. God only knows what's gone on in here. The middle aged man in the front seat doesn't look at me as he adjusts the buttons on the console.

"Where to?"

"Nowhere, I just have a couple questions about one of your rides this afternoon."

He turns around, his bushy mustache and beard is a harsh contrast to his bald head. His thick brows are narrowed as he barks, "I don't have time for this. Either tell me where to take you or get out."

The guy looks like he should be on a Harley, not in a cab. I pass him a hundred dollar bill. "You picked up a girl here about an hour ago. Where did you take her?"

His fingers stroke at his beard as he tosses the Benjamin on the console. "Today you say? I'm not sure… I have a lot of fares and my memory is a little hazy."

I narrow my eyes while digging out another hundred. "Does this clear things up?"

He takes it and throws it next to the other one as I see his baseball bat on the floorboard, causing me to scoot closer to the door.

"Actually, I was here earlier. A pretty brunette I think it was. Took her to the south side."

"Do you remember the address?"

He clicks his tongue. "You know, it's on the edge of my mind, I just can't quite grasp it."

"Oh for fuck's sake, here." I toss him the last of the hundreds as he rips a piece of paper off a notepad and clicks through his phone before scribbling down the information. I yank it out of his hand with a less than friendly 'thanks' and finally get out of that disgusting cab.

Smoothing out the paper, I read the address:

**8326 S. Morningstar Ave**.
**Shadoebox City, CA 95478**

I can't make myself go see Tavin immediately after work, so I stop at home and eat the delicious roast Cara Jo made. I'm a little worried that I'm going to weird her out by just showing up, even if I don't feel she's giving me much choice. I need to know why she left or else I will always wonder. I'm prepared to find her with kids or married, and regardless, I want an explanation.

It's after eight before I finally get myself into my car and enter her address into the GPS. Her neighborhood reminds me of the one Silas grew up in. It's your average suburban middle class community. The address is to a blue Victorian styled house that really needs a paint job and a couple cracked windows replaced. I park on the street and lock my car before I climb up her steps. Her yard has grass, even though it isn't looking too hot, and there aren't any bushes or flowers. The house looks bare and a few of the shutters need straightening. Oddly, a shiver crawls up my spine despite the warmth of spring.

I knock on the door, and as I do, it slightly creaks open. My palm is pressed against the worn wood of the door when I open it the rest of the way.

"Hello? Tavin?"

The house is quiet and it takes my eyes a moment to find the unmoving girl on the floor. Shit. I run over to her and kneel next to her body. She's lying on her side, her feet bare. I desperately look for the rise and fall of her chest, while concentrating on the pink unicorn zombie t-shirt she's wearing, but I can't tell if she is breathing or not. I feel for her pulse and there's nothing at first, so when it does happen, it's glorious. Just a little jump on her wrist to tell me she's still alive.

I can't believe this is her. This isn't the bright eyed girl I remember from the carnival. She's pale with dark circles under her eyes, her lips are dry and cracked. My gaze makes it to the floor, making my stomach climb into my throat.

A syringe.

She's a junkie? How is that possible?

"You fucking stupid girl," I tell her even though I doubt she can hear me. I rip out my phone, my hands are surprisingly steady as I call an old friend.

Marie's chipper voice comes on the line. Too bad her night is about to take a turn in a real shitty direction.

"Oh hey Al—"

"How do I fix an overdose?"

"Are they breathing?"

"She is, very slowly."

"Do you know what she's on?"

"Jesus, I don't know! I assume heroin—what else do people shoot?" I look up on the table to see white powder on a tray, along with a spoon, a lighter, some cotton balls, and God knows what else.

"Make sure she's on her side, pull out her tongue, and tell me how it looks."

"It looks normal."

"Look at her eyes. Is she conscious or responsive at all?"

I try to get a reaction, any reaction, "Tavin! Wake up!" I shake and slap her. Still nothing happens. I spread apart her eyelids to see vacant violet.

"I'm not getting anything, her eyes are dilated and she isn't responding."

"You need to call 9-1-1. Get her to the E.R. now."

"I can't do that. I don't know what all she's mixed up in. I'm taking her to my house. Will you come over?"

"Christ Alex, you cannot be serious."

"Are you gonna help her at my house or not?"

"Well, I'm not going to let her die because you're an idiot," she snaps. "I'll get there as soon as I possibly can. Keep her on her side. Got it?"

"Yeah, got it. Meet you at my place."

Carrying her to my car, I follow Marie's directions. I drive faster than I have in all my life and I can't believe I don't get pulled over.

My tires squeal as I turn into my driveway and I barely get the car turned off before I run to the passenger's side. Lifting her out of the car, I carry her inside and bring her up to one of the guest bedrooms. My heart is pounding in my chest as I make her comfortable and check that she's still breathing. The doorbell rings and I sprint down the stairs to answer.

Marie and I don't speak to each other as we hurry up to the guest bedroom. Within seconds, her gloved hand pulls a needle from her bag and screws it onto a syringe. She's a fantastic doctor and has been my personal physician since she graduated. I trust her completely, which is fortunate considering I'm doing just that with Tavin's life.

Removing a bottle of liquid from her bag, she pops off the orange lid, lifts the bottle upside down, and inserts the syringe into the bottle, pulling down on the plunger.

"Help me with her jeans."

We peel the tight denims from Tavin's body before Marie cleans the injection site on her thigh and sticks in the needle.

"What the hell is that?"

I know she's aware of what she's doing, even so, shoving more shit into Tavin's body makes me nervous.

"It's *Narcan*. It will reverse the effects of the heroin."

I expect the reaction to be instant, similar to how you see in the movies. Even after thirty seconds, there's no change and I start to panic. She cannot die in this house.

"It didn't work! What do we do?" I choke out.

"Okay, Alexander. Hey! Look at me." I'm staring at the motionless body on the bed as Marie is snapping her fingers in my face. "You need to relax or you need to leave the room, understand? It could take a couple minutes for her to respond."

The minutes feel like hours with still no reaction. Marie begins to prepare another dose when I hear a huge inhalation of breath from the bed. It takes Tavin a second to absorb her surroundings as her confusion becomes apparent. I let myself fall into the chair next to the dresser.

"Oh thank God." I finally exhale.

She looks up at me and mortification curtains her face. She turns away and won't acknowledge me even when I ask her if she is alright.

Marie touches my arm, "Hey, will you please step out for a minute? I need to speak with my patient."

I cannot believe she's a motherfucking junkie. That's why she wouldn't take off her sweater, because she didn't want me to see her track marks. I sigh and look at Tavin one last time before I relent and go downstairs to pour a double shot and wait.

This is insane and the last thing I expected. The waiting is driving me mad and just as I'm about to head back upstairs, Marie comes down.

She sighs, "I'm going to hang out for a couple of hours. There is a slight chance she could overdose again after the *Narcan* wears off..." She pauses, clearly having much more to say and contemplating on how to say it.

"Spit it out, Marie."

She scowls, crossing her arms. "How do you know this girl?"

I rake my fingers through my hair and blow out a breath. "Honestly, I don't really know her at all. We went out once about a week ago and...I don't know. I just can't stop thinking about her. I've kind of been obsessing so I tracked her down." I sound like a stalker. I can hear it now. "I called you moments after finding her."

"What are you going to do with her?"

That is an extremely good question. Her going back to her house is not an option right now. If I learned anything from Sasha, it's that a junkie is incapable of making rational decisions, and Tavin is clearly into something heavy. I have the space and I'm the one who found her.

"She can just stay here until we figure this whole thing out."

She scoffs, "Wow. You really are an idiot."

I actually don't think it's that bad of an idea. Maybe that's why I felt so drawn to her. "No really, I could help her get clean, back on her feet."

She shakes her head and rolls her eyes, "You have no idea what you're getting into. Her withdrawals could last for over a week. She can't be alone, she needs someone to stay with her constantly. Otherwise, she has zero chance of rehabilitation, and that's if she even wants to be clean. She will be in pain, and she will beg and plead for you to let her go." She sighs, "Even if you can handle all that, you have Vulture. You can't stay with her day in and day out. Do you really think Cara Jo will be up for that task?"

Cara Jo would not appreciate that responsibility, though I know exactly who would be ideal for this situation. The only problem is, she hates my guts.

# *Tavin*

I need to breathe...

Someone is gasping for air... Wait, is that me?

My head hurts. I'm on something soft... a bed? My eye-lids weigh a thousand pounds and I use all my strength to push them open. I don't know this room. Where the heck am I? And where are my pants? I'm not high. Why aren't I high? I just prepared that rig not... dang how long has it been?

"Oh thank God."

I know that voice, it's *his* voice...

My neck is stiff. I ignore it as I turn my head to see a pretty blonde with her lips down in concern. I wonder what's wrong. I want to ask her what she thinks is so horrible that would make her look so sad. It wasn't her who spoke though. I let my eyes leave the blonde lady to see...no...

Alexander.

No. No. No. Shit! I should have listened to Toben. He was right, the date was a bad idea.

Wait... Am I back in his house? No, no, no, this isn't sup-posed to happen. This is not good, not good at all. How did he find me? Why did he find me? Did he come to my house? How does he know where I live?

"Tavin are you okay?"

His voice is tinged with worry. What am I doing here? His gorgeous green eyes look scared and the mouth that has kissed me so sweetly is turned down into a frown.

I remember putting the needle to my skin, and then that rush. Oh my God that rush was epic, completely in-sane. I mean it's always amazing, but it's never been like that. Something went wrong though, my blood was being frozen in my veins. I don't remember anything after that.

Hold on… Did I overdose?! Ha! Oh my God, wouldn't that be hilarious? After everything? I thought I might have been pushing it. Seeing him earlier just made my day extra crappy and I needed to make sure I got high. Super high.

God, I'm too humiliated to even look at him. He wasn't ever supposed to see my reality. He was supposed to remember me as I was that night: a normal girl on a normal date with a normal guy. All I wanted was one night! One dang night! Was that too much to ask? I let it go too far, I don't know what I was thinking. He made it stop though. He temporarily took it away.

"Hey, will you please step out for a minute? I need to speak with my patient."

The blonde lady is talking to Alexander and I think he's going to yell at her. He looks angry as he glances at me and sighs before leaving the room.

"Tavin? My name is Marie. I'm a friend of Alex's. Do you know what happened?" Her voice is kind and she smiles at me as she pulls out a stethoscope from a small leather bag and places it around her neck. I hate those things. She can't possibly know that though. Maybe she's another doctor. Still, I can't stop myself from shifting away from her. Hold on. She asked me a question… what was it?

"Tavin, sweetheart, do you know where you are?" She walks over to me and her hands are soft when she places them on my arm.

"Alexander's house." A whisper is all I can manage to get out. I don't know what they want from me yet.

"You overdosed. Did you know that? You would probably be dead if it wasn't for Alex."

She almost sounds upset or angry. Why? She's never met me before in her life. I don't know what to say. If he saved my life then I know I should be grateful, but what I really feel is cheated.

I nod so she'll stop looking at me and it works because she goes back to looking through the leather bag. "Do you mind if I take a blood sample?"

Shaking my head no, I watch her as she cleans a plastic tray and fills it with medical things like a syringe package, a plastic tube, a blue tourniquet... just like The Doctor does. She rubs some kind of disinfectant on her hands and the latex snaps as she pulls on the gloves. Picking up the tray, she places it on the bed and pulls up a chair to sit in front of me. Her gloved fingers rub over my track marks and she ties the tourniquet.

I hate how loud silence can be. I shift on the bed as she lightly pushes against my skin to find a good vein. Once she cleans my arm and has the needle at the desired angle, she pushes in the syringe and I relax as I watch my blood splash against the walls of the plastic vile.

As she finishes, she presses the cotton against my arm to stop the bleeding and tapes it. She smiles at me as she throws the needle into a plastic container and puts the tube of my blood into her bag.

"Almost done," she says as she walks behind me. I feel the bed dip as her hands grab the bottom of my shirt and the fabric begins to push up my skin. No! She can't see. I jump away from her so she won't lift it.

"I won't hurt you Tavin, I just want to listen to your heartbeat. I need to check you over and make sure you won't relapse."

Even though she seems nice enough, things are rarely as they seem. She comes toward me slowly, with her hands up, like you would a vicious dog. Does she think I will hurt her? The thought would make me laugh if I wasn't so mad at myself for being so stupid and letting this happen.

"Will you please sit on the bed and let me listen?" She

can't see. She'll ask questions. I hate questions. "Whatever goes on in here stays between us. I promise. It's illegal for me to tell anyone if that is what you're worried about. I can't even tell Alex anything. Please, just let me make sure you're alright."

While I'm hesitant, I would rather not fall back into an overdose and die in this house, away from Toben. Slowly, I sit on the bed and she scoots behind me to lift my shirt. She doesn't make any noise and she stops moving for a long time before pressing the stethoscope to my back. After a couple of silent moments, she puts down my shirt and sighs.

"Tavin, are you in danger?"

What a funny question, one that I can't begin to answer.

*The correct answer is no, you fucked up freak.*

I shake my head. "No."

She frowns at me. "When was your last doctor's appointment?" At least she is still talking to me in a soft voice.

I think it has been two weeks since The Doctor came to see us. "Two weeks ago."

"What is your doctor's name?"

"I just know him as 'The Doctor.'"

She narrows her eyes. "Do you have any identification? A driver's license?"

Why does she need my ID? I don't understand what is happening. I reach down to the floor and into my jeans pocket, I think it might still be in there. Feeling the flimsy plastic, I pull it out and hand it to her. She looks at it and frowns before glaring at me.

"Are you going to give me a real one?"

How the heck can she tell? Toben and I go to bars all the time and they've never once questioned it.

"It is real." Well… it's as real as it's going to get.

She puts her fingers against her temples and rubs. "Okay, I'm going to get Alex." She steps toward the door.

"No!"

I don't mean to yell, but I have to stop her. I don't want to see him. Not like this. The night of the carnival, he looked at me like he wanted to live in my soul and eat my thoughts. He confuses me and scares me in ways I'm not accustomed. I just know I never wanted this.

I need to get the heck out of here.

# Alexander

This is not going to be a pleasant conversation. I've been holding the phone in my hand for ten minutes trying to fig-ure out the best way to present the situation because I am all too aware of its irony. Swallowing my pride, I dial the number.

"Well don't you have balls of steel, calling here?"

I roll my eyes. I've met this guy once and that was more than enough to know he's an asshole.

"Drew, this is important. I need to talk to her."

I can hear Sasha in the background asking who it is.

"I'll give you a hint. You look alike and he's a dick." He enunciates the last bit right into the mouthpiece.

I hear her shout, "What the hell does he want?"

"What do you want, Alexander?"

"To talk to my sister! Now put her on the damn phone!"

I hear the rustling of the phone being passed. "What?" She barks in my ear.

"Look, I know I'm the last person you want to talk to, and honestly this wasn't an easy call for me to make… I need your help, Sash."

She scoffs, "I remember needing your help too, and

I believe your exact words were, 'Fuck off, junkie bitch'...
among other things."

"I tried to fuc-" I stop myself because arguing with her
isn't going to help. I sigh and lean my head against my fridge.
"I know, and believe me, I've regretted that for a while.
I didn't understand it then and I don't understand it now.
I just..." I groan at my inability to find the right words. "I
have a girl in my house that had an overdose tonight. I want
to help her and I can't do it alone. I have to work and you
have been through this first hand. You can understand her
in ways I can't." I'm rushing through my words, so I take a
deep breath, "Will you help me? Please?"

She is quiet for a few minutes and I don't think I exhale
to breathe. Finally, she huffs out, "I'm not doing it for you.
I'm doing it for whoever this girl is."

"Thank you. I'll pay you."

"Yeah, yeah, let me pack some stuff and I'll be over."

She hangs up and I head back upstairs to the bedroom
Tavin is in. Just as I'm about to enter, Marie comes out.

"She doesn't want to see you right now." She pushes me
back down the hall.

"What? Why?"

"She's had a rough night, just give her some time."

"How long has she been doing this?"

This is all too much. A couple of hours ago she was the
girl of my dreams, now she's a drug addict?

"That's between her and myself. If she wants to tell you,
that's her choice."

"Then let me talk to her." I try pushing past her when I'm
stopped by her hand.

"Not tonight Alex. Did you find someone?"

"Yeah, she'll be here soon."

"I'm pretty sure Tavin is okay for now. I still want to stay
until your help gets here."

"My 'help' is Sasha."

Her eyes widen. "Oh… well, isn't that ironic?"

~

I take a deep breath and ignore the pit in my stomach as I swing the door open. Even if I won't admit it out loud, I've missed Sasha horribly. We've barely spoken for almost three years and I haven't even seen her in over a year.

The last time she was here, I severed our relationship and I can't help myself from remembering all the terrible things I said to her.

**Three years ago…**

*This view. I knew when I saw this view I had to have this house. I can see all of Shadoebox City and it's abuzz below me. Beyond that, the ocean disappears into itself and takes the blue sky with it. The scotch burns my throat as the pool laps in the wind next to me and I hear the sliding glass door open. Cara Jo must have finished dinner.*

*I turn to her and her face is creased with uncertainty.*

*"What's wrong?" I ask as she licks her lips and takes a breath. When she holds her hands out to calm me, I know for sure something is up. "What's going on Cara Jo?"*

*"Alright, I need you to promise me you are going to do your best to remain calm."*

*"Oh Jesus. Why?"*

*She takes another deep breath and I'm starting to worry. "Your sister is here."*

*Instantly, my heart doubles in speed. "Oh hell no."*

*I storm past her and through the open door to see Sasha's long, uncombed blonde hair, which probably hasn't been washed in days, as I come up behind her. I think my air* conditioner might be broken because it's suddenly incredibly hot in here.

"What the hell are you doing here?"

I may have already had a few drinks tonight, which doesn't always mix that well when I'm as pissed as I am at her right now.

She jumps at my voice and spins around. She looks even shittier than the last time I saw her. This must be her new look: 'The Walking Dead' chic. Her skin is nearly translucent and I wish that was makeup causing the dark circles under her eyes.

"Alex…" She scratches her arm and is all fidgety. "I know I fucked up…please. I don't wanna do this shit." She looks at me with the same look that has made me fall for her games a hundred times before. "I really do wanna get clean. I don't wanna live like this anymore."

"I can't believe you actually have the audacity to come here after what you did. Out of everything you could have stolen from me. That was all I had left of her and you knew that."

"I know. I'm sorry Alex. I hate that it has this control over me. I don't know why. Please, I need you. I want to beat this. I truly do, but rehab…it costs money…I need your help."

She can't even make eye contact as she shifts around on her feet. Well, I can't look at her either.

"Fuck off, junkie bitch. Why don't you go fill up your needle and do what you've been attempting to this whole time. You aren't my sister. My sister wouldn't have stolen the most important thing that I own, for a few moments of freedom. I've tried to help you and you threw it all back in my face. If I never see you again it will be too soon." Her expression breaks my heart. Ignoring the ache in my chest, I get close enough to almost touch her nose. "Get the fuck out of my house."

"Alex…please…"

"I will never forgive you, I want you to know that. You chose the high over me."

"I'm sorry."

"Fuck you. Get out."

I can't believe she's actually producing tears. "Alex, you're my twin, I need you..."

"GET OUT!"

"I'm sorry," she barely whispers as she sticks her hand in her designer jeans and holds out a few bills. "This is all I have left."

Is she serious with this?

"Go put it in a needle." I nod toward the door. "Don't make me say it again."

Her tears run down an expression that I can't quite place, before she finally leaves.

I need a drink.

Cara Jo's hand covers mine while I pour my whiskey, "You have every right to be angry—"

"Yeah, I know."

"—but she's struggling and she needs you. She's your sister."

"That?" I point to where she had been standing a moment ago. "That was not my sister. That was a lifeless, selfish, bitch in a Sasha suit."

Her hand grabs my chin and jerks it down to look at her, "I do not care what she has done to you. I do not want to hear you speak of her or any other woman that way. I know I raised you better than that. You're a good man, Alexander, so act like it." She releases me, "Now sit down. Your dinner is ready."

She puts my plate in front of me. Normally I love her chicken, today though, my appetite has vanished.

"So I'm assuming you heard all that. I was pretty harsh, huh?"

She squeezes my shoulder before untying her apron. "You definitely weren't kind, even though I understand your reasons for your feelings. She IS your sister, Alexander, your twin sister. She's...Sasha."

*"I know. That's why this hurts so much."*

Sasha has a bag, her purse and a cup of coffee. I have no idea what she's wearing. I stopped asking about her outfits years ago.

"Hi, Sash."

She won't look at me. "Hey."

This is awkward. I move to let her in, and as she enters the kitchen she is greeted by Marie.

A genuine smile spreads across her face, "Hey Sasha! How have you been?"

"Hey, it's been awhile. I've been great, thanks. How about you?"

They go back and forth for a couple minutes catching up. It's been a few years since Sasha has really been around. She and Marie were inseparable in high school, so it's nice to have them here together. Kind of reminds me of old times.

"So what exactly is going on?" Sasha places her bag on the ground and Marie gestures at me to explain away.

Sighing, I speed summarize, "She's a girl I went out with a couple weekends ago. She kind of got into my head, so I looked her up. When I found her, she was unconscious. I saw the drugs, called Marie, and here we are."

She looks confused. "Okay...so why is she here and not in a hospital?"

Marie snorts in response. Why are they giving me so much shit about this? Sasha, especially, should understand.

"I know absolutely nothing about her. I didn't want the police to get involved in case she's in some type of trouble."

"So why not take her to a methadone clinic? Why is she your responsibility?"

I glare at her. I can't believe she actually just made that suggestion.

"We both know how well that works." I shouldn't snap

at her and I clearly piss her off because her body goes rigid and her fist balls up. I try to rationalize, "Look, if I found a hurt dog I would nurse it back to health until I found a home or took it to the pound. It's essentially the same concept... right?"

Sasha and Marie are both looking at me with disgusted expressions and Sasha shakes her head. "Idiot."

Marie snorts, "She's not a dog, she's a human, you moron. Your analogy doesn't even make sense anyway. If you find a wounded dog, you take it to the vet not keep it in your damn guestroom." She actually looks pissed. "Whatever your reasons for wanting to keep her here, I just want to be on the record saying: this is a bad idea. And just so you know, forcing her to stay against her will is illegal."

Why can't they see I truly just want to help her?

"I don't know what the hell I'm doing okay? I haven't had a lot of time to think this through."

Sasha sighs, "I'm going to go meet her." She looks to Marie. "It's good to see you again. If you ever want to grab lunch," she reaches into her pocket and hands her a card, "hit me up."

Her face lights up with a smile. "I will. I would enjoy that."

Sasha picks up her bag and heads upstairs as Marie tightens her ponytail and rubs her temples. She's stressing out.

"Are you okay, Marie?"

She glowers. "Stop worrying about me, and worry about the situation upstairs." She walks toward the door. "I'm going home. Call if she needs me. I'll have my phone on."

"Thanks, Marie."

After letting her out, I go upstairs and pause at the guestroom door before going to my own room to get some sleep.

*Tavin*

Marie the Doctor said I didn't have to see him tonight. I like this room. There is a window with a window seat. I like windows. This house is a lot wider than it is tall, and I'm upstairs, but I bet it isn't that far of a climb down from up here. I could do it.

When I do figure a way out, will he just come find me again? I guess I have to wait and cross that bridge when I get to it.

Footsteps rip me from my thoughts.

Is it Marie the Doctor or Alexander? This is his house, why would he care what I want? If he wants to see me, what's stopping him?

The door opens, and it isn't Marie the Doctor or Alexander. It's the most beautiful girl I've ever seen. I wish I looked like her. Then I immediately take it back because things would probably be worse for me if I did. She is tall with long, light blonde hair and lean, sleek curves. Her cherry red lips are slightly upturned into a gentle smile.

"Hi, Tavin, my name is Sasha." Her voice sounds like music and she has the same subtle accent that Alexander does.

When she comes closer, I see her eyes are the same shocking Emerald City green as his. I feel my head cock to the side.

"You look like him."

Her mouth opens into a wide smile showing her incredibly white teeth. "Yeah, it's a stupid side effect of being a twin."

I can't think straight. It feels like I don't have a single

drop of dope in my system or anything else for that matter. My skin itches. I shouldn't be feeling this yet, I just shot up a couple of hours ago.

"Oh."

"I'm going to be staying with you for the next week or so while we get you cleaned up. At least until you get through the withdrawals."

Whoa…wait, what? I can't stay here for an entire week! My heart is pounding. This is bad. So, so bad. Crap, crap!

I feel my head shaking violently. "No, no, no, no. Please don't do this, I can't stay here." Hot tears burn the rim of my eyes.

*Dry it up you pathetic cunt.*

I wipe them away quickly. What am I going to do? She looks sad. I don't like to see those eyes sad.

She sits next to me and puts her hand on my leg. "Alex just wants to help. Honestly, I think this has as much to do with me as it does you. I know this is scary. I also know living for the high isn't living at all. While I'm sure you can't imagine it now, life truly is better without it…if you spend it with the right people."

She thinks she knows, but she doesn't. She doesn't have the capacity to know, and he doesn't know either! Who does he think he is? I'm angry with him even if I shouldn't be. He has no right. What is he planning on getting out of this?

"I need to leave."

She sighs, "Even though he can't force you to stay, I doubt he'll willingly just let you walk out, at least not without some answers." She shrugs and combs her long blonde hair back with her fingers. "You can always call the cops if that's what you want to do."

Did she actually just suggest that I call the police on her own brother? That's horrible. Doesn't she know what they will do to him? How bad they are? While being here is dangerous, getting the police involved will be much worse.

"I could never do that to him." I shake my head. "We've already had sex. What else does he want?"

"I told you, he just wants to help." She flops onto her stomach. "There's obviously something about you that has his attention, and trust me that doesn't happen with him."

Yeah well, his attention is going to get me killed.

# Alexander

Sleep is apparently wishful thinking because I lie in bed tossing and turning until around one-thirty when I am awoken by a shout.

I get out of bed and jog down the hall until I hear crying and the sound of vomiting. Opening the guestroom door, I see Sasha and Tavin on the floor with Tavin leaning over a large bowl throwing her guts up.

"Please," she's shaking and crying, "You don't understand…" When she looks up and sees me, her face twists in anger. "Why are you doing this?" She stands up to lunge toward me before Sasha grabs her arm. "If I wanted you to find me I would have left you a message or a note. You had no right to come looking!"

I know she isn't blaming me when she's the one shooting shit into her arm.

"Well it's a good thing I did! You would be dead right now if I hadn't!"

"I told you that you didn't want this," she cries.

She's seriously going to throw that in my face? Fuck that. She's the one who lied to me.

"Maybe, if you would have told me in the first place that

you were a Goddamn junk—"

"Okay, okay," Sasha stands up and pushes me out the door. "I can tell you're revving up for a mean one. She's in pain and sick. You called me here because I've been where she is. So trust me, right now she knows two things: one, there's something out there that can take away this pain, and two, you're the one keeping it from her."

I wipe my hands down my face. I can hear Tavin crying and gagging through the door. Jesus, what am I doing? I clearly know nothing about this girl. I don't understand how I already feel such a pull to someone who is a stranger, and a strung out one at that.

"This is going to last a whole week?"

"Yeah, it can and probably will. There are a lot of factors. At least she's young and small so she has that in her favor." She rubs her arm where her track scars are. "What's the real reason you're doing all this? Does it have anything to do with me?"

"God, I don't know…maybe. I didn't handle things very well with you, and I do regret it. I should have been the one person that could get you away from all that and I failed. Still, you did some ruthless things too. You have to admit that. I could deal with you stealing money and even *Mormor*'s silver, but Aslaug's tiara? That was incredibly low, Sash." She opens her mouth to speak and I hold up my hand to stop her, "Look, now is not the time to talk about it. I know it sounds insane. I can't explain it. The moment I laid eyes on Tavin I felt something. It's as if she's more alive than everyone else. She disappeared after our date and I tried to forget about her, but I just couldn't. I had to find her again."

"Well, you did." She rubs her face. I wonder if this is difficult for her. "Just give it some time and she'll be closer to normal."

I don't have the slightest clue what normal is. She could

have been doped up our entire night together. How could I not tell?

"Yeah, whatever that is."

"Come on, you did a good thing tonight. You're obviously already invested in this girl. Don't give up on her like you did on me."

That's a hit to the chest. "Sasha I—"

"I have to get back in there." She opens the door and I can hear Tavin weeping louder now.

"Don't you want my help with her?" I start to follow her into the room.

She does her annoying sarcastic laugh. "You're clearly not her favorite person at the moment, so why don't you try to get some rest and just let me do what you asked me here to do." She disappears behind the door and shuts them both in the room.

I groan and let my head hit the wall in the hallway.

A hundred different scenarios crossed my mind about how this would play out, and being locked out of a room in my own house by two girls that hate me, was not among them.

# CHAPTER FIVE
## Withdrawal

*Tuesday, May 12th*

I'M SO EXHAUSTED MY EYES CAN BARELY FOCUS ON MY computer screen. I got zero sleep last night and my nerves are shot. I'm giving serious thought to my decision to take on Tavin. What made me think this was in any way a good idea? She refuses to talk to me and that's fine, but she can't avoid me forever.

My stomach rumbles and I need to get out of here for a while anyway. As I lock my door, I look to Eric's office and the thought hits me.

Holy shit. Is she Eric's drug dealer? Or the other way around?

I march to his office and knock on his door. He opens it immediately as if he was on his way out.

"Mr. Sørensen, hi. How can I help you?"

"In your office, now," I bark at him through clenched teeth.

Yeah, I'm pretty damn livid. That's why he was all twitchy when I asked him about her. He knows I will not be okay with drugs in my damn building.

"Take a seat."

He gestures to a chair as I cross my arms and remain

standing. This isn't a friendly visit. "Tavin is apparently a heroin addict. Were you aware of this?"

He exhales as his shoulders relax. "Well, yeah." He ambles to his desk and sits down. "I mean, she's hot and all, but she's a total smack freak."

Why is he so chill all of a sudden? I don't know exactly why his comment pisses me off so badly. She's definitely hot and apparently a 'smack freak', still, it takes all of my self-control not to hit him.

Slamming my hands down on his desk I grate out, "If I find out you have been doing anything illegal in this office you will not only be immediately removed, I will also do everything within my power to destroy your career in this city."

He gives me a silent nod as I turn on my heel. Refraining from slamming his door, I storm out of his office and into Silas'. I'm not going to get anything done today. I'm too tired, wired, and angry.

Silas jumps when I swing his door open. "Jesus Christ, knock much?"

"I'm taking a sick day."

I don't wait for him to respond, I just see his confused face before I turn around and leave. It's probably good that I cool down before I get home because I'm pissed at her. She's all sweet and perfect, acting as if she's my fantasies-come-alive, then I find out it's all bullshit. What was the point? Yes, I basically only have one night stands, but the difference is, both of us know what's going on and emotions are never involved. There are with her, and I'm not crazy, I know she felt something too. The way she looked at me, touched me, and kissed me was anything besides casual. However, now that the drugs are involved, it's very possible that she was so stoned that whatever she felt was from the high, not me.

If she's going to be staying with me for a few days, she'll need some things, so I stop at Whittaker's to get her some toiletries. I don't know what all she needs, but I do have a sister and have seen a ton of girls' bathrooms so I get toothpaste, floss, a toothbrush, deodorant, shampoo, conditioner, body wash, nail polish, nail polish remover, lotion, and a brush. Even though Sasha brought clothes last night, she'll still need underwear.

I can honestly say I have never bought underwear for anyone before. Even though they're cheap and just to get her through the next few days, I still get a bit of a thrill picking them out. I look in my basket trying to remember what else I could need.

Tampons. Girls always have endless tampons.

I'm seriously standing in the 'feminine hygiene' aisle. There's got to be forty different kinds to choose from and I have no clue what she uses, so I just get one of each.

At the checkout, the lady who is ringing me out is staring at me as if I'm a serial killer.

"House guest," I chuckle.

She clears her throat and takes a step away from me. "One fifteen forty-seven."

⌒

I'm not even inside yet and I can hear some kind of commotion going on. I push the button to lower the garage door as I walk into the entryway and find Tavin screaming at Sasha.

"No! God! I told you I'm not hungry." Tavin swipes her arm across the table, and a plate crashes to the floor.

Sasha throws her hands up as if she's considering strangling her. "Well then it's a good thing I don't give a shit! You are going to eat and then you are going to clean that up."

She shoves a banana in Tavin's face and I look down to see the shattered plate and bits of sandwich everywhere. I'm so glad I gave Cara Jo the day off, she would have flown off the handle.

"Tavin!" I shout. They both look up at me startled, and Tavin goes white. "Eat the damn banana, you'll feel better once you do." I turn my attention to Sasha. "I'm going to lie down for a few hours, then you can go home to spend some time with Drew and get some rest."

She nods in relief as I glance at Tavin, who refuses to acknowledge me. Shaking my head, I climb the stairs to my room and drop the shopping bags on the floor. I don't even take off my suit. I just fall onto my bed and crash.

Once I awaken, I take a quick shower, and change into some jeans and a tee. Bringing the bags from the drug store, I go to the guest bedroom and find Tavin curled up in a ball on the floor, crying as she clutches her stomach. Sasha lies next to her, rubbing her back and humming a melody. I sit the bags on the dresser and cross the hall to prepare her a bubble bath in the guest bathroom.

When I return, I kneel next to Sasha and whisper, "I started a bath for her. Help me get her in and then you can go."

She nods her agreement as we lift Tavin to standing and she helps her into the bathroom while I wait in the hall.

Moments later, Sasha emerges with a dazed frown and I ask, "Is she okay?"

"As okay as can be expected," she murmurs as she stares back at the bathroom door.

"What's wrong?"

She shakes her head as if she can jiggle away whatever thought she is having. "Oh nothing, why did you come home so early?"

I know she thinks it's because I don't trust her. Nodding my head toward the stairs, I gesture for her to follow me.

"I was never going to be able to focus today. I'm tired

and she has me all backwards, I can't think straight. I don't know what I'm doing here." I run my fingers through my hair. "I just need to talk to her."

We walk into the kitchen and I turn to see her raised brows.

"Wow, you're really mixed up over this." She shifts back and forth on her feet, clearly anxious to get out of here. "She's definitely got me curious though."

"Right?" At least I'm not the only one. "Sasha, I can't thank you enough for this. Take the day and get some rest tomorrow. I'll text you what time to be back tomorrow night."

She slides her purse strap over her shoulder. "Okay. Well, call me if she needs anything. She's a handful, so good luck."

As she steps away to leave, I place my hand on her arm. "Hey, I almost forgot." Reaching into my pocket, I pull out the key and hand it to her. "I had this cut for you this afternoon."

Her eyes go wide and her eyebrows nearly hit her hairline. "Wow."

"I'm not doing this lightly, Sash. I'm trusting you. And I need you."

"No, yeah, I know." She looks at me and gives me a smile I haven't seen in over three years. "Thank you, this really means a lot."

I follow her to the front door and our good bye isn't shaping up to be any more comfortable than our greeting. We don't know whether we're supposed to hug or what, and eventually we just wave as she leaves.

I stand at the base of the stairs for a moment, composing myself. This is the first time Tavin and I will be alone since this whole thing happened.

When I walk into the bathroom, the tub is so full of bubbles, it takes me a minute to realize she isn't in there.

Shit.

"Tavin!"

She can't have gone far, I would have seen her if she tried to leave from the main floor. I run across the hall to the guest bedroom and there she is: dripping wet in a little tee and shorts, bent over the window seat, attempting to climb through the window. She sees me and just tries to scramble out faster. I grab her arm and jerk her away before forcing her to sit her ass on the bed.

"Were you seriously just trying to climb out the window?" She still won't acknowledge my existence. "Goddamn it, look at me. I want to help you."

"I don't want or need your help." Her angry eyes finally meet mine. "How did you even find me? Eric doesn't know where I live."

She's going to think I'm a psycho. "The cabbie that took you home yesterday wasn't that difficult to persuade."

She gapes at me for a moment before murmuring, "We've already had sex. What more do you want?"

I sit down next to her. "This isn't about sex. At the moment, my main concern is getting you clean, but you've been in my head from the beginning. I don't think I ever wanted it to be only one night with you."

"Well that was all it was meant to be. I should never have agreed to go out with you in the first place. It was a mistake, a selfish, stupid mistake." My stomach clenches. No matter what happens, that night will never have been a mistake to me. "If you knew what I was you never would have looked at me twice."

"The drugs are not who you are, Tavin."

She releases an eerie laugh and it's unnerving to say the least. "You have no idea what I am."

"Well, you're right about that." I tuck her hair behind her ear. "I want to though." She scoffs and yawns. With a trembling hand, she covers her mouth. "Are you tired? Have you slept?"

She shakes her head. "I can't."

Getting off the bed, I retrieve the bags from the dresser and set them next to her. "I picked up some things for you today. If you need anything else, just let me know and I'll get it."

She digs through them and raises an eyebrow. "What's with all the tampons?"

"I didn't know what kind you needed."

"I don't need any of them, hopefully you can return them." She closes the bags and rubs her arm as she shrugs. "I don't get a period."

"Are you on a shot?"

"No, I never got it in the first place."

"Oh." That can't be good. She rubs the back of her neck and shakes out her hands. She's fidgety and keeps yawning. "Why don't we get you back in the bath? It might help you relax."

I take her hand to lead her back to the bathroom. Giving her privacy so she can get undressed, I wait until I hear the sound of the water splashing before I walk back in. Her head and neck are all I can see. She is covered in bubbles.

"Is it still warm?"

She nods, "Yes."

"How are you feeling?"

"Sore mostly." Her trembling hand covers her mouth as she yawns. "I've done this before you know. Gotten clean, I mean."

It's disconcerting to hear her sultry voice coming from such a broken version of her. Her head makes a small twitchy motion as I sit down on the bench against the wall.

"Then you know this is all temporary. It hasn't even been twenty-four hours yet. You have to give it time." She leans back in the tub and her shoulders seem to slack a bit.

We sit in silence for a couple of moments before I ask, "Were you high when we were together?"

She doesn't look at me as she speaks. "I was on coke in the beginning. I hadn't been high from any heroin for a couple of hours by then though, if that's what you're asking."

That makes me feel somewhat better. I tried coke in college. It didn't seem to do much, it just gave me a ton of energy.

"Are you hungry yet? You really should eat."

"Please don't make me. I get queasy just thinking about it."

"How about some tea? It might at least help you relax." Her eyes are focused on the water as she nods in agreement. "I'm going to give you some time alone, just don't try to run again, okay? I'm asking you to trust me. Once you're clean, you're free to go. I promise."

I wait for a response that doesn't come before sighing and leaving her to go downstairs. After pulling the white tea kettle from the cabinet, I choose a lemon blend from the pantry and as it brews, I grab a padlock and key from the garage for her window. Yes, I know this is crazy. I also know I'm just trying to do what I think is best. What I should have done for Sasha.

While I want to give her time to herself, I still stand next to the bathroom door every few minutes to make sure I can hear the water splashing. The kettle screams as I retrieve Cara Jo's floral tea cup and fill it with steaming tea. I bring it up the stairs and I barely step into the hall when I hear the sounds of retching. Pushing open the bathroom door, I look down to see her trembling, nude body kneeling over the toilet. Setting the tea on the vanity, I grab a towel off the rack. When I go to wrap it around her, I suck in my gasp and I'm grateful she can't see my face because I'm sure it looks horrified.

I don't know which is worse, the black, blue, and yellow bruises scattered all over her back or the cuts and gashes. Again, some are old and healed while others looked as if she could have gotten them within the last few days. Another reason for her not wanting to take off the sweater. I rush to cover her with the towel before I stand and wait in the thick silence.

When her vomiting has completely ceased, she whispers, "You should have stayed away. You weren't supposed to know about any of it." She coughs and looks at me with such a tortured expression. "I just wanted the one night, a fantasy, something to dream of. The way you looked at me that night, I wanted to lock it away and save it. Now, all I'll see is your disappointment." Anger overtakes the sadness in her voice when she adds, "You took that from me."

I feel like an asshole because it's true. I am disappointed. She isn't who I imagined her to be. It isn't fair to be upset at her for being less than truthful because she never expected me to become invested.

"Come on, even though you can't sleep, it'll be more comfortable if you lie down."

I help her back to the guestroom and let her get dressed while I get the tea from the bathroom. She's sitting on the bed when I return, so I turn on some music and help her get beneath the covers. Her skin becomes slick from the sweat and after a moment she pushes off the blankets. Shivers almost immediately overtake her body and I hate that I can't stop this for her. Climbing into the bed behind her, I wrap my arms around her and pull her against my chest. After a few seconds, her harsh shaking turns to slight vibrations. I kiss her neck while I hum along with the music, hoping my sister's technique will help calm her and possibly allow her to sleep.

"I'm not sorry that I found you. You're alive because of

it." I run my nose along the back of her neck, her scent a welcome reminder of the girl from the carnival. "Your back, Tavin…what kind of trouble are you in?" I whisper in her ear.

She jolts away from me and covers her mouth with her hand. "I'm gonna puke."

I jump out after her, pick up the bowl Sasha left on the nightstand and return just in time. I hold her long hair back as she convulses over and over until all that's left is dry heaving.

"Do you know how humiliating this is for me?" She cries.

"How long have you been using?"

Falling backwards on the bed, she rolls over so her beaten back is facing me.

"A long time."

I pause in hopes she will elaborate and not be so damn vague. She doesn't, so I clean the bowl before getting a cloth from the closet and running it under cold water.

I return to the room to find her curled up on the window seat, leaning up against the glass crying.

I'm not prepared for this. I want to take it all away from her, I want the girl from the carnival, and I want to do the right thing. Kneeling beside her, I wrap my arms around her shaky body.

"You locked the window," she finally gets out between sobs.

I try to conceal the amusement in my voice, she's just so defeated from a simple locked window.

"You tried to get out again? After I asked you not to?"

She gazes down at me with those sad eyes. "I know you are trying to do what you think you're supposed to, but you aren't listening to me. If you don't let me go I could die."

I roll my eyes. "Stop being so melodramatic, you can't

die from heroin withdrawal."

Her chest lifts with a sigh as she leans against the wall, staring vacantly out the window. I stand to wipe the wet cloth over her face and neck, watching the water roll down her destroyed back. The skin is raised beneath my fingers as I lightly caress over a couple of the cuts that appear so fresh they had to have been put there this week.

"What's happened to you?"

She shakes her head. "It's not what you think."

"I don't know what to think," I snap. "You haven't told me a damn thing. All I know is that our night together was incredible. I thought for sure we had something, and then you bail. When I do find you, you're half dead and beaten with a shit habit." I dab the cloth lightly across her back. "Do you owe someone money?"

She shakes her head. "No."

"Do you need to let anyone know where you are? A boss? Family?"

Her long eyelashes flutter as she shifts awkwardly. "No."

"Am I imagining something between us?" Big violet eyes look at me through wet lashes. "I can't get you out of my head."

She appears a bit stunned, at a loss for words or maybe just choosing them carefully. Finally she says, "I don't know what I feel, it's…jumbled, and it doesn't matter. I just…you don't want this, Alexander. You need to leave it alone."

"Seriously, stop fucking saying that. I decide what I want, no one else." I put a finger under her chin to make her look at me. "Is that why you left? You thought it was fair to make my decision for me?"

Her perfect eyebrows knit together as she stands up and sits on the bed. It's cute how she's too short for her feet to touch the ground. "I have nothing to give you."

"You don't know your own worth, *Lille*."

"My name is Tavin. Don't call me Leila."

I lie down on the bed behind her. "I am well aware of your name and I said *Lille*, not Leila. It's Danish. It means 'little'. It's a nickname my *Mormor* used to call Sasha. I think it fits you."

"What the heck is a mor-mor?"

"My grandmother. My mother's mother."

"Oh."

We lie in bed together for over an hour, not even speaking as I comb my fingers through her hair and we listen to the music kill the silence. I stare at her marks and bruises. They vary in size and shape as well as their stage of the healing process. The majority of them are long and thin, however there are shorter thicker ones next to small round ones. I also notice two sets of four perfectly symmetrical holes across her shoulder blades, as if her back has been pierced.

What is this girl's deal? Right now I'm going to tackle one thing at a time, and at present, it's getting her detoxed.


### Wednesday, May 13th


The rest of the night is a series of vomiting, crying, and shaking. I do the best I can to calm her, which really just amounts to holding her. She never sleeps, so I don't either. By six a.m. I'm beyond hungry, so I run downstairs to grab a bagel. I already called Cara Jo last night and told her to take a paid day off, so we will have the house to ourselves today.

If I take a shower there's no way Tavin won't jump on the opportunity to skip out. While Cara Jo goes home on nights and weekends, I still prefer she have her own space here and that's where she keeps the master key. After starting the coffee, I go to her bedside table and retrieve the key before walking to the guestroom to lock the door.

I go back to my room and stare longingly at my bed before getting undressed. Though I find it necessary to lock her in the room, I still feel a bit guilty about it so I rush through my shower as quickly as possible. Yanking on a pair of jeans, I grab a white tee shirt and pull it on as I hurry down the hall back to her room.

The lock is quiet as I turn the key and when I swing open the door, I see her standing in the far corner in nothing other than her green underwear and camisole. Her palms are against the wall and her shoulders rise and fall with heavy breathing. My gaze can't help traveling down her body. Below her right butt cheek, high on her thigh, are three red lines that stretch across the back of her leg, directly above the dotted band of scars. Jesus.

"Are you okay?"

"It's so hot." She pushes off the wall. "It's like a thousand degrees in here!" She whips her head in my direction and slightly raises an eyebrow. "Did you just shower?" She looks me up and down.

"Uh yeah…"

"Oh, it's just your hair is still wet." She bites her lip and exhales slowly. "You look good with wet hair." Seemingly just realizing she's still uncomfortable, she yells, "God, it's so hot!" She lifts her hair off her shoulders as she begins to pace the floor.

I place my hand on her back, leading her to the bed. "Lie down, I have an idea. I'll be right back."

I hurry to the kitchen and grab a large mixing bowl from the cabinet before filling it with ice cubes. When I return, I find her still on the bed and drinking from a bottle of water. At least she's been pretty good about her liquid intake. After placing the bowl on the bedside table, I tell her to arch her back so I can slide the towels beneath her. I climb on the bed and hover over her with my knees on the outside of her hips. Lifting the camisole to her naval, I reach in the bowl and remove a piece of ice. Her stomach has a few healed, thin, white scars that I wouldn't have even noticed if I hadn't been looking. When the ice makes contact with her skin, she takes in a sharp breath. It melts quickly as water pools in her cute little bellybutton.

I push up her shirt little bits at a time, letting the water drip down her sides. I have her shirt halfway up her ribs before she stops me.

"Please don't."

Jesus, how much worse could it get?

"There's more?"

Her beautiful, flawless face fills with shame making me feel like a prick. I pick up another ice cube, move to the end of the bed and pull her foot into my lap. Starting on her right calf, I glide the cube under her knee, over the top of her shin, and up to her thigh. When I switch to her other leg, I glance up at her, and she's watching the ice. God, she's sick as hell and still looks incredible. Her hair is a mess, which is darling, and her bangs are sticking against her forehead. Her eyes have dark circles beneath them and still they are so beautiful. Her ivory skin is a little washed out, though it's improving.

I reach over to the bowl to pick another piece and place it on the inside of her left wrist. There's another scar... and a tattoo. The handwritten script reads: *When you bleed, I bleed.* The large diagonal wound directly above it is long since healed, beginning at her wrist and ending a couple inches below her elbow. I trace the ice along the raised skin before switching to her other arm. There are a couple of cigarette burns as well as much larger burns, inside her forearm. I move up to her shoulder only to find more proof of her secrets. With a new piece of ice, I place it at the top of her neck, move it down and across her chest to the other shoulder as she sighs with quiet moans of relief.

She closes her eyes. "Oh yes, this feels better, thank you."

The way she says it along with the arching of her back, I have to kiss her. I lean over and place my lips lightly against hers.

"Please, let me help you."

She opens her eyes. "I don't understand why you're making your life so hectic for a junkie you stuck your dick in once."

I jerk my head back in shock at her words. "Hey! I don't want you to talk that way while you're in this house, got it?" She just stares at me with borderline defiance. Finally, she gives me a harsh nod and a frown. I sigh as I get more ice and continue trying to cool her off.

I spend the rest of the day running baths, fighting with her about eating, and holding her. She starts freezing again so I give her my sweatshirt. We lie in bed for hours listening to music while I lightly trail my fingers across her thigh.

At some point I doze off because I'm startled awake by a crash. Bolting upright, I see a broken lamp on the floor and her lying next to it as if she fell. She turns back to look at me, and when she sees me watching, her eyes widen as she scrambles to her feet. The bedroom door hits the wall as she throws it open and sprints into the hall.

That little shit.

I jump up and fly off the bed, staying right on her heels. She takes two steps at a time down the stairs and so do I.

"Goddamn it! Stop!" I yell as I turn the corner at the landing.

Silas is standing in the kitchen, and she isn't expecting him so it throws her off balance. Her arms instinctively go out to break her fall before he catches her.

A smile spreads across his face. "Hi, Angel."

Oh hell no. I know that look and he better stop fucking giving it to her.

"Tavin, get upstairs," I snap.

She stands up straight and speed walks past me. While I'm thankful she's wearing my sweatshirt so he doesn't see her back, I wish she was wearing a little more than just her underwear and a camisole beneath it.

Silas points up and smirks. "So that's what's been going on with you?" I rub my hands over my face and can't respond with any more than a groan. He pulls a beer from my fridge. "Uh, well no offense, but I get the feeling she doesn't want to be here." Popping the top he adds, "Maybe I could take her off your hands for a couple of hours."

I know in the past we have occasionally passed girls back and forth, but not this time, definitely not this time. I glare at him. "That's not going to happen. Get that idea out of your head right the fuck now."

He holds his hands up. "Okay, Jesus."

I explain the situation the best I can and if he thinks I am being foolish he doesn't say so. Once he leaves, I stop by the guest bedroom to ask Tavin if she wants to eat anything which is swiftly answered with a scowl. I'm too tired to argue anymore today so I slip out, shut the door, and lock it with the key.

As I walk down the hallway I hear her banging and yelling, "You can't lock me in here!"

I shake my head as I walk to my room to finally get some sleep. What the hell am I doing?

*Tavin*

I want to scream at his stupid, gorgeous face that he's putting us both in danger. He thinks this is about the freaking heroin. I can't believe I brought him into this.

*Stupid, selfish, fucking bitch.*

I need to relax. I technically have three and a half weeks before this gets too serious. I mean it's already extremely bad and I'm sure Toben is freaking out. If I'm still in this mess when the three weeks are over and Logan gets back...things will get bloody.

I want to call Toben. I know I can't though because then Alexander's number will be on the phone bill. I have to find a way to let him know I'm okay so he doesn't do anything stupid.

I can't believe the jerk locked me in here. The last time I was locked up to get clean, I was at least in my own house with Toben. I hate being locked up, I think it makes the withdrawals worse.

My skin, my teeth, my dang eyelashes ache and I just feel so irritated. I don't like this. Why did I have to get another habit? Even if it is a small one. It's Toben's fault, he's the one always bringing it home even though he knows it's against the rules.

I need to stop thinking about it.

The lock clicks and my heart still stops when I see him, no matter how mad I am.

"You locked me in?!"

I don't know if I'm angrier that he's doing this without any right whatsoever, or the fact that it's him doing it in the first place.

"I can't trust you right now."

He makes me want to pull my hair out! Well, more than

normal. Why does he need to trust me? There can't be anything between us. If he thinks he is going to clean me up and then I'll be his girlfriend, he has a lot of disappointment to look forward to. How do I tell him he is wasting his time?

I just want out of this room.

"Please, I want to go outside, can we go on a walk?"

He laughs and it isn't the light, sexy laugh from the carnival, this one is heavy with distress. "Nice try. That's not happening."

"I need fresh air."

"And when you've earned it, you'll get it."

Arrogant ass. He has no power to do this. That much I know. He sure acts like he does though. Well, I don't have to do a dang thing he says without a fight. I don't feel good, I'm scared of the repercussions of this, and he's pissing me off.

"You're making me so mad!" I yell it at him so maybe he'll understand.

He crosses his arms and his muscles bulge from the movement. He may currently be acting like a dick, but he looks so good doing it.

"Well, you can get glad in the same pants you got mad in." Immediately, he looks disgusted with himself, "Oh God that sounded like Cara Jo." Am I supposed to know who that is? He shakes the thought away and emerald eyes shine down on me. "Will you just relax? Chill out and be proud of the fact that you've been clean for nearly forty-eight hours? And will you please just lie down?"

I blow my bangs out of my eyes and comply. He gets on too, sitting at the foot of the bed and bringing my feet onto his lap. His warm touch sends his heat through the rest of my body and when it stops, I know his fingers are brushing over the piece of missing skin inside my ankle.

"What happened here?"

Oh Lord what a question. His fingers keep brushing

over it causing his burn to disappear and reappear. It's kind of funny how many people ask questions they don't really want the answers to.

"I don't remember."

His hand stops moving and when I look up at him, his mouth is pressed in a hard line and his jaw is twitching. I swallow instinctively. He's mad at me. He sighs and his face softens as his fingers trail over my heel across the pad to my toes. It feels so freaking good, a whispered moan slithers between my lips.

His strong, warm hand moves up my leg. "You do want to be clean, right?"

*You will never be clean. Disgusting, repulsive girl.*

I inhale deeply before letting all the air rush out. "I don't like getting sick if I don't use, so I guess I don't like having a habit, but I love heroin. It's…" How can I explain this to him? How do I tell him it's the heroin that helps me and Toben get through the days? It's what allows us to live for each other and without the heroin, I don't know if we are strong enough anymore.

"What is it like?"

I close my eyes and feel myself smile. What is peace like? What is nothing like?

"It's kind of difficult to explain…" His hands are massaging into my flesh and talking about it makes me miss the high. "Mmmm, imagine the happiest you've ever felt multiplied by like…a jillion. It takes you away and holds you tight. It's kind of like flying or sleeping on a cloud. Floating away from all your sadness, where it keeps you safe. It's a beautiful numbness. It's love where none exists. Heaven is a heroin high." I can almost feel the needle going into my skin when his warm hand moves higher up my thigh making me hyper aware of his touch.

My eyes fly open and match his. I never thought I would

see him again and if I did, I never dreamed it would be under these circumstances. He doesn't know what he's doing to me in more ways than one. My skin is tingling and it isn't associated with the sickness. He still touches me with gentle, arousing fingers even after he saw my back, even after he knows that I'm an addict. He still looks at me with curiosity and wonder and passion. What is wrong with him?

What's really sad is that I want him to want me, even now. It's so ridiculous it's tragic. His hand is on my leg, his eyes are burning into mine, and his beautiful face is turned on. I want his body in mine, I want to pull his soft, light blond hair, I want to taste his mouth and feel his lips on my skin.

A harsh breath escapes me as his hand massages higher on my thigh. I watch his fingers move and I can't help myself from wondering if our night together was a fluke. Would he still be able to keep the dirty fear away? I know I promised Toben I wouldn't do it again. He would be so angry, but Alexander is touching me and I've thought about his touch every day since our night together.

Why does he still want me? My back alone should turn a normal guy like him right off. I don't know what I'm doing or why I torture myself when I open my legs for him. I have to know if he can do it again. I almost want it to crawl over me so I know it was just that one time, and maybe he won't consume my thoughts anymore once I get out of here. I wait for his repulsion, and instead his large bulge shifts in his pants, giving me a rush. I'm so filthy, I know it, yet somehow, while he's touching me, I don't feel it. I brush my fingertips over his hand on my thigh before trailing them toward the ache between my legs. I lightly touch myself over the fabric, gauging his reaction. He has the same smoldering heat across his face as before.

"Do you still want me, Alexander?" I whisper. I let my fingers find my cunt beneath my shorts and it's slippery. He makes me ready just by being near. He doesn't answer, his stare is searing into my moving hand so I continue, "Now that you know I'm a mangled junkie?"

His face flashes and I think he actually growls at me when he's across the bed with his mouth nearly on mine so fast my heart free-falls into my stomach. I jump and he pulls my hand away from in-between my legs and replaces it with his.

"I told you..." His long fingers trace along my wet folds and his deep voice rumbles against my lips. "Don't..." He smells like sunshine and I can feel myself clenching in anticipation, "...fucking..." He rams two fingers inside of me and I welcome them, "...talk that way."

He pushes them in again, hard and deep. Yes he's intimidating, they all are, but he's also tender and...kind and... Oh God...

I can hear the sounds my wetness is making and I can't believe he can do this. It wasn't a fluke, it wasn't just the one night. It's him. He makes me feel like I'm not covered in repulsive memories. He makes me confused. He makes me want to forget the consequences and just see what happens. He makes me wish...Yes...

"Hey, nobody answered so I just let m- Oh Jesus!"

Sasha's voice startles me and he jumps back from me so fast that he falls off the bed. I slap my hand over my mouth so I won't laugh. He's so sexy getting all flustered and I feel the tingles drumming throughout my body.

He clears his throat and he straightens. "Hey Sash."

The accent that tints his voice seems heavier with his embarrassment as he runs a hand through his light hair. He speed walks out, leaving the room without another word.

I'm staring after him through the empty doorway when Sasha's laughing grabs my attention. I yank my head in her direction.

"Wow, girl, I haven't seen him blush in ages. That shit is

hilarious." She sits her purse down on the tall dresser. "Just be careful, okay? My brother can be…fickle. This is a sensitive time in your recovery and letting your emotions get out of control is the quickest way back to the needle."

Actually, the quickest way back to the needle is out of this house.

She comes over and sits on the bed. "I know that he can be somewhat charming, even if he is an idiot."

That makes me mad. She shouldn't talk about him like that. "He's not an idiot."

She laughs, even though I don't see what's funny about it. My stomach is starting to get queasy and I want to scratch away the itchy flesh and burn away the grime. I have to get out of here.

"Hey I brought some ointment for your back." She digs around in a bag. "Oh damn, I forgot a cloth, I'll be right back."

I don't know why I do it. I've never stolen anything in my life. I don't even know what I'm expecting to find. Regardless, when she leaves, I look through her purse. There's a pill bottle near the top and the label says *Valium*.

Oooh! Those will help! I try to open the bottle, but before I can, I hear her footsteps coming down the hall, so I throw it back in her purse before running to jump back on the bed.

*Thursday, May 14th*

# Alexander

I wish I could at least text Tavin. I want to see how she's feeling and it would be nice to talk to her whenever I want. I send a quick email to my assistant instructing her to pick up a phone and call Sasha to let her know how late I'm going to be tonight.

"Okay. You might have wanted to give Cara Jo a heads up about Tavin though. I stepped out to call Drew for five seconds and she found her in the guest room. She tried to throw her out and of course Tavin didn't protest. If I hadn't gotten there in time, she would be long gone."

"Shit. She came in late today so I didn't see her this morning. What did she say when you explained the situation?"

She laughs—a sound I have missed.

"She was shocked. Other than that though, they took to each other pretty well. She had Tavin laughing at the old photos she keeps of us in her purse and how you could never say the word 'individual' right." She laughs again. "Invididual."

I roll my eyes. I'm glad that I'm so damn entertaining. "How is she?"

"She has ups and downs. She's anxious, sore, and irritable. Still, it could be so much worse."

I don't even want to think about what 'worse' entails. "Do you really think locking her in is necessary though?"

"If it keeps her from getting out and overdosing again, then yeah, I do."

"You know she can still overdose whether she's clean or not right?

"I'm aware of that, but right now wanting to get high is her top priority. If she leaves now, the first thing she'll do is use."

"That's not going to change in a week."

"Jesus, Sash, are you trying to discourage me?"

"No, I'm actually proud of you, but I'm trying to make you be realistic."

I know she is trying to help, I just can't think that far ahead right now. "I need to get back to work."

My heart is racing from the anticipation of seeing Tavin. I shut my car door and as I walk into the entryway from the garage, I'm pummeled by a little body and skinny arms around my waist.

"You're back!"

I'm thrown off by her enthusiasm, yet I wrap my arms around her just the same. My stomach flips and I feel a smile on my face.

"And you must be feeling better." I tuck her hair behind her ear.

Before she can respond, Sasha comes barreling down the stairs. "Okay, don't be mad." she holds her hands up in surrender.

"Oh God, why would I be mad?" Tavin releases me then, and smiles up at me. As she does, I see glossed over violet eyes with almost nonexistent pupils.

Oh I'm mad alright.

"Is she fucking high?!"

"Okay, I know you're pissed and it was my fault. I left my purse in her room. I had a bottle of Valium in there aaand… she found them."

Grabbing Tavin by the arm, I pull her upstairs. "So, you are still using then?" I yell to Sasha over my shoulder. I hear her audibly gasp and I can see her face in my mind's eye, scrunched up in offense.

"It's a prescription, you dick!"

She follows us up the stairs and as we arrive at the guestroom, Tavin looks up at me. Her large eyes appear even bigger with the dilation, so she kind of looks similar to those *Precious Moments* dolls, when she takes my hand.

"Don't be mad at her. Please?"

I point inside the room. "Get on the bed." She huffs, but hightails it once she looks at my face. I storm to the dresser, get Sasha's purse and throw it to her. "Either leave the drugs at home, or do a better job of keeping them away from her."

She pulls her purse strap over her shoulder. "God, they're just Valium. They prescribe them to addicts all the time." She tries, mostly succeeding, to stifle a laugh. "She just took a few too many."

"It isn't funny Sasha. Could she OD again?" I don't even want to think about that.

"Xander! Chill. No. She didn't take the whole bottle."

"Don't call me Xander."

She doesn't miss a beat, "I'm not saying she should have done it, I just don't think it's that big of a deal."

"The whole point of you being here is to prevent this from happening and she's over there high as hell."

She throws up her hands. "She's a sneaky shit! I was literally gone for two seconds, I don't even know how she knew I had anything in there. She had them gone and taken before I knew what she was doing."

I hear soft laughing from the bed. "You guys know I can hear you, right?"

# CHAPTER SIX
## *House guest*

A FTER WALKING SASHA OUT AND TELLING HER WHEN to return, I go back upstairs to the guestroom. Tavin is sitting in the middle of the bed and as I walk in, she jumps up on her knees.

"Don't be upset. It was getting really bad."

I sigh. To be honest, I'm happy she's able to get some relief.

"I'm just trying to be a decent guy here. I'm not trying to hurt you."

"I want you to…" she mumbles seemingly to herself.

"You want me to what?"

She ignores my question and suddenly, the hem of her shorts become extremely interesting because she's inspecting it as though it holds the answers to the entire Goddamn universe.

"You do see that I'm trying to help you, right?" I take off my jacket and drape it over the chair before I sit on the edge of the bed.

She crawls over, moving to sit next to me. "Yes, I do. It's just things aren't as simple as all that and right now my thoughts are cloudy." She scoots closer and nudges my shoulder. "Well… partly."

She winks as her hand moves to my thigh, gripping it lightly.

The fucking wink. I turn to face her and groan. "You have no idea how much I want to do this," gesturing between her and my lap where my erection has turned against me, "but you're sick right now."

She gets off the bed and kneels on the floor between my legs. Looking up at me through her long eyelashes, she moves her little hands up my thighs.

"I feel okay right now. I want you to do it again." Her hands rub my cock over the top of my suit trousers.

Wait…what? Do what again? I can't think while she's touching me. I shouldn't do this while she's high and sick. I shouldn't do this when I don't know what her situation is.

"Tavin, I…"

I'm not even trying anymore as she unzips my fly and pulls my underwear down enough to free me. I have been fantasizing about this for what feels like forever. Her warm little mouth consumes me. Her perfect pink lips encase me. Oh my God, even better than I remember. Without a doubt, she gives the best head I have ever had.

She pulls away, withholding her suction and my eyes fly open.

"I don't want you to be mad at me," she whispers.

"I'm not mad."

I push her back down as I thrust between her lips. Damn, I keep hitting the back of her throat and she barely makes a sound. I have no idea how she's able to fit so much without gagging. I'm actually nervous. If I don't get her off this time I might lose my mind.

I rub a piece of her silky hair in between my fingers before I cup her cheek and lift her head to begrudgingly take her off of me.

"Stand up."

She does what I say and I reach up to the waistband of her shorts, clawing my fingers around the elastic. I want to rip them off, yet again, I take my time. I'm going to enjoy what I have been waiting for. I slide them down her bare legs, letting them drop to the floor before placing my hands on her hips and pulling her to me. She's so short, even with me sitting, I have to bend down to shove my nose into her pink low rise panties. I inhale deeply and her erotic aroma brings more blood to my already throbbing cock. Her arousal wets my nose through the fabric.

"God, you smell so good." I kiss her stomach above the hem of her panties and push them down her body to drop them on top of the shorts. "I want to taste your come."

Her eyebrows twitch as her mouth sets into a line. She leaves me so clueless sometimes. I lift her left leg so that her foot is on the bed next to my thigh, opening her up for me. I reach between her open legs to get a handful of her incredible ass and pull her pussy onto my mouth. I have to lift her up so that I can reach her center with my tongue, causing her to grasp on to my hair to keep her balance. I eat her out as if I'm starving because I am. Her taste, her smell, her voice, all of it is more overwhelming than I remember, if that's even possible. I moan into her before I lean back a bit, allowing my tongue more room. Her breathing gets heavy as she rocks her hips. She whimpers as I squeeze her clit between my pointer and middle finger, flicking my tongue over the little button.

"Yes," she whispers and grips my hair a little tighter.

Licking her bottom lip, she watches me with intensity as I pull my mouth away. "Come for me."

She draws her eyebrows together and I want to reach up and smooth the creases. What is going on in that beautiful head of hers?

I lean forward and kiss her pussy before sliding in a

finger and sucking her clit between my lips.

This is quickly becoming a repeat of last time. Does my tongue need to tie itself into a fucking bow to get this girl off? She's biting her lip, hips are quickening their tempo, and still she watches me.

I put my hands to her waist before I throw her on the bed and push her legs as far apart as they will go. With two fingers, I pump them in and out of her as my tongue begs her pussy for climax. Nothing. I am not letting this happen again. I force a third finger and ram them into her so hard, my knuckles are hitting her pelvic bone and forcing a gasp from her throat.

Her voice is as soft as a cloud. "Yes, Lex."

My stomach jumps and pulls a smile across my lips. *Lex.* That's a new one. I kiss her stomach before pushing myself up to be face to face with her.

"You are going to come this time, because I won't stop fucking you until you do."

I quickly unbutton my shirt and throw it to the floor. She watches me and exhales a shaky breath. How does she make me feel like a God and so weak at the same time? I get up to get a condom before I toss off the rest of my clothes, rip the package open, and roll it on. I hover over her to make sure I'm locked in with the most beautiful eyes I have ever seen as I run the tip along her drenched slit, and push into heaven.

Her slickness is hardening my cock more with every thrust. I want to rip that shirt off and suck on her tits, though I settle for groping her over the tee. I kiss her neck and nibble on her ear lobe. My lips crash into hers and my tongue enters her mouth as soon as she opens for it. Cupping the nape of her neck, I bring her closer. She's kissing me with such passion, it forces the need to be deeper. It's essential to be deeper. Her little gasps fuel my fire as I grab her thigh to put it around my waist and she follows my lead by wrapping the other. She shoves herself onto me as hard as I push myself into her, our bodies slamming against each other as quiet, raspy moans escape her swollen lips.

Hoisting her up to straddle me, I sit on my knees and slide her back onto my body. Using my grip on her neck, I enforce my thrusts by digging my other hand into her waist and slamming her down. The wet sounds are so damn hot that I have to bite my tongue so I won't get too close to the edge. She watches me, never breaking eye contact. When she does that, it makes me feel untouchable and in control as much as it does powerless and under her spell. I keep her body stationary while I tear her apart with violent plunging from below. She brings her arms around my neck and her mouth is next to my ear so I can hear every shaky breath, raspy moan, and impassioned whimper. The way she rolls her body and rocks her hips with such soul is incredible. She is so quiet during sex, it's such a contrast to her extremely intense movements.

She has a look of pleading and confusion and I hate that I have no idea what she's feeling or thinking. She won't talk to me. Her soft little hand comes to my cheek and her lips delicately touch mine in a sweet kiss. She kisses my neck before resting her head there and bringing her body down on mine so hard it's starting to send to me too close. I need to switch it up. Lifting her off of me is torture.

"Get on your knees."

She does what I ask, and it's the first time I see her bare ass. More scars. There are new red angry marks along with the old healed ones that seem to be the common theme. My eyes travel down to the adorable little diamond gap that exposes her pretty pussy. Just like her face, it's flawless and without scars.

With her in this position, it makes me think, maybe she

didn't get off last time because I didn't touch her ass. I lean down to lick in between her folds before I run my tongue over her tight puckered hole. I slip my thumb into her pussy while I rim her. Her body does sway a little, though for the most part she stays still. Other than the little sighs and grunts making their way out of her mouth here and there, anal licking doesn't seem to be doing much. I straighten and slam back into her without warning. Fuck, she's even tighter in this position.

This is starting to get ridiculous. Don't get me wrong, this feels—wow, but what the hell does a guy have to do? I pull out of her and push her onto her back in one motion, before sliding back into her body. I want to see her eyes and I'm getting to the point that I don't think I can hold off much longer.

"Your tight little cunt is going to make me come and I will be beyond pissed if I finish before you do this time." I ram in hard. "Tell me what to do."

She doesn't respond and after a moment she starts making this weird, forced moaning sound.

Now, I know she didn't just do that.

"Did you seriously just try to fake an orgasm?" I'm still powering into her and barely audible sounds are leaving her mouth as she looks away. "Damn it, Tavin."

I don't necessarily want to snap at her, but I'm going to get off if she doesn't hurry.

Her eyes shift down to watch me thrust in and out of her.

She moans, "I…uh…"

"Spit it the fuck out!" This girl is killing me.

"God! Fine." She closes her eyes. "Cover my nose and mouth." She snaps them back open to connect with mine. "You can't let me breathe."

I'm sorry what?

"Are you serious?" The question comes out before I can think it through.

She looks away and I can see her closing right back up. I'm not really sure how I'm supposed to feel about this, but I finally got something out of her and my desire to get her off wins out by a landslide. My hand easily covers most of her face. I press down with my palm to sever all the airflow as my thrusts bring me closer and closer to finishing. All I can see are her burning eyes locked onto mine. After a couple moments, they take on a sheen as her eyelids droop. I have no idea how long I'm supposed to do this. She is giving me complete control, and while it's overwhelmingly erotic, I'm clueless as what to do with it. Her life is quite literally in my hands.

Is this what she needs? Asphyxiation? Death flirtation? I have never done anything remotely close to this before. This is so fucked up and Jesus help me, I love it. Her body jolts beneath me and I'm scared for a moment that I'm suffocating her to the point of danger when I feel the wet choking tightness around my cock. Finally. She's soaking me. I'm so relieved it finally happened that I know I'm smirking.

"There you go, let it out *Lille*."

When I'm positive the throbbing has completely stopped, I release her mouth and she gasps harshly to regain her composure as the floodgates open with my climax. Oh my God…fuck yes… fuck…I'm going to overflow the condom with how much she's pulling out of me. I exhale a breath as I place the hand that just deprived her of oxygen onto her cheek.

Still reveling in how incredible that was, I groan, "Wow."

I let out a small grunt when I slide out of her and her chest is still heaving while she tries to squirm out from under me. During sex she will keep eye contact almost constantly. Now that I'm not inside of her anymore, she's looking everywhere other than me.

I grab her arm. "Hey relax, what's wrong?"

"You think I'm a freak now."

I don't think it's a good idea to tell her I think 'freaky' showed up long before her asphyxiaphilia came to light.

"There's nothing wrong with being a bit of a freak, Tav. Everyone has something." I put my mouth over hers and give her lip a nip, "Besides, that was hot as hell."

And I want to do it again.

She gives me her half smile and her cheeks flush. As I stand to remove the condom, I pick our clothes up off the floor and remember her cell phone is in my jacket. "I got you a phone today."

She sits up in bed, confused. Her head makes a little jerk. "A phone? Why?"

I pull it from the pocket and when I go to throw it to her, she's obviously staring at my ass.

"Like what you see?" I laugh. She turns crimson and looks away again. Kneeling on the bed, I kiss her jawline. "It makes me feel good when you stare." I hand her the phone and get back in bed with her. "I got it so we can text while I'm at work."

"Oh."

I hug her to me with her back against my chest, so I'm talking to the top of her head. "The alcohol had nothing to do with your inability to come the night of the carnival did it?"

I feel her shoulders shake a bit. The little shit is giggling. "Nope."

She falls asleep before I'm able to try for a second round. Combing my fingers through her hair, I watch her slightly parted lips. Her steady breathing causes her tits to rise and fall beneath her shirt. I want to see what's under that tee so damn bad. I keep thinking the worst, such as deep gashes or horrible burns. I trace my finger over the burns on her arm. It's becoming more unsettling to not have a clue as to what I'm really dealing with here. My heart races just from looking at her. If I'm truly honest with myself, I know what I'm doing probably isn't right. She may benefit from a clinic more than she will here. I never said I wasn't selfish.

A loud banging noise comes from the hallway and I sit up, rolling my eyes at Sasha's ability to throw her one hundred and ten pound body around like a gorilla. Just as I think her name, the doorknob turns and she peeks inside. I nod in greeting and she glances at Tavin before wiggling her fingers at me in a wave. She closes the door and pounds her way back down the stairs to the guestroom.

Lying back down, I kiss Tavin's head. I just need to see this thing through and do what I should have done with Sasha. It's a bit of a foreign concept for me, not wanting to let her go.

### Friday, May 15th

I'm jolted from sleep at two a.m. by crying. I push open my eyes to find Sasha sitting in the lamplight on the bed with her arms around Tavin.

"Tavin, are you okay?" I ask. Her response consists of vomiting. "Can I get you anything?"

Sasha answers, "Get a cold, wet washcloth."

I grip the comforter to toss it off before realizing I'm naked. I rub the back of my neck and nod towards my dresser. "Mind handing me a pair of underwear? I'm going natural over here."

Her lip lifts in a snarl as she scoffs in disgust. "Ewe."

She still gets the underwear though because neither of us wants her to see that. After she throws them at my face, I slide them on beneath the sheets and walk to the bathroom for the washcloth.

I return to see Tavin shaking, sweating, and vomiting all at once. I would literally do anything to take this from her.

I hand Sasha the wet cloth. "Let's get her in the bathroom and I'll run her a bath," I say as I put my arm under Tavin's legs and lift her off the bed. Her body is convulsing with dry heaves on top of my arms. "I'm sorry you are going through this, *Lille*."

My twintuition allows me to feel Sasha's gaze on my back at the use of the familiar nickname.

"Obviously the Valium wore off," Sash grumbles.

I make a mental note to call Marie tomorrow to ask her about a prescription to help ease through this transition. I know I'm running hot and cold here, it's just unnecessary for her to suffer more than she needs to.

I place Tavin gently on the bathroom floor and turn to start the bath. Sasha sits on the floor next to her and looks up at me.

"You should go back to bed." She glances down at Tavin, "This is why I'm here."

I nod and kneel down to kiss Tavin on the head before I go to my room.

Seventy-two hours down.

# Tavin

Sasha is sleeping, Alexander's probably getting ready for work, and Cara Jo hopefully isn't here yet. I think for a split second about staying for a few more days. He surprised me last night. Clearly he was a little shocked, but he wasn't horrified or disgusted. His actual words were: *that was hot as hell.*

I can feel myself smile. Sasha gave me another Valium a couple hours ago and I'm still feeling pretty decent.

No, I have to leave. I need Toben, I need a fix, and the more playdates I miss the worse it will be.

I look over at the girl that looks like him. I like her except for when she talks about Alexander like he's stupid. I have never really spent much time with women. She and Cara Jo are so nice though. I blow my bangs out of my eyes as I sneak out of bed. Tiptoeing across the carpet, I peek my head out the door. Good, I don't see Lex.

I creep down the hall to the top of the stairs. Dang! My jeans and tee shirt are still in the bedroom. Oh well, they're gone now, I'm not risking waking up Sasha to get them and I'll find a way to give her back the clothes I'm wearing.

As quietly as I can, I take each step slowly. Just as my foot is about to touch the landing, I hear his deep voice.

"I'm sorry I didn't warn you about Tavin. It's been an insane couple days."

Well that's not my fault. He's the one calling the shots here.

Dishes *clank* as Cara Jo speaks, "Don't apologize. She's a wonderful girl. She's the one from the carnival right?"

My stomach pangs. He's talked about me?

"How do you know that?" He sounds surprised.

"You told me you had a date and you told me her name. Usually all I get is 'I'm going out'. A blind man could see that you were excited. It's been years since you have shown real interest in anyone." I feel the hot tears burning and press the heels of my palms to my eyes. I'm not used to hearing people talk about me like this. "Then of course she mentioned her name. Tavin is not one that is easily forgotten."

I can hear his smile. "No, it's not."

"Eavesdroppin' huh? Nice." A voice whispers in my ear. I jump about ten feet and clasp my hand over my mouth. Sasha is standing there grinning. "Hear anything good?" She laughs and nods her head toward the kitchen as she holds my hand. "Let's go get breakfast."

I roll my eyes. She knows I don't feel like eating.

We sit at the island and Alexander keeps smiling at me over his coffee. I can feel my face get red. Considering everything, a smile should most definitely not make me blush.

After breakfast, Sasha and I go back upstairs and I take a shower. She's sitting on the bed when I get back into the room writing in a notebook. I feel myself get excited. Does she draw too?

"What are you doing?" I ask her.

"Sketching. See?" She turns the paper to show me. It's a picture of a tall skinny woman in a long dress. "I'm going to make this dress."

"You can make clothes?"

She smiles and it reminds me of him.

"Fashion is my love. My life." She sighs, "Ironically, it had as much of a hand in getting me hooked on the needle as it did getting me off." That doesn't make sense. How can clothes do either of those things? "Art. She's a bitch sometimes."

"What do you mean?"

She sets down the notepad, crosses her arms and leans back. "I want to be famous for my designs. I want to see my gowns on the red carpet, someday." She closes her eyes. "A few years ago, I got invited to an elite party. There were models, fashion photographers, designers, magazine editors… We're talking some big names." She groans, "You would not believe the buffet of drugs they had at this place. I wanted to get in with these people so I allowed myself to shoot up for the first time that night. I know it doesn't always hook people instantly, the way they warn you about, but it did me. I began to love the heroin more than art. More than life."

I lick my lips. That sounds wonderful. "Do you not do it at all anymore?"

She rubs her arm. "I can't."

"Well I can. It's just gotten out of hand the last few months."

She frowns at me. "You have no intention of staying off when you leave here, do you?"

I wish I could make them understand. "No. Not completely anyway. I will try to not get a habit again though. Quitting completely isn't an option."

My life is impossible to live without at least a little heroin.

She rolls on her side and props her head in her hand. "How long have you been using?"

I debate whether to tell her. I don't know if that part is a secret and I don't know why, but I want to tell her things.

"Since I was ten."

Her mouth falls open. "Whoa what?! Does Alex know that?

"No."

"And you're how old?"

"Twenty-three."

"How is that possible? How do you look like…you?"

I shrug. "I never used heavily until recently."

She's staring at me like she is waiting for something to come into focus. "I have so many questions…" And I have no answers. "What's the deal with the…" She rubs her hand over her sternum.

I shake my head. "I can't tell you."

She narrows her eyes. "Hmm. Curiouser and curiouser"

"Please Sasha, I feel like crap."

"No. I shouldn't have given you one this morning, I'm not trying to make Alex pissed at me anymore than he already is. And you feel like crap because you haven't eaten."

Shut up about the food!

I roll my eyes at her. "Why is he mad at you?"

"No way, bitch. You don't get my dirty laundry without handing over some of your own."

Even though I don't like being called a bitch, or any names for that matter, for some reason the way she says it doesn't bother me. My attention is caught by the buzzing from the phone Alexander bought me. I pick it up and touch the 'message' notification.

**How are you feeling?**

I look over at Sasha painting my toenails. "Lex is texting me."

She snorts. "Wow, you guys already have pet names for each other? That's actually kind of barfworthy."

I type out my response.

**Like crap.**

He responds quickly.

**I'm going to try to get you a Valium prescription tonight so you can ask Sasha to give you ONE.**

Wow caps and underlined? Think he got his point across?

"Hey, he just said I can have a few of your Valium, he's getting me a script."

She squints at me and her fingers fly across her phone screen. A moment later mine goes back off.

**Nice try.**

I gape at her and she shrugs before digging in her purse and giving me ONE.

**I didn't realize twins could be identically a pain in my ass.**

I hit send and down the pill.

# Alexander

I call Marie when I get a minute and she answers in her constantly happy tone.

"Hi Alexander, how's Tavin?"

"Hey, she's why I'm calling, actually. What are the chances you could write her a script for Valium or something similar? She got a hold of some of Sasha's last night and it really helped."

Her sigh fills my ear. "She would need an ID to be able to pick up a prescription."

"So?"

"Her ID is fake. I had planned on writing her one the first night. She never would admit to it, but trust me, it's fake."

"What would a twenty-three year old need with a fake ID?"

"That was kind of my thought."

Shit, shit, shit. I'm trying not to freak out inside. Even though she's extremely small, she still looks old enough. I'm sure there's a reasonable explanation for this. I swear to God she better at least be eighteen.

I'm way too pretty for prison.

After some coercing, Marie agrees to write a prescription for me that I can just give to Tavin and I pick them up on the way home. I'm not looking forward to talking with her about her age. I'm a little scared of what the answer might be.

When I walk in to the house from the garage, the downstairs is empty. I take off my suit jacket, drape it over my forearm and start up the stairs.

I see Sasha in the hallway just as I climb the last step. "Hey Sash, where's Tavin?"

She gestures toward the bathroom. "Taking a shower, poor thing can't stop sweating and shaking." She combs her hair back with her fingers. "Oh and she started a fun new one today."

My shoulders drop and I let out a breath. "What now?"

She points to the skin below her cuticles. "She's been picking at her fingers. They were bloody before I even realized what she was doing." She tilts her head. "A nervous habit, maybe?"

I wish I fucking knew. She's hurting herself now?

Walking around her, I shrug. "Your guess is as good as mine." I nod toward the stairs. "I'm going to change. You can head out for the weekend. We should be good until Sunday night."

"Okay, just call if she needs me." She waves as she descends the stairs and I unbutton my shirt and head to my room.

After I change and wash my face, I check to see if Tavin's out of the shower. Once I cross the threshold out of my room, she's entering the hall from the bathroom and our eyes lock. Her face lights up with a smile, even if her eyes look tired. She's dripping wet, her long hair sticking to her arms, face, and chest. She has on the teeniest towel. Where did she even find that?

God, please let there be an explanation to the ID that doesn't make me a perv.

"Hi," she rasps.

"Hi."

She continues across the hall to her room and I follow her. When I walk in, her back is to me and her little ass cheeks are poking out from under the tea towel she has on.

"Get dressed. We need to talk."

And I need a drink.

I go downstairs and pour a double shot of bourbon. Who knows what will come of this conversation. When I get back, I knock and ask, "Are you decent?"

The door flies open. "Am I decent? You've had your head between my legs, what's considered 'decent' after that?" She's wearing a baby tee with those short-ass shorts and her hair is still sticking to her skin. She puts her hands to her hips. "So, what do you need to talk about?"

I pass by her as I enter the room. "I'm going to ask you a question, and do not lie to me, Tavin." She leans against the door frame and I cross my arms, "Besides, I'm pretty sure I figured out your 'tell', so I'll know if you do." I take a deep breath. "How old are you?" She opens her mouth to speak and I cut her off to save her from more lies. "Marie told me about the fake ID."

She holds up her hands. "Okay, yes the ID is fake, but I'm pretty sure that I'm twenty-three."

"How the fuck are you only 'pretty sure'?"

She sighs and shakes her head. "The birthday I celebrate is a day I picked. My parents never seemed too sure. They would always say different stuff so I don't know the exact date. I do know I'm in between the ages of twenty-two and twenty-four." She stands up straight and draws an imaginary X on her chest, with her finger. "Cross my heart."

She doesn't flutter those long, beautiful eyelashes, so I have no real reason to not believe her, however…

"So then why the fake ID?"

Her eyes shoot down to the floor when she pushes off the door frame passing me to the bed.

"I grew up kind of off the grid. I only got the ID to get into bars and to buy alcohol. I've never needed it other than that."

I gesture my fingers in air quotes. "'Off the grid'? What does that even mean?" I turn to follow her. "The only thing you live 'off' of is the damn freeway." She just shrugs and sits on the bed. "You need identification to go to school, where did you go?"

"Um…" Her eyelashes start going.

"The truth Tavin."

"Jeez! I didn't go okay?"

Wait. What?

"I'm sorry, you didn't go to school? Were you home schooled?"

Somehow parents that don't know their own child's birthday don't strike me as the type to home school.

She considers it and a sweet smile stretches across her face. "Yeah, I guess I kind of was." Flopping backward onto the bed she groans, "Ugh! I just took a shower and I'm already sweaty again!" She lifts her head to give me a dirty look. "You might want to leave, I'm about to get 'indecent.'"

She sits back up and rips off her shirt. I get excited before I see she has on this bralette thing. Still, it's the most I have seen of her torso, and I barely get to see it for a whole half a second before she quickly flips to her stomach.

"Oh don't get all pissy," I snap. "You're the one with the secrets. How am I the asshole just because I want to make sure you're legal?"

"I'm sorry, I just can't get comfortable. I'm irritable and I feel like crap. You…you're not an asshole, I'm just…"

"Hey," I sit next to her on the bed. "I brought you something for that."

I take the pills from my pocket and her face suddenly goes green.

"I don't feel—" She lurches toward the ever present vomit bowl, getting there just in time. Her shoulders are shaking when I lean down next to her to hold her hair. The bruises are taking on a sickly shade of yellow, and I can see her spine all the way down her battered back.

After about ten minutes she seems to finally be finished.

"Why are you really doing all this? What are you expecting to get out of it?" She cries through shaky lips.

I trace my thumb across her jaw. "Is it not obvious? I'm crazy about the very little I know about you. Sure, this partly has to do with my guilt over Sasha, mostly though I just want to help. I felt connected to you the night of the carnival. I was even drawn to you when you first knocked on my office door. I haven't felt something for anyone in a long time and even then, I don't remember it being this way." I give her head a soft kiss. "You make me feel powerful yet vulnerable. Things with you somehow feel simultaneously ancient and new."

"Please don't say things like that."

Her scars are bumpy under my fingers as I rub her back. "Why?"

When my eyes meet hers, they are full of disgust. "Because, I'm trash, Alexander, I'm dirty and worthless and this isn't fair to you."

I grab her chin, not hard, just enough to get my point across. "I have seriously had it with that. I've told you not to talk that way, so do it again and you lose the Valium. I don't care how much you vomit."

She's staring daggers at me, but I don't give a shit. She can be pissed at me all she wants; I won't listen to that. I pull out the Valium bottle and unscrew the lid to the water. "Hold out your hand." I drop it in her palm.

"Still only one?" She looks at it sadly.

"Yes, only one."

When I glance down at her hand I see what Sasha was talking about, and she had undersold it terribly. Beneath her cuticles, the skin has been picked away, leaving bloody red patches in its place. I grab her hand to inspect it closer. They are clawed to shreds.

"Oh my God, what the hell did you do to yourself?!"

She pulls her hand free from my grasp, tucking them beneath her arms. "I don't even know I'm doing it."

I pick her up and carry her to the bed, climbing in with her. We lie facing each other as I comb my fingers through her hair.

"I want to be here for you, in any way that you need. I don't want to pressure you to tell me anything, just don't lie to me, okay?"

She doesn't answer other than a slight nod.

We stay there for a couple of hours before she finally falls asleep. I slowly and quietly slip out of bed to go to my office.

I type her name into Google and every social media platform I can think of, I get zilch. All I find is a Tavin Winters in Phoenix, Arizona and she's a six year old who apparently won her region's spelling bee this year. There's nothing. No social media, no birth announcements, not even a Yellow Pages listing.

I go on to search the word 'asphyxiation'. The first results are mostly about the amount of people that die each year from strangling themselves while masturbating. Good to know. I'll have to remember to not hang myself next time I jerk off. I mean seriously, what the hell?

I'm realizing that this is an extremely dangerous fetish, even with a partner. How will I know if her brain has been deprived of oxygen for too long? I find some blogs that cover topics such as where to apply pressure and how to avoid injury, and a few sites mention a safe word, but how is she supposed to talk if she can't even breathe? We need to come up with a signal, and even then it's still risking the very thing I'm trying to save. I sigh and go downstairs for a past-due drink.

As I flip through my DVR, a scream from upstairs can be heard all the way in my basement. I bolt up the stairs as the wails get louder with every step. Sprinting up the staircase to the top level, I rush to unlock Tavin's door. She's in the bed, weeping in heavy cries. When I get closer, I see she's still sleeping. Her face is covered in sweat and contorted in agony. I slip into the bed and take her hands. "Hey, Tavin, shhh. You are okay, hey, wake up."

After a couple of tedious moments, she wakes, frowning in confusion until she gets her bearings.

"What's wrong?" She looks at me as though I'm the one having an issue.

"You had a bad dream, you were screaming and crying."

She sits up and rubs her eyes. "Oh, I'm sorry. It's been a long time since I've had one."

It's a good thing I stay with her because it doesn't take long for the hot/cold sweats, shaking, and vomiting to all come back with a vengeance. The night is spent helping her to and from the bathroom. She never falls back asleep and at around five a.m. I feel myself dozing off. I kiss her forehead, lock her door, go to my room, and fall right to sleep.

### Saturday, May 16th

*Crash!*

I force open my eyes at the sound. Is that glass breaking? What's going on now? Looking at the clock, I see it's ten in the morning. I throw off the covers, pull on some sweat pants, and storm down the hallway to Tavin's room. There are more crashes as I unlock the door. Swinging it open, I see there is another broken lamp on the floor, along with a bookend, and a now shattered ship in a bottle. She's about to go for the ivory box on the dresser.

"What the hell are you doing?!" I yell at her.

Her long hair is frazzled and her eyes are red rimmed. Her cheeks look puffy and her fingers are worse than last night.

"I need to get out of here! I don't like to be locked up!"

She tries to push past me and so I grab her, however, she anticipates it and my jaw has a little sting all of a sudden.

"Did you just hit me?"

She covers her mouth and calms her little ass down.

"Um…I'm sorry… Now I'm thinking that was too much."

Her facial expression is confused, as if she feels bad for hitting me, but she's still mad and can't decide which one she feels more at the moment.

I don't know if it's the absurdity of this entire situation, because I'm tired, or because I just got punched by Thumbelina, regardless, I start cracking up laughing. She looks up at me, clearly not sure how to react to this response of mine.

"Whew, I needed that."

Her ornery smile is fucking adorable. "You needed a punch in the face?"

# CHAPTER SEVEN
## Art Fair

W E WALK DOWN THE FRONT PATHWAY AND EVEN though I can't exactly put a leash on her, I would be lying if I said I didn't entertain and get slightly turned on by the idea. I lace my fingers in between hers.

"Keep a hold of my hand and don't think I'm beneath chasing your ass."

She drops her head back and holds her hand to the sky. "Oh my gosh! Fresh air!" Inhaling as if she had been indoors for months, not days, she sighs theatrically. It's amusing, so I can't help myself from smirking at her.

We walk around my neighborhood and she points out all the houses she likes. As we pass a small park with just swings, monkey bars, and a slide, she points. "Can we swing?" I shrug and follow her as she sits down and immediately starts using her feet. "I love swinging. It feels like flying. My best friend and I still go sometimes." A yellow corvette drives by when she pipes up, "Hey that kinda looks like your car."

I laugh. Other than the color they don't look alike at all. "My car is sick, huh?"

She snorts. "Yeah sure, it's cute."

Cute? What a terrible thing to say.

"The Alfa is not fucking cute. It is a bad ass piece of machinery that makes women wet."

Her eyes roll as she snickers. "It's called an Alfa? How cheesy."

Oh wait until she hears the full name.

"It's actually an Alfa Romeo."

She is full on laughing now. "Wow, that's bad." She releases a breath and slows her hysteria before she smiles at me. "Besides, it wasn't your car that made me wet."

I shut my open mouth and adjust myself. "Are you ready to head back yet?"

The exercise looks to have done her some good. She has more color in her cheeks and seems to feel better, even though I'm sure the Valium has a part in that. When we get back to the house and pass the kitchen, I try to get her to eat something. I know she hasn't had very much since coming to stay here.

"How would you feel about a snack?"

"Not hungry."

I put my hand on her arm and pull her into my chest. "Come on Tav, you haven't been eating enough, just something small? Crackers?"

She sighs, "Fine, I'll try."

I look through a cabinet for some saltines. With no luck I try another one, and notice her staring at the cookies Cara Jo baked, inside the glass serving dish on the counter.

"Do you want one?"

She tries not to smile when she says, "Yes."

Happy as a clam with her treat in hand, we climb back up the stairs. "How are you feeling?"

Cookie fills her mouth as she mumbles, "Axuay, pety goo."

"God, Tavin don't talk with your mouth full."

She swallows and smirks. "Sorry. I'm actually feeling pretty good."

We take our separate showers, and I have her take hers in my room so I can lock her in and still allow her to get around.

After I finish, I realize I forgot clothes so I wrap the towel around my waist to go back to my room. She's a sight to behold in an oversized tee shirt that hangs off her shoulder, barely covering her perky ass. She combs her hair and the little purple panties I bought her peek out with each brush. She turns to me and when I drop my towel, I'm rewarded with a huge grin. I flash her one right back before opening my drawer to put on some underwear. Throwing on a pair of faded denims, I add my Zegna belt.

"Since you're feeling better, how about checking out my playroom?"

A gray cloud comes over her face. Her eyes lose their shine and I feel I may have hurt her feelings when she chokes out, "Okay."

Her response causes me to hesitate. What's with the attitude whiplash? "I promise you'll like it."

She's gone somber as she says, "Okay."

I don't know what just happened so I say nothing as I take her hand and lead her to the basement. Her shoulders are tense and she isn't speaking as I turn on the light at the end of the staircase. The entire expanse of the space becomes illuminated and I look down at her.

Her gaze drifts over the Foosball table and air hockey table, she scans the gaming station, ping pong table, and seating area by the bar and the theater room.

I jump a little when she starts busting up laughing. A doubled-over-holding-her-stomach kind of laugh and I'm standing here completely missing the joke.

"Oh, Lex."

She tackles me, knocking me off balance to the floor. She kisses me with purpose, deep and hard. Her tongue finds mine as her fingers pull at my hair. My hands go straight to her ass and I squeeze. Her shirt is so big, it would be so easy just to rip it off. I want to see her completely from head to toe, but that isn't fair. She needs to be comfortable enough with me to take the shirt off herself. I rock my pelvis against her when she removes her hands from my hair, places them on my chest, and begins kissing her way down. Looking up at me, she slowly undoes my belt as her hair drags along my chest and abs. I cannot accurately describe to you how incredibly hot that is. Reaching into my underwear, she releases my erection. She lightly flicks the head with the tip of her tongue and softly kisses it before sending me into ecstasy with her mouth. I can't stop myself from thrusting while I run my fingers through her hair, gripping a chunk of it.

"Good God, you give great head." She makes absolutely no noise besides the sounds of her sucking and that just spurs me on more. Eventually, I tug on her hair. "Get on your knees."

She pulls her hair over her shoulder and gets on all fours. Now that's a motherfucking view. I trail my hand over her left butt cheek. I don't usually rip off a girl's underwear because some of them spend good money on their lingerie. These cheap little panties though, these are mine.

I grip the thin waistband and tear them off her body with a *rip*. She jolts a little as she leans back, giving me a glamorous view of that shiny little cunt. I can almost feel my mouth salivating when I press it into that perfect diamond window.

I have no idea how I'm supposed to safely, well safely as possible, cut off her airflow while I'm all the way down here. I'm not even going to try right now, I'm beyond ready to be inside of her again.

Oh shit…my condoms are upstairs. I've never brought a girl down here so I've never needed them. I look down at her pussy and it's just waiting for me. Fuck it. I don't even bother pulling my jeans all the way down as I place the tip of my dick at her entrance and slam into her amazing body.

Dear Christ, Gaia, and Krishna. She feels like silk. Squeezing, tight silk.

"Fuck, *Lille*. You feel so amazing," I groan.

Her body freezes and she turns her head to look back at me. "Did you put on a condom?"

I'm pounding into her and she's as still as can be. "No."

Yeah okay, I know that was a dick move. I'll own that. I should have at least asked her even if she can't get pregnant. The damage is done now though and she must have come to that conclusion as well, because after a second she begins pushing herself back onto me.

Oh wow, I haven't had sex without a condom since high school and this is fucking incredible. So incredible in fact, that I'm already about to come. I dig my fingers into her hips as I drill into her with such force I would worry I was hurting her if she wasn't matching me thrust for thrust. Still, all I get out of her are soft moans and quiet grunts. I'm not really sure if I'm supposed to just grab her face or throat or what. We never talked about a signal. I'm about to go for it when her hand reaches behind to my belt and tugs on it.

"Take this off," she shoves her little body harder onto me, "and hit my back with it."

I can almost hear the proverbial record screeching.

"What? You want me to hit you?"

She rocks her body back, her pussy clenching around me as she rasps, "If you want me to come, then yes."

"What if I seriously hurt you?"

"I want you to hurt me."

For some twisted reason, that I don't really want to think about, her statement in her soft husky voice, almost does me in. I do what she asks, I yank the belt through the loops with a *whoosh*. She's so drenched, she is dripping down her thighs. I lift her shirt, exposing all the scars.

Oh my God. This is what the scars are from? Things just officially got fucked. It still doesn't stop me from folding the belt in half and bringing it down on her with a *whack*. She barely makes a sound so I bring it down again and again. I find myself wondering if the marks have all been inflicted by a single lover or multiple partners. She bucks harder with each hit and my cock is loving this.

"Damn it, Tavin, would you come already?" I growl into her ear.

"Hit me harder," she moans.

I do too. I swing down full force onto her back. When I do, the end of the belt slips from my hand and wraps around her side. She throws her head back with an erotic whimper and her pussy constricts around my dick so tightly I don't know if I can last through her orgasm. It's miraculous that I do too, because she keeps coming for what seems like forever. It's almost too much to bear.

Since I already stuck my condom-less dick in without asking, I'm not too sure how she'll feel about me pumping my come into her too. The paleness of her fair skin changes into rose as I pull out and semen streams all over her ass.

"Oh my God, Alexander! Did you just jizz on me?!" She looks back to her ass with a disgusted expression. "You could have warned me."

A laugh pours from my belly as I kiss the marks I just gave her, "You want me to hit and suffocate you, but a little come on your ass is unacceptable?"

I get a towel from the bar to clean her off as I look her over to see how much damage I've done. I don't know if I feel guiltier that I left new marks on her, or because I love the physical proof of me on her body.

Similar to writing: *Alexander was here.*

I lie on the floor next to her, propped up on my elbow. "So this is how you got all the scars?"

She rolls over to lie flat on her back, looking to the ceiling. "Uh huh."

I trace her jawline with my finger, "So…" bringing it over her chin and down her neck, "to be able to climax, you need what? Pain?"

"Yes," she pauses before jerking her head and looking at me, "I don't deserve pleasure without pain. It's always been that way. It's part of what I am."

Half the time I have no idea how I'm supposed to respond or feel about some of the shit she says. I have thought more than once that I'm in over my head with her. Still, I want more.

I turn her face so she has to look at me. "Why do you do that? It's part of *who* you are, not what, and *who* you are is the kindest, most fascinating, and most beautiful girl I have ever met." I release her and stand. "I'll go get you a new pair of underwear since I destroyed the other ones." I grin at her and am relieved when that half smile peeks out. "Why don't you pick out a movie to watch?" I point her to the theater door. "There is a big binder on the bar with a list of all the movies I have on reel. Or you could just pick out a Blu-ray from one of the wooden cases in the back."

I jog upstairs to her room and pick out a pair of blue boy shorts. Once I'm back in the basement, I walk into the theater room and she's leaning over the bar flipping through the binder. Her shirt is only covering half her ass cheeks and I kick myself for even mentioning the underwear. The thought of her walking around bottomless is an enjoyable one. I come up behind her, move her hair to the side and kiss her neck before I drop to the floor.

"Lift your leg." She places a foot in the hole of the panties before doing the same with the other leg. I pull them up over her calves and thighs before securing them over her perfectly curved ass. Pressing my nose into her hair, I smell the coconut shampoo mixed with her natural scent. It's so amazing that I groan into the silky strands. "Find anything?"

She holds up a Blu-ray and oh God. It's 'Teacher's Pet', a Japanimation porn. "What about this one?"

I actually consider it for a second before grabbing it out of her hand and an awkward laugh leaves my mouth, "No, not today."

She sees the back and her mouth drops open. "Are those cartoons fucking?" She scrunches her face up and flicks out a finger as she points.

I laugh again, though more at her expression. "Yeah, I should probably keep the porn separate. Pick something else."

She must be in the mood for an animated movie because her next choice is Tim Burton's 'The Nightmare Before Christmas'.

This will be fun, I haven't seen this movie in years. As soon as it starts she is in a trance. She can't take her eyes off the screen. Her face lights up as she gets closer and closer to the edge of the seat.

At one point she whispers, "Oh my God. Jack and Sally." She looks at me and laughs. "We can live like Jack and Sally if we want."

"What?"

"And we'll have Halloween on Christmas."

Now it's my turn to laugh. "Are you quoting Blink 182?"

She's so excited about this, she's nearly bouncing. "It's like the song!"

Her enthusiasm stays and I keep catching myself smiling

at her childlike awe. After it's over, she falls backwards on the seat and sighs. "That was incredible."

I laugh. "You really don't get out much."

She sits back up with her hands clasped together. "Can we watch it again?"

"Maybe later, I think we need to go shopping. You can't wear the same four outfits Sasha left you."

"I have clothes at home," she smarts off.

"And they will still be there when you get back," I mock her tone.

She rolls her eyes and smirks. "Fine."

We go to the Shadoebox City Galleria and she's in the dressing room for forever, trying stuff on. I buy her a few dresses, skirts, shorts, jeans, tops, shoes and of course stockings. Gotta have the stockings. She keeps saying it's enough, but everything she tries on makes me want to see it in a pile on my floor. She never attempts to run. She actually seems to be enjoying herself, having fun even.

By the time we get home I'm withering away from hunger so I throw one of Cara Jo's pre-prepared meals into the oven. When it's done, I bring some up to Tavin, hoping to get her to eat an actual meal. I unlock her room and she's crashed on the bed with her chest slowly rising and falling. I decide I'm going to give her free reign of the house, a test of sorts. She earned it today.

My phone vibrates against my leg in my pocket. As I pull it out, I see Sasha's picture light up my screen.

"Hey Sash, what's up?"

"Hi, how is she today?"

I close the door and take my food to my office. "Actually, we had a great day. I think she's really feeling better."

"Good. I'm glad to hear that." She inhales deeply. "So,

I got a call today. Some big shot plastic surgeon saw my clothes on a colleague and wants me to design a collection for her honeymoon. She wants to meet Tuesday at four to discuss it. Would you hate me for skipping out at three that day?"

"Of course not, that's amazing. I'm happy for you."

"Thank you, Xander."

"Don't call me Xander."

Tavin has been sleeping all evening and I'm about to turn in myself when the wailing starts. I run to her room to find her in the same state as last time.

"Toben!"

She calls out the name over and over. I hold her tight so she can't flail around anymore. "Tavin, shhhh, calm down. You're safe."

She's shaking and it isn't from withdrawals. She takes a long time to catch her breath. Inhaling harshly for so long I'm worried she will hyperventilate. I can already tell I'm going to go insane wondering who this Toben person is, and honestly it causes fury to snarl in my stomach imagining what he could have possibly done to cause these nightmares.

*Sunday, May 17th*

*Tavin*

I smell him. Sunshine. The Sun God. He's touching me, kissing me… Oh… yes. I feel his warm tongue as his strong fingers barrel into me. I wish I could come just like this. Show him the proof of what he's doing. My hands find his soft hair, and my gaze shifts down. I love watching him. His light blond head moves with determination as he consumes me like I'm the best thing he's ever tasted.

"Alexander," I breathe out.

He kisses, bites and licks his way up my body. He tries to lift my shirt again. I know he wants to see, and while I want to let him, then he might know. If he doesn't then he will ask and he doesn't want me to lie, but it's hard! What am I supposed to say to all of his questions? I shake my head at him. I see his irritation, yet he responds by taking a nipple into his mouth through my shirt. Oh God, his mouth is amazing, everything it touches comes alive with energy and I feel myself clench. He moves to my neck, biting with teasing pressure. Goosebumps appear down my body and he leans over me to reach in the nightstand.

I can't stop my thoughts from wondering how mad Master is right now. This is his weekend. I'm supposed to be with him, not here. Inevitably, my fear of the outcome of my actions and Logan's wrath stabs my chest until I feel soft lips on my neck, kissing away my anxieties. I turn my head to face him and press my mouth to his. I stretch out my legs and arms as he laughs at me while rolling on a condom. Not sure what the point is after what he pulled yesterday.

"Lie on your side." His voice gets deeper when he's aroused.

I obey and he slides off my panties before lying behind me and running the tip up and down my slickness. He fills me up and as I take a moment to adjust to being stretched, he fists a chunk of my hair, wrapping it around his wrist as he pulls.

His mouth is next to my ear when he gruffly says, "If you feel yourself losing consciousness, draw an $X$ on my thigh right here." He grabs my finger and makes a crisscross motion on his leg as he moans, "No orgasm is worth dying over, so if you still haven't achieved climax, we'll keep trying. Don't let it go too far." Ramming back into me, he pulls on

my hair and forces a grunt to fall from my lips. "Do you understand?" I nod and he yanks again. "Say it."

"I understand, Alexander."

His huge hand wraps around my neck, tightening away
the oxygen and he doesn't slow his pace as the burning in-
tensifies, crawling up my throat. The need for air is wonderfully agonizing. His thrusts are deep and I can feel my head
lighten as the slow thrumming rolls of my orgasm shock
through me. The sexy noises he makes as he comes causes
me to tighten around him, milking him further.

Black dots are dancing behind my eyes and I reach for
his leg just as his hand disappears from my neck. It always
takes a second for the oxygen to reach my lungs as deep
gasps fight their way from my throat. His hot breath is on
my neck while his lips tickle my skin with his whispers.

"God, you're incredible."

His heat and touch evaporate as he gets up and disposes
of the condom. Jumping back in bed behind me, he wraps
his arms around my stomach. I softly trace my fingers over
his tattoo. I have been curious about it since The Necco
Room.

"What does this mean?"

His body tenses against my back as a regretful sigh slips
into the room. "When I was in high school my girlfriend
Carrie did something...malicious."

"What did she do?"

"She ripped out my heart, sliced it up and shoved it back
in, but that's a story for another day." He kisses my shoulder
and squeezes me a little tighter. "It screwed with my head
for a while, though from that pain I gained inspiration." He
laughs nervously, "You should feel special because not a single person knows this other than Sasha. I've wanted to be
a screenwriter for as long as I can remember. After everything with Carrie, I started toying with an idea for a story,

and before long it kind of overtook my brain. I couldn't stop thinking about it." His chest presses against my back when he sighs, "I finally wrote my first screenplay. It's about a girl named Shaya who dies from a rare disease, and because of a spell done by creatures in another world, she doesn't go to heaven or hell. Instead, she awakes in their realm and slowly ages over hundreds of years. There are actually three volumes in the series for each part of her afterlife. The tattoo represents each stage."

He rotates his arm to show me and I see a little, sad, blonde girl surrounded by scaly mermaids and fairies with torn wings. It fades into a fierce blonde closer to my age holding a sword and fighting with big monsters, and finally a gray haired, old woman sitting on a throne made of bones and wearing an intricate crown. It makes me very sad, while at the same time, it's so incredible. The whole thing has a dark, twisted, almost horror feel to it. It's such a contrast to the intense color of the tattoo and the bright, warm, light aura he naturally gives off.

"Once I finished it, it was as though I physically felt the weight lighten and I was finally able to move on. The tattoo is more about the inspiration behind the story, not so much the story itself."

"Oh."

I don't know what else to say to that. What am I doing? Am I really going to hurt him and Toben just because he makes me feel good? How selfish is that? Have I not done enough already? I could have gotten away yesterday. I could be with Toben right now calming him down, because I know he is probably going ballistic. I know that and I'm still here with Lex, lying and deceiving him. This will not end well for anyone, but when his arms are squeezing me tight and his warmth makes me feel safe, it's easy to push away my worries.

I wonder if his screenplays are kind of like my draw-ings or Toben's lyrics. Hearing about him talk about his high school girlfriend makes me wonder about his life. I honestly cannot even fathom living the way normal people do. What it must be like. I roll over to face him. I want to look at his strong, stubbly jaw, his bright green eyes, and his mouth that I constantly want to kiss. I don't know how much longer I'll get the chance.

"What were you like as a kid?"

He sticks his nose in the crook of my neck and inhales deeply as his lips brush against it while he speaks. "I don't know, normal I guess. Cara Jo pretty much raised us. When we were in elementary school, she talked our parents into letting us go to public schools instead of the private tutors. That was when I met Silas and we've been best friends ever since. I played a lot of sports, partied, straight A's... My life was kind of boring until Vulture."

I smile. I'm glad he had a boring childhood. Boring is good. Boring is safe and it comforts me to know he was safe. He and Sasha grew up always knowing each other. That is just crazy to me. I've never once thought about having a sibling.

"What was it like growing up with Sasha? Is it fun being a twin?"

I like how he smiles when he talks about her. "We've al-ways been close and we join forces when we need to, but with my temper and her stubbornness we butt heads a lot too. We'll beat anyone's ass to defend each other though. We also had the same friends in high school." He laughs one of his perfect laughs that makes my mouth go dry, and between my thighs not so dry. "We were actually Prom King and Queen together our senior year," his thumb touches over my lip, "Yeah, that was humiliating."

What the heck is he talking about? "What is Prom?"

Shoving himself up to sitting, he gets serious all of a sudden. "Why didn't you go to school?"

Stupid questions. What am I supposed to say? Even if I did tell him, the only thing it would do is provoke more questions. I hate questions. "My parents didn't want me to."

"Why?"

Ugh! See what I mean? I can't think of a single thing to say. I try to imagine some kind of normal, reasonable explanation.

"Um… Because, I…"

I can see his face change from soft and curious to a hard, twitching jaw and flaring nostrils. He harshly rubs his hands down his face before glaring at me. "If you don't want to tell me something, say 'pass' or tell me you don't want to talk to me, but for the love of God. Do. Not. Lie to me."

I huff, "I'm sorry, there are just some things that I can't explain. That's why I left in the first place. I knew this couldn't work because…of everything."

He brushes my bangs out of my eyes. "I want to know you. It's getting harder to cope with the whole mysterious thing. While it's hot and all, I'm actually into you. I want to know what your life is like…are you sure you aren't in any danger?"

That question is so funny I can't stop the laugh falling from my mouth. The truth is, I will be in danger if I stay here. At least he has given me an out.

"Pass."

He twitches his lip and knits his brows for a moment before relaxing. "Do you want breakfast?"

I usually like to eat. A lot. Toben used to say I was like those miniature pigs, but when we are using I don't eat much and neither of us ate last time we went through withdrawals. It's the same this time, food is kind of bleh right now.

"I'm just not hungry. Sorry."

He narrows his eyes as he kisses me and jumps off the bed. He's barely out the door when my skin starts to feel like there are bugs crawling all over me. I don't like this. I'm not usually violent or angry, and right now I want so bad to hit something! I want to scream, cry, and rip off my skin more than normal. I tear off the blankets and pace the floor. This is when I need the shit. It would take this away. It takes everything away. I need to go home. I need Toben. I need heroin.

I'm still pacing as Alexander walks back into the room holding a cup and a bowl. "Hey are you alright?"

No I'm not alright! You are confusing me and making me feel weird!

I squeeze my eyes tight. "I'm fine," I grate out.

"Do you need a Valium?"

Oh my God, yes! I don't wait for the question to fully leave his lips before I rush out, "Yes."

He's trying to look disapproving, even though his smirk kind of takes away from the effect. I hold out my hand and he gives me the *one* dang pill.

He hands me the glass and it's full of strawberry milk. I laugh and smile up at him. It's my favorite drink in the whole world. He takes a big bite of his Marshmallow Mateys. I love that cereal. Well, the marshmallow part at least.

The pill gives me relief and I feel a little more like myself when he asks, "I'm going to hit the bag and do some jogging, do you want to come? I think I might have some yoga videos. Some exercise would probably be great for you if you feel up to it."

I shrug. It will be fun to watch him workout. I don't know what the heck 'yoga' is though. Whatever it is, it can't be that hard.

⟵

What the crap is this? The woman on the T.V. is literally

bending herself backwards. Her feet are tickling the top of her head…that's not going to happen.

"How the heck does she do that?"

I hear Alexander chuckling as he punches a big, black bag hanging from the ceiling. He is obviously strong, he could destroy me if he wanted to.

I know I want him to.

He keeps grinning at me as he continues his workout, while I attempt all these crazy things I'm supposed to be making my body do. Okay, so this position isn't quite so bad. I just have to spread my legs super far apart and touch the ground. Lex is behind me on the treadmill and when I bend over, I can see him upside down staring at my ass while he runs.

Honestly, by the end of the video, I feel pretty good, all stretchy and limber. He wraps his sweaty arms around me and it somehow isn't disgusting. It's actually insanely sexy because I can smell his scent much stronger right now.

I've never met anyone like him before. He's so vibrant and he smiles a lot. The longer I'm here, the more dangerous it becomes, yet the less I care about the repercussions from Logan.

It's hard to believe that I yearn touch…well, Alexander's touch. Every time he puts his strong hands on me, my whole body crackles and I can feel the swirls all the way to my toes. He says such nice things, and it hurts to hear them because I know they aren't true. Not really. He thinks they are, but he doesn't know that he's saying them to a toy.

He makes me feel different. Not quite so dirty. I know my face can be seen as attractive, it's the rest of me that is disgusting, and still he doesn't recoil or sneer and that's what makes me hope that he truly does think I'm beautiful.

*Why would a man like that want your mutilated, used up body? You're nothing but a novelty, to him and all the others.*

I'm being dumb. Even if he does really think he wants me, it's not fair to him. I let him put himself inside me without telling him what he's doing. He doesn't deserve that. It's cruel for me to let him touch me, but I'm weak. I like it. The way his eyes roam over me makes me feel big and tall. There are moments this almost feels real. It's not though, real I mean, and every time I remember that, my heart twists up so tight I can feel the blood being wrung out of it. I know what I'm doing is terrible, I've just never felt like this and I don't want it to stop. He is the only one that has ever been *mine*.

We leave his gym and as we walk into the hall, his phone rings. He answers and after a moment he says, "Uh, yeah sure." Looking over at me, he raises his eyebrow in question before hanging up. "Marie wants to come talk to you, do you know why?"

How should I know? "Nuh uh."

"Well, she's on her way." He kisses my head and turns to go into his room. "I'm going to shower."

He still hasn't come back when Marie the Doctor walks into my room.

"Hello, Tavin, you are looking well. How do you feel?"

I don't know how I feel. I'm not really sick anymore. My stomach bubbles when Lex is around. I miss Toben, I need to talk to him. I'm scared about what happens when Logan gets back in town, and I find myself wanting a hit frequently. It's not constantly sitting in the front of my head anymore though, so I guess I feel good.

"I feel okay."

I shift on the seat as I look out the window. He has a pool? How did I not notice that before? I've never been in a pool.

"I'm glad to hear that." She sits next to me on the window seat. "I came by to tell you that I ran some tests with your blood sample. This whole situation is unorthodox, so I may not have gone about this the right way, but am I correct in assuming you're still having sexual intercourse with Alex?"

'Sexual Intercourse'? I want to giggle at her. What a funny way to say fuck. I can feel my lips lift into a bit of a smile that I can't contain and nod.

"That's what I thought, and I have to admit I was half expecting positive results." She sighs and shakes her head. "Regardless, you're clean. Of everything. Have you never shared needles?"

Never. Never ever share a needle. I know that. Always a new one. Always. Logan made sure we knew that.

I shake my head. "No way."

Her face softens and she smiles. "Can I ask you something personal?" Uh oh. I don't respond so she continues, "Are you sleeping with another man besides Alex?"

My throat swells. "I-uh… I mean, I have…" Oh no, now I can't think of what to say.

She puts her hand on my arm. "Okay, Tavin. It's okay. You don't have to tell me anything. I shouldn't have asked. Alex is one of my closest friends and I have a tendency to get a little protective of him, and honestly this whole thing between you two makes me uneasy…" She stands up and gets into her medical bag, "but you are both adults." She pulls out her stethoscope again. I feel a chill run up my arm. "There's something else I want to ask you. Have you ever heard of Tourette syndrome?"

"No."

She nods. Lifting up my shirt, she places the stethoscope to my back. "You aren't experiencing any pain, shortness of breath, or difficulty breathing, correct?"

"Only when Lex is around."

She laughs at me. "Lex, huh?" I turn around to look at

her and she is shaking her head as she rolls her eyes. "Lord, I get it okay? He's 'dreamy.'" She's making fun of me. That's okay though. I like how he makes me feel. "Well, if you notice anything out of the ordinary, tell 'Lex' okay?"

"Okay."

After Marie the Doctor is gone, I go across the hall to take a shower. I don't even try to leave. The damage is already done. What's one more day really gonna do?

She said I was clean. The irony in that is so sad it's funny. I'm anything other than clean. I know she's referring to the needle disease, but I already know I don't have diseases. Alexander did break rule number one though. I still can't get used to the idea of wanting him to touch me. Wanting to pleasure him too, take him in my mouth and body.

*Filthy, nasty whore.*

Turning the hot water all the way up, I moan as the burn scorches my skin. I hear the bathroom door open. "Is everything okay?" Alexander's voice warms me on the inside like the water does on the outside.

"Yeah everything's fine."

Everything is so not fine.

"When you finish, will you put on that blue dress we got yesterday and meet me downstairs? The Art Fair is going on and I thought we could go if you're up to it."

A fair? I think those are like carnivals! I'm so excited I can hear it in my voice.

"Okay!"

I put on the baby blue, lace dress he wants me to wear. It falls mid-thigh and I match it with the cream knee highs he bought me because I know he likes them. A lot. They reach about an inch above my knees and have three little brown buttons on the outside. I yank on the light brown boots that cover most of my calf, brush my hair, and run down the stairs to meet him.

"You must be wanting to get fucked wearing those."
I laugh, and I'm sure blush, when he takes my hand.
Just one more day.

# Alexander

I barely have the car parked before she jumps out and bee-lines for the fair. Running to catch up, I grab her hand.

"I'm not going to run away, you know." She says it as though she hasn't already tried three times.

"I just want to hold your hand, Tav."

The vendors are all over the place, selling items of every extreme and she wants to stop at all of them. Every single one.

"Please tell me what possible reason there could be for needing to look at homemade dog treats?"

"They were cakes for dogs, Alexander." She emphasizes every word with her hands, "Cakes. For. Dogs."

She makes my chest ache and my pulse jump. Sometimes it feels as if I have known her for years, until I'm reminded of her obscurity. God, she's gorgeous.

We watch a performing shock artist sticking pins and screws in extremely uncomfortable looking areas. His hair is blue, his tongue is forked and his entire body is covered in tattoos and piercings. She's completely enamored and claps enthusiastically after every act. He has quite a bag of tricks between the fire blowing and the sword swallowing. I'm quite impressed myself until he taps her nose and winks at her.

"There's a lot to look at Tavin, let's keep going."

She doesn't want to leave, but she complies and within

moments he's forgotten. When she spots a rainbow colored painted horse, she pulls free from my hand and goes straight for it.

"I've always wanted to see a real horse!" She kisses his neck. "He's like the one in Oz." It's so sweet how tender she is as she runs her fingers over his mane. "Your eyes have always reminded me of the Emerald City."

A split second after she says it, she closes her eyes and the color of embarrassment blossoms across her fair cheeks, making my heart thump. She's thought about my eyes.

I get her to eat something even if it's just a funnel cake. This girl has a serious sweet tooth. I'm going to have to get her to eat some real food very soon.

The day is an amazing and eventful one. We hear beautiful poetry, see some stunning photography of children around the world, and watch a street magic show. During the show, her face is hysterical, I don't think she stops gaping the whole time. The magician asks her to pick a card and shows it to her. After he places the card back in the deck, he takes off his shirt. He then turns around to reveal a tattoo of her card on his back. Very impressive.

We continue on to check out some seriously dark paintings of ripped open chests and stomachs. They all have large eyes with something pouring out of them such as rain or smoke, and she loves them. It's apparent she wants to touch them and probably would if it wasn't for the sign that says, 'Do Not Touch'.

Stopping in front of one, she gasps. She holds a hand out before yanking it back to keep herself from caressing it. She's lost in it.

The brushstrokes create a little girl with curly hair sitting on the floor in the corner of a dark room. Her head is thrown back, mouth open in a silent scream, and her little fists are balled up. She is in a puffy, pink dress with pink buckle shoes. Her stomach is torn open and a black gooey substance oozes out onto her dress and the floor.

I look to the vendor. "I'll take this one."

She spins around. "No, please don't. It's too beautiful, and it won't be safe at my house."

I want to ask what the fuck that's supposed to mean. Why she says she isn't in danger if the painting would be. I let out a sigh. I don't want to argue with her right now so I just say, "Well, it will be safe at mine."

She looks pained for a moment when a scowl crosses her face. Is she angry? Finally she whispers, "Thank you."

The sun has begun to set, so the place glows with a variety of light sources, from Christmas lights to Tiki torches. A band has started playing and a large street dance has emerged. Off she goes, jumping into the crowd, unconcerned about anything other than dancing. People of all ages, lifestyles, and sizes are together celebrating their love of art. I watch her as she throws her head back and laughs. She's so stunning in her elation.

In that moment it's as if my foot takes that first step off the edge and I feel myself begin to fall.

# CHAPTER EIGHT
## *lotus*

I'T'S GETTING LATE, SO I LOOK OVER TO WHERE SHE HAD been dancing just moments ago and she isn't there anymore. Shoving through the crowd, I scan for her and she's nowhere to be seen. My stomach turns with every passing moment and my feet pick up the pace. Checking in between the venders, I retrace our steps. Damn it! Obviously, I've trusted her too quickly, given her too much freedom. People are beginning to break down their booths and I pull my phone out to call her when I hear her sweet laugh. I follow the sound to find her watching a Capuchin monkey in overalls flipping around and doing tricks. Her long, brown hair hangs down the back of that blue dress and my throat opens up, allowing me to breathe properly again. She turns around grins at me as she runs over to grab my hand and pull me toward the damn monkey. I laugh with both relief and amusement at how she's so easily excited. Once we get there her arms hug my waist as she looks up at me with those killer eyes.

"Thank you so much. This is just…wow."

Her innocence and purity bleeds through whenever these mundane things give her so much pleasure. I move her bangs out of the way to kiss her forehead.

"I had a lot of fun too, but I'm sorry, we do need to head back."

She waves to the monkey and laces her fingers between mine as we walk back to the parking lot. I press the button on the remote starter and the Alfa roars to life as the headlights beam through the darkness.

She climbs into the car while I put the painting in the trunk. I barely slide into my seat before she is undoing my pants. She kisses me hard as she climbs up to straddle me. Her pelvis is hovering above mine as she uses her knees to hold herself up. These stockings are so hot that I place a hand on each thigh and trace a finger under the hem. Unzipping and reaching into my jeans, she takes me out. "Thank you for the painting, Lex." She keeps eye contact as she uses her other hand to move her panties and guide me inside. No condom again and I'm savoring every inch she takes. She's so wet and warm as she slides up and down at an excruciatingly slow pace. She softly kisses my lips before climbing off of me.

"What are you doing?!"

I try to grab for her, you have no idea how bad this sucks. The little tart straightens her dress and puts her seat belt on.

"You better drive fast, Alexander."

And drive fast, I do. We don't make it past my kitchen. I lift her onto the island at the same time I lift her dress. Again, she's wearing the panties I paid for, so I tear them off. I don't tease and I don't play games, I just push open her legs and go straight for her clit.

"Do you want to taste my come, Alexander?"

How the hell does she make that sentence sound so innocent?

"That coy shit is going to get you wrecked."

She smirks as she reaches back and pulls a small knife from the caddy on the island, She holds it out to me as her fingers trace along the inside of her thigh.

"Just a little cut," she whispers.

Whoa. Okay. Ooookay. This is crossing a line. I know that. There is no going back after this. I'm fully aware of how twisted it is and honestly, while the idea would have never turned me on before, she does turn me on. I feel as if I'm in a backwards version of *Alice in Wonderland*. I'm the white rabbit following Alice down the hole. I know this is wrong, yet I take the knife anyway.

"Are you sure?"

She nods as she swipes her tongue over her bottom lip. Next to the other faint scars, inside her thigh, I use the sharp edge of the blade to put pressure on her skin, careful to not break it yet as I work my tongue. After a few moments, I take a mental breath and slice into her flesh with a swift swipe. She yanks my hair as she begins to grind against my face. "Alexander," she gasps. When the vibrations begin beneath my tongue, I drop the knife and slip a finger inside of her convulsing pussy. Finally, I'm getting a taste and it's well worth the wait. Her soft moans get slightly louder as she wets my tongue with every pulse of her orgasm. Her body sags with completion and I look at the cut. The three inch line is red and there's thankfully, not much blood. Heavy-lidded eyes and flushed cheeks make her look angelic as I pull her off the island.

Wrapping my hand around the nape of her neck, I slam my mouth against hers before I undo my pants and shove her to her knees.

I thrust between her lips and enjoy her mouth for as long as I can without reaching climax. When I can't take anymore, I grab her arm and yank her up to standing before I flip her over the edge of the island. Her feet are dangling a few inches above the ground and her thigh highs are killing me with her bent over like that.

Squeezing her hips for momentum, I push into her body. She wants to fuck me back, but the angle I have her at makes it nearly impossible. It doesn't stop my dick from twitching inside of her when she wiggles her ass trying. I lean forward so my chest is against her back and move her hair so I can bite the crook of her neck. I smile against her skin when the little goose bumps make their appearance.

"Why can't I get enough of you?" I murmur.

Reaching for the drawer handle, I jerk it open, hoping for something I can use. I feel a wooden handle and when I pull it out, I see it's a large spoon with holes in it. Bingo. I pull a section of her hair, yanking it around my wrist and jerking her head back.

"I need your safe word."

She turns her head to the side and I see her scrunched up nose. "What the heck is that?" I release her hair and stop moving. How is she in to all this and not have any idea what a safe word is? That doesn't sit right with me at all. She tries to turn her body to see me better. "Why did you stop?"

"How am I supposed to know if I'm going too far? That I'm hurting you too badly?"

She turns back around as she wiggles her ass and laughs a soft, sinister laugh. "Oh Lex, that's cute and sweet, but you won't go too far. We don't need a safe word."

The way she says it pisses me off, as if I'm not capable of causing her real pain. It's a little hard not to take it as a challenge. I bring the spoon down as hard as I can and all I get is a gasp that melts into a moan. It feels like I'm wailing on her. Her ass is going to be so messed up tomorrow. There are already angry red welts and I'm almost positive she will bruise. Why does that make me want to fuck her harder? Her back arches as she comes and the sounds she makes while drowning in her pleasure are intoxicating. I beat her ass until I break the spoon and I never let up on the abuse

I'm giving her pussy either. Still, she pushes into the blows and presses harder against my body.

I shove the blue dress up her back. "I'm going to come." Pulling out just in time, I let my semen stream across her little round ass.

"Oh my God, again?" She gapes at me.

It cracks me up how that grosses her out so much. She'll swallow the shit, but God forbid she gets it on her skin.

"Hey, I warned you."

She laughs as I wipe her back with a dish towel and lower her from the counter. She smooths her dress down and I barely get my pants up and buttoned when Sasha walks in the front door.

"Hey guys, what's up?"

Tavin and I grin at each other as I walk toward the garage. "I was just about to hang up Tavin's new painting."

After retrieving the painting from the trunk, I meet them upstairs and hang it in her room, directly in front of her bed. I want her to be able to look at it when she wakes up in the morning.


*Monday, May 18th*


I'm scarfing down the incredible eggs Cara Jo made as Sasha walks into the kitchen with a sigh. "So now she's having night terrors." She picks up my coffee and takes a drink.

My mouth is full, so I can't tell her to get the hell off my coffee other than my glare. I take it out of her hand as I swallow. "There's a whole pot, get your own." I check for lipstick residue. "I should have warned you about the dreams. She's had them a couple of times."

"So, who is Toben?"

I point my fork at her. "I tell you what, as soon as you

figure that out, you let me know, okay?"

She scoffs, "Yeah, she tells me just about as much as she tells you."

As she walks to the cabinet for a coffee mug, I stand to put my plate in the sink. Wrapping my arm around her neck, I kiss her head as she pours her coffee.

"I got to head to work, I love you. I'll call you later."

"Yeah, I love you too, Alex."

I grab my keys from the bowl and before walking into the garage I add, "And when Tavin wakes up, get her to eat some eggs."

I arrive at the office forty minutes later to find my assistant Lauren waiting for me to discuss the charity event that Vulture's hosting. It brings a smile to my face to think of Tavin being my date.

Before I head out to run some errands, I print off a few pages of information on getting a GED. I don't understand her situation since she won't tell me anything, nevertheless, I said I'd help her and that's what I'm trying to do. Any education is better than none.

The printer is still going as I lock my door and head to the elevator. Once I push the button for the main floor, I take out my phone to text Tavin.

**How do you feel?**

My phone vibrates as I'm getting inside my car.

**I'm a little anxious. My ass hurts though and it makes me miss you.**

My stomach jumps while an idiotic grin spreads across my face.

**Just wait till I get home. I have a surprise.**

I stop by the shop to get her 'surprise' and let's just say I learn a lot. Grabbing a quick coffee on my way back, I check my phone and she still hasn't responded. I'm back at work for over an hour before my phone pings with her message.

**Did you say something to Sasha? She won't give me a Valium and I REALLY need it.**

I told Sasha this morning about withholding them if she hears Tavin talking herself down.

**Uh huh, and did you say something that would have caused her to do that?**

In the silence I can visualize her scowling at the phone.

I call Sasha to hear her yelling into the background, "Christ, you're like a damn toddler, I said no! You knew the rule." Her voice finds the mouthpiece and is back to normal, "Hey what's up, Bro?"

"So, what did she say to lose it?"

Her holler echoes through the phone, "Snitches get stitches, Tavin!" A small laugh comes from faraway, so she must not need it too much if she's in the mood to play around. "I don't know, something about being dirty and waiting on you to see that."

Maybe I should feel bad for her because she has such low self-esteem, really though it just pisses me off.

"Yeah, she doesn't get anything until I get home. I can hear that she isn't doing that bad anyway."

Sasha laughs, "She is milking you babying her, you know."

I do know and I don't care. I enjoy taking care of her and 'babying' her. Though I may not know anything specifically, whatever it is, I doubt it includes much doting.

---

Tavin's door is closed when I get home so I shower and pick through my bag of purchases. After I separate what I want, I put on a t-shirt and jeans and walk to her room. She and Sasha are both sitting on the bed, clearly in a deep conversation when I open the door.

Sasha jumps a little and scowls at me. "Jesus, Alex,

maybe knock next time? I could have been naked for all you knew."

"Didn't need that mental image, thanks." I lay the bag on the dresser before leaning against it and crossing my arms. "So how was your day?" I'm asking them both, but I can't force myself to look away from Tavin when she smiles like that.

"It was good," Sasha answers.

"That's great… Well, I'm here now so you can head out."

"Are you trying to get rid of me, brother?"

"No."

Yes.

I follow Sasha to the door as Cara Jo says dinner will be ready in a little over an hour, so I grab a bottle of water and bring it up to Tavin. The way her eyes brighten for that very first second that she sees me makes me feel like I'm made of steel.

She swings her legs around to sit on the edge of the bed. "Hi."

"Hi."

Her head turns to the dresser as she asks, "What's in the bag?"

"Something I hope you'll like."

I pick it up before getting on the bed with her. Rubbing my knuckles over her cheek, I kiss her and discard the bag as I move my kisses to her neck.

She's wearing one of her new outfits. It's a white, linen shirt that has big wooden buttons up the front. She paired it with the cutest jean shorts that are about to get ripped off. She isn't wearing shoes and her dark blue thigh highs have little bows on them.

Fucking thigh highs.

I take the Valium from my pocket and give it to her with the bottle of water.

"Sasha told me what you said this afternoon. Why do you talk about yourself that way?"

She swallows her pill and chugs some water before throwing the bottle on the bed.

"Because I honestly don't understand why you like me. You know all these smart, beautiful, successful women and I'm just…"

I stand up and reach down to pick her up. It's so natural how she wraps her legs around my waist. I grab the bag, carry her down the hall to my room, and into my bathroom. Standing behind her, I sit her down on the large vanity and turn her body to face the mirror. Her ass is pressed against my erection and with her knees bent, her toes are touching the bottom of the glass.

"You're poking me." She smirks.

I kiss her jawline before making eye contact in the mirror.

"You are the sweetest person I have ever met. You have this pureness about you, like you can only see beautiful things." Moving her hair, I kiss her neck. "When you're happy, I swear you glow." I kiss her shoulder before meeting her eyes in the mirror. "And you are smart. Just because you aren't educated, doesn't mean anything. You can change that." Her eyebrows are creased and her bottom lip is between her teeth. "Your eyes were the first thing to take my breath away the day you knocked on my door." I softly touch the pad of my fingers over her mouth. "Your lips are that perfect shade of pink and they match that precious pussy of yours. They are so soft and taste of honey." I move my touch to her cheek. "When you get turned on or embarrassed, your cheeks take on the same blush they are right now." I continue along her jaw. "You are the most stunning creature I have ever seen." Her face flashes with disbelief. "I'm dead serious about that. It kills me that you actually feel otherwise about yourself, I mean, Jesus, look at you. You're breathtaking."

"But...all the scars."

I place both hands over her knees, running my fingers over her thigh highs and spreading her legs. "They make me hard, Tav. Do you understand that? Everything about you makes me so hard it's almost painful."

I can tell she's struggling internally. I can almost see her mind working things over.

"Lex, I'm not... I'm not a normal girl."

Normal. I already know she isn't normal and that's the last thing I want her to be. I place my hand in between her legs, over the shorts.

"Good. You make me want to abandon everything I know about what's conventional and normal. I don't want to be normal and I don't want you to be either. Fuck. Normal. I want to hurt you because you want me to, I love watching the way your body curves beneath my belt. I just wish I could make you trust me with your secrets like you do with your skin."

Something switches in her eyes when she whispers, "Please, please Lex don't ask questions."

Her gaze locks into mine in the mirror as she reaches down and lifts the hem of her shirt, pulling it over her head and making my heart slam against my rib cage. She's finally going to show me. She has on a bralette, so I still can't see anything until she takes a deep breath, and in one swift motion, it's gone. First, I see her tits. When reality exceeds fantasy it is a wonderful sight to behold. They are exquisite, absolutely perfect. I want to suck on those little nipples so bad. My eyes shift to her sternum. In the space nestled between her breasts, I finally see what she's really been hiding and I'm having difficulty swallowing.

She's branded.

It's a lotus flower and it's completely healed so it sort of resembles a white ink tattoo. It's about three inches wide and five inches long including the scrolled stem. It is so Goddamn sexy I think I'm going to lose it right now. What's odd, is the familiarity of it. Where do I know that flower from? Although it does raise a whole new set of questions, I will honor her wishes and not ask.

I reach up and lightly trace my fingers over the raised skin. "Oh my God, Tavin...it's gorgeous."

She smiles a sad and sweet smile. Whatever she expected my reaction to be, it isn't the one I give her. Finally, I palm my hand over her bare tits. I squeeze and pull and massage. They fit in my hand as if they were made for me. I keep touching her as I reach into the bag.

I pull out the 'wand'. It releases electrical currents, and when I touch it to her ankle, her eyes widen.

"What is that?"

"The lady at the shop said it's called a 'violet wand.'"

It's shaped in a slightly upward curved *T* and is purple as the name suggests. The lady said to turn it up full power or it won't actually cause any real pain. It crackles when it touches her and that alone is getting heavy breathing out of her. I drag it up her calf to her thigh before I put it down and flip her around so she is facing me. When I lean in and kiss her, I pull her to the edge of the vanity.

Down her neck my kisses travel until I pull a little, perfect, pink nipple into my mouth, sucking as I tug on the other with my fingers. She has deprived me of them for so long, they are going to get the appropriate attention. I kiss her brand before switching.

I may be spending a little too much time on them because she laughs, "They aren't going anywhere."

I stand and grab a fistful of hair to pull her to my mouth. I wish I could absorb her. I already feel her in my skin and pulse. It's as if I finally found her even though I never knew

I was searching. I pull back and undo her shorts, yanking them off along with her underwear before I pick up the wand again.

After kicking off my jeans, I nestle myself in between her legs, her wet center begging me to enter. When our lips are almost touching, our bodies connect and our gasps collide.

Between the high I get from her finally trusting me with something and being able to feel her tits for the first time, I'm feeling impatient. She slides her fingers into my hair and pulls. Dear Jesus, I love that.

"Turn around and spread your legs. Lean over the vanity. I want to see those eyes, so keep them open."

I reach back into the bag and trade the wand for the whip. Her eyes flash when she sees it. We watch each other in the mirror as I bring the whip down and her skin instantly flushes red. She bites her lip as I continue to hit her. I don't know or understand how this is doing it for me. I've never fantasized about hurting anyone before. I mean, yeah sure I've jerked off to some BDSM porn, but really, who the hell hasn't?

I cut her a couple times and after a few blows, I'm learning how much strength is and isn't necessary. Her back and ass are lit up in lines and it drives me wild as I slide back inside. Placing my hand against her brand to bring her closer, she has to stand on her tip-toes and for some reason that riles me up even more. I trail my hand from her brand to her neck and squeeze. It feels so small.

She never stops watching me, even when she reaches her climaxes.

"I'm going to come inside of you." She nods and I fall into the forever of her eyes as my body ignites.

We lie in my bed as I trail my fingers lightly over her brand, tugging erratic breaths from her lips. I lean forward to place a soft kiss on her shoulder and run my fingers down her arm, stopping at the small red track marks, rubbing my thumb over them.

"How often were you using?"

She exhales harshly. "It only got kinda heavy again within the last few months." She rolls to her side and props her head in her hand, facing me. "I try to keep it to every other day, but occasionally I'll push it."

"That must get expensive, how do you pay for all that?" From what I've learned, I'm convinced she's a drug dealer. I haven't mentioned it because I want her to tell me. Her face falls, turning white as a ghost as her head makes that sharp twitchy movement. She won't make eye contact so I reach for her arm. "Hey, what is it?"

She gives me this pained look and I can almost see the wheels in her head turning.

"You're going to hate me, but you have to swear you won't tell anyone." She speaks in hushed tones and for the first time, I think I see a flash of fear. "I'm not supposed to talk about it. It's important okay?" Her eyes look at me with a little bit of sorrow and a whole lot of shame.

I grab her hand and nod as she takes a long, slow breath and whispers, "I'm Sweet Girl."

"Okay? What the hell is that?"

Her breathing becomes shaky along with her hands. I'm about to comfort her when she rasps, "Wealthy men pay to hurt me… and fuck me."

It actually takes a second to sink in. When it does, my body temperature shoots through the roof. My palms instantly sweat and my voice sounds eerily calm even to me.

"What?"

"Rich men pay to—"

It takes every ounce of energy to keep my chest from

exploding. The idea of her being with so many men brings my blood to a boil.

"I heard what the fuck you said." I push off the bed and shove my hand through my hair. I need to try and calm down so she can explain herself. "You choose this? Why?" She doesn't respond as I shove my leg into my jeans. "Is it the money?"

She shakes her head and mumbles, "No."

"Then why?"

Silence. My fists ball up and I wish I was in the gym right now so I could beat the shit out of something. I can't close my eyes without seeing all the men who have touched her, hurt her, kissed her, smelt her, fucked her…

"Fuck, Tavin. Give me something. Please."

She swipes away a tear and I want to hold her. I don't understand why she would want to be used that way, assuming she does since she won't fucking tell me otherwise. The fury that she won't talk to me about what the hell is going on keeps me grounded. Her teary eyes meet mine and her mouth opens without words, before she shakes her head and looks away. My frustration, anger, and confusion leave me with nothing else to say as I grab my shirt and throw it over my head. She doesn't try to stop me as I storm out and slam the door.

I cannot look at her right now. I know she'll bail the first chance she gets and she's not getting off that easy. Cara Jo is in the kitchen finishing dinner.

"You might as well put that away, I need you to watch Tavin like a motherfucking hawk until I get back. She's not to leave this house."

"When should I expect you back?"

"I don't know, call Sasha if it gets too late. I need a drink," I yell over my shoulder before slamming the door. How does this happen?

I order a double and sit at the bar. The Necco Room has been my favorite bar for the past three years and now all I see is Tavin standing on that booth seat over there kissing me. I down my drink and I gesture for another. I can't look at the dance floor without seeing her body moving to the music.

The drugs I can deal with and the masochistic tendencies are hot as hell, I'll give her that, but a prostitute? Not just any prostitute either, oh no, not only do random men have sex with her, they also rip apart her flesh.

Oh my God.

Oh fuck. I've been inside her without a condom.

Downing the second whiskey, I motion to the bartender. How had I let myself become so careless?

*Oh you know, a little of this, some of that.*

That had been her response when I asked her what she did for a living—in this very bar that first night. Even then I had known it was a shady answer. I'm scared to think about what else she's hiding. Down goes my third and the bartender refills my glass.

"You might want to slow down." I glare at him and he backs off, throwing up his hands. "Just saying, you won't last long at this rate."

And there goes the fourth. He refills, shrugs and walks away. How could she not tell me? Am I really supposed to get past this? What am I supposed to do? I can't just stop caring about her. My stomach is twisted up in knots. I remember I have her Valium in my pocket. They're for anxiety right? Well, right now I am feeling pretty fucking anxious. I pop one and wash it down with my next drink. She purposely withheld this information from me.

*Wealthy men pay to hurt me… and fuck me.*

At least there's the silver lining that she isn't a street

walker. Thank Christ for that. More of a call girl, I assume. An expensive one if it's only wealthy men. She's says it's not about the money, so why? Does she go out on actual dates with them first or is it just sex? Where does she meet them? Hotels? Offices?

Holy shit.

Holy motherfucking shit.

Is *that* what she was doing with Eric? She panicked when she saw my name plate because she was at the wrong door.

My hands are shaking when I finish the next drink. The bartender is on top of things so I up my tip on the next ones.

**In my own Goddamn building? Is that how you're 'acquainted' with Eric?**

It takes me four times to type it and as soon as I hit 'send' I wish I hadn't. I don't know if that counts as drunk texting, regardless, I need to have this conversation in person. I want to see how many times she flutters those fucking eyelashes. My phone pings with her response.

**Your building? Are you his boss?**

I don't respond. I empty my last drink and I'm pretty sure I walk straight to the valet before handing him my ticket. The kid looks around as if he's uncomfortable.

"Maybe we should send for a car," he squeaks.

I protest a bit because I wouldn't be a very good drunk if I didn't, but I also relent easily enough.

The driver arrives to pick me up and is silent as he takes me home. For that I am grateful. I have no idea where to go from here. What to say to her.

When I get inside my house, I hit my elbow hard on the edge of the kitchen counter and the pain shoots through my arm. "Argh! Damn it!"

"Oh, Alex. Are you drunk?" Sasha's hands are on her hips. "Cara Jo said you left in a mood."

I glare at her and hold up my hand. "Don't start, Sash,

you have no idea what happened with Tavin today."

She rolls her eyes. "Nor do I care. You found her over-dosing a week ago. Does that stop you from shoving your dick into her? No, of course it doesn't." She shakes her head, "You're a dumb ass and I'm going to bed."

She turns toward the guest room she's been staying in and disappears down the hall. I pour myself another drink and bring the bottle upstairs. When I walk by Tavin's room, she's sleeping on top of the covers and her arm is draped over her eyes. Her breasts that I now know are impeccable are rising and falling with each breath. Why does she have to be as fucked up as she is radiant?

I go to my room and a few drinks later, there's a knock at the door. My stupid sister. She pissed me off with that comment earlier.

I yank open my door. "I am not just 'shoving my—"

It isn't Sasha. It's Tavin. She's standing there in a white baby tee that shows her naval and she isn't wearing a bra. Seeing those little nipples poking through the thin fabric makes me want to bite them. Her hair is down and she has a bit of bed head. Damn it. Why does she have to look so incredible?

Her shoulders slump as she lets out a harsh breath. "I just wanted to tell you that I don't have anything. I get test-ed frequently and Marie the Doctor tested me too."

Marie the Doctor? That's cute. Shit, no it isn't.

"Well that's good to fucking know."

I wonder how she gets tested without any identifica-tion, though it's not exactly a concern right now.

"I should never have told you, but I guess it's for the best." She jerks her head and her sexy-ass voice drops. "I'm sorry, Alexander, you picked the broken toy to play with."

This hasn't changed a thing. I'm more pissed than I have been in a long time and still my feelings are the same.

It's beyond *want* at this point. I *need* to touch her, taste her…fuck her. It's as if I'm barely being sated, I'm always needing more.

*I want you to hurt me.*

I adore the way her body orgasms at the presence of pain and at this point all I can think about is making her pay for lying to me, for letting herself be used by God knows how many men, and for that last ridiculous comment.

She turns to leave and I grab her arm, jerk her into my room, and slam the door. I pull her to the bed and release her.

"You had literally just slid off of Eric's dick when I asked you out in the elevator, hadn't you?"

"Alexan—"

"Yes or motherfucking no?

"Yes." She nods.

My pulse spikes as I unzip my jeans. I clutch a fistful of her hair and jerk her head down so her lips are inches away from where I want them. I have never in my life been so vehemently aroused. The more I give in to my anger, the harder I get.

"Open." She obeys and looks up at me. I shove in and out of her mouth. "You're done. Done with the drugs and fucking done with your 'Sweet' bullshit."

I shove between her lips and my current state makes me care a lot less about hurting her, although according to her I'm not capable of doing so.

Oh, we'll see about that.

"You are with me now, and I'm not sharing." I pull out of her mouth and grip my hand around her neck to jerk her up. This is way past liberating. Anger and lust have taken over and she *wants* me to take it all out on her. I kiss her hard. "Get naked and turn around."

She responds by lifting her shirt over her head. How many men have done this very thing to her? How many have touched her, heard their name in her raspy voice and tasted her come? I unbuckle my jeans as she pushes down her shorts and licks her lips before turning around. I kick her ankles so she spreads her legs and I slide my fingers inside feeling how ready she is. I stroke myself as I fuck her with my fingers.

Rubbing the head along her slit, I slam inside of her as hard as I can and she lets out a small grunt. I spread one hand across her stomach while the other one is on her throat pressing her back to my chest.

"Alexander, I—"

"Do not say a single fucking word right now."

I bend my knees to maximize force while tightening my hand to cut off her airflow. I'm drilling into her so hard I can tell it is causing her pain, and I'm glad. Her body slacks as she comes with such ferocity that I can feel it dripping down my shaft. I love the little sounds she makes and I can't hear them with my hand squeezing her neck.

I remove it and she gasps, moans, and whimpers all in the same insanely erotic sound. Trailing my hand down her chest, I feel her brand beneath my fingers before I push her away and shove her face down on the bed. As my hands grab her wrists, I press them to the small of her back and see they're bloody from her shredding them. I lightly touch her fingertips and bend over to pull them into my mouth.

"You need to cut this out." I hold her wrists together with one hand while the other caresses the curve of her buttocks. "You have such a perfect little ass." I trace my finger over the tight orifice.

Ripping the belt off my pants, I accidently knock my laptop off the night stand giving me an idea.

She wants pain? Oh, she'll get pain.

I rip the charging chord from the wall and slam it down across her back making her actually yell. She never makes loud noises during sex and that just revs me up more. I'm trashed and seeing red, so the rest of the night is a blur of sex and cries.

# CHAPTER NINE
## *Control*

*Tuesday, May 19th*

FEEL LIKE DEATH, SO WHEN THE ALARM STARTS BEEPING, I hit snooze and skip my workout in lieu of getting out of bed with Tavin. As far as I know, she didn't have any night terrors, so we at least got to sleep for a couple of hours. Rolling over, I reach my arm out for her when the scene before me comes into focus and my heart sinks into my nauseated stomach.

Her entire back is shredded and bloody, bruised and welted. My white sheets are smeared in scarlet. I rip my fingers through my hair.

Oh my God… What the fuck did I do?!

Reaching out to touch her, I think better of it and pull my hand back. I wish I could wipe it all away. She moans and turns her head to look at me as she smiles.

"Mmm, good morning."

I am horrified. I did this? My voice comes out shaky. "Tavin…I…I'm so sorry."

She slowly leans up on her elbows. "For what?"

"What do you think? For tearing you apart!" I scream at her, I cannot believe I let myself completely lose control. I shove off the blankets and as she sits up, she's clearly in pain.

"Don't, Lex. I liked it, and you needed to let it out. Please don't do this guilt thing." I shake my head and when I look to the floor I see the whip. I must have taken that to her too. She climbs out of bed, and can't stand up completely straight. "You don't get it. I need the pain. You didn't do anything wrong, Lex. I love what we did last night."

"You can't even fucking stand up! This is not okay, Tav! How can I want to hurt you and protect you at the same time? It doesn't make sense. If someone else did this to you, I would want to slit their Goddamn throat."

She smirks and places her hand on my arm. "You're so sweet."

Pulling my arm back, I twist away from her. I can't handle her affection right now. This is so fucked up. I'm confused and I need to clear my head. That isn't going to happen with her naked, beaten body standing in front of me.

"I need to get ready for work."

I glance at the bloodied sheets and shake my head before disappearing into my bathroom to shower.

She isn't in my room when I finish and her bedroom door is closed as I walk by. I almost stop to say goodbye when I glance at my watch. I don't have enough time.

Cara Jo is in the kitchen when I run through. "I'm running behind today, I'll just take an orange." I'm being short with her and she ignores it as usual.

She hands me the orange. "Don't forget I'm leaving at one today for my appointment."

I did forget about that and today is the day Sasha has to leave for her client consult. I can't very well tell either of them no, so I'll just try to skip out early. Even if I can't, the truth I don't want to admit is that Tavin is technically clean. She's still a little anxious, but she isn't having withdrawals anymore. My reason to keep her here is gone. What she does from here has to be completely up to her.

"No problem. I'll see you tomorrow."

I can't decide if last night makes me a bad person and that freaks me out. This should be a no brainer. I literally beat her last night. I have never hit a woman in my life, and have never desired to until Tavin. I still can't believe I let myself lose it like that. She makes it all twisted because she likes it so damn much, and I like that she likes it.

When I get to work, everyone is abuzz about the children's home benefit. It's in less than two weeks and there's a lot that still needs to be done. Lauren meets me as I walk off the elevator.

"Good morning, Mr. Sørensen. There are a few insurance documents that need your signature," she hands me a paper-clipped stack of papers, "and South Shadoebox Bowl just signed off on the three lane agreement for the children's home."

Thank God. We've gotten a pool and a basketball court already donated. Of course we're donating the equipment and the money for a theater, so the bowling alley is the caramel on the sundae.

"That's fantastic. I'll have these ready for you before I leave for my rounds."

There are a few theaters I need to visit today, and as promised, I have the necessary paperwork on Lauren's desk before I leave.

All day I keep wanting to text Tav, yet every time I try, I can't find the words to say. I don't even know what to feel. She makes me crazy. I'm having contradicting emotions and it's driving me nuts. She makes everything upside down and backwards and I'm not used to this. I love the way she gives her body to me to do whatever I want with it, while guiding me toward what she needs. The idea of her being in pain twists my gut, yet I want to inflict it on her. How demented is that? My initial reaction this morning was remorse and trepidation, so why does my dick stiffen when I think about last night? What is this girl doing to me? I seriously hurt her and all I can think about is getting home and doing more.

The day is madness, so I don't get to leave as early as I would prefer. I arrive home to find the main floor empty. Dropping the papers for the GED on the island, I take off my suit jacket and climb the stairs to her room, which is also empty. "Tav?" I check the bathroom across the hall and she isn't there either. I call for her again and the silence responds.

She actually did it. She left. Part of me wants to get back in my car, drive to her house, and demand she tell me why she left again. While I know she couldn't wait to get out of here at first, at this point I thought things had changed. She was basically in a post-coital glow this morning. I did promise her she could leave when she got everything out of her system, still, it doesn't make sense. We were becoming something real. She showed me her lotus brand last night, why would she do that if she was just going to leave today?

*I'm Sweet Girl.*

She said it as if I should already know what it was. I feel as if there's this giant hidden puzzle piece, and if I find it, she will finally make sense. It makes me sick to think she probably went right back to the men and the drugs.

Goddamn it, this actually hurts. I shouldn't feel this way, we haven't known each other for more than a couple weeks. My fingers wrap around my bedroom door handle as a quiet noise sounds behind me. Standing perfectly still, I listen.

There it is again.

Quick un-patterned sounds. I follow them down the hall to the gym. As I get closer, I hear whimpers and moans. *Tavin's* whimpers and moans. My heart leaps because she stayed.

By choice.

I push open the door and see her on the floor. She found one of my old iPods and the earbuds are in her ears, which is why she didn't hear me calling. The main menu to the yoga video is on the flat screen so she must have been doing that before…she started doing what she's doing now.

She has her right hand down the front of her shorts shifting in fast movements as she rocks beneath her hand and more erotic noises escape her lips. Her shirt is pushed up above her naval and her left arm rests across the floor above her head. After a couple moments, her hand beneath her shorts paces even faster as her breathing becomes choppy and erratic. She reaches beside her and by the time I realize what she's about to do, she picks up a pair of scissors, slicing them across her stomach.

It's beautiful.

She's turned me into a sick bastard.

Laughing to herself, she removes the earbuds and stands to her feet, moving much easier than this morning. When she sees me, she jumps and her ears flush pink along with her cheeks.

"What are you doing here? You aren't supposed to be back yet."

She's embarrassed and it's cute as hell. I slip my hand beneath her shirt over her cut before sliding it down her shorts.

"Were you thinking of me?"

"Yes." She smiles and whispers, "I've never done that before."

I shouldn't laugh, but really? "What? Masturbated?"

Her cheeks get pinker. "Last night was just…"

She needs to stop smiling that way.

I remove my hand from between her legs and lift her

chin. "'Fucked up' is the phrase you're looking for. That can't happen again. Not that bad. I love marking you, I want to make you sore for days, but last night was brutal."

"You don't understand. I need it."

"Not to that extreme you don't, and I should have known better."

Walking to the closet, I get the resistance bands and point behind me. "Bend over the Roman chair."

I walk around to the front of the chair, crouching to the balls of my feet as I fasten her wrists with the bands. Her long hair falls over her head and I brush it out of the way to kiss her.

God she's exquisite.

"There has to be a middle ground, Tav."

Standing and circling around behind her, I examine the view. Her legs are closed with her feet resting on the foot-rest. Her ass is up in the air with her little shorts on. I slide them down with her underwear and discard them.

That's better.

I loosen my tie and undo my trousers, not bothering with anything else before I stand behind her. With her standing on the footrest, she's the perfect height for me to slip into her little body.

Kissing her neck, I murmur, "You mean something to me, you know."

I bite down and am quickly rewarded with a shudder before I lift her shirt to look at the damage. She's showered, so it doesn't look quite as harsh as it did this morning. Still, it looks pretty bad.

I did this to her.

I need to find our balance and what feels right for us. Find how much she needs and how much I can give her.

The chicken dinner Cara Jo left for tonight is amazing, even though Tavin has barely touched it. I take a drink of my whine as I grin at her and reach for the GED papers.

"I got you some information for school."

She looks at me as if I just told her we were eating human flesh. "Why would you do that?"

This isn't exactly the response I was going for. I hold them out to her and she doesn't even look at them. I drop them back on the island and sigh. "I thought I was being supportive."

"It was a nice thought, Lex, but I'm not getting a GED."

She's so final it takes me aback. "Don't you want an education? Have you never even considered it?"

Her lip is going to start bleeding if she chews on it any harder. "It's not possible." She shakes her head and continues eating as if it's the end of the conversation.

"Why not?"

"Because it isn't," she snaps as she drops her fork on the plate. "Just forget it."

I really thought she'd be more excited about this. "Is this because of the Sweet Girl thing or your identification issues?"

She lets out a groan and crosses her arms. "What do you want me to say? I already told you I can't explain everything and you don't want me lying. Would I like to go to school and become smart? Of course I would, but it isn't going to happen, so please, let it go like I asked."

I take her hand and squeeze it, smiling at her so she knows I'm not upset. At least not at her. "Okay, Tav."

*Wednesday, May 20th*

*Tavin*

"Tavin, sweetie, will you stir this so I can go to the cellar?"

The coolness of the floor seeps through my stockings as I hop off the island. "Sure." I like Cara Jo. She always talks nice about Alexander and she calls me nice names. She lets me help her sometimes and she never asks questions. She is tall and thin, and her silver hair is almost shorter than Alexander's. I think she's so pretty. I take the spoon and do what she asks while Sasha is drawing in her notebook. "What are you drawing?"

"It's not drawing, it's sketching."

She flips her notebook around and the same long, skinny woman with no face that's in all her pictures, is wearing a sleeveless short dress. It just looks like a bunch of lines to me. One time though, she showed me pictures of what she designs and I couldn't believe it. She knows how to make clothes and they're so beautiful.

When Lex brought up school, I wanted so bad to grab the papers to see what they said. I wonder how many things I could learn there. Maybe I could learn how to make my drawings better or how to make clothes like Sasha. Wondering just makes me sad though. There's no way Logan would let me do that. Especially not now.

My mind keeps slipping to Toben. I miss him so much. I'm hurting him and Alexander both and I still can't stop. I even snuck out yesterday when I was alone, and Toben wasn't even home. I didn't get any of my things or else Alexander would have known that I left, I just looked everywhere for my cell and still couldn't find it. At least I got to do a couple lines of coke. To be honest, I was going to shoot a little, just a teensy weensy bit, but Toben must have cleaned us out again because it was gone. I still can't believe I actually came back here.

It amazes me that Lex has the power to get me aroused when he's not even around me. I don't understand it. I keep thinking about the other night when I told him about being Sweet Girl. He didn't recognize my title, so he's not in Logan's circle of associates, and knowing that makes me happy. He wanted me to give him an explanation that would make him feel better about what I do, and I wish I could have. He asked me why I do it and as hard as I tried to think of something that would have been enough, I kept coming up blank. It makes me feel terrible that he was so upset, but oh my God, when he came back, it was incredible. Every time I think about it, I get achy.

I like it here and I really like him. I'm having fun even if I'm ignoring the fact that every day I don't talk to Toben things get worse. He might get me in more trouble just because he doesn't know where I am. I have never been away from him this long. Dang it! I should have written him a note. What if Logan already knows I've been gone and comes back early? That scares me too much to think about.

On top of it, Lex thinks we are together.

*You are with me now, and I'm not sharing.*

It took everything I had not to cry when he said that. I even tried to explain, he was mad at me though and didn't want me talking. He knows I'm a whore and he knows I'm a junkie, and he still looks at me like it's painful to not touch me. I catch his eyes staring at my lips, my neck, my ass, my tits, and whatever other body part enamors him at that given moment. He says amazing things and don't get me wrong, Toben has always spoken to me in that special way that he does. I don't know…it's just different with Lex. I haven't decided when I'm going to leave yet and am worried about how I'm going to explain this to Tobe when I can't even really explain it to myself.

Cara Jo and Sasha know the song on the radio too and we all sing it together. It's so weird to be surrounded by girls, but I like it. I like girls.

The sound of the garage door opening up drones in the background and my heart leaps.

He's back.

His beautiful smile is on his face as he walks into the kitchen. "Hey, what are you guys making?"

The warmth of his voice wraps around me, making me sigh. I want to kiss him all over, the way he looks in that suit.

"Salmon," Cara Jo answers and she smiles at him.

He gives her a side hug and grabs my wrist to pull me upstairs as he says over his shoulder, "We'll be back."

I half laugh at Sasha rolling her eyes while her pencil is still moving feverishly. He pulls me into his room and against his chest as his mouth slams against mine. Good Lord, someone's worked up. He takes off his jacket to put it on the back of his chair before his fingers fly to each button of his shirt.

I smirk. "What's goin' on?"

He laughs and he's on me, his large hands cupping both sides of my face. "Nothing, you're just beautiful. You know what those knee highs do to me, *Lille*." I bite my lip so I don't laugh because yes, yes I do. He tosses his shirt to the floor and is popping open the button on my jean shorts. "I will make you a deal." He yanks them down. "If you eat a real meal tonight, I will give you a treat." With impressive swiftness, he pulls my shirt over my head and pops off my bra. His mouth is on me in an instant. I laugh because he's so overzealous when it comes to my tits. He has my back arching and I'm leaning into him like the whore I am, when he murmurs, "Do we have a deal?"

I don't tell him that I started feeling hungry today

anyway. I can't make myself say anything right now other than a breathless, "Yes."

I eat my dinner. All of it. I'm gonna get my dang treat. He says we have to go somewhere to get it and I think it's so sweet that he wants to surprise me. He makes me forget that I might be signing my death warrant with every day that passes and every touch we share. We get ready in our separate rooms and he only has one request for my outfit selection. I curl my hair and match my short, cream t-shirt dress with boots and the desired gray knee socks. Sasha even helps me put on the eyeliner he bought me. I never wear eyeliner. When I meet him downstairs, he's in a dark blue, faded t-shirt and jeans. I don't have a dream of staying dry when the man puts his sexy ass in jeans.

We get into his car and I grin at him. According to Sasha, he's just as wealthy as the Clients. She says he is the CEO of Vulture, and even though I don't know crap about business, I have picked up from the Clients that the CEO is the big shot. It surprises me that he has that kind of responsibility, just because he's usually so laid back. Don't get me wrong, he definitely has his intense moments, but he is also carefree, light, bright, and warm.

I can see the glowing neon yellow lights that say 'Vulture' from pretty far away. I've seen his theaters before, even if I've never been inside one. Movies aren't exactly mine and Toben's source of entertainment these days. Getting fucked up when we're not getting fucked—that's our life.

I'm so excited to see it. This is his creation, his reality. Pride isn't a very common emotion for me and I feel it for him in this moment. He saw what he wanted and took it. I wish I could have the strength and the bravery to do that because I would take him.

We walk up long, cement steps before he swings open one of the many sets of doors. Gray is the main color and bright yellow punches out in accents just like at his office. Movie posters are everywhere. A huge *L*-shaped snack bar lines the entire back wall with a large, neon yellow sign above it that reads: **Concessions.**

As I take it all in, my eyes land on the most delicious sight and my jaw drops. There are rows of glass jars filled to the brim with cotton candy in every color of the rainbow.

Oh. My. God.

I hear his deep laugh. "Found the cotton candy bar, huh?"

"Is that my treat?" Please say yes.

"No, but you may have some."

I had pink last time so I pick purple. It's grape flavor and it is so freaking good. I love the way it dissolves into sugar the moment it gets in my mouth. Mmmmm.

We walk by a huge entryway that has a yellow *V* above it. He says it's a restaurant and he'll bring me back to eat sometime. I won't be around that long though, even if I don't say that.

Directly next to it, is a nearly identical entrance, except instead of the *V*, there's a picture of the Vulture logo. He holds my hand as we go inside. It looks like it could be a store in the mall. There are graphic tees, toys, posters, phone cases...pretty much everything you can think of is covered in movie names and characters. I recognize a few of them. He introduces me simply as Tavin. He doesn't give any explanation at all. I could be his cousin for all anyone knows.

I throw away the paper handle from my cotton candy as we walk past the concession stand toward the back of the building. He leads me down a long hallway with a bunch of theater rooms until we finally come to the desired one. He's taking me to a movie like normal couples do.

Too bad we aren't normal…or a couple.

He kisses my head and murmurs in my ear, "Pick a seat in the front row. I'll be right back," before turning back the way we came.

As I walk in, I realize the theater is completely empty. I'm the only one here. There is quiet music playing and the dim lights are bright enough for me to see the golden swirls in the carpet. My eyes scan for the first row and when I see it I grin. Of course. The front consists of only four seats and they aren't really seats at all, more like beds. There are even pillows. My laugh sounds loud in the empty room. Is this really my life? Well no, but it is happening to me. I choose right now that no matter how this turns out, I will save the way he makes me feel in these moments. I will take out these memories and gorge on them in my darkest hours.

When he comes back he's carrying a box with popcorn and sodas. "What do you think?"

"It's neat."

"Oh stop, you're making me blush." His sarcasm is in monotone before flashing that incredible smile and making me laugh.

He lies down next to me as the curtain lifts. The room goes dark and the screen casts a glow onto his face. Stuffing the popcorn in my mouth, I stare at the gigantic screen as it flashes with trailers of movies that will be out soon. He situates the pillows before shoving his hand into the popcorn bucket and grins at me.

When the trailers are over and the intro to the movie starts, I slurp my soda with anticipation. I am so excited to see what he picked.

What was he thinking? This is a war movie and it isn't even in English! The thing hasn't even been on for fifteen minutes and I'm bored out of my skull.

"Alexander?" I whisper.

He keeps his eyes on the screen. "Hmmm?"

"What the crap is this?"

He laughs his full belly laugh and his body shakes. "Not getting into it, huh?"

I feel bad. He's trying to be nice. "Sorry. It's just kind of dull."

He jumps up to sitting as he reaches into his pocket. "Good, now I can give you your treat. I don't want you sidetracked."

Did he pick this dumb movie on purpose?

He chuckles as he hovers over me and kisses my gawping mouth. "The first two times I saw you, you had a lollipop. Now I can't look at one and not think of you." He hands me a sucker. "This one's yours. Save it for whenever you want."

His kisses trail down my neck as he pushes up my dress and takes down my boy shorts. He lightly touches his fingers across the hem of my knee sock and fondles it for a moment before opening my legs. He reaches into his pocket again and takes out another lollipop.

"This one...this one is mine." He rips off the wrapper and puts it in his mouth while his incredible long fingers rub along my slit. "Always so wet for me."

He has barely done a thing and my chest is almost heaving. He licks the sucker once more before he rubs it over my clit. He brings it across my entrance a few times before sliding it inside of me. The shallow penetration is punishing, paired with his slow pace.

He takes it out, pops it into his mouth for a second time before putting it back again.

"Mmmm. Tavin flavored. Now that's good." His crooked smile makes me clench around the candy. The final time he removes it, he hands it to me. "Here."

I smirk at him and slip it between my lips. He's right, it does taste like me. He moves up my body to kiss me and then gets right back down there. I eat my treat and watch him while he licks and sucks, murmuring how good I taste.

He even brought a paring knife.

After we give the technician guy a show of our own, we lie there, wrapped up in each other, eating popcorn and drinking soda.

Everything is perfect until he clears his throat. "So the whole Sweet Girl thing... How did that work?"

Dang it.

I'm not supposed to talk about this. The list of things that is going to royally piss off Logan is getting longer by the day. I don't think Lex will tell anyone though, I already told him not to and he doesn't seem like he would go against his word.

I let out a breath. "The men are called Clients. The only way they can hire me is to be referred. They have to sign a contract and they can schedule either an hour, a full, or a weekend playdate."

There it is. The disgust I've been waiting for.

"A playdate? That's what you called it?"

I don't want to talk about this with him! "Um...yeah."

His jaw twitches. He's trying to act like this isn't bothering him, yet he's squeezing the crap out of my hip right now.

"What did the contract say?"

He is referring to it in the past tense and it makes my stomach twist. If only he knew how badly I wish that was an option.

"I don't know exactly. There are rules that apply to them though."

"What were the rules?"

I'm not usually an irritable person, but he's driving me crazy!

"Rule number one is that they always have to wear a condom. Always. You broke that little rule by the way." He forces a smile and waits for me to continue. "Rule number two is that they can only mark me from the back of my neck to the top of my thighs. The bottoms of my feet are okay too."

I can't put a finger on the way he is looking at me. It isn't necessarily bad, more... odd. A shift of fury, curiousness, arousal, and sympathy all crossing his face at once.

"Rule number three is that I can't have sex with anyone other than with the Clients." I may be paraphrasing that one. "I shouldn't be doing this with you." His eyes fill with sadness and I can't bear it.

"You don't want to know all this, Lex."

"No, I need to know. Keep going." He finally loosens his grip on my hip to rub tender fingers along the side of my body.

I sigh, "Rule number four is that I have to be prepared for penetration. They have to lube me up. No dry fucking." His hand stops for a moment before gently starting up again, and his picked up breathing slows. "Rule number five is more of a guideline. They can do most things, as long as I'm able to walk out when they're done. They can't break bones or remove chunks of flesh. They can't cut anything off or anything."

His mouth drops open. He's repulsed. I knew he would get grossed out eventually. "The sick assholes have to be told not to cut shit off?"

I try to hide my offense. I just knew this would happen. "Oh, then wait till you hear rule number six. You will really think I'm sick."

I don't want to look at his horrified expression anymore so I sit up and he grabs my arm.

"Hey," he snaps. Releasing me, he rubs where his hand had just squeezed. "Do not put words in my mouth, okay? I did not say you were sick, I said *they* were sick." His arm feels so big when he wraps it around me and pulls me against him. "What is rule number six?"

This is so humiliating. I can't believe he knows this stuff about me.

"No bodily fluids. They can't get anything besides come, saliva and my blood involved."

He tucks my hair behind my ear and when I look up at him, he doesn't seem repulsed anymore.

"How did you even get into this?"

Uh uh. No way.

"Pass."

"Do you have a pimp or a Madame?"

I can't keep looking into his eager eyes. He wants answers that I can't give. He doesn't understand I'm protecting us both by keeping my secrets. I scoot away from him to reach for my soda. "Pass."

His sigh is full of frustration. "How many other 'Sweet Girls' are there?"

"There are no other girls. I'm THE Sweet Girl. I'm exclusive."

Well, since he said 'girls' I'm not lying. I drink my soda and watch the muscles in his arms as he combs his fingers through his hair. He is clearly lost in thought and I want to ask him, but I'm hoping this is the end of his interrogation.

"Weren't you ever afraid of getting raped?" Oh my God, he has to stop! I just shrug. How am I really supposed to answer that? "What the fuck? Have you been raped?!"

His voice booms over the movie causing me to jump. I want to touch his face and take away the worry.

"Pass," I manage to croak out.

"Oh no you don't. I ask if you're a victim of a brutal crime, and you shrug it off? Like if it did happen, it's nothing more than an inconvenience? You have somehow made all of this seem normal, as if it's not completely insane, but you officially just freaked me out."

He's mad and I don't know what I'm supposed to say. I feel the tears burning. I see his exasperation and I hate that I'm doing this to him. Grabbing his hand, I squeeze it tight.

"I'm sorry. I can't tell you anything. Please don't look at me like that. You said I could say pass if I didn't want to talk about it. Please Alexander, I didn't mean to say that. Can you just forget it?"

*Stupid bitch! Keep your dirty mouth shut!*

He gives an incredulous glare. "Forget that you basically just told me you've been raped? No Tavin, I can't."

It's all of his stupid questions! He asks and asks! I don't want to spend the little time we have fighting about this. I can't stop the tears.

I pull my hand away to wipe my face. I hate how easily they fall. "Please, it's not how you think, I can't explain…just please let it go."

"Was it rape or wasn't it? Did you want it or not? It's not that complicated."

"Yes it is!" I throw up my hands as I yell at him. He will never understand and I don't think I want him to. I try to get up when he grabs my arm to pull me into his chest.

"Okay, okay, calm down. We'll drop it for now, I just hate knowing that you have obviously been through something bad and I can't do anything to help you because you won't let me in."

I never will either. If he knew everything, it would not only put him in danger, but he would never look at me again, let alone touch me.

Something dawns on him because he releases me as fury overruns his features. "Did Eric hurt you?!"

I can't contain the laugh that falls out from my mouth. "Have you not been listening? Hurting me is the dang point!"

His hands become fists as he presses them against the seat cushions. "He's fired first thing in the fucking morning."

No! He can't do that!

"No, no please, Alexander! You aren't supposed to know! If you fire him then…"

He leans toward me, forcing me to pull back. "Then what?!" I can't give him his answers. His body is on top of me instantly as he slams me down on the bed seat and whispers, "This is getting intense, Tav, in a lot more ways than one, and we haven't been at this long. I feel as if you're going to disappear and I'll never see you again."

If I'm being completely honest, if it wasn't for Toben, I might handle this a little differently. I still don't know what the heck I'm doing. The way he looks at me and the things he's saying are crushing my heart. While of course I don't want it to be like this, I don't have a choice. Well, I guess that isn't true. I could leave tonight and tell him to leave me alone. I could stop this now and Logan will never know anything other than I've been missing my playdates. I avoid thinking of what my punishment will be when Logan gets back, and I completely ignore the thoughts of what he would do to Lex if he ever found out about him. I've seen what he does to those who steal from him.

I need to talk to Toben.

He hovers over me, his blond hair soft beneath my fingers as I brush it away from his face. His strong and gorgeous face. I touch his cheeks so softly I wonder if he feels it.

"Can't we just enjoy this? The right now? I don't want to think about anything past tonight."

His eyebrows narrow as his jaw ticks and it's like he thinks if he looks into my eyes deep enough, he'll get the answers he thinks he wants.

"That's what I'm talking about. Whenever you say stuff like that it feels like every moment with you could be my last. You have this way about you, as if you see something the rest of the world can't. Sometimes you feel almost... magical." He presses his forehead against mine and laces our fingers together before pulling our hands above our heads. "Please don't disappear," he whispers against my lips.

He really isn't going to make this any easier on me, is he? I almost hate him saying these things. It just confuses me more. I don't know these emotions, not exactly. This is different from Toben. I can't do this to him anymore. He's given me so much more than I thought I would ever have. Actually, he didn't give it to me. He gave it to *Lille*. She's not me. I stole those things from him by lying.

I have to go home, I miss Toben.

I'll leave tomorrow.

# CHAPTER TEN
*Toben*

## Alexander

"TOBEN!"

My eyes flip open. She's having another nightmare. Forcing myself out of bed, I rush down the hall to her room and find Sasha shushing her cries.

"Tavin, who is Toben?"

Sasha asks the question that has been burning in my skull for days. Standing in the doorway, I watch Tavin's silhouette sit up and lift her hand to wipe her head.

"Can I have some water?" Her voice strains.

It unsettles me that she's ignoring the question instead of just saying 'pass', which she clearly has no problem doing.

Sasha sighs and raises her eyebrows while she walks past me to go to the kitchen. As nice as it's been having my sister back again, her being here has become pointless. Tavin isn't having withdrawals anymore and she ate really well last night.

As I cross the threshold into her room, she pushes off the bed and gives me a weak smile as she walks by me to go to the bathroom.

She splashes water on her face as she hunches over the

vanity. Her back is gently lifting and falling as her heavy breathing slows. Leaning against the door frame and crossing my arms, I watch her. Why can't I figure out how to get her to trust me?

"Are you okay?"

I can see her face in the mirror so she can't hide the fluttering. "I'm fine."

It's late and I don't want to fight or upset her more, but even little lies piss me off. "No lying."

Her knuckles are white from gripping the vanity as her eyes meet mine in the reflection. "I need to go home."

My stomach drops. It's not that she wants to leave that has me worried, it's what happens after that.

"You want to leave?"

She shakes her head as she turns around and takes a step closer to me. "It's not a matter of want. This was always temporary." She gestures toward the hall and all around her, implying the rest of the house. "I am grateful to you for not leaving me to die and I'm even glad you made me stay here. I've enjoyed my time with you. I really, really have." She takes a step closer and her eyes look darker than I've seen them. "I need you to understand, I *have* to go back."

I feel hot. I'm not liking the way this is sounding.

"We'll still see each other right?"

She closes her eyes as she sighs and turns back to the sink. "Lex…"

No, absolutely not. She's not getting away this time, not without telling me flat out I'm not what she wants. I stand behind her and turn her around, by her shoulder. She's going to face me during this conversation.

"You told me yourself that the painting wouldn't be safe at your house, how do you expect me to not worry about you going back?" I have avoided thinking about the fact that she has never once said she's finished being 'Sweet Girl'. "What are you going to do for work? You could always stay here while you look for something. I enjoy having you here and now you don't have anywhere to be."

Okay so maybe that was kind of a dick thing to say. Regardless, she's going to have to tell me to my face that she would rather be with her 'Clients' than me. I'm not ready for her to leave. I've grown accustomed to knowing she'll be here. The details of her life I can be patient and wait for, her safety however, I'm having a harder time with.

She freezes for a minute, her body as still as stone until she slowly melts back into a living girl and her head nods. Did she just say yes? Seriously? That was way easier than I thought it would be. I still wish she would lift her head and look at me.

"I need to take care of some things at my house, but yeah sure, maybe a few more days would be okay."

She mumbles it, yet I hear every word. I'm not missing the way she completely skips over the part about finding a new job. Honestly though, I can really only deal with one thing at a time with this girl and right now I'm just glad she's staying.

I wrap my arms around her and kiss the top of her head.

"Let's go back to bed."

I follow her out of the bathroom back into her room where Sasha is waiting with a glass of water. She takes it as I kiss her head and leave her with Sash.

My mind drifts as I try to sleep, and the more I think about it, the more I want to go with her to her house. It has to answer some of my questions.

It's immature, horrible work ethic, and irresponsible management, nevertheless I call in 'sick' to work, or rather text Silas that I won't be in tomorrow.

Sasha is sitting in the corner of Tavin's room, sketching by lamplight when I walk in. I look over at Tavin's sleeping body. Her light breathing and Sasha's pencil are the only sounds in the room.

"Hey," I whisper and Sasha looks up at me as I nod for her to follow me into the hall. She has her arms wrapped around her sketchpad as she meets me and I ask, "Can't sleep either, huh?"

"No, this line I'm working on is stressing me out." She yawns, "So what's got you up?"

"I'm taking the day off tomorrow, so I'm gonna crash with Tav tonight. You can take the guestroom and have the day tomorrow to work on your designs."

Her shoulders drop as she exhales. "That would be so awesome. Thanks, Bro." She wraps an arm around my neck and kisses my cheek. "Goodnight." As she heads downstairs, I slip into Tavin's room and into her bed.

I'm pretty positive she's going to be less than enthusiastic about my presence tomorrow and honestly, I don't really care. I said I wouldn't force her to talk to me, not that I wouldn't take advantage of a possibly enlightening situation.

*Thursday, May 21st*

I'm enjoying sleeping in late when Tavin starts spouting off about the time.

"Holy cow, it's eight o'clock! How do you run a company?"

"Like a bad ass." I roll over and drape my arm over her. "I stayed home to spend the day with you."

She narrows her eyes at me and points a finger. "You get all angry if I lie, and you're full of crap. You stayed home so you could come to my house."

I laugh and rub her arm. "What do you expect? I'm so far beyond curiosity at this point. I need to know more about you."

She mumbles, "Fine. Just don't expect to get anything out of it."

We shower and eat breakfast before we get in my car to head to her house. As I drive onto her street, she sits straight and fists the door handle like she's ready to jump out. I pull in front of her house, and I'm surprised to see a brand new Ferrari parked out front. Who the hell's car is that? Pretty sure she wouldn't be taking cabs if it was hers. I'm also pretty sure she wouldn't be living here if it was hers either.

I barely get the car stopped before she jumps out. Pushing the lock button on the key fob, I hurry out to follow her as flashes of finding her overdosing dance around in my mind. We climb the steps to her house and I'm surprised to see her front door slightly ajar; someone is obviously here. God, I hate this fucking house. It gives me an eerie feeling and sets me on edge.

"Oh, it looks like Toben's home."

My head snaps in her direction. "Toben?"

She flicks her little hand to wave me off.

"He's my roommate."

Oh you know, no big deal.

"I'm sorry, you have a dude for a roommate?"

I push open the door to step across the threshold into her house and dear God, do I wish I hadn't. A young man, who I assume to be Toben, is wearing nothing other than a black beanie, getting his ass rammed so hard I can almost feel it. The man doing the ramming is much older and for the split second I see him, resembles Mayer Wallace.

"Fucking hell." I spin on my heel as Tavin grasps my forearm.

"I'm so sorry!" She calls over her shoulder. She pulls me back outside and shuts the door. Her hand is covering her mouth as she giggles her little ass off.

"Oops."

"Toben is gay," I say with a sigh. Well, that's a relief.

She laughs, "Oh no, Toben is sooo not gay."

"What do you mean by *sooo* not gay?" I mock her tone and she smirks at me. "I'm pretty sure what I just saw falls somewhere into the gay category, but you know, I'm no expert."

She leans in and whispers, "That guy is just a Client. Toben is Sweet Boy."

"What? You said you were the only Sweet Girl or whatever."

"I said I was the only Sweet *Girl*. Toben is a boy."

I glare at her. She's not stupid, she knew exactly what I was asking.

So the guy she screams for in her nightmares is her straight, male, roommate...oh and he's also a hooker. Fucking fantastic.

"This isn't something you thought you should have prepared me for?"

I'm trying to speak in hushed tones, she's just so...Tavin. Before she can answer me, the door swings open and Toben, thankfully with clothes on, looks as though he's about to break down in tears when he grabs her arm and pulls her inside. I step in after them as he hugs her tight and presses his forehead to hers.

Hmm. Not a fan of this.

The man who was with Toben when we arrived is no-where to be seen. While the house is rundown, it's large and spacious, leaving a still, empty feeling that makes me uneasy. The living room and dining room are combined in one and it reaches all the way to the back of the house. The ugly-ass green couch that Toben was just sodomized on, is directly in front of me sitting behind the worn coffee table I saw all the drugs on the first time I was here.

My teeth clench as I watch them lace their fingers and

press their forearms together in some kind of secret hand-shake. He brings both of his hands to her face tightening his hold and like a light switch, his face twists into fury.

"Where the fuck have you been?!" He bellows. "Do you have any idea how terrified I've been? Do you?!" When he releases her face, it's with way too much force.

Oh hell no.

"Hey," I don't quite yell as he whips his head in my direction. "Take it back a notch."

He completely ignores me as he scowls at her and throws out his hand. "Who the fuck is this?"

She cups his face for a moment before turning to me. "I need a minute. Will you go into the kitchen, please?"

I don't know what's going on here. So even though I most definitely don't want to, I do what she asks, because right now I feel like I'm walking on glass in the dark. I clench my fists and nod to her before throwing a warning glance at him. He glares at me and if he could get away with flipping me off without Tavin seeing, I'm sure he would.

I pass behind the couch, to the kitchen, and see the dining room table piled high with a bunch of random shit. I wonder if it's ever been used for its intended purpose. Passing under the archway that leads to the kitchen, the first thing I see is the refrigerator to my right. It's covered in Polaroid pictures of the two of them together. Written on the white strips across the bottom are dates and names. There's a blond boy who is occasionally in some of the later photos and he's always smiling bigger than either of them. His name is Christopher, according to the writing.

I find the photos a little anomalous. I mean Polaroids? Is this 1998? However, everything about Tavin has a dash of anomalous, in my opinion.

She and Toben are touching in every single photo, in one way or another, they have their hands on each other. They are really close in age if not the same age, yet I still hoped he would end up being her brother. It's apparent though, especially in the more recent ones, that isn't the case. In most of the photos, their ages range somewhere around fourteen or fifteen, to the present. Toben must really dig stocking caps because there are only two photos that he isn't wearing one and it looks as if his hair has almost always been long. I guess if something works stick with it.

There is one photo however, where they are much younger, around nine or ten.

### Tavin and Toben—October 2001

Even as a kid she was stunning. Granted, she looks like an orphan with her dirty face and unmanaged hair. She's smiling a big cheesy grin that makes the whole photo almost comical. Toben had the whole dark and dreary thing going on even then. I think they're on the boardwalk and Toben has his arm around her as he cracks a smile. He looks so starkly clean next to her.

This little trip is raising more questions than its answering.

Toben's voice raises loud enough to hear him from the living room. "Yes Tavin, I'm fucking pissed and I don't even want to think about what Logan is going to do!"

Wonderful. Who the hell is Logan?

I don't hear her full response other than a loud whisper of, "And be quiet!"

My eyes roam the bare kitchen to see a tray of cocaine sitting randomly between black bananas and an empty paper towel roll. I wipe my hands over my face when I hear Toben yelling again.

"What?!"

Panic has made its way into his tone so I sneak a peek into the living room. Biting back the string of profanities I want to yell, I release my clenched fists and watch as he sits on the couch, smoking a cigarette, while she is across his lap running her fingers through his shaggy, brown hair. Her lips move as she whispers in a rush and his hand rubs up and down her arm. The way they touch each other with such familiarity and intimacy makes me grind my teeth. He's clearly accustomed to her body.

The self-control it's taking for me not to walk over there and sit her ass on the opposite end of that revolting couch is quickly waning. This is ridiculous. I am not going to stand in her kitchen while she cuddles with her not-gay-whore-maybe boyfriend-roommate. She leans forward and when she presses her lips to his, I shove my hands into my pockets to physically stop myself from hitting the wall.

Okay. Now I'm mad.

She has to know this isn't alright. My come is basically still warm inside her from this morning as she's kissing someone else right in front of me? Hell fucking no. I take a deep breath to calm down before I go back out there.

She climbs off him as I walk back into the living room. Not as if she's trying to hide it, just as if she was getting up anyway.

"Well," Toben nods his head toward the ceiling, "I better get back to it." Wrapping his arms back around her, he murmurs, "I sure do hope this is worth it, Love."

I'm sorry, what was that? Love? Did he just call her Love? Leaning down he kisses her a little deeper and longer than last time. I cross my arms as I involuntarily exhale out of my nostrils and I can feel my teeth grinding again. The whole cool and contained thing I've been pulling off is about done running its course.

"I love you, Toben." She says it softly, as an apology.

"I love you too, Tav." They once again, lace their fingers together and touch forearms. "When you bleed, I bleed."

That's what her tattoo says. He separates his hand from

hers and places it on her cheek allowing me to see the same words written across his wrist. They have matching tattoos. He kisses her forehead and disappears up the stairs.

She turns to me, finally acknowledging my presence and holds up a finger.

"Wait here, I'll be right back." Super casual, as though she hasn't been hanging all over another guy.

Turning on her heel, she's in a hurry all of a sudden. She walks behind me to a door opposite the kitchen, rips it open, and quickly pounds her way down a set of stairs. After the scene I just had to witness, I don't really care what she says so I follow her.

I see a concrete floor and parts of the mostly unfinished wall. There's a bathroom next to the landing and a washer and dryer are in the back of the room next to a stack of boxes. When I'm far enough down to be able to look through the staircase, I see a refrigerator and a table next to the window well on the opposite side. She's flying around the room shoving clothes into a bag on her cot-type bed. Between us is a dog cage.

"Do you have a dog?"

She jumps about ten feet in the air and when she turns to me, she looks pissed.

Oh *she's* pissed?

"I told you to wait upstairs!" She yells at me.

"And I told you I wasn't fucking sharing."

She throws on those gigantic sunglasses and brushes past me up the stairs. "I'm ready anyway, let's go."

I follow her as she stomps up the steps and rushes across the living room. For someone so insistent on coming home, she sure is ready to leave. She doesn't speak to me as she rips open the front door and speed walks across the lawn to my car. She's waiting for me to unlock it as I walk around to the driver's side. Putting my fists on the roof of the Alfa, I ask through gritted teeth, "What in the hell was that?"

Her arms cross. "What?" She asks as if she really has no clue.

"Oh I don't know, maybe the fact that I just watched you make out with another guy." She drives me so fucking crazy sometimes.

Her head shakes. "I wasn't—"

I unlock the car door and slam it once I'm inside. How could she not mention this guy? She gets in and I don't even let her door get all the way closed.

"Who is he to you?"

Her shoulders sag as she turns to me. "He's my oldest and dearest...everything. I'm sorry I made you uncomfortable, but I honestly didn't think much of it. That's just the way we are. The way we've always been."

"Have you slept with him?"

She sags into the seat and turns to get her seat belt so I can't see her eyelashes.

"No."

"If you truly didn't think you were doing anything wrong then why didn't you tell me about him?"

Tossing up her arms, she leans back against the seat. "I did!"

She sounds all exasperated, though I'm pretty sure I'm the one with the exasperation rights here.

"Oh really? When was that? Because I can guarantee you I would remember that conversation."

"When I told you my best friend got sick of me playing the Nirvana album and when I told you we still go to the park sometimes."

"Yeah well, I assumed your 'best friend' was a girl."

I turn the key and the engine roars to life as she shrugs and mumbles, "That's your fault, sexist."

"Don't give me that bullshit and stop being petulant.

You were vague on purpose and you know it."

Oh no response to that? Yeah, that's what I thought.

⟋

She's in a weird mood all night. Whenever I try to talk to her, her thoughts are somewhere else. I have a lot of work to catch up on from today, so I get comfortable in my office. I have an important meeting coming up with a major investor and I have not been putting the time into preparing for it like I should be.

The screen burns into my retinas making it nearly impossible to focus. I just can't get the way they were together, out of my head, and why she didn't already tell me about him.

Exhaustion seems to consume me as I close my eyes. Why am I letting her affect me this way? I've let myself get too wrapped up. Yes, I like her, a lot. I want to see where this goes, I just still have no idea what her situation really is.

Regardless of how things end up with us, I don't want her in harm's way. She is an adult so ultimately she has a choice if she wants to go back, I just need time to get more of her story. I can't get away from the feeling that she's going to spontaneously vanish.

I rub my hands over my face to wake myself up and when I open my eyes, she is standing in front of my desk with her hair down and messy. She's in an off-the-shoulder t-shirt with pink cotton boy shorts. Lifting the shirt over her head, she exposes her bare breasts and the brand nestled between them. When my breath disappears, my erection shows up.

"I know I should have told you about Toben, it's just that he and I are nothing like you and I. Toben and I are...complicated to explain. I have known him almost my entire life."

She lowers her boy shorts revealing her glorious nude

body. Once she circles my desk, she climbs up and straddles me. I don't say a word as she slowly unzips my pants. Her eyes are locked into mine just as always, when she hovers over my cock. It takes every single drop of energy I have to refrain from piercing up into her. She is sliding down in an extremely slow motion so I tear my eyes from hers to watch her envelop me. Her quiet little moans roll out from her lips as she slides to the base. Her arms wrap around my neck when she brings her mouth to my ear.

"You are the only one who has ever been mine. Please know that you are special to me."

She gasps as she rides me harder. I'm not one hundred percent sure what she means by that, I just know that hearing her call me hers causes a warmth to spread in my chest.

*Friday, May 22nd*

*Tavin*

Cara Jo is humming to the music and bustling around the kitchen as my blue colored pencil dances across the paper. It's weird without Sasha here and I miss her, although I feel better after talking with Toben last night. He was furious and hurt and as much as I hate that, I will never get this opportunity again.

*"What? Have you completely lost it?!"*

*His ears are getting red…he's angry and he needs to stop yelling! "Be quiet!"*

*"Do you have a death wish? You have already missed a ton of playdates and now you want to miss another two weeks of them?"*

This is impossible to explain. I just want him to understand. "What will be the difference other than I get two more weeks to pretend? Logan will punish me the same. It's like living a fairy tale, Tobe."

The smoke floats through his lips as he shakes his head and scoffs, "It can't be too fantastic. You've been sober the whole time."

"Please, I despise that I hurt you and I know this isn't fair. I just really like him. I don't understand why or how, but the filthy fear disappears with him. I want to make it last."

"Not that I give a fuck, but if you like this guy so Goddamn much, how do you think he's going to feel when you ditch him in two weeks?"

I brush his hair back and look at his beautiful midnight eyes. "I never said it was perfect, and I hate that he might get hurt. At this point, though, he will probably be a little hurt no matter what, so can't I just have two more weeks without Clients?"

"I don't want to be the asshole to stand in the way of this, just remember, you promised me you would never see him again, that it was just that once. Yet you've been shacked up with him for over a week now."

I know I broke my promise, but I didn't plan this! "That's not fair. It wasn't like that."

"I can't help how I feel, Tav."

"Neither can I! This is temporary. In two weeks it will be back to normal, okay?"

"Logan will know you're lying about where you've been and I'm fucking scared about how he'll react to this."

So am I. My fingers caress his lips before I kiss them. "As long as he doesn't know I've been with Lex is all I care about. I love you Toben, okay? This changes nothing between us, alright?"

I wish I could hug away his sadness as he sighs, "Yeah,

*alright, Love."*

*This will be my last chance for a while, so I ask, "Hey, do we have any coke or anything? I want a hit before he comes back out here."*

*He snorts before he chuckles, "This guy is so fucked."*

*I sigh in relief as he digs in his back pocket, even though I still look at him through narrow eyes. "Shut up."*

Yeah, so maybe it was kinda messed up to do the blow with Lex right there. It was just a little bump though, and he never even suspected. I needed to see Toben, touch him, and explain everything, even if there was a small part of me that had hoped he would be away at a playdate so he didn't meet Lex. Neither of them liked the other, and it still went a million times smoother than it could have. There's no way for Lex to fathom what Toben and I are and I sure can't explain it to him. We are deeper than any friends, siblings, or even lovers could be. He's my lifeline and if it wasn't the heroin that got us through, it was each other. He is the only person that has ever loved me. We are the same. We are half people.

The blue pencil clatters against the island as I switch it for the red one.

I've already told Alexander way too much. It was stupid to tell him about the Clients. Logan has warned us plenty of times what would happen if we told anyone. At least now I have a plan. I will spend my last, free, two and a half weeks staying here, and now I have my cell phone so I can text Tobe and I'll know if Logan tries to call me.

I'm going to live inside the moments. I don't want to waste my thoughts on the bleakness of my future or precious time on the torment of my past. I want to bathe in his light instead of drowning in the darkness. I will never feel this again. I am sure of it to my core.

A loud ringing startles me so bad I almost fall off the

bar stool. I look down and I have drawn a picture of a girl in a blue dress rolling the skin off her arm like a sleeve. Her brown hair is straight and she is smiling at me.

Cara Jo picks up the phone and uses her shoulder to hold it to her ear. "Hello, Alexander Sørensen's residence." Her smile falls from her face as she stops stirring and glares at the pot of food. "I'll tell him, Carrie, but I can just about promise you his response will be the same as every other time you've called." Carrie...that's Lex's old girlfriend's name. Cara Jo sighs as she rolls her eyes and turns to dig through a drawer. Pulling out a notepad, she begins scribbling down whatever she's telling her. "And what room number? Alright I'll pass it along... Mmm hmm, bye." She hangs up and drops the pen on the counter next to the notepad before she wipes her forehead with the back of her wrist. "You'd think someone that studies people for a living would learn to take a hint."

"What did she say?" The words come out before I realize how rude the question is. That's none of my business.

She scoffs as she turns back to the stove. "She wants Alex to meet her for drinks while she's in town for a conference." My heart pounds so loud at the thought of him going to spend time with another girl that I barely hear Cara Jo speaking to me. She tilts her head and waves the spatula around. "He won't go though. He never does. She's tried dozens of times over the past nine years."

The questions pile in my brain and spill from my mouth. "Why not? What did she do?" I pick at the edge of my paper. "Does he love her?"

She sighs as she adjusts the heat on the stove and wipes her hand on her apron before sitting next to me at the island. "If you don't know, then it's not my place to tell you the details. What I can tell you is, she lied to him about something and it broke his heart." She rests her head in her hand and lifts the corner of her mouth into a small smile. "He did love her, very much at one time. They were each others first love, and Lord knows those are always the worst. After she did what she did, he shut himself off from everyone, even me. He never was really the same boy after that. He became... harder."

"Has he never fallen in love again?"

What if he can't love me? The thought comforts and crushes me at the same time. If he can't love me then I can't hurt him. That would be perfectly ideal, so why is there a pang in my heart that desires him to?

She scoffs, "Not even close. I never liked Carrie to begin with, and even less after what she did. The thing that I really have issue with is how she broke him so bad emotionally. It's as if he intentionally picks girls he knows he would never be able to be with." She groans, "And believe me, he's brought back some doozies." I've been asking myself this whole time why Lex wants me around. Now I know. I'm safe to him because he won't ever be able to have real feelings for me. This shouldn't bother me. I have no right to be upset. What I am doing to him is way worse. Cara Jo covers her mouth and wipes her hand across my cheek. I didn't even know I was crying. "Oh sweetie, I wasn't talking about you, you're changing him." She lifts my chin to look at her. "Listen to me, I don't think I've ever seen him this taken with anyone. Not even Carrie. You are different to him. Do you understand?"

I want the words she is saying to be true so badly that in this moment, I let myself believe them. I nod to her and smile. "Yes."

She squeezes my shoulders. "Good. Now, help me finish dinner."

# Alexander

I sink into the seat of the Alfa and close my eyes as I drop my head against the headrest. Thank God today is finally over and it's the weekend. The vibration against my leg forces my eyes open and I pull my phone out to see my sister's picture.

"Hey, Sash, what's up?"

"Do you have plans for Sunday?"

I put the call on the car speakers as I adjust my air conditioner. "Not that I know of, why?"

"We're having dinner with mom and dad at six."

We haven't had a family dinner in years. I scoff, "Why?"

"Just be there alright? Are you going to bring Tavin?"

I want to and that in itself surprises me. However, I do worry that my parents, my mother especially, will make Tavin uncomfortable.

"I don't know, you know, because of…Mom."

"Mom." She says it with me simultaneously and we both start laughing.

"Yeah, exactly." Making sure the lane is clear, I pull into the street. "I'll talk to Tavin about it tonight. So, I guess I'll see you Sunday."

"Cool, later."

I end the call and get on the freeway feeling the same excitement at seeing Tav that I have felt every day since she started staying with me.

After pulling into the garage, I walk into the kitchen and grin at her smiling at me from her seat at the island.

Cara Jo sets down two plates of spaghetti and wipes her hands on her apron. "Just in time, dinner's ready. How was work?"

"It was fine. Did you guys have a good day?"

She nods. "You have a message though." She says

'message' as if it tastes bad on her tongue.

I tilt my head in question as Tavin slides a notepad across the counter. "Here."

I pick it up and even seeing her name makes me angry.

**I'd love to catch up. Call me if you're interested in meeting for drinks.**

**-Carrie**

**555-436-0843—North Shadoebox Suites #901**

"Ugh." I toss it on the island. "Will this bitch ever give up?"

Cara Jo's mouth falls open as she furrows her brows.

Shit.

"Alexander Henrik Sørensen!"

At almost twenty-nine years old, I still flinch when she uses my full name. "Sorry...I just honestly don't see how someone so crazy can be a licensed therapist." I sit next to Tavin and hold the free hand that isn't using the fork to twirl up her spaghetti.

Cara Jo slips the apron over her head. "I need more wine from the cellar."

I nod at her as I brush Tavin's hair over her shoulder. She seems a little off. "Are you okay?"

She looks up at me and scrunches her eyebrows. "Why do you hate her so much?"

"You know, it's a little unfair for you to get answers about my past when I'm not getting anything in return."

She slurps up the noodles on her plate. I've learned she's actually quite a big eater and I have no idea where it all goes.

"Fine, ask me a question."

I don't even have to think about it. "Who's Logan?"

Her fork stops mid stab and her whole body is completely unmoving. She doesn't look at me. "Any other question."

Uh huh. I'm already pretty positive he's her pimp.

"Where are your parents?"

"Lacie is dead and Brian is...gone."

First name basis isn't usually good. I'm not surprised they aren't in the picture and I almost ask how her mother died before deciding that's a heavier conversation than I want to get into right now.

"Do you know where Brian is?"

"Yes." She shoves another bite in her mouth.

She really overdoes it on the elaboration doesn't she? I have something at least, even if it is vague as hell. I want to tell her about meeting my parents on Sunday. I'm just anxious about what her reaction will be and I want to keep things light. I decide to direct the conversation away from parents completely.

"Have you ever been on a boat?"

Her head pops up and finally she has a huge smile on her face making that little dimple appear on her right cheek.

"No! Are we going on a boat?"

"We can take mine out tomorrow if you want."

"Oh my God, you own a boat? Do you have a jet too?"

I chuckle, "No. No jet, just a lame yacht."

She dives back into her spaghetti with gusto. "Oh man, Toben is going to be so jealous." I try not to cringe at the sound of his name in her voice. "We used to always go to the pier and watch the boats before..."

The smile slips from her face and the sudden change in her demeanor is jarring.

"Before what?"

"Pass."

# CHAPTER ELEVEN
## *Parents*

*Saturday, May 23rd*

WE'RE BARELY A HALF MILE AWAY FROM PORT when Tavin comes running into the control room, spinning as she looks around the boat. The sheerness of her short, white dress allows me to see the silhouette of her body.

"This is so awesome!" Her feet are bare since she abandoned her flip flops the moment we got on the boat and her hair is up in a top knot making her neck look simply bitable. Pulling her huge sunglasses over her eyes, she grins. "Thanks for bringing me."

"You're welcome, *Lille*." I gesture to her linen cover, "It's just us. You don't need that anymore." She smirks as she grabs the hem of the dress and pulls it over her head.

Her suit is exquisite. It's a solid black haltered one piece and has a high waist short with a plunging neckline that gloriously reaches all the way to her belly button, putting her brand on display. She turns in a slow circle to show me the back, which is completely open exposing her scars. I'm one hundred percent erect right now.

"That's quite the suit."

"Do you like it?"

"It'll be better when it's off." She laughs and kisses my cheek. I have a damn pool, I'm an idiot for not getting her into a swimsuit sooner. I just never thought about it, and she never asked. It's been an eventful couple of weeks. I wrap my hand around her wrist and pull her in front of me to place her hands on the steering wheel. Her neck is too irresistible not to kiss. "Do you want to steer?"

"Yes, but what if I break it? I don't even know how to drive a car, much less a boat."

"All you need to do is steer, I'll control the throttles. It's a still day and there's nothing around to hit. You'll be fine."

Her hands clutch the wheel as she spreads her feet apart like she's rooting herself to the floor and nods with determination. "Okay." After a few moments her shoulders relax. "This isn't so hard."

Once we come to a favorable spot, I drop anchor as she runs out to the cockpit, looking out onto the ocean. I follow her out and smack her ass before going down into the galley to grab a beer.

Just as I open my mouth to ask her if she wants a drink, I hear a splash. Climbing back onto the lower cockpit, I sit on the port side jump seat near the edge of the boat as she pops her head out of the water. She has taken her top knot out, so her hair is covering her face. When she throws her head back, she splashes a stream of water from her hair to my chest.

"Whoa!" I chuckle as I reflexively pull my beer away from the water.

She laughs, "Oh, I'm sorry. I wouldn't want to get your swimsuit wet...while on a boat...in the ocean."

"Uh huh. Just wait till I finish this beer; you'll pay for that."

"Don't make promises you don't intend to keep, Lex." She winks and goes back under.

Dog paddling around the yacht, she splashes her way to the front of the boat. I finish my beer, take our clothes into the galley, and wait for her to circle back. Once she does, I jump behind her making her squeal in surprise.

She climbs on my shoulders and when she gains her balance, she jumps off, cannon-balling into the ocean and laughing when her head comes above water. I love the way she acts as if everything is the most magnificent thing she has ever encountered. She makes me see the beauty in the things I take for granted. She tries to dunk me, laughing the whole time, so I allow her to and then dunk her right back. We race around the boat and she tries so hard to win that I eventually give in and let her.

She tries to frown so she narrows her eyebrows, but she can't seem to get the smile off her face. "It's still cheating if you lose on purpose you know."

I haven't played around like this in ages. I laugh as she climbs up the ladder to get back on the boat and I can't stop staring at her ass. Once she's standing by the port side jump seat, she gives herself enough room to get a running start and then plunges back into the ocean. Swimming over to me, she wraps an arm around my neck and kisses me hard. She slips her tongue into my mouth and flattens her hand against my abs as she slides it inside my trunks and strokes me.

I grab her forearm to stop her motion. "It isn't time for that yet," I murmur against her mouth.

She runs her tongue along my lower lip. "I've never done it in the water before."

I groan, "I swear I'll change that. Tonight though, I have other plans." Her suit is so low I can slide my hand easily down the front. "Until then, think of how good it will feel when I make you come with my tongue."

"Alexander." She smiles as she softly moans.

Will I ever get used to her voice? If I don't stop now, I won't stop at all, so I take away my hand. She lets out a subtle huff in frustration and I smirk at her before kissing her head. Climbing onto the boat, I lift her up and toss her a towel before walking down to the galley to retrieve the steaks, our sunglasses, and the wine.

When I get back into the cockpit, I find her sunbathing on the swim platform. After pouring our Moscato, and throwing a couple steaks on the grill, I sit next to her and hand her the glass.

"Lex, this has been like a dream. You don't even know."

I smile and kiss her, but I do know. I still wake up and think I just imagined her. She's a fantasy. Yet, at the exact same time this feels more real than anything ever has before.

When the steaks are done, I put the wine, crackers, cheese, grapes, bread, salad, and petit fours on the table.

"Lunch is ready." She bounds over to me and immediately reaches for the petit fours. I grab her wrist before she touches them. "Real food first."

Scowling, she grumbles, "How is cake not real food?"

I comb my hair back with my fingers as I lean back. "So my parents are having a dinner tomorrow. Would you want to go?"

Her lip lifts as her face twists into disgust. "You want me to meet your parents?"

Now she has me thinking this is too soon. "Well, yeah."

"Why would I want to meet your parents, Alexander?" Slouching in her seat she adds, "I hate parents."

Ever since she told me her parents' names, I have been dying to Google them, I just prefer to get my information from her. Right now, I'm kind of wishing I had. I have my theories of abuse and abandonment, and that's exactly what they are: theories. I reach across the table to hold her hand.

"They aren't perfect by any stretch, Tavin, but I do love them. I want them to meet you more than the other way around."

"Will it make you happy if I go?"

"Yes."

Pulling her hand free, she stabs a piece of lettuce and sighs, "Okay, I'll meet them."

After dinner, I take her below deck into the salon. We are on our third bottle of wine sitting on the couch as Nirvana floats in the background.

"Are they your favorite?" She asks.

"They have been for a long time. Kurt Cobain was a God to me growing up."

"He did heroin you know." She raises her eyebrows and her fingers tap her glass as if she just made a valid point.

I narrow my eyes at her. "I also know he died when he was twenty-seven years old and I'm pretty sure he didn't advocate it... nice try though." She rolls her eyes and smirks while my hand rubs her thigh. "How did you get into them?"

"My favorite singer, Otep, did a cover of *Breed*. I thought if she likes them, then I bet I will too. And I did."

"Who's Otep?"

She smiles, "If Kurt Cobain was a God, then Otep Shamaya is a Goddess. She doesn't even know me, and still she knows exactly how I feel."

Her hair is down and dried into loose waves while her face is sun kissed and her eyes are a bit glossy with her buzz. Without the drugs she really doesn't hold her liquor well at all. She's all giggles, and every time she smiles, it makes me proud that I put it there.

"God, you're gorgeous." With the wine and being constantly turned on around her, it comes out a bit gravelly. She looks at me as a tear rolls down her face. "What's wrong? What did I say?"

She gestures between us. "This…you…it's all so overwhelming sometimes. I've never felt this way. Toben has always been the only person I cared about, the only person who cared about me, but we have just always been. This, with you, it's all new and I don't understand it. You're normal and I'm not and you still want to be around me. It's more than how you make me feel though. Sex has never been a good thing. It's just what I do. With you it's…" She sits up to meet my eyes and whispers, "Every time I look at you I get wet, when you touch me my flesh burns, and when you're inside of me, I feel like I could die right then and be happy."

She may have had more to say, but I don't give her the opportunity. Grabbing her face, I press our mouths together. I put my hand on the small of her back and push her to lie down. Unhooking her halter causes the fabric to fall exposing her beautiful breasts, and my tongue is on them instantly. She wraps her legs around my waist as I make my way back to her mouth. I lift her up and carry her to the master stateroom at the front of the boat.

Lying her on the bed, I kiss her neck as I remove her swimsuit.

"Touch yourself," I order as I light the candle on the nightstand. I stare for a moment, watching her little fingers disappear. "Don't stop. I want to watch you make yourself come."

I climb on the bed with the lit candle, kneeling between her legs and tipping it slightly so the wax drops off. As soon as it hits her stomach, she gasps and her breathing gets harsher. I flick her nipple with my tongue and drip the wax over it. She moans softly and becomes more aggressive with her fingers. Slowly, I let the wax drip over her brand and then her stomach.

I grab what the lady at the sex shop referred to as a 'tail tip crop'. Basically, it's a stick with a leather strap at the end. I put the candle back on the table before trailing the crop down her neck and across her chest. I let the tail softly drape over her nipple before hitting it hard and instantly earning a pretty pink shade on her fair skin.

Shattered breathing escapes her lips while I bring the implement over her brand, in between her ribs, and over her stomach. *Thwack.* I'm putting some serious strength behind these blows. When the leather comes in contact with her flesh, it makes the color bursts from her skin, and my body hums.

As she comes, she arches her body through the pleasure and it's beautiful. Her chest is still rising and falling as I pull her hands up over her head and cuff her wrists together before attaching them to the headboard. I yank each ankle to opposite ends of the bed, spreading her legs as far as they could comfortably go before cuffing them as well.

My erection is throbbing as I kneel on the mattress by her head, lifting her enough to wrap her lips around me. I increase the pleasure by pushing her head down and trailing my thumb across her jawline to feel how hard she works to please me. Her little tongue is licking in between her suction and it almost hurts to take myself from her mouth. I run my fingers down her nose, her lips, continuing across her chin, and down her body until they reach the evidence of her orgasm. I use my free hand to reach over her head and grab a throw pillow to slip beneath her ass. With her legs spread this way, she is begging to be eaten. Leaning between her legs, I softly blow on her pretty pussy and she pulls on the restraints as she pushes herself onto my tongue. I stop occasionally to bite the crap out of her thigh and she bucks her way back to my mouth.

After she comes, I climb into her body and feed off the

sounds she makes. The water rocking the boat acts as an aid as I take my time, savoring every moment until I give her the pain she needs and feel her succumb beneath me.

I kiss each ankle as I unfasten the restraints and my lips brush over the piece of cut away skin inside her left foot. After I finish peeling the wax from her body, I reach inside the nightstand.

"I've been meaning to give you this." As soon as I wrap my hand around the necklace, I question the gift. I'm not exactly middle class and I buy the girl of my dreams a cheap trinket? "It's nothing much, I just saw it and it made me think of you."

Insecurity has never been an emotion in my repertoire before. It's supposed to be more sentimental than anything. It's a little vintage carousel that turns on a bronze chain. I'm an idiot. Why didn't I get her diamond earrings or an emerald bracelet?

"You got this for me?"

"It reminded me of our first night together."

Her head jerks. When she looks up at me, her eyes are sad.

"I don't deserve this, Lex."

She frustrates the hell out of me sometimes. I grab her chin so she can't look away.

"You deserve this and so much more."

It crushes me to see the heartbreak that comes out every once in a while. It shows through her eyes and bleeds through her pores.

I move behind her to fasten the necklace around her neck and kiss her shoulder. We lie down on the bed and I wrap my arms around her until she falls asleep.

When I look at the clock on the nightstand and see how

late it is, I slowly slide out of bed to pull up the anchor.

As I drive back to port, her screams cut through the silence of the night. Without thinking, I turn to run to her before realizing that would result in crashing the yacht. We are close enough to port for me to see the docks, making dropping anchor again impossible. I have to sit here and listen to her torment until I'm finally able to dock the boat.

Leaving the keys in the ignition, I sprint to the stateroom and find her still crying as she calls for Toben and bows her back. I jump on the bed and hold her tight to stop her from moving so much.

"Tavin, wake up. You're safe, just wake up." She blinks open her eyes and they are glittering in the moonlight with tears. I don't understand why she screams his name. She isn't afraid of him that much is obvious, so why? "Did Toben hurt you?"

Sleep is quickly taking her back when she murmurs, "He didn't want to."

### Sunday, May 24th

Tavin slips into my office just as I shut down my computer. She's wearing mint, tribal print palazzo pants, a white lace halter, and hemp flip flops.

"How do I look?" She holds her hands out and spins around. Her ass looks killer in those pants, but the halter shows every scar and bruise on her back. There is no way my mom won't mention that.

"Sexy as sin." She grins at me. "You're comfortable in that shirt though right?"

Her smile slips away. "The scars."

Getting up from my desk, I walk to her. "Hey, I like them, remember? I just want you to know if you wear that shirt, be prepared for my mother to say something about it."

She makes a weird expression that I can't quite place. "Of course. I don't know what I was thinking." I reach out to touch her when she turns back to the door. "Just give me a minute."

When she meets me downstairs, she has traded the halter for a white fitted tee that is tucked into her pants. She still looks perfect, I just feel a little guilty for mentioning it.

Her mouth is hanging open as I pull up to my parents' estate.

"This is a house? I've seen mansions before, but jeez."

I try to ignore her reasons for having 'seen mansions before'.

"Yeah my great-grandfather's fishing company in Oslo made my family really rich."

"Don't you have a funny name for great-grandfather? Like *For-For* or something?" She grins at me.

"Close, it's *Oldeforeldre*."

She shakes her head and laughs. "You're so weird."

I stop the car in front of the house and am greeted by my parents' servant, Baker. I hand him the keys before opening Tavin's door and grabbing her hand.

I open the front door and walk us inside. My mom enters the foyer with a half empty tumbler in her hand.

"Hello, dear."

"Hi, Mom."

She pecks me on the side of the mouth. "I need a drink and Bridget is never around when I need her."

I bite my tongue from telling her she definitely does not need another drink. She turns away without acknowledging Tavin at all.

"Mom?" She looks back and I hold my hand toward Tav. "This is Tavin."

She scrunches her nose as she looks her up and down. Tavin gives her a pathetic little wave and I'm mortified at my mother's lack of basic manners.

"Mmm hmm."

Jesus Christ. My fucking mother.

"Is Sasha here yet?"

"Is your sister ever on time? No. As if the whole world wants to wait on her." She turns back to the kitchen and hollers, "Bridget!"

Squeezing Tavin's hand, I smile at her and she smirks, assuring me she's unaffected. I lead her to the back of the house and out a set of double doors to show her my mother's garden. Her reaction is exactly what I hoped for. Her eyes are big and bright as she allows her fingers to lightly caress the petals. We walk along the stone path under the floral archway as I pull her against me to kiss her. I meant for it to be quick, but once I start, I just want more. I grab her ass to bring her closer as she slips her tongue into my mouth.

"Ahem."

I sigh against her lips because I know it's my father. I turn from her and place my hand against the small of her back as I look at him and roll my eyes. It bugs the shit out of me that he wears suits on the weekends.

"Hey, Dad."

"Alexander."

He looks at Tavin and he tilts his head to the side. Suddenly, his face goes from questioning to horrified.

"Tavin?" He whispers.

Her body goes rigid next to me and I feel her head jerk. When I glance down, she's white as snow and has the same freaked out look he does.

"Bjørn?" She squeaks.

They know each other? How in the hell would they... Holy fuck.

"No fucking way." I look between them and the way they stare at each other.

His chest lifts with his breath as his voice turns much softer. "Tavin..." He holds a hand out to touch her. Yeah, that's not happening.

"Stepping between them, I put my back to him and separate her from his gaze. "Tell me you did not fuck my dad, Tavin." My fists are so tight, my nails are digging into my palms.

I hear my father sigh as her head jerks and she tries to find somewhere to look besides me. "He..." She bites her lip as she squeezes her eyes shut and whispers, "He was my first."

Fuck my life.

"Are you seriously telling me you lost your virginity to him?!" I yell as I throw my arm toward my father, though I refuse to look at him right now.

My mind is fighting whether to be more pissed about my dad cheating on my mom or about who he cheated with. She shakes her head and there are tears in her eyes.

"No. He was my first Client, but that was like eight years ago!"

"Tavin!" My father scolds her as he steps beside us. "What are you doing?"

She ignores him as she grabs my forearm. "Please don't hate me. I didn't know he was your dad. I just...shit!" She shakes her head again as she looks up at me, squeezing my arm tight. "I'm so sorry, Lex."

I sigh and brush her hair over her shoulder. "Alright, calm down." Like a punch in the gut, what she actually said sinks in. "Wait...eight years ago?" My attention immediately shifts to my father. "Are you fucking kidding me?"

Playdates.

I think I'm gonna puke.

Shoving his chest, I get in his face. "She was fifteen? She was just a kid! How could you do this to mom? How could you do this at all? You're a fucking pedophile for Christ's sake!"

Though I've lost a lot of respect for my father over the years, he's still my dad and I love him. I feel like knowing this changes that. I knew he wasn't I good man, I just had no idea he was capable of this kind of disgusting shit.

He gains his footing and steps in front of me, nearly toe to toe. "Keep your Goddamn voice down! I didn't know how old she was until she showed up at the hotel, and your mother and I were separated at the time. You need to calm down."

Oh, I'm calm. Believe me. The fact that his face is still in place attests to that. "Did you fuck her after you found out how old she was?"

His jaw ticks and his shoulders tense. He wants to hit me, I can see it, but he won't. It's been almost twenty years since he last put his fists on me and he knows he would lose that fight. He glares at me as he gives me the slightest of nods.

I scoff and shake my head. "You repulsive fuck. Mom is going to be heartbroken when she finds out."

Tavin jumps between us and shoves her hands against my chest. "No! You can't tell her!"

I glare at my dad as I speak to her. "She deserves to know, Tav."

Her eyes are panicked as they flip to my father, and I swear I see him shake his head. She takes my hands and holds them to her chest. The tears fall down her cheeks as her gaze is pleading. "I can't be the one responsible for breaking up your family. I'm not worth it, Lex."

When she says things like that, my chest gets hot and it hurts. Why can't she see how amazing she is? I reach my hand to touch her face when I hear the clicking sound of footsteps on the cobble pathway.

"What is all the yelling out here?" My mother's voice causes all of us to freeze and watch her walk toward us. I glare at my dad. He's going to be the one to tell her. Not me.

I grab Tavin's hand to pull her from my parents. "Nothing, Mom. Is dinner ready?"

She scrunches her brows and looks at Tavin. She leans in to her and inhales a breath. Did I just watch my mother smell my girlfriend?

Her face goes hard as she takes a sip from her glass. "Not yet, but your sister just arrived. She's asking about you."

I peck her on the cheek as she stares at my father.

This cannot be happening.

I lead Tavin back to the house and once we are inside and alone, I hold her out in front of me by her arms. She is moments away from breaking down and she looks like she wants to disappear.

"You know I'm angry with him, not you, right? He was the adult." She's staring at her feet, but the top of her head moves with her nod. I reach beneath her face to lift up her chin. "*Lille*, look at me."

Tears are streaming down her cheeks and I wipe them as Sasha's voice carries across the house. "Hey, guys." She walks toward us with Drew behind her. "What's goin' on?"

I want nothing more than to drag Tavin out of this house, be alone with her, and talk about this. She's been doing this Sweet shit since she was a teenager. I don't want to deal with anyone else right now and I really don't want to explain this to Sasha.

"You really don't want to fucking know."

Tavin's face is marred in humiliation and she won't look at any of us. Sasha glances at her and frowns before she puts her hands on her hips and snaps at me, "Uh, yes I fucking do." She reaches her hand out and rubs Tavin's arm. "What happened, Tav?"

Tavin's hair curtains around her face as she drops her head down and destroys her fingers, pulling little pieces of skin off each time.

I wrap my hands around hers. "*Lille*, please stop doing this. You have no reason to be ashamed. He does."

"Who?!" Sasha throws her arms up.

I know she's just concerned, but I really wish she would shut up. "Dad, okay? He cheated on mom." Again.

"What?"

I ignore her as I pull Tavin toward the front of the house wanting so bad to take her out the front door. Instead, I lead her into the parlor as Sasha follows behind. I hear Drew close the door and Sasha rushes around to stand in front of us as she narrows in on Tav. "Wait. What does that have to do with you?"

Tavin's head jerks and she still refuses to take her eyes off the floor. I squeeze her hand and give Sasha a look begging her to figure it out without making someone say it.

She whispers, "Because I'm what he cheated with."

I huff because I want to correct her for referring to herself in that manner, honestly though, right now there's enough going on.

"What? Are you serious?"

Sasha looks to Drew as he joins us and his eyes are as big as his mouth when he says, "Whoa."

Okay this needs to stop, Tavin is about to have a nervous breakdown. I kiss her head before dragging Sasha to the corner. "Come here." I glance at Tavin before I whisper, "She was fifteen, Sash. Fifteen. How could he do that?"

She covers her mouth and looks rightfully disgusted. Her eyebrows lift as realization hits. "Oh…her little Sweet thing… He hired her?"

"You fucking knew about this?" I could strangle her.

How long has she known?

She holds her hands up. "I know what you know. I had no idea she started that young and obviously I didn't know about dad. She just told me about being a call girl and your reaction." She crosses her arms. "Way to be a dick, by the way."

I rub my head and look back at Tavin who hasn't moved a muscle. I want to get her out of here so bad, but my mom will know something's up, if she doesn't already. We just have to make it through this dinner.

Opening my mouth to try to defend myself, I'm interrupted by my parents' maid, Bridget, peeking into the parlor. "Dinner is ready to be served."

I turn back to Sasha. "Not a word to mom."

She glares at me as if I'm the village idiot. "No shit, dumb ass."

I march back to Tav and hold her hand as we all follow Bridget to the dining room. My parents are already sitting at opposite ends of the table and I can't stand to look at my father. I feel as if I don't even know the man. His infidelity is unacceptable, and I have already caught him once before, but that isn't even what upsets me the most. What bothers me is that he was able to do what he did, with a child. The fact that the child was Tavin makes me about to explode.

The subtle glares my mother is throwing at my father makes me uneasy as Bridget places our food in front of us and fills our drinks.

The *clanking* of silverware on plates is the only sound in the room when my mother lifts her glass to her lips. "We are all here as requested, Sasha. Now that you decided to show up, what is this all about?"

Sasha smiles an odd smile that even I can't figure out, and looks to Drew. He shrugs and she stutters, "Uh, well…" Sitting up straight, her hand flies out as she blurts, "We're getting married!"

She's seriously marrying this guy? Just because she's my sister, I'm not blind to the fact that she's beautiful, educated, confident, and a fucking catch. I think Drew's a manipulative prick who took advantage of her when she was in a vulnerable position. Now, that's just my personal opinion, and I could be way off base. Honestly, all I want is for her to be happy. I just don't think he's that great of a guy. Nevertheless, she has a huge smile on her face and in this moment she seems to be excited, so I guess I'm happy for her, even if it does mean Drew is here to stay. At least something good is coming out of this dinner.

"Well, it's good you won't be living in sin anymore." My mother waves her off. And that's about as excited as she gets over anything that isn't alcohol or money related.

Sasha's face falls for just a moment before she goes off on her plans for the wedding.

I glance at Tavin poking around at her food and I'm pretty sure she hasn't taken a single bite.

"Bread roll?" My father holds out the biscuit basket to her.

She lifts her head to meet his eyes. "No thank you, Bjørn."

"You're on a first name basis with my husband?"

My mother's voice slices through the room and all heads turn to her. It's the first thing she's said to Tavin all evening.

"I-um…uh…" Tav gets all blinky.

Oh God.

"I told her my name when I introduced myself, Caterina." His lies spew out so easily. My mother knows him well, though, and she doesn't believe a thing out of his mouth.

"Mmm hmm." She sets her sights back on Tav. "So what is it you do…Traven is it?"

"Mom, you know her name is Tavin." She ignores my

silent pleas to not be herself today, as she waits for her response.

Tavin scrunches her eyebrows in confusion and her head makes that harsh little yank that she does, especially when she's overwhelmed.

"Uh…what?"

"Are you stupid girl? What is your occupation?"

"Mom!"

"Mom!"

Sasha and I simultaneously scold her and give her matching expressions of distaste. Even though we rarely twin out much anymore, you aren't going to talk that way about Tavin around either one of us and not hear about it.

"I…I don't. Work I mean." I hate this, she wants to crawl out of her skin.

"You don't work? How do you pay for food and rent?"

God, please, shut up! She is relentless and I'm done watching this.

"She is staying with me for the time being."

I cringe as her eyebrows raise and her fingers steeple. "You live with my son and eat his food, yet you do not bring in money? You may not have a job my dear, however you most certainly are *working*."

"Jesus Christ, Mom!" I throw up my hands in disbelief at her crassness.

"Caterina!" My father's voice bellows across the room. He never corrects my mother, so he is solely defending Tavin.

And my mother knows it.

Tavin's hands are under the table and I know she's probably ripping them up. This is done. I'm not putting her through another moment of this.

"Well this has been bloody fantastic as usual, but we're leaving." I grab Tavin's now torn up hand and glance at

Sasha. "I'm happy for you, congratulations."

She nods while she looks at Tavin. I scoff at my mother and ignore my father as I march us out of the dining room and through the foyer. Baker is sitting on his perch and hops up as we walk out the front door.

"Leaving already, sir?"

"Not soon enough. Would you pull the car around please?"

"Certainly."

We stand in silence. I want to wait until we are alone to have this conversation. Baker brings around the Alfa and hands me the keys.

"Have a good day, sir."

Once inside the car, I slam the door and take a slow breath. "How did you become Sweet Girl, Tavin?" She doesn't respond as she turns and looks out the window. "Fifteen? I mean, motherfucking fifteen, are you kidding me with this?"

No response.

This has to stop.

I take her chin and force her to look at me. "No fifteen year old wants to be a whore. Where were your parents then?" She jerks her head away with tears in her eyes and looks back out the window. "Goddamn it! What do I have to do to get you to talk to me?"

I know I shouldn't be screaming at her, I have just grown attached and I care for her. I want her safe and her life sounds anything besides safe. She has either been forced or willing to let men beat and use her since she was barely a teenager. She doesn't say a word and I honestly don't know what to do at this point. She scoots closer to the car door, distancing herself as much as possible.

I wipe my hand over my face and put the car in drive. The only sound is the music turned down low, as we drive back to my house. I can't find any words that seem right.

I glance over at her to see her wet face, as she picks at her bloodied fingers.

"Seriously, stop doing this."

I take her hand and pull it across the console into my lap to keep her from doing any more damage.

As soon as I pull into the garage, she flies out of the car and sprints inside the house. I hurry after her, catching up to her in her room. She's throwing her stuff, not the things I bought her, into her bag.

I grasp her wrist. "Hey, *Lille,* stop."

She spins around to me, anger darkening her eyes. "How could I not have seen it? What did I think this was?" She's crying and shaking, though she's clearly more pissed than sad right now. "I'm your live in whore! A ready-hole to fuck. That's all I'll ever be." She shakes her head. "I can't be that to you. Not you." Pushing past me, she murmurs, "I'm leaving, Alexander."

I grab her arm. "Damn it, Tavin. Stop! I told you not to take anything she says to heart."

"But she's right!"

"No she fucking isn't! You mean something to me. I don't see you that way. I can't see you that way."

She pulls herself away from me as she hoists her bag over her shoulder. "I need some time. I'm going home."

My gut twists. I'm scared to let her go. She just got clean and she's upset. If the opportunity presents itself, I'm almost positive she'll do it again.

"Don't go."

"Are you forcing me to stay?"

I want to say yes. I almost say yes. "No, b—"

She cuts me off and brushes past me. "Okay then."

"Do you have any money? How are you going to get there?"

"I'll walk."

I glare at her for even suggesting that. "You most certainly will not walk." I pull out my wallet and hand her a credit card. "It's yours, now get a cab." She rolls her eyes while still taking it from my hand. "Please be careful, Tav."

# Tavin

*You disgusting, demented freak!*

Even though my eyes are burning, I won't cry anymore. I've done this to myself and now I have to pay the piper. I watch the palm trees out the window of the cab as the foreign music the driver's playing, fills the car. The world around me is so bright and sunny when my mind feels dark, black, and sludgy.

I'm humiliated. Bjørn is his dad. I hate what I am. Why can't I be like Sasha or Marie the Doctor? I want to be like them, a girl he deserves. I'm not though, and I never will be. I believe him when he says he cares about me. He truly thinks he does, he just doesn't know.

Admittedly, he has been handling what he learns way better than I could have ever foreseen. Even Lex has his limits though, and he showed that today. Just because neither of us knew it was being done, it doesn't change that she's right. He hasn't paid for me in the traditional sense, instead he gives me affection, and brings me to fun places. He helps me escape and takes away the disgusting, repulsive fear. In return, I open my legs for him without him asking. I even fantasize about his touch, the way he kisses, licks and fucks.

Before he kidnapped me into his world, I didn't care about what I wanted, I didn't want anything. I was beautifully numb, and now I'm *always feeling*. There are times when it's so incredible I think I might die from the flutters in my stomach and the heat in my chest. Then other times I feel so sad...deep angst that I haven't felt for a long time.

I need Toben.

When the cabby drops me off at my house, I run up the steps. I can't wait to be in the familiar comfort of my closest confidant.

Slayer is booming from the speakers as I open the door to see Toben on the couch wearing his ever present beanie with a red head bobbing between his legs. He has his hand on her head, pushing down. He's with girls all the time, but he never does this stuff in the living room unless he's with a Client. What's really shocking me though, is the look of loathing on his face as he forces himself into her mouth. He looks like he hates this girl.

"Swallow it you ridiculous bitch."

I can't believe my ears.

"Toben!"

His eyes shoot up to me and his face loses its color. "Shit, get out."

He pushes the girl off and she smirks at me as she passes. Adjusting his stocking cap, he stands and pulls his pants up as I smack his arm.

"How could you talk to her like that?"

His fingers lace in mine, bringing our scars and our words together once again.

"Some girls are into that sort of thing. She didn't look too broken up did she?"

Why anyone would want to be talked to that way is beyond me, but I need pain to come so I can't exactly judge. I lay my head against his chest as he brings his arms around me. Oh I've missed his smell, his touch.

"I miss you," I whisper into his shirt.

"Then come home and stop this defiant bullshit." I lift

my head from his chest and he presses his forehead against mine. "Remember the last time you decided to be disobedient?" Wow. We haven't spoken of that day in over four years and I was under the assumption we never would again. I pull my head back and regret instantly covers his face. "I can't believe I just said that. I'm sorry Love, do not give me that look."

"This isn't about defiance Toben and you know it."

He cups my face and kisses me "He won't see it that way and this is so much worse than not answering his call. I'm scared, Tav. I haven't been scared in a while."

"I hate that you're scared and I know this is hurting you. I know everyone involved will end up getting hurt, I just don't want it to be over yet. I don't know why I feel this way."

He steps away from me to sit on the couch and light a cigarette. "I don't understand what all this will get you besides a broken heart and a taste of what you can never have."

"Memories. I'll remember when I actually got to feel what it's like to live a normal life. I will never ever get the chance to feel this again. I have less than two weeks until Logan gets back and I lose all of it."

He wipes down the table and opens a new needle package. "If it's so great, then why are you about to cry?"

I sit behind him so I can lay my head on his back as he gets out the works kit.

"Do you remember my first Client, Bjørn?"

"Uh huh."

"He's Lex's dad."

The dick head actually chokes on smoke before I feel his back shaking with laughter. This is really upsetting me and his hysteria is making my lips curl up. I'm about to start laughing with him. I smack his back. "Shut up, jerk, it isn't funny. It's mortifying."

He turns so I can see his profile. "I'm sorry, Love, I

shouldn't laugh but…" one more chuckle escapes, "oh God that's epic."

I tell him the whole story about dinner and how Alexander freaked about how old I was when I was with Bjørn. I tell him what his mom said.

"I don't think you have any idea what you're doing. I get that you like this guy, but this is why we can't mix worlds. They can't know about our life."

"It works with Christopher."

"We have to lie to him constantly and he knows it since you're the suckiest liar on earth. He just doesn't give a shit. This guy sounds like he does and that is not fucking good. Can you imagine what Logan would do to him?"

I groan and flop on the couch. "You're right. I don't know what I'm doing and I don't know what I'm feeling and I hate it."

He mixes the water in and cooks it. After setting the spoon on the table, he drops in the cotton. I watch in anticipation as escape fills the needle.

Dang it.

Part of me is so ready for this and part of me feels bad. I know this isn't what Lex wants. He would be so disappointed. I don't want that. God, I just miss the nothing and right now I need it. This is what I am and after two weeks I won't ever see him again.

Toben hovers over me, his dark hair peeking out beneath his hat. "I can take that away, Love."

I feel my head nodding.

"Let's go."

I'm going to be sick. I push off the wooden porch step and stumble into the yard. My fingers grasp at the blades of grass as my body jolts and repulses the mass amounts of vodka

I've consumed.

That's a little better. I'm so trashed and the noise from the party is beginning to get to me. Where's Toben? What time is it? I wade through the bodies to go back inside. God, there are so many people here.

Christopher is on the couch getting straddled by a tall, ebony, model looking girl with dark hair streaked in baby blue. They're making out like they're going to die if they stop.

I sit next to them and snap my fingers next to their connected faces. "Hey, take a break."

His blond hair falls in his face as he glares at me. "What the fuck, Tav?"

"Tere's Woben? No, I mean—"

His hand flicks toward the staircase. "He's upstairs with a chick. Now shoo."

I can't go back to Lex's like this. I need to lie down.

I'm halfway down the stairs to my room when I fall the rest of the way. Crawling across the floor, I climb up on my bed. Ahhh, that's better...Ugh. No it's not. Stop spinning, room!

What did I do? Am I trying to make him hate me? He isn't going to take much more. I need to talk to someone and Toben isn't here. I need someone to understand all of it and tell me what to do. Nobody knows everything besides him and he doesn't understand the stuff with Alexander. He's my only dang friend other than Christopher, and Christopher doesn't know anything. Besides, he's busy anyway. I wish Sasha knew it all. She would be perfect. She told me she won't ever tell Lex anything I don't want her to.

I take out both cell phones. I have to make sure I call her from the right one.

It rings seven times before her groggy, pissy voice comes on the line. "What the shit balls, Tav? It is four o'clock in the fucking morning."

"I shot up tonight."

She sighs, "Oh, Sweetie. Have you called Alex?"

"No. I can't talk to him right now, I'm too wasted."

"Yeah I can hear that."

"Will you come get me?"

"Of course, where are you?"

"Eighty-three twenty-six South Morningstar Avenue."

*Monday, May 25th*

*Alexander*

My alarm goes off, and the first thing I do is go to her room. Admittedly, my heart sinks when she isn't in there. I sit on her bed and let out a breath as I fall back against the pillows. I don't know what else to do to get her to open up and trust me. I've always known there is something hollow and obscure inside her that she has tried to hide. I want to see the magical girl who is full of wonder, but that's only one side of the coin. She has another part—a twisted side. I can't just want half of her, loving her means loving all of her.

Well, not love. I don't mean love. I don't think... I can't be in love with her yet, it's only been a few weeks for Christ's sake. I thought I loved Carrie until she betrayed me in a remarkably cruel way. This is nothing like that. I feel as if I'm in a whirlwind—flying and not knowing where, just knowing it's with her.

Cara Jo's guidance is exactly what I need right now. She doesn't know much other than the drug addiction, so it will be entertaining to see her reaction when I explain the prostitution, the pain thing, the weird guy roommate, the secretive past, the sex with my dad, and of course, the brand.

I go downstairs and find her in the kitchen.

"Hey, Cara Jo... Can I talk to you for a minute?"

Her eyebrows twitch as she smiles and drops her rag on the counter. "Of course, I'm always here for you."

She follows me to my gym and talks to me while I work out. Well, listens mostly. She takes it all remarkably well. If she's shocked or disapproving she isn't showing it. Her advice is honest as always.

"She's such a wonderful girl, Alex. I have enjoyed having her here as much as I've loved seeing this side of you. I just know that there are clearly some emotional, and possibly psychological issues she's dealing with. You need to decide if you're ready for the kind of commitment being with someone like that can entail, and you need to stick with that choice. She's not the kind of girl to be wishy-washy with."

She's right. It will be hard, it will be frustrating, and it will be heartbreaking at times.

She will piss me off and push me to my limits, so I need to decide if I'm willing to deal with all of that to have her.

She will bring chaos into my organized world and that is absolutely what I want. This is real. I don't know what the future holds, I just know I want her in mine.

As I slip on my jacket, my phone lights up with Sasha's photo. "Hey, Sash."

"Hey, I just wanted to let you know that Tavin is at my place. She's drunk off her ass, but she's fine."

I can tell by her voice she's been crying.

"Are you okay?"

"Yeah, I'm just tired."

She is my damn twin, I know when she's lying to me, but I'm too spent to pull it out of her. She'll talk to me when she's ready.

"She was really upset when she went home last night. She didn't use or anything did she?"

Her heavy sigh comes through the line. "Alex…"

"She fucking did, didn't she?" I can almost hear crickets. "Your silence tells me everything I need to know."

"Okay, calm down. You didn't think it was going to be that easy did you? She has an addiction, and obviously a pretty rough life, so she's going to struggle. You're lucky things have been as smooth as they have been."

"Smooth? That's how you describe how things have gone the last few weeks?"

"Yes. I have some insane stories from rehab. She's nowhere near some of the addicts in there. She feels horrible about it and she knows she let you down so don't rub it in, alright?"

One night away from me and she sticks it right back in her arm. She should feel horrible about it.

"I have to go to work."

Damn it, Tavin.

Everything is irritating me and it's becoming harder to keep on my happy face when all I want to do is punch a hole in the wall.

There's a knock on my door before my assistant, Lauren, slips inside. She brushes her hair over her shoulder with a seductive smile. "Hi."

I've always tried to remain somewhat professional, so I've never slept with her. That doesn't mean I haven't flirted pretty hard with her in the past.

"Hi, Lauren, I don't need anything at the moment."

She leans forward on my desk, showing me her cleavage and I actually avert my eyes.

"I just want to thank you for the great reference. I got the job."

Good for her. She has worked her ass off in law school.

"Congratulations."

I know I should probably be more enthusiastic about it, I just can't seem to muster it at present. Thankfully, she doesn't seem fazed.

"Thank you." She straightens her posture and smooths her skirt. "You know, that does mean you aren't my boss anymore."

I'm about to say something to the effect of being disappointed to lose her, when she stuns me into silence. Untying her wrap dress, she lets it fall to the floor, exposing her nude body. My mouth is probably hanging open while I try to think of what to say.

I don't have time though, because my office door opens and of course... Tavin.

"Hey, okay so I kno—"

She sees Lauren and takes in a quick breath. When she looks at me, I want to die. Spinning so fast her hair flies out, she bolts from the doorway.

"Shit," I groan.

I chase after her to the elevator where she's smashing the button over and over.

"Please just open."

I slow my pace as I come up behind her and grab her arm to turn her around. "You have to listen to me, what you saw was not my doing."

She tries to keep it together as she holds her hand out and gestures to my office. "It's fine, Alexander. She's the kind of girl you're supposed to be with. Not me. This whole thing with us is absurd anyway."

She turns away from me and that pisses me off. All the shit she's pulled and she won't even let me explain myself?

Well, guess what? She doesn't get to let me. I grab her arm and yank her into the stairwell.

"What are you doing?!"

Her voice echoes through the stone stairwell as I ignore her and pull her down the stairs to the first landing. Shoving her up against the wall, I lift her long maxi skirt. She is going to understand.

"You are who I want. Only you."

I'm still pissed about the heroin and I hate that she had to see that shit with Lauren.

"What you saw was her hitting on me, not the other way around."

She frowns as she bites her lip. Her doubt is clear. I pull her panties to the side, fingering her as I simultaneously undo my pants. My fingers are already soaked in her arousal and when I push my thumb against her clit, her body jolts beneath my touch. Pressing a hand against the wall for support, I slowly slide out my fingers and wrap her leg around my waist before lining up and pushing into her tight body.

"I don't see other girls anymore, just you. You've gotten into my head, beneath my skin. I'm hooked, Tav. I have been from the moment I first saw you." Her breathing is heavy as I finally see her anger turn to lust.

"Please, believe me."

I shove in deep as I dig my nails into her thigh, scratching her as hard as I can. Long, bleeding red lines appear, leaving skin under my nails as she softly moans.

"You are it for me. Tell me you believe me." With wet rimmed eyes she nods. I wrap a chunk of her hair around my wrist. I need to hear it. "Say it."

Her hand comes to my cheek as she whispers, "I believe you, Alexander."

I am fully aware that someone could walk in the stairwell and see us. I won't care. Let them watch me take her. She may have been with more men than I care to think about, but she's with me now. I grab the back of her neck and press my forehead to hers. With our unbroken eye contact the surge rushes through my body, and for the first time in my life, I mutually come with someone.

Putting her leg back on the floor, I let her maxi skirt down. Her face is flushed as her chest rises and falls.

"I have to get back to work," I rub my fingers over the track marks, "and we need to talk about last night. You'll be there when I get home right?"

She's still breathing heavy as she gives me her half smile and rasps, "Yes."

<hr>

After greeting Cara Jo, I head upstairs and as I pass the guest bath, I hear the shower running, and singing. While she isn't perfectly pitched, her voice is soft and sweet. I open the door and lean against the door frame as I listen.

The sound of the shower being turned off is my cue to slip out and go to my room. Trading my suit for basketball shorts, I go to her bedroom. I smile as I watch her towel dry her hair, in a tank and boy shorts, while she shakes her ass to the music she's playing.

How did this happen in only a few weeks? She makes my heart beat, and gives my soul a home. She makes my blood crash through my veins and every time I look at her, my skin hums. She brings colors I've never seen, into my world. I'm in a constant state of wanting to touch her, taste her, and smell her.

She looks over her shoulder and gives me an awkward smile, still unsure about where we left off.

"Hi."

"Hi." I kiss her head and lie down on the bed with my hands behind my head for support. "So you did it, huh?"

She gives me this sad, pathetic expression. "I know I let you down…"

"You let yourself down, Tav. I've told you, I'm not trying to be this big fun-hater. You almost died and I know the toll drugs can take."

"So you're not mad?"

"Oh, I'm mad as hell, but yelling at you isn't going to help either of us." She gets on the bed and lays her head on my chest as I run my hand over her hair. After a moment I ask, "Was my father cruel to you?"

She rolls on her stomach and rests her chin on laced fingers, "No. I was so scared and I didn't know what to expect. He was nice to me and didn't say mean things. It could have been really bad, Lex, and he was kind."

"How long was he a Client?"

She breaks eye contact. "Two years."

That selfish bastard, he and my mom were never separated for that long. "Yeah, we wouldn't have wanted you to turn eighteen or anything."

I may be a little bitter about this.

⟜

Being careful not to wake her, I slide out of bed and quietly shut the door. I'm not waiting anymore. I sit at my desk and search for a Brian Winters in and around Shadoebox City. After wading through a few that are clearly not him, I find an article.

It states that he's been incarcerated since April 2004 for the murder of his wife, Lacie Winters, with no mention of the child they left behind. There's a high school picture of her mom, and the article says it was her most recent photo. She has similarities to Tav though without the striking eyes. I hate the way I feel when I think of the kind of things Tav could have been exposed to.

I go back into her room and pull her into my chest. Whatever happened to her, whatever she suffers, and whatever she fears, is all in her past. I am her future and no one is ever going to hurt her again.

Well, besides me and not unless she wants me to.

# CHAPTER TWELVE
*Surprise*

*Tuesday, May 26th*

'M A LITTLE LATE GETTING HOME FROM WORK AND THE sight that greets me is an amusing one. Tavin, not Cara Jo, is cooking dinner. She's wearing blue jeans made for that tight ass, a tank, and an apron. She's tapping her little bare foot to the music with a hip sway. I have a quick flash of ripping down those jeans and tying the apron strings around her neck while fucking her over my counter.

"Where is Cara Jo?"

"I decided that I wanted to make you dinner, so I told her to go home." She grins. "She didn't seem to like it much."

No. I bet she didn't.

"Oh really?" I come up behind her, kissing her neck. I could get used to this. "So what are you making?"

"Tavin surprise," she emphasizes with spirit fingers.

"Well that definitely sounds like something I'd eat."

I smack her ass and go upstairs. When I return, she's pouring a couple glasses of wine. Cara Jo better watch out, she might be getting replaced. I sit down and stare at my plate, it's some sort of casserole. I honestly can't figure out what's in it. I think I see noodles. I pick up my fork and shovel a big bite into my mouth…and I think I might die. I can't spit it out fast enough,

"Oh God, Tavin, that's terrible. Where the fuck did you learn to cook?"

It's not easy keeping the gagging at bay. I drink over half the glass of wine in one drink. She scrunches her nose and lets her mouth drop open looking insulted. She takes an equally huge bite and tries for two seconds to act as if it's edible before she spits it out and scrapes her tongue.

"Yeah, that is pretty bad. I've never really cooked anything before."

Cara Jo's job is definitely safe.

"Hey, at least the noodles were done." Her eyes slit in an unamused expression making me grin. "Do you want to order pizza?"

Her lips turn up at the corners and answers with an approving nod.

We eat the pizza and drink beer as she draws a beautiful, yet somewhat disquieting portrait of a two headed girl with no eyes. I have never actually looked at her art before, I guess I just assumed she was doodling, but she has tangible talent.

Once she adds a few of the shadowing and highlighting details, I am blown away. It's stunning. I don't get to admire it for long when she shuts her notebook.

"Can we watch a movie?"

"Sure, what do you want to watch?"

She taps her chin for a second. "I don't know yet."

We head down to the playroom and as we pass the gaming station, she walks over to the case of games. Her fingers trail along the cases until she pulls one out and holds up an old Dance Dance Revolution game.

"What's this?"

"It's a game. You follow the dance moves to the beat of

the music."

Her eyes widen in excitement and curiosity. "Can I play?"

I laugh because I know I'm going to enjoy watching this. "Absolutely."

Once it's all set up, I sit on the couch to watch the show. I'm not disappointed either. She loves it. Her joy and laughter mixed with that amazing ass hasn't allowed the smile to leave my face.

"Oh dang, oops," she giggles as she finds her place. "Oh my God, Toben and I are so getting one of these."

I try to be mature and not get all pissy because she talks about another guy, but I hate whatever is between them. It's weird and a little creepy to be honest.

The sound of someone coming down the stairs breaks my attention away from her. I turn to see Sasha stepping onto the landing.

"Hey, Sash. What are you doing here?"

"Just stopped in to say hi." The quick expression that passes across her face before she laughs at Tavin worries me. "Dance Dance Revolution, huh? How retro of you."

Tavin turns her head and grins. "Do it with me!"

"Oh why not?" She shrugs as she tosses her purse next to me on the couch.

They click together well; Tavin is different around Sasha. I don't know, it's as though her guard is completely down. She's more relaxed, more natural. The friendship is good for both of them.

After three rounds, Tavin falls back on the couch beside me with an expelling breath while Sasha subtly jerks her head toward the stairs and silently mouths: *I need to talk to you.* Whatever she has to say, she clearly doesn't want Tavin to hear.

"Hey, Tav, do you want to play another game or watch

a movie?"

She lets out another breath. "Movie."

We all go to the theater and eventually she settles for 'Repo! The Genetic Opera' again. She apparently loves musicals.

I let it get to the second song before mentioning a reason to leave. "I'm gonna grab another beer." Nodding for Sasha to follow, I climb the steps. Once we are in the kitchen, I pour a shot. I have a feeling I'm going to need it. "So what's up?"

"Mom knows everything about Tavin and dad." She points to my glass. "Give me one of those."

I nearly choke on my drink. "What?!"

She sighs as she grabs the bottle. "Mom isn't stupid, she knew something was up. She heard the familiarity in the way Tavin said his name. It doesn't exactly roll off the tongue of most people. It just further confirmed suspicion when he jumped in to defend her." She shakes her head in disbelief. "He admitted to it."

"Shit."

She throws back her shot and shakes her head from the harsh taste. "She kicked him out. They're getting a divorce."

Even though we both know their marriage has been more about convenience for a while, I can see the idea is unsettling for her. I grab her hand and squeeze in a pathetic attempt at comfort.

"We cannot let Tavin find out about this."

"I'd be more worried about mom coming over here and confronting her."

I run my hands over my face. "I need to go see her and smooth this out."

She snorts, "Oh, yeah, sure. Good luck with that."

It's too late to go tonight, but I will need to make that unfortunate trip tomorrow.

*Wednesday, May 27th*

I want to take Tavin out for a nice dinner tonight, so during my lunch break I call Cara Jo to let her know there's no need to cook. I make reservations at Lucian. It's the best I can get on such short notice.

On the drive home, I go see my mom. I'm sweating this conversation. My mother is not a forgiving woman and I'm sure she puts the blame on Tavin.

The house is silent when I walk in and the foyer is empty.

"Mom?" Pulling open the parlor doors, I see her on the divan with a drink in her hand. She doesn't acknowledge me as I sit next to her. "I am so sorry, Mom."

"You better not have brought that *jävla hore* back into this house."

I clench my fists and bite my tongue to keep from exploding on her. Even though I feel she has the right to be angry and drunk, I'm still not letting her talk about Tavin that way.

"Of course, Mom, Dad is completely innocent. Just blame everything on the girl that was fifteen years old when he paid to fuck her. Did he tell you that?"

She looks at me with so much pain in her eyes. "How could he have done this, Alexander?"

All I can do is hold her while she cries. This is exactly why I kept my twelve year old mouth shut.

*Sixteen years ago...*

*"I'm telling you, 'The Big Lebowski' will be a classic. Just watch."*

*I mean seriously, who doesn't love The Dude?*

*He shakes his head with a mouth full of chips. "No way,*

'Something About Mary' is way better."

"I can't even talk to you, Silas."

He chuckles and throws a Cheeto at me.

"Excuse me, Silas Hamilton. This is not the middle school cafeteria. Pick that up."

"Sorry, Cara Jo."

He obeys and I laugh because it's always funny when someone else besides me gets in trouble from Cara Jo.

"You're both wrong. 'Armageddon' is better than both of those dumb movies," Sasha pipes up from the table as she and Marie look through girl magazines.

Marie swoons, "Mmmm Ben Affleck…"

Ewe. Girls are so weird.

"Gross, he's old."

Cara Jo rolls her eyes. "Oh Lord, Alex, he is not—"she scoots us all out, "Never mind, everyone out of the kitchen."

The girls follow us into my room. "Don't you have to curl your hair or paint your nails or something stupid?"

Sasha gives me a dirty look. "Shut up loser, mom says we have to share your computer until I get mine fixed and we want to look at Leonardo DiCaprio pictures."

I almost ask what the point in that is, but this is Sasha we're talking about.

"We're supposed to ask if we can get online in case dad needs the phone."

"Then go ask him."

Silas chuckles as he looks through my video games and I glare at him. I cross my arms. "Why would I ask him? You're the one who wants the computer."

"Because I still haven't told on you two…" she points to Silas and me, "for watching dad's pornos."

"Ugh sick. You guys are pervs," Marie spouts off from my bed as she still flips through that dumb magazine.

I give them both a frown before shrugging. I'm still hungry

*anyway. "Fine, whatever, I'll be right back."*

*Sweet talking Cara Jo into handing over the six pack of Surge isn't that hard and I grab a handful of Slim Jims, stuffing the Dorito bag under my arm. Now to find dad. I can almost guarantee he's in his study. He's always in his study.*

*I open his door, and Sharon, one of our maids, is just sitting in one of his chairs. Why is she—*

*Oh…*

*Her legs are open and my dad's head is between them. I know what he's doing.*

*Why is he doing that? What about mom?!*

*She's moaning, but the noise that jumps from my throat is loud enough to get his attention.*

*"Alexander!" He barks.*

*I have to get away from him, from this. I don't want to see this. I back up and run away, ignoring his yelling. I don't know what to do. I slide into the parlor for a second to think. What am I going to do?*

*"Alexander, darling, are you alright? You look pale."*

*I jump at my mother's voice and drop the chips. She looks at me with concern, completely oblivious to what he's doing in the other room. She would be so sad. She would cry and I hate it when she cries. I can't tell her. I know I should, I just can't. I don't want her in pain.*

*"I'm fine, Mom…I was just looking for my Gameboy."*

I hate him. They have been together for almost forty years.

"He's a selfish man, Mom. He always has been."

Her manicured hand wipes her tears as she shakes her head. "I knew her smell was familiar. I've smelt her on him before." Her face hardens as she turns to me. "I don't know what you are doing with that girl, just make certain I never see her again. The way your father looked at her… he was smitten, Alexander."

She's furious and hurt. I'm never going to get her to see Tavin's side when she's feeling this way. Her feelings might not ever change. All I can do is let her cry on my shoulder until she falls asleep. I adjust her on the divan before I leave. At least I know she probably won't show up at my house. I wish I could fix this for them both. My main concern about it now is that Tavin doesn't find out about the divorce.

She's playing Dance Dance Revolution again, when I come home. She must have been at it awhile because her hair is sticking to her face and neck. The soft pink sports bra she's wearing matches the waistline of her gray yoga pants. Good God her ass looks great in those pants. She spins to the side to see me watching her. A grand smile lifts her face and she doesn't skip a beat. The song ends and her score flashes across the screen.

She pumps her fist. "Yes!"

Bounding over to me, she stands on her tip toes and I lean down so she can wrap her arms around my neck.

"How do you feel about going out for a fancy dinner?"

She grins. "How fancy? Do I get to dress up?"

"Oh yes, *Lille*, I'm counting on it."

I wear my black *Brioni* suit and I'm ready before she is, so I have a glass of scotch while I wait. She finally comes down thirty minutes later and is dressed to the nines. She has her hair pinned up and has on full makeup complete with lip gloss. The classic little black dress she's wearing fits her superbly. It has cap sleeves and slightly bells out at the waist, falling mid-thigh. The entire ensemble is complete with her carousel necklace and sexy as sin black pumps.

Whoa. I've never seen those legs in heels.

"Wow." I meet her and put my hand on her ass. "You

look incredible."

She smiles an ornery, coy smile. "So do you."

# Tavin

I can't believe he's still letting me stay after finding out about me getting high at the party. He's actually been pretty chill about it which in turn makes me feel more like crap. I need to stop this, I know. I'm getting too attached too fast and I think he is starting to feel real feelings for me. I'm going to hurt him no matter what I do. The only thing I can do to make up for it is give him as many good memories as I can, to help him through his bad days when I'm gone.

I feel so pretty in my dress and shoes. The way he looks me up and down in his kitchen and the movement in his pants makes me feel warm all over. He always acts like I'm the most stunning thing he's ever laid eyes on. He's convincing too. I find myself believing it.

On the way to the restaurant, he tells me to pick a song and since we both like Nirvana, I pick *Polly*. I sing along with the words and Lex even joins in. He has a nice voice. Even though it's not quite as perfect sounding as when Toben sings, it's still soothing.

This is one of those moments that I almost forget this isn't real. He's holding my hand and when he flashes that incredible smile, I feel myself clench and refrain from sighing.

I stare into his bright green eyes as I lean back and lift my dress. I can't believe I'm doing this. It's something that Master always makes me do, and it drives him wild, so maybe it will with Lex too. His gaze pulls from my eyes and travels to my hands slowly raising the fabric up my thighs.

He quickly glances through the windshield then back to my skirt.

"What are you doing?"

I'm glad I'm not wearing panties because the subtle ascendency glazing over the amusement in his voice would have them soaked.

"I just want to show you something," I say. It's getting harder to stop my mouth from smiling.

This is fun. I've never had the power to do this. I have never wanted to before either, but still. I pull my skirt the rest of the way up and as soon as he sees that I'm bare, his jaw twitches. I bet if I were to touch my hand to his lap, I would find him stiff.

"I just thought you should know." I push my skirt back down. "Something to think about during dinner."

His laugh is deep and happy. "It's cute you think I'm actually going to wait until after dinner."

As I watch the palm trees dancing in the sunset through the car window, he holds my hand and doesn't let go until we're seated at the restaurant. He gives me a sexy smile that brightens his eyes. Dang he looks good tonight. I mean, he always looks freaking amazing, tonight though, he bumped it up a notch.

"You know, looking at you in that suit makes me wet."

I almost start laughing. I can't believe I actually just said that, and his facial expression nearly makes me burst. At first glance he appears almost angry, until his lip twitches and he looks like he's about to jump across the table.

"I know you're just trying to tease me, but one more comment like that and I promise you, I won't be doing any waiting."

I do laugh then. As I take a drink of my wine, a pretty red head comes up to our table. Lex cocks his head to the side like he's trying to figure out who she is.

"Alexander! Hi!"

Well, she obviously knows him.

"Um, hi?"

"I haven't heard from you, we had such a fun time I was surprised." His face goes from uncertainty to apprehension. He knows who she is now. "You know, I left my underwear at your house. Maybe I can come get them sometime?"

Oh really?

Just because I have zero right to feel jealous, it doesn't change the fact that I do. He's been with this girl. He's kissed her, smelled her, felt her. And she wants him to again. Um no. Not while I'm still around. She looks at me like I just arrived.

"Oh hi, are you his sister?"

I have never had much experience with jealousy. While it was hard with Toben at first, his being with girls doesn't faze me anymore. This is different. I feel angry that she has experienced him, has known his body. Now she's trying for a round two with me sitting right here?

"I'm not his sister and he isn't available, so back off before I make you."

Lex spews out his wine and the girl looks at me with offense. I would normally feel so bad, right now though, I just want her away from him.

Lex starts busting up laughing as she walks away. "What the hell was that?"

I feel the need to claim him, which is ridiculous considering he isn't mine to claim.

For tonight, he is.

"We aren't waiting until after dinner."

I throw my napkin down and get up to march to the bathroom knowing full well he's going to follow. After a couple of minutes, he enters the hallway and it's almost like I'm high on the desire for him to tear me apart. I jump on him and wrap my legs around his waist. His hands instantly find my ass to hold me up and squeeze. His finger is already inside me as he carries me to the bathroom. I feel him fumbling in his pocket with one hand while the other hand still holds me up. He kisses my neck as he kicks open the stall, and I see the money he's thrown on the floor so the bathroom attendant will give us privacy.

He puts me on my feet and his hands get to his belt faster than mine do. Once he's accessible I grab hold of him with one hand, turn around, lift my dress, and use the other hand to brace myself against the wall as I shove him inside me. God he's massive. His grunt meets my gasp as our bodies connect. Pressing my hands against the cool tile for momentum, I push myself around him.

"Jesus, Tav, I almost feel violated. Damn."

His voice gets so deep when he fucks. He presses down on my body to reach deeper. It isn't meant to last long and it doesn't. He pulls my sleeve down and bites my shoulder so hard he breaks the skin, finally letting me fall into the steady rolls of ecstasy around him.

"You were jealous weren't you?" He murmurs as his lips move against his bite mark.

He pushes in hard and it forces out my moan. "Yes."

I feel him grow before he empties everything into me. He kisses my neck and tears off some toilet paper to wipe me clean. That action alone somehow gets me wet again as he rights my dress and puts himself back together.

"Oh God," he groans. "That is so hot."

"What?" I turn back to see what he's talking about.

"You left a wet spot on my fucking suit."

I laugh from embarrassment and it's cut off by his kiss. Holding my hand, he leads me back to our table. We sit down and he tells me about a big party he has coming up. It sounds fancy, like a ball.

"Sasha's making your gown."

"That I can keep?"

"Yes, silly, it's literally being created just for you."

I can feel the excitement bubble up. Even though Master gives me gowns to wear, they stay at his house. They aren't really mine. Of course I won't keep it, but he doesn't know that.

*You don't deserve any of this.*

A waitress stops at our table and takes our order. As she walks away, he's giving me a sarcastic expression.

"Really Tavin? Spaghetti? At a five star restaurant? That's two hundred dollars' worth of noodles and sauce." I shrug. He never gave me stipulations so he's lucky I didn't just order the chocolate cake.

### Thursday, May 28th

He still isn't back. Cara Jo says she has to leave, and dinner will stay warm in the oven. Toben and I text for a while, but he has a playdate, so I'm getting kind of bored by myself.

I wonder what Lex would do if he came home and I was standing here naked. I bet his expression would be so funny.

I'm gonna do it.

After pulling off all my clothes, I run downstairs to wait. When I finally hear the lock, I hurry to stand in the entryway. I grin as I look up at him and...

Uh oh.

"Damn, Angel." His friend Silas is staring me up and down. His eyes find my logo. "Whoa."

My hand jumps to cover my mouth. "I am so sorry."

"Oh no apology wanted here."

Jeez, I'm still standing here naked. I don't know rather to run or walk up the stairs, so I speed walk. Crap. I know Lex will not like this; accident or not. I throw on a pair of shorts and a camisole before going back downstairs.

I'm hoping he left now that he knows Lex isn't here. No such luck. He is sitting on a stool in the kitchen drinking a beer.

He brushes back his black hair when he sees me. "We really don't need to say anything to Alex about that. He will freak and we didn't do anything wrong. It'll just cause un- necessary drama. For some reason he's all teenage crushin' on you."

Maybe he's right. Lex really doesn't need to know that yet another man from his life knows what I look like naked.

"Um…okay."

"The reason I came by is because Alex and Sasha's birth- day is next Friday and their surprise party is tomorrow." His birthday is the day before I have to go home? That sucks. "He will obviously want you there since you guys apparently live together." He's judging. He doesn't trust me and he shouldn't. "It's at The Necco Room and we should all try to be there around six thirty. He's going to work late again tomorrow, so just text him around then and tell him to meet you there."

"Okay."

"As long as you're able to keep a secret, he won't have any idea. He is too preoccupied with the fundraiser this week- end and his meeting with an investor, coming up. And of course you, so mums the word alright?"

I nod.

He starts going on and on about the decorations and the food and I just keep nodding because I honestly don't care.

"Oh and I also g—"

"Uh, hey guys." I jump about five feet, I didn't even hear the garage door open. Lex's eyebrows are knit together as he loosens his tie. "What's going on?"

Thankfully Silas answers, "Damn, you're home late."

"Yeah…so what's up?"

"I was going to see if you wanted to go get some drinks."

He gestures to me. "The point in drinks is to get a girl. I have mine."

My chest twists. It eats at my gut when he talks about us like we have a future together.

"Suit yourself." Silas shrugs and Alexander narrows his eyes at us. The stool scrapes as Silas stands up. "Alright, I'm out." He smacks Lex's shoulder. "See you tomorrow."

The front door closes and I'm nervous all of a sudden. I can't tell him about the party and Silas said not to tell him he saw me naked.

"How long have you two been hanging out?"

He looks upset.

"Uh… maybe thirty minutes."

"So what was with the guilty expressions when I walked in? What were you guys doing?"

"Talking."

"Wearing that?"

What do my clothes have to do with anything?

"What's wrong with my clothes?"

"I can almost see your ass in those shorts."

I know my mouth drops open. I can't believe he just said that.

"Say what you really mean, Lex: I'm dressed like the whore that I am."

"Don't put words in my mouth, I just don't want you alone with him, half naked. I know nothing happened—" He cuts himself short and glowers. Crap. My face must have given something away because his voice takes on an aggressive undertone. "Nothing happened, right?"

Something technically *did* happen. "No…"

His shoulders drop and he looks defeated for a moment. I want to hug him. It wasn't anything. Maybe I should just tell him so he doesn't think anything worse. "That was a Goddamn lie!" He bellows and it startles me so bad my heart flutters. "Something did happen. Tell me right fucking now what went on between you two."

He's mad, well so am I. He has every reason to think this way, and it still makes me furious that he does. Until him, I never understood how having sex for fun was even a thing. It hurts so bad that he could think for a second that I would willingly sleep with his friend.

"I know what I am, so it makes sense for you to think I will just open my legs for anyone at any time, but I won't."

He sighs, "Tavin—"

"He saw me naked."

"What?!"

"I thought he was you!"

"He saw...all of you?"

I nod. "Cara Jo left dinner in the oven." I turn around to head upstairs. "I want to be alone tonight." I'm being unfair, but my feelings are hurt. If Toben wasn't gone at a playdate I would consider going home.

"Tavin, come on."

He grabs my elbow and I yank it free. "Good night, Alexander."

*Friday, May 29th*

Alexander

I don't know why she's so mad at me, exactly. She was going to lie to me about it, I'm the one that should be upset. I need to leave for work and I want to see her before I go. I don't want to leave while we are in a fight.

I knock on her door. "I'm going to work. Will you at least say good bye?"

When she swings the door open, she's in yoga pants and one of my shirts that's so big, it almost comes to her knees. I know the ensemble is courtesy of the comment I made about her shorts.

"Bye." She doesn't have a major attitude, though the fact that she's still unhappy with me is apparent.

"What is this ridiculous outfit you're wearing?"

She shrugs. "Something a little less slutty."

Oh my God, she drives me insane. "You infuriate me sometimes. You know you are blowing this out of proportion."

"Yeah well, I'm a whore remember? I blow a lot of things."

Oh no. Oh hell no, that does not fly. I grab her arm. "I know you're pissed, but do not ever say shit like that again. Do you understand? I'm fucking serious." She nods. "Answer me."

She glares and grates her teeth. "Yes, Alexander."

Once I get to Vulture, I head straight to Silas' office and walk right in just as he loves to do at my house. He's balls deep in a little pony-tailed Korean number.

"Wrap it up Silas, we need to talk."

I can't believe he would do anything to intentionally hurt me. Since the first day I met him, he's been nothing less than an amazing friend.

*Nineteen years ago...*

*This place kind of stinks...and it's hot. I thought I wanted this so much and now that I'm here I don't want to be. Every time Cara Jo drives by the playground, Sasha and I watch them all running and chasing each other. They always look so happy.*

*The only friends we have are the ones we're forced to have because of our parents. We thought this would be fun.*

*"Class, we have a new student." The teacher talks through her nose and all the kids are staring at me. I wish they would stop. Even though Sasha is the most annoying sister in the world, I would do anything to have her here with me right now. Why would they put us in separate classes? We only know each other. "Say hello to Alexander."*

*"HELLO, ALEXANDER."*

*I almost jump because they all respond...at the exact same time.*

*"H-hello uh...fourth grade."*

*Oh great, now everyone is laughing at me. I don't like this. This was a bad idea. Maybe Sasha will ditch with me at lunch and go to the Boardwalk.*

*The teacher smiles at me as she pushes up her glasses.*

*"Alright, everyone calm down." Her hand softly presses against my back as she points to a boy with thick, black hair tipping back in his chair. "My name is Mrs. Tykes. You may take a seat next to Silas Hamilton."*

*"Yes Ma'am."*

*"Mr. Hamilton, all four legs need to remain on the floor."*

*I walk down the aisle and it feels like everyone is looking at the way I'm dressed, my backpack, my hair, my lunch box...I didn't think it would be like this.*

*I sit next to the boy named Silas and hold out my hand. "How do you do? It is a pleasure to meet you."*

*He snorts at me and holds his hand into a fist. "What's up, dude?"*

*That is a weird question, but I look up to see. "Um...the ceiling?"*

He chuckles and drops his hand. "Jeez, that's so old it's almost funny again." His eyebrow arches as he whispers, "You might want to unbutton that top button, you kind of look like a dork."

Oh man really? Sasha was right?

"Okay." I do it and it actually does feel better.

"What school did you go to before here?"

"My sister and I had private tutors."

He looks a little horrified. "Don't tell people that." He shakes his head and his dark hair flops around. "Home school kids get a bad rep. Say you went to… East Shadoebox elementary." He nods and tips back in his chair again. "Stick with me, Alex. You will be the second most popular fourth grader in less than a month."

"Actually, it's Alexander."

"Trust me, Alex is cooler."

I think I like this kid.

"Silas Hamilton!" He grins back at me and puts his chair back on the floor when Mrs. Tykes sighs and rubs her forehead. "You know the drill…Principal's office."

He stands up and puts on his backpack.

"Sit with me at lunch, okay?"

"Okay."

On his way up the aisle, he slips a note to a girl in the next desk before turning back to me, "Welcome to North Shadoebox Elementary, Alex."

My cheeks lift. Maybe it won't be so bad here.

I watch the clock as Ms. Tykes drones on about stuff Sasha and I were already taught last year. The bell ringing is loud, and I'm happy for it as I throw my bag over my shoulder and rush to the lunchroom.

There are so many kids that it's hard to look for Silas. I'm getting awkward looks from passing students so I toss my backpack on the closest table and look from there.

*Something hits my shoulders so hard my head snaps back.*
*"You're sitting at our table, new kid."*

*I look up to see who spoke, and find a boy much too large to still be in elementary school. Behind him are two smaller boys holding trays and snickering.*

*"I apologize, I didn't know there was assigned seating."*

*I try to stand, but one of the smaller boys pushes me back down. The large boy shoves my bag off the table and kicks it across the floor.*

*"Well let me make sure you don't forget."*

*He laughs and reaches behind him, scooping a handful of baked beans off the smaller boy's tray. I can't get out of the way fast enough as the lukewarm gunk squishes up my nose and into my eyes. Fingers dig into my arms before I get the chance to wipe it away. I am shoved to the floor as pain shoots up my leg, just as I hear Silas' voice.*

*"What have I told you about messing with my friends, Franco?"*

*"He just started today, how was I supposed to know he was your friend?" The large boy 'Franco', doesn't sound so tough anymore.*

*"Well now you do," Silas says.*

*I hear a grunt and a groan before a napkin is wiping off my face. Silas is kneeling in front of me and over his shoulder, I watch the three boys shuffle away.*

*"Thank you," I tell him as I take the napkin and try to clean my own face.*

*He laughs as he stands. "Come on, I don't live far from here. You can't walk around looking like this. Besides, if my mom feels bad enough for you, she might let us skip the rest of the day."*

*He slides his arms through his backpack straps and I do the same. We walk out of the cafeteria and across the playground before we are on the street to his house.*

*"So Alex," he asks, "Do you like movies?"*

Once the girl leaves, I walk in to him tucking in his shirt. "Tavin told me what happened between you two last night."

Throwing his head back, he groans, "This is why I told her not to mention it. It was an accident, so chill." He looks back at me. "While we are on the subject of your naked girlfriend, what the hell is the thing on her chest?"

I'm not getting into that right now.

"Then why did you both look as if you got caught doing something wrong? That's what doesn't make sense."

"Jesus, will you relax? You just scared us, that's all."

There's something going on. I can feel it. I hate knowing she is mad at me. It wasn't that bad of a comment though. She's the one who is making it a huge thing. It's as if she expects me to just automatically know whatever it is she's feeling and thinking.

I call her and she doesn't answer, I text with no reply. For lack of a better term, she's being a brat.

I call my house phone and Cara Jo answers, "Hello, Alexander Sørensen's residence."

"Hey, Cara Jo, can I talk to Tavin?"

"She's not here."

"What? Where did she go?"

"When I asked her, her exact words were: 'To make Alexander feel like a jerk.'"

I roll my eyes. "You don't have to sound so damn amused you know. Let me know if you hear anything."

She snickers, "Alright, Alex."

On my way home I call again to see if Tavin is back yet, and there's no answer. I'm beginning to really worry. Cara Jo's cell is the same thing and I get home to find an empty house with no dinner.

What the hell is going on?

I climb the stairs to my room, taking my jacket off and throwing it on the bed when I hear buzzing. I reach across the bed to pull out my phone and it's a text from Tavin.

**Cara Jo went home early, there's no dinner so we need to go out. I'm at The Necco Room, see you there.**

That doesn't make sense. Why would she not wait for me? And Cara Jo leaving early without telling me is not something she does. Something is definitely off. I turn right back around and get back in the Alfa.

Pulling into The Necco Room, the valet opens my door and I hand him my keys just as I see Sasha getting out of her car in the parking lot.

What is Sasha doing here?

"Sasha?"

She looks up and gives me a confused wave. "Hey."

"You hang out at The Necco Room now?"

The door is held for us as we walk inside.

She scoffs, "No. I have no clue why Drew wanted to come here."

It hits me at the exact moment before I see the balloons, streamers, and happy birthday banner.

Oh my God, of course, our stupid birthday.

So that was why they were startled at the sight of me yesterday.

There's a huge cake and a ton of food. Both our social groups are in attendance along with several colleagues. Silas must have rented the whole place. They all see us and a loud "Surprise!" rings through the bar.

I see Silas in between two girls, and then I see Tavin. She's in a purple maxi dress with her hair down. She looks beautiful, even if the dress hangs off her and hides her perfect figure. Her arms are crossed as she smirks at me.

I close the distance between us. "So you succeeded. I feel like a jerk."

"This is why he was even over in the first place. And he just walked in! He didn't even knock. I threw on the first thing I saw, I didn't think about it."

"I'm sorry. It was an idiotic thing to say." I take her hand and lower my head to look into her eyes. "Are we okay?"

She smirks. "Yes."

Wrapping my arm around her waist, I kiss her temple. "Come on, I'm starving. Let's go get some food."

I fill my plate and meet her at our table to see hers piled high with cookies, cake and ice cream.

"Jesus, Tavin, you can't just eat that. Get your ass up and go get a burger."

This crazy girl is going to give herself diabetes. She throws out a huff while still doing what I ask.

After we eat, we kick things off with a couple of double shots and then I follow her to the dance floor.

The party is a blast. Both Cara Jo and Marie stop by to give us birthday wishes and take a birthday shot, though neither stay long. Benny has had Tavin laughing all night. I feel bad for not being at the gym these past few weeks. He says he isn't bothered by it and his lack of sensitivity is one of the things I love about him. Maybe I'll get her a membership and we can go together.

He has her trash talking me as we play beer pong because she's beating my ass into next week.

"Ooh, ouch! Now that has to sting." She isn't exactly a humble winner.

Her wispy bangs have started to grow and are in her eyes, sticking to her face from the sweat. She punches her fists out in a little victory dance, and I shake my head at her.

"Two outta three, you won't be so damn cocky."

Her head falls back as she laughs causing her hair to

reach her ass that I can't see in that gunny sack of a dress.

Sometimes I swear I see a glow coming off her, when she laughs that real, honest, true laugh that she does. These are the moments that I just want to pounce on her. I mean, I always want to, but when her vibrancy bursts through, I have to physically stop myself and remember that there are other people here.

"Bring it on, Lex. Your ass is gonna be so sore tomorrow from all this kicking."

"Someone's ass is going to be sore and I can promise it won't be mine."

She smirks as she sets herself up for her next shot and I groan when the beer sloshes over the rim as the ball lands in the cup. She throws her arms up in triumph before dancing around and giving Benny a high five.

I shake my head at her theatrics and hold out my hand. "Give me the damn ball."

She snickers at me and when it bounces off the rim of the cup to the floor, I drop my head in defeat. Just because I'm not a sore loser doesn't mean I don't prefer to win.

She comes up beside me and holds my hand.

"You tried your best and that's all that matters." I think it's sweet that she's trying to give me a pep talk until she says, "At least that's what Benny says we're supposed to say to losers." She bursts out laughing so hard her whole body is shaking. Benny laughs with her until she finally calms down enough to say, "I was just joking, I don't really think you're a loser, just that you're not very good at beer pong."

I laugh and wrap my arm around her neck to kiss the top of her head as she sways a little against my chest. I pull out my phone and see it's a quarter till two. As much as I want to drive my car, seeing as I was hoping for one of her incredible blow jobs, we have drank way too much for that.

I call us a car and as soon as we are in the backseat, I lift her dress to slide my fingers beneath her panties and keep them there the entire drive home.

Once I unlock the front door, it swings open, causing us to fall inside as our tongues remain intertwined and we laugh against each others lips. The stairs are just too far away, so I guide us to the couch in the living room. Her foot fumbles in front of mine and I don't want to step on it, so I lose my balance, causing both of us to fall on the couch. I smile at her soft giggles as I kiss her neck. She's so wasted. Our lips touch and I reach down to pull this unflattering dress over her head.

She stops kissing me, pushes me off, and moves to the opposite end of the couch.

"We aren't having sex tonight."

"The hell we aren't!" I growl as I go for her.

She shakes her head. "It really hurt my feelings that you could even think I would do anything with Silas. You said you were sorry, and I'm going to make sure of it. I want you to stroke your cock and I'm going to watch. You got to watch me, now it's my turn. You can't touch me, but you can look."

She has to be joking. "Seriously?"

Crossing her arms she gives me a curt nod. "Seriously."

"Come on, it's my birthday."

"Your birthday isn't until next week. Don't whine, I want to watch you ejaculate."

That voice saying the word 'ejaculate' is adorable. I glower at her, while I undo my pants and push them low enough to let my cock spring free. She's staring and biting her lip. Clearly she is anticipating this, so what the hell. I'll give her a show.

I undo my shirt, slowly, so she has to wait for what she really wants to see. She grins as I grab the base of my dick, starting with a few short pumps. She takes off her dress and is wearing little pink and purple striped boy shorts with a purple cotton push up bra. The damn bra unsnaps in the front and I'm not going to get to unsnap it. I pump higher up my shaft, taking longer strokes. Her fingers are lightly brushing her thigh and her breasts are rising and falling with each heavy breath.

I run my thumb over the tip before I thrust into my hand. Her pelvis slightly moves forward into a nearly invisible rocking motion and I bet she's drenched. I've never been with a girl that gets as wet as she does. She reaches her hand up to her neck, slowly dragging her fingers across her chest, taking her sweet-ass time as she brushes a soft touch over the top of her bra clasp. *Please, please pop it open.* She moves past the clasp and begins tracing her finger along the outline of her brand. I'm pumping myself as hard as I can now. This is not what I expected. She continues trailing her fingers down her stomach to the waistband of her boy shorts. She releases an almost silent moan as she allows herself to softly rub her mound over the top of the underwear.

"Say my name, Tavin."

Her lip twitches into a crooked smile when she leans forward. The tip of her little tongue brushes over her bottom lip.

"Alexander." She says it slow and raspy and oh my God, I pre-come.

I want to pump faster, instead I actually slow down. I'm enjoying myself very much and I want this to last. She touches her bra and with a flick of her finger, it springs open, allowing her mouthwatering tits to bounce into view. This is the most gratifying torture I have ever endured. Of course I want to touch her, while at the same time I want her to watch me come for her.

She stands up and points a finger at me. "Don't come without me, but don't stop."

"Oh I won't."

She disappears into the kitchen as she lets her bra fall off her shoulders to the floor. I don't stop pumping my fist while I await her return and I don't have to wait for long. She hurries back into the room, slowing her pace once she sees me still jerking off. Her little tits bounce with every step.

She sits back down, opposite of me, placing a small paring knife on the shoulder of the couch. She puts one foot on the floor and uses her other foot to push into the cushion, lifting her ass to remove her boy shorts. She spreads her legs, giving me full view of her gorgeous cunt. Lunging forward to taste her, I am stopped with a foot to my chest.

She shakes her head. "Uh uh" and points to my erection. "Do it."

Her bossiness, while cute as a button, is insanely erotic. I start again fast. Her fingers trail over her stomach to her thighs. It's as if years pass before her delicate hand is over her pussy. Her middle finger disappears as she slides it inside. Slow, small pumps in and out. She removes it as she kneels forward on the couch and brings her finger to her lips, winking as she takes it into her mouth. More pre-come seeps out. I'm not going to make it much longer.

She cocks her head to the side. "Do you want a taste?"

I don't answer, she knows I do. God, this feels so damn good. She dips her finger inside a few times before bringing it to my mouth. I lick as much as I can before she slides it out from between my lips.

Lying back, she rubs quickly over her clit. We become each others audience as we deprive ourselves of the others touch. Her rocking quickens and she picks up the paring knife. Her raspy moans become whimpers as she presses the knife to her flesh. It's almost too much, it's about to happen. I can feel the pressure rising as she yanks the knife across her flesh and throws her head back.

Oh, God, yes. The electric pulse runs up and down my

body as my semen flows over my hand and onto my stomach.

"I'm gonna come, Lex," she softly moans as she trembles through her orgasm.

She sighs and drops the knife on the floor. After leaning forward to kiss her, I glance down and there's blood everywhere.

"Shit!" The thumping in my chest batters my rib cage as I jump off the couch and rip up my pants.

"What's wrong?" As soon as she says it, she sees her thigh and covers the cut with her hand. "Oh no, it's all over your couch. I'm sorry."

I'm trying to find my phone in my pants and I wonder if this is what a panic attack feels like. "I don't give a fuck about my couch! You're bleeding! A fucking lot!"

She waves her hand as though I'm being ridiculous. "It's okay, chill. I've had much worse than this before. It's fine."

I finally find my phone, searching for Marie in my contacts. "There is a major artery there Tavin, this could be really bad." I'm shaking—I'm actually scared here. The line rings and I point to her. "Don't move."

"Hey, Ale—."

"Tavin sliced open her thigh and she's bleeding everywhere." I rush out my words as I hurry to the kitchen for towels.

Her voice switches to 'doctor' mode. "Is the blood spraying out?"

"No, seeping would be more accurate."

I hear a relieved sigh, allowing me to relax a bit as well.

"Okay, that's good. Put pressure on it and keep her leg elevated. I'm on my way."

I get back into the living room and she's trying to put her underwear on without getting blood on it.

"Tavin, stop. Sit down, I'll help you."

"God, I'm sorry."

"Stop apologizing."

"Sorry."

I glare at her and she gives me a contrite smile.

"Are you feeling light headed?" My heart is pounding and I'm still drunk. Bending her knee, I raise her thigh.

"I'm fine, really."

Oh yeah, she's frickin' fantastic. Maneuvering her underwear around the wound, I slide them back on.

"Hold these here."

I place her hand on the towels and throw my shirt over her head. When I lift the towel again, I see that even though the bleeding has slowed, there's a nasty gash.

"Jesus, you are going to need stitches. I just about guarantee it."

"Would you relax? You didn't need to call Marie."

"Are you not grasping the fact that you hurt yourself? Don't get me wrong, the whole pain thing is hot and it's been quite the experience, but we can't be seriously hurting you this way. I mean, this is fucked up, Tav."

She narrows her eyes and snaps, "I'm so glad it's been 'quite the experience' for you because I can't be sexually satisfied without some type of affliction. So for me I guess it's been 'quite the experience' as well."

"Whoa, look. You've barely told me anything and I've tried not to ask too many questions because I want to give you time, but you can't bite my head off whenever you feel I should just psychically know something." I run my thumb over her chin as I lift it up. "You can trust me. I promise."

I never knew a laugh could be gloomy and yet hers is.

"The sad part is, I do know that…I'm sorry everything is so complicated. I just wish your touch was enough."

I do too, sometimes.

"I want you to tell me everything there is to know about you, more importantly though, I want you to *want* to tell me about it. Until then, maybe you should talk to someone else. Maybe Marie?"

Her head jerks and her posture becomes withdrawn.

"No. I'm fine."

She is a pendulum swinging from impassioned to insufferable and it's going to make me lose my ever lovin' mind. Before I can reply, the doorbell rings. I exhale a large breath as I get off the now blood stained couch and answer the door.

I swing it open and gesture behind me. "She's in the living room."

She rushes to Tavin and I follow her. "Hi, Tavin, how are you feeling?" Marie kneels in front of the couch, setting her medical bag on the floor.

"I'm sorry he made you come out tonight. He's over reacting, it's just a cut. I'm really okay."

She sounds embarrassed and I can't decide if it's because she truly doesn't believe it's necessary for me to have called Marie or if it's because it happened in the first place. I narrow my eyes at her even though she isn't looking at me.

"Well, let me see it." Marie removes the towels and draws in a breath. Tavin doesn't even wince as the wound is cleaned, she sits perfectly still and allows Marie to work. "This is not 'just a cut'. I'm going to have to sew this up." I raise my eyebrows in a nonverbal, *told you so* and Tavin rolls her eyes. Marie leans over to her bag and her voice changes completely. "How did this happen?" She barks as she holds the knife in front of Tavin's face.

"Uh…"

Marie stands up and faces me. "What happened here, Alex?"

I can't help myself, a smile spreads across my face of its own free will. She's pretty conservative. She won't like this. I lace my fingers together behind my head and let an awkward laugh free.

"It's a sex thing."

Her eyebrows shoot up. "Oh—" she clears her throat. "Oh, I see."

Shifting her attention back to Tavin, who has a hand over her mouth, trying unsuccessfully, to hide her smile, she sighs.

"I know you guys were just having some fun, but this is dangerous, so try being more careful okay?" Tavin gives her a nod and we are all silent for a few minutes as she sews her up. "It's clear from all the scars that you have done this numerous times, so this is obviously something you're into…" She trails off in thought as she finishes sewing up the cut. Reaching into her bag, she takes out a card and hands it to Tavin. "If you ever need me for anything, just call me directly. Anytime. I mean it."

"Okay."

Marie stands and brushes past me as I follow her and walk her to the door. Stopping dead in her tracks, she spins around on me. "I do not approve of this at all. The girl is clearly in some type of trouble. Everything about her suggests abuse; the scars, the secrets. And you're over here playing house and indulging her."

Her lack of understanding is infuriating. "First of all, she's safe here. I'm not 'playing house'. Second, I have asked her, but I cannot nor do I want to force her to tell me anything about what she's mixed up in. Lastly, I'm not indulging her. She is an algolagnist, it just got out of hand this time. I'm doing my best. I appreciate your help and I'm sorry you don't approve. I'm just not sure what you expect me to do."

She huffs and wipes her eyes. "God, I don't know. I just know, this," she points toward Tavin, "tonight, cannot happen again."

"Well we agree on that."

She gives me the same look she's given me since high

school, the one where she shakes her head and closes her eyes, as if she just doesn't know what to do with me.

"I'm going home. Good night, Alexander."

"Good night and thanks again."

"Uh huh."

Tavin is still on the couch, gripping the cushions and seemingly deep in thought as I walk back into the living room. I slide an arm under her knees while wrapping my other around her waist, lifting her off the couch and startling her.

"What are you doing?"

"I'm taking you to bed."

Her mouth twitches and her eyes are sad when her soft, pouty lips lightly press against mine.

Her head rests on my shoulder, and her long hair tickles my back as I climb the stairs.

I carry her to my room and place her on the duvet. With her sleepy eyes, hair a bit messy, and the way she rocks out my shirt, I can't take my eyes from the beauty in my bed. My hand envelops her cheek and her skin is so soft. Leaning close, I slip my hand to the nape of her neck as I press my mouth against hers.

I want to tell her the way she makes me feel equally excites and terrifies me, that I never know what to expect with her. Every day is a new adventure and I love it. I want to tell her how beautiful she is and that she's made my world brighter and more vibrant than ever before. That I care deeper for her than I think I have for anyone. My heart beats so hard for her, I can physically feel it.

I don't tell her any of those things though. I just lay soft kisses on her neck as I unbutton her shirt. Her fingers pull my hair that is so far past the need of a haircut it's an entirely new style.

"Lex," she whispers. I remove my lips from her clavicle

to look at her face. She's sad. Her eyes are shining bright and rimmed with tears. "I…" She wants to talk to me, I can see it. Still, for some reason she's holding back. Her expression changes quickly, from anguish to compliance as she climbs back into her castle of secrets. "Will you lick me?"

That wasn't her intended statement, I know that, nonetheless it's an offer I can't refuse. I push the shirt open, bringing her beautiful breasts into view. Reaching into the dresser for the wand, I trace it over her fresh wound as I kiss, lick, and taste her. It doesn't take long before I hear her whisper, "I'm going to come." She nearly pulls my hair out as she sighs, "Lex."

"You're going to kill me with that voice."

Lying next to her, I lift her on top of me as I lift and lower her, pumping her on and off my cock. She leans forward to pick up the wand. She trails it along her arm, moaning all the while. I close my eyes as I get lost in the incredible feeling of her when all of a sudden, a sharp jolt of pain stabs my leg. I jump with her still on me.

She covers her mouth and tries, unsuccessfully, to not laugh. "So…no? You don't like the wand?"

"Oh you're gonna get it for that." I flip her around on her back, and turn that giggle into a moan as I slide right back in.

She's falling apart around me as my hand grips her small neck. She may not trust me with her secrets, but she trusts me with her life and those gasps for air are the proof that causes my adrenaline to pump and my come to flow.

# CHAPTER THIRTEEN
## Punish

**Saturday, May 30th**

I RETURN FROM GETTING COFFEE AND MUFFINS AT THE perfect moment to watch her doing her major production of the stretching she does every single morning, and it makes me laugh every time.

"Good morning." Her voice is somehow even sexier when she first wakes up. She gazes up at me and raises an eyebrow. "Don't give me that look, I at least get to drink the coffee you got me first."

"Well drink fast."

Her laugh brings out a smile that makes it impossible not to kiss her.

After sex, breakfast, and exercise we're on our way to take a shower when my cell rings with Sasha's number. I nod towards the restroom. "Go ahead and get in, I'll be there in a minute."

As soon as I answer, Sasha starts going off about how perfect Tavin's dress is for tonight.

"Yeah, yeah. Tavin's waiting for me in the shower. Be here around two-ish to do all the girlie shit."

I hang up and open the bathroom door to have steam blow over my face. I undress and climb through the curtain when my skin nearly melts off.

"Christ, Tavin!" I jump across the tub to get out of the water. "That's scalding!"

"Sorry, I just don't feel clean if it doesn't burn."

I push through the pain as the boiling stream hits my hand and I reach for the knob. She has the cold water nozzle turned completely off.

"I don't think that's good for you."

She laughs her dark laugh, that if I'm completely honest, can give me chills from time to time. "Yeah, worrying about what's good for me has always been my main priority."

I give her a dirty look. "Okay Miss Sarcasm, it's a priority now."

Since the water is no longer six thousand degrees, I slip inside of her and kiss her until there's no heat in the water at all.

We eat takeout sandwiches for lunch and watch 'Repo! The Genetic Opera' again. She's starting to mouth the words to the songs. Even if I'm really not sure why she is so obsessed with this movie, seeing her face light up every time is worth the repetitiveness.

Sasha arrives and takes Tavin to get her nails, hair, and makeup done while I go to my own appointment, making sure the stylist leaves some length so Tavin still has something to grip onto.

They are holed up in her room when I get home, so I shave and shower to get all the little hairs off of me. Once I'm dressed in the cream *Ravazzollo* suit I bought last month for the occasion, I do the last minute touch ups on my hair and head downstairs.

I glance at the clock on the stove and it's almost time to leave so I pour myself a shot while I wait. Their talking and laughter trails down the stairway as they come downstairs. I turn to tell them we need to get a move on, and suddenly my voice refuses to come.

The lilac gown Sasha made expertly fits every perfect curve of Tavin's body. The hem falls right above the floor and it has a low neckline with sheer straps that hug her shoulders. Her hair is loosely pinned up in curls and she has makeup on that enhances every one of her flawless features. She spins around and the back of the dress is even more breathtaking. It is cut low to her waist and technically open, however the hood that is currently down, dips across her back. When Sasha lifts her hood, I grin. She looks equally adorable and bad ass. I never would have guessed a hood on a gown could look so stunning. My eyes are glued to the visibility of her scars. If it doesn't bother her, it sure as hell doesn't bother me.

I hold her chin and kiss her before I finally find my voice. "You look incredible."

We walk hand in hand to the main hall of the event and she tilts her head in surprise. "There are a bunch of kids here."

"They are why we're here."

The event is centered around them so there's a bouncy house, games, and a movie playing in the next hall. The 'adult' section is off in a side room with alcohol and a quieter place to brush shoulders. The dance floor is toward the back of the room past all the tables.

Along with movie popcorn and the soda fountain, there is also a full candy buffet. She hasn't seen that yet. I take two glasses of champagne from a passing waiter and hand her one.

Silas and I see each other from across the room. He waves us over with the arm that the blonde woman isn't hanging off of. He keeps silent as his gaze travels down the length of her body. He's not being sleazy about it, but I still beyond loathe that he's seen her body.

I tell him we are going to check out the rest of the party, and we almost immediately bump into Eric. The way he looks down on Tavin is pissing me off to the point I'm about to say something. His face is disgusted as if he can barely stand to be around her while she refuses to acknowledge him. Her grip tightens around my hand as I forcibly greet him.

"Hi, Eric."

"Hello, Mr. Sørensen."

I grit my teeth. "And you know Tavin."

There is so much more I want to do than just fire this asshole and I have to stand here as if everything is fine. Not only did he pay to fuck my girlfriend, but he did it inside my building. Even if it wasn't Tavin, prostitution is illegal and I don't want anything like that associated with Vulture. I'm not going to lie though, I am curious how much he paid for her.

With tight lips, he nods to her and I am able to pull her away without a scene

She's been receiving compliments on her dress since we arrived and it makes her smile every time. Once we empty our second glass of champagne, I decide we should probably eat before we drink anymore.

On our way, she finally spots the candy buffet. There are about forty different types of candy. Jar after jar is filled with brightly colored treats, creating a rainbow effect. She bolts right toward it before I grab her wrist to lead her to the actual food.

"Real food first."

Sticking out her bottom lip, she bats her eyelashes, all dramatic. She's only playing around, and still that little pout just made the list for sexiest facial expressions ever.

As we finish our food, the music gets turned down while the president of SafeYouth takes the stage. She tells her story of being the child of an alcoholic and what it was like to have adult responsibility at such a young age.

It's about time for her to introduce me and I'm feeling a little shallow because I have never experienced anything remotely close to that. I have always had everything I ever needed or wanted. Nobody ever hurt me as a child and I have led a privileged life. I can't relate to these kids at all.

"Please give a warm round of applause for the man that made this night possible, Alexander Sørensen."

The entire room begins clapping as I whisper to Tav, "I'll be right back."

While I'm giving my speech, I notice our table is empty. My eyes flick over to the candy buffet, and I try not to grin. Of course she's going to town on a super rope.

Once I'm done, I head toward her to get her to ease up on the damn sugar. On my way, I get stopped by multiple people thanking me or talking about the cause in general. When I finally get to her, she holds out the rope to me and I take a bite. I lace my fingers in hers and lead her to the photo booth.

"Come on."

"What is this?"

"You've never seen a photo booth?" I pull her inside and onto my lap. "We're getting our picture taken."

I start the machine, and the first one is just of me smiling at her laughing with her hand over her mouth. There is one of her kissing my cheek, one with the big glasses prop, one with us touching the tips of our tongues together, and the final one where she spins around to straddle me, turning her face so I can see her smiling profile and the back of her dress. They are perfect and I slip both copies into my pocket.

I love how it feels to have her by my side through this stuff. My hand remains on her lower back as we mingle until eventually, she slips off to the bathroom.

Just as I finish talking to Mrs. Trove, who will probably be the one giving the largest donation of the evening, I feel a hand tugging my arm.

"Let's go dance."

"Hold on. I promise I'll dance with you later." She's looking at everything and everyone other than me. "There are people I still need to talk to... Hey, Tav, look at me." She turns her head toward me, yet refuses to make eye contact. Something is off. I grab her chin. "Look at me." She finally does and Goddamn it.

She's high.

"Are you fucking kidding me?"

I need something much harder than champagne. I turn away from her and march to the bar.

"I'm sorry! It was just a little coke." She holds up her dress as she tries to keep up with me.

"Where did you even get it?" I bark.

"A girl in the bathroom was doing a line; it was just right there. Then she asked me if I wanted any. I don't know why I did it, I know you don't like it, it's just- it's only coke!"

I suddenly want to get out of here, so I grab her hand. "We are leaving, now."

She pulls away from me. "Don't leave your party for me. I'll go." She looks so defeated.

How is it, every time she screws up, I end up being the asshole?

"Oh my God, fine. We'll stay, but I promise we will talk about this once we get back."

I really want to hit something. Why would she pull this? Nothing bad has happened, we were having a good night. She had absolutely no reason.

"I'm sorry, Lex. Ple—"

"I said we will fucking talk about it later!" I'm madder about this than the heroin. A few people glance our way and I force out an assuring smile.

She furrows her brows and throws herself against me. "Please. I have been getting high for so long it's just part of my life. I'm sorry! Can't you just punish me and we get past this? Please, I don't want to fight. I don't want to spend any time fighting."

I hear every word she said, though only two ring in my ears: *Punish me.*

Holding her wrist, I pull her to the candy buffet and grab another super rope. I take her into the elevator and hit the button for the next floor.

"Lex—"

"Don't."

When the doors open, it's to an office lobby. I lead her to the coffee table. "Bend over and place your hands flat on the glass."

She does what I say without question, causing my arousal to almost overtake my anger. I'm able to push it back though because this time, it's not about sex. It's about getting her to stop putting this poison into her perfect body. When I lift her gown above her waist, a breath expels from my mouth. Her legs look incredible in those champagne pumps. Her pussy is visibly wet when I remove her sheer panties. I caress her little ass before standing.

Silas hit me hard in the back with one of these once, and it left a mark that lasted around three days.

I leave the candy in the wrapper so it doesn't break when I put all my strength behind the first strike. A surprised squeal escapes her lips and even though I'm irate, that almost makes me smile. She gets so damn cocky about her pain tolerance; she wasn't prepared for the candy to sting that badly.

"How many times do I have to tell you I care about you? I don't get pissed because I'm trying to be a jerk. I get pissed because you could die from it, Tav. You already almost have!" I hit her again. "I don't know what your life entails because you still don't trust me, but I do know that you need to make the effort to not get high at every Goddamn opportunity!" I hit her six times in a row causing a nice red glow and a few whimpers to escape. My body relaxes as I calm down. "Why did you do it? What happened?"

"You just don't get it, nothing happened Alexander. I. Am. An. Addict. I want to get high because I want to get high. It was right there for the taking, I didn't go looking for it. I messed up. I wish I wouldn't have done it, and that right there is something, because I have never regretted a high before you. This won't be my last mistake though, I promise you that."

I kneel next to her as I pull up her panties. "You're right. I don't get it and I'm going to need a little more information real soon. We've been doing this for almost three weeks now. I still feel as if I don't know hardly anything about you and what I do know is all filed under 'what-the-fuck.'" I lower her dress. "Now stand up and let's go back to the party."

She smooths herself out and blows her bangs out of her face. "Do I get the rope?" She points to the candy.

I laugh and roll my eyes as I hand it to her. "Here. Jesus Christ."

Keeping my promise to dance with her, I lead her into the middle of the floor. Watching her dance will always bring a smile to my face and it's clearly an outlet for her. I love that I can touch her without restriction, letting my hands fall to her waist, arms, hips, ass, neck, and wherever the hell else I want. I pull up her hood and since I'm already semi-hard from 'punishing' her, that's all it takes to get my cocks attention. That dress is definitely not coming off. She's keeping that thing on when I fuck her.

Around three, we are pretty trashed and she's returning from yet another trip to the damn candy buffet, sucking on a lollipop.

"Remember this?"

"I don't see myself forgetting."

She comes closer and lowers her voice. "I love that you did that. I kind of have a… thing for candy."

The way she says it is kind of weird, I'm just too drunk to worry about it.

"Oh yeah? I hadn't noticed." I laugh into her hair as I wrap my hand around her waist and lead her to the car I called.

She tortures me the entire way home. She's wasted, so her inhibitions have high tailed it. She's trying to slut it up, sucking the candy with exaggerated licks and moans. That isn't what makes me about to jizz myself though, it's that she can't do it without cracking herself up every five seconds. She has her hood still on, and one knee up in the seat causing her dress to hike up, showing me her sheer panties.

When we walk in the front door, I smack her ass. "Go up to my room, I'll be up in a minute." Her dimple appears with her smile and I add, "And leave the dress on." She laughs as she kicks off her heels and bounds up the stairs. I pour us each a shot before following her.

When I cross the threshold to my room, she's holding the phone I got her in my direction.

She bites her lip and smiles. "Let's make a movie." I'm pretty sure she's already filming. My eyebrows rise as I hand her the shot. My own porn of her? Yes and hell yes. She hands me her empty glass and I throw back my own. Her fingers caress my collar as she focuses on the phone screen. "Undo your shirt, but leave it on so I can see your abs."

Fucking little tart, she gets so bossy and bold when she drinks and I adore it. I already took my jacket off downstairs, so I start on the buttons and smirk.

"So are you the director of our little flick?"

"Yup."

Grabbing the phone, I flash her a smile. "Then I'm the videographer."

I turn it so she's in frame. Her hood has come down at some point so she smirks, pulls it back up and drops to her knees. Looking up at me through the camera, she undoes my pants, taking her time pulling me out. She flicks the head with the tip of her tongue before giving it a little kiss and taking me all the way in her mouth. The way she pulls off looking innocent with a cock in her mouth is almost too much.

"I love...how good you are at this."

I almost said it, I almost told her that I loved her. Thank God I recovered quickly. That would have been romantic, telling her she owns my heart while she's swallowing my dick. She likes hearing it though because she sucks harder and with more aggression. It drives me crazy sometimes how quickly she can make me come. She brings me to my knees and I melt at the sight of her.

"Okay, that's enough. I want to come in your pussy not your mouth."

She stands up and looks into the camera doing a faux pout. "Oh, dang. I wanted your cock in my ass."

When she says that vulgar shit in her sweet little voice, I just want to tear her apart.

I groan, "Go get on the bed on all fours, take off your panties, and lift that sexy-ass dress." She does what I ask and I let the camera get a good view before handing it back to her. "Come in my mouth, Tav. I want that on video."

I slide my head between her legs as she sits up straight

to look down at me. She bites her lip and focuses the camera as she rides my tongue. She's so wet she's dripping down my cheeks as I lap up as much as I can. I force three fingers inside and push them as deep as they will go as she tightens around them. Her moans are a little louder tonight as she pumps her hips down on my mouth. I lay her onto her back before spreading her legs and running my tongue across her slit. Since she can't come without something 'extra' I can eat her for as long as I want before getting her off, and I'm enjoying myself by doing just that.

"Can you reach the drawer in the nightstand?" I ask.

Reaching behind her, she is nowhere close so she grunts in frustration, "Argh. No."

I laugh into her pussy before I stand to get what I want. I hold it up to show her. "A pinwheel."

It's a small chrome handle with a spiked wheel to roll along the skin just as the name suggests. I push the spikes into her leg as hard as I can without breaking skin and roll it down her thigh while I continue licking her clit. She angles the camera above my mouth and she watches. I press harder onto the pinwheel until I feel the skin break. Now she's quiet as a mouse as she rocks little thrusts against my face.

When she finishes and I taste her fill my mouth, I yank away the camera and turn it so it's back on her. She does a little wave and I press my mouth forcefully against hers, momentarily forgetting the video. Sitting up, I prop the phone against the lamp so neither of us have to hold it.

"I want to watch you fuck me."

I roll onto my back and lift her on top of me. Her dress is hiked up to her waist, the hood is still on, and her face is flushed while her scent of arousal infiltrates my senses. She settles over me, sliding herself down and moves her hips in fluid steady motion to start as she quickly picks up speed. I trail my fingers over the exposed skin of her neckline which is cut so low, it almost shows her brand. I am glad it doesn't, I'm oddly protective of people seeing it. Maybe because she made me wait so long before I got to. I bite the crook of her neck and bury myself into the girl I finally can admit that I have fallen crazy, insanely, and terribly in love with.

# CHAPTER FOURTEEN
## Blind Mag

*Sunday, May 31st*

"CAN I INVITE SASHA OVER TO GO SWIMMING?" I look up from my computer to see Tavin standing in my office doorway in her swimsuit. Well, I'm definitely not giving her a reason to take that off.

"Sure I'll be done in about an hour and I'll grill us some steaks."

Once I finish up my work I go out to the pool to find Sasha, Drew, and Tavin splashing in the water. Of course Sasha brought Drew.

I greet them before I pull out the steaks to throw on the grill. As Drew and I drink our beers and make forced conversation, Sasha and Tavin race across the pool.

"Having a pool party without me?" I look up to see Silas walking out onto the patio.

"Hey, what are you doing here?"

He walks over to the cooler and takes out a beer before popping off the top and helping himself. "I was going to see if you felt up to taking out the yacht." He points to the pool house. "You still have my extra suit in there?"

I nod to him and he disappears inside. The next thing I

know, he's running across the pavement and plunging into the pool, causing a huge splash.

Sasha squeals and covers her face. "Watch it, dick."

Tavin's little laughs are making me grin and I love seeing her so happy. After we eat, I join them in racing across the pool and glare at both Silas and Drew when I catch them staring at her brand. I will never ask her to cover it, I just hate it being out on parade.

Swimming to the ladder, I call over my shoulder, "I'm grabbing a beer."

I pop open the cooler when my phone pings with a text from my mom.

**Your father still hasn't moved his things. I need help packing. Will you come over?**

I hate that she's going through this and I want to help her. I don't have any idea what excuse I'm going to use though. I don't want to lie to Tavin, I just hate imagining what her reaction would be if she found out what was going on.

**Of course. I'll be there soon.**

I hit send as Silas jogs past me to the pool house. "Need to pee."

"Hey, hold on."

I follow him inside and he snorts, "You're spending way too much time around women. I don't need a bathroom-buddy, dude."

I sigh and spill, "Okay, long story short: Tavin and my dad had sex so my parents are getting a divorce, but I don't want Tavin to know that and I need to help my mom pack my dad's shit. So when I say we have work to do at the office, don't blow my cover, okay?"

His mouth is in a perfect circle making a face that's pretty priceless. "Wh-what?!"

I rush out the short version of the whole story. Regardless of his shock, he easily goes along with what I say and for that I'm grateful.

"Hey, we need to run into the office for a bit." I tell them as we walk out to the pool. I look to Sasha. "You and Drew can stay as long as you want."

Tavin swims to the edge and kisses me goodbye and Silas follows me back into the house.

"Do you want some help at your mom's?" he offers.

I can always count on Silas.

His help probably cuts the time I would have spent, in half. It's after eight before I get back home and once I'm in the door, I call for Tavin getting silence as an answer. I climb the stairs and peek into her empty room.

"Tavin?" I call down the hall as I pull out my cell. My phone is flashing with a notification. She already sent me one over an hour ago and I somehow missed it.

**Hey, I'm going to hang out with Toben. Don't wait up.**

Don't wait up? Who does she think I am?

I push the button to call her and as the ring sounds in my ear, muffled music plays behind me. I follow the music back into her room and it's coming from her bed. When I move around the sheets I find her phone beneath them. I roll my eyes and pick it up. What is the point in a cell phone, besides making smutty movies, if she isn't going to carry the thing?

My skin is sticky from sweat, so I peel my shirt off as I head to the shower. She is crazy as hell if she thinks I'm just going to let her spend her whole night with her incredibly touchy, junkie, male best friend without any way to get a hold of her.

After my shower, I dry off and I toss on my jeans and gray Nirvana shirt before jumping back into the Alfa. I turn up the music to slow down the pounding in my chest even though it's futile. The closer I get to her house, the more anxious I become. My fingers keep tapping the steering wheel and I wish this stupid light would turn green. She shot up the last time she was with him and I honestly don't know what I'm going to do if she's high again.

As I turn onto her street, cars are lined up along both sides of the road. Her driveway is packed and so is any free space around her property, so I have to park a few houses down. Apparently they're throwing a house party. She left out that little tidbit.

I can hear Die Antwoord before I am even up the steps. I'm definitely nervous about what I will see behind the door, considering what has been behind it on previous visits to this creepy-ass house. I knock, though I'm guessing nobody hears it, so I let myself inside.

There are probably thirty to forty people spread throughout the long living room, people ranging in age from early twenties to mid-thirties. The first thing I see is the coffee table littered in pills, beer, lighters, weed, and an array of trays and powders. I look to the back of the room to the dining room table that currently has a topless girl across it, getting drugs snorted off her stomach. There's a couple in the back corner dancing, though if her hiked up skirt is any indication, they're doing more than that.

I finally spot Tav sitting on the floor with a group of people in front of the couch. She's in-between Toben's legs, smoking a joint and laughing with the blond boy that I recognize as the third kid in the pictures on her fridge. She leans forward, crawling on all fours toward him, and I think for a second she is going to kiss him. Instead, she shot guns the hit into his mouth as Toben stares at her ass.

I really don't like that kid.

Releasing my clenching fists at the fact that she's obviously not high on heroin, I wade through the people to walk toward her. She sits back as the blond boy picks up yet another tray off the floor with lines already cut and holds out a rolled up bill.

Her shoulders slump as she rests her hand on Toben's knee. "Christopher," she sighs.

The boy named Christopher urges the tray toward her. "I haven't seen you take as much as a bump since I've been here. Catch your crazy-ass up."

She leans forward and I think she's going to take it, when her hand stops right before Toben looks up and sees me.

"Um Tav..." He taps her shoulder.

"Hold on." Her attention is focused on the tray of coke. "Uh...well..."

Christopher frowns at Tavin, in confusion. "What's your deal? Are you gonna take the blow or what?"

Toben raises his voice to get her attention. "Tavin. Y—"

Her hand flies out to silence him. "I said hold on! Give me a second." She's stressing this. It shouldn't be this difficult. "I can't believe I'm saying this..." She shakes her head. "No, I'm good."

Toben yells at her as he grabs her arm. "Tavin!"

"God, what?!" She snaps. He points to me to guide her gaze. She takes another pull off the joint as she sees me and her eyes go wide as she shoves the weed behind her back. She lets out a huge breath of smoke and closes her eyes when she mutters, "Crap."

Honestly, I could care less about pot, but she doesn't know that. I stare her down, having fun messing with her. Stepping in front of her, I sit to face her on the floor.

"Okay, Lex, before you say anything, it's just pot. I mean it's basically legal, a lot of people say it's safer than alcohol and you let me drink all the time."

She's really trying to save her ass here. I glare at her, reach behind her and grab the joint out of her hand. I take a long pull and her reaction is hilarious. It goes from a jaw drop, to stunned, to a full on smile.

Christopher snorts, "He 'lets' you drink?" His gaze flips to Toben when he points to me. "Is she dating this douche?"

Tavin glares at him. "Christopher! Be nice."

He can think I'm a douche all day long, I couldn't care less. It's her quick defensiveness of me that makes my heart flip. Toben just shakes his head as he lights a cigarette, as if the whole thing is too ridiculous for words.

"That's why you wouldn't do the coke? Or the meth?" This Christopher kid is testing my patience too. She didn't do it though. I feel so proud of her. I don't care if she parties and smokes a little pot, it's the hardcore drugs that are dangerous and unacceptable. So no, as long as we are together, I won't allow it. He shakes his head at her. "What the shit, Tav? You never date. I literally haven't seen you with a guy since you broke up with doom and gloom over there." Toben takes a drag and flips him off. So they had been more than friends at some point. Tavin's eyes are wide in a death stare while he ignores her and adds, "And you're just going to completely change for a guy you've known for how long?"

He is talking about me as if I'm not here and that…well that pisses me off.

"I found her overdosing in almost the exact spot you're sitting. So yeah, maybe I am a bit of a 'douche' when it comes to hard drugs."

Concern drapes over his face as his head whips to Tavin and Toben. "Is that true?"

I didn't realize how strung out Toben is until now. I'm pretty sure he would be a lot more involved in this conversation otherwise. He just takes a drag and nods along with Tavin. I pass him the joint and call her to me with a jerk of my head. She smiles and crawls out of his arms and into mine, where she should be. The look on Toben's face, even trashed, is a furious one. I just knew he was her ex.

"Christopher, kitchen," he snaps.

I wait until they are out of earshot to not embarrass her further. "You left your phone."

"I texted you first."

"Tavin, the point in the phone is to talk to you whenever I want."

She bites her nail. "Sooo, wanna beer?"

"Nice subject change." I roll my eyes and laugh, "Yes, get me a damn beer."

After a few bong loads, a blunt, six beers, and a couple of vodka shots, I'm just as faded as Tavin. Toben and Christopher get over their issue with me enough for us all to have a good time and it's fun to see her in her element. I've met quite a few colorful people tonight.

Currently, we're talking to Shay Shay, apparently a transvestite hooker.

"And I tol' that busta, nuh uh, no way, Shay Shay don't play that way."

Tavin thinks that's pretty funny, though truthfully, I'm not exactly sure what she's talking about. I got lost around the mention of anal fisting.

Pulling out my phone, I look at the time as Tavin jumps back in my lap. "I'm having fun."

I kiss her forehead. "So am I, but I have to work in the morning and it's getting late." I move my lips to her temple. "You can stay if you want, though I would prefer it if you came back with me."

She nods and smiles. "Okay. Let me say bye to Christopher and Toben."

Finding them quickly enough, she also stops to talk to a few people before following me out to my car. We grab some fast food on the way home, and she helps me carry it up to her room. We set it all out on the bed and I grimace at her drowning her fries in ketchup.

Popping a fry in my mouth I ask, "How long were you and Toben dating?"

She shakes her head and rolls her eyes. "Dumb Christopher." She groans dramatically, "I don't know when it started exactly. It was gradual. It just happened. I guess we were always kind of together. God, I don't know Lex. I suppose you could say we 'broke up', but it wasn't really like that. There was a…shift in our relationship and that happened when we were around eighteen so it's been five years I guess."

"And you're telling me that you never slept with a guy that you have basically dated your whole life, yet you slept with me right after we met?"

I hear a little choke and she looks as though I hit her, and not in a good way.

"Sometimes I forget how little you know me. You have no clue what I am."

I wipe the grease and salt from my fingers with a napkin. "It's *who* not what and whose fucking fault is that? I'm trying here, but you can't logically get mad at me for not knowing something about you when you refuse to tell me anything. It's maddening."

She drops her burger onto the wrapper and murmurs, "I don't know what I'm doing."

I hate the sound of defeat in her voice especially when I don't understand why it's there. My fingers squeeze the bridge of my nose because at this point I feel as if I'm going into these conversations blind.

"Can't you just tell me what you need? I will literally do anything, *Lille*."

She smiles a sad smile. "See, that's the thing about you, you're a genuinely sweet, good person. I am a bad person. You deserve so much more than me, Alexander."

"I'm so fucking tired of you saying shit like that." The

whipping actually worked with the drugs, maybe it will work for this too. "Get up and take off your jeans." She tilts her head and immediately obeys.

I watch as she stands in her purple bikini cut panties and t-shirt. Jesus, this is almost more torturous for me than her. As much as I want to rip her up right now, she would enjoy that too much and then it wouldn't be much of a punishment now would it?

I get off the bed and point behind her. "Place your hands flat on the nightstand and spread your legs." She does it as I slide the belt through the loops and stand directly behind her perfect body. Her ass is nearly begging to be hit. "I want you to stop talking about yourself like you're shit." I fold the belt in half and swing it against her ass. "You're not any of those things and I don't want to hear it anymore. You're mine, and nobody talks about who's mine that way. Not even you. You are part of who I am now, and I'll never be the same now that you've turned my life into…this." Her shoulders are shaking as I hit her twice more. "You've brought back the beauty and color that's been gone since I was a kid. I feel things with you I've never felt ever before, about anyone." I'm getting emotional and with her beautiful bright red skin I can't stop myself. I drop the belt and rip open my jeans.

"I care about you so much, Tav." I yank the panties over her ass before I slide into her.

*And I think I love you.*

### Monday, June 1st

Mr. Franklin's bald head shines with sweat as we ride the elevator back to my office. We've had our lunch, so now it's time to delve into numbers. If he invests the money he's talking about, Vulture has a very lucrative future. To be frank, I'm kissing major ass right now.

We walk across the lobby and I unlock my office door just to be shocked frozen as I stare at the scene before me.

Tavin is atop my desk wearing nothing other than panties and stockings, kneeling with her hands on her thighs. She looks up at me with a sexy as sin smile on her face. When her gaze flicks to Mr. Franklin, she startles herself so badly, she falls backwards off my desk.

"Crap," she squeaks.

And now I'm fucked.

I sigh as I move to help her up and put some clothes on her ass so I might be able to salvage this fiasco. Just as I am, Mr. Franklin passes by me and beats me to it.

Kneeling down, he offers her his hand. "Are you alright?"

She looks up at him and places her hand in his as she stands with a flush across her face. "Uh, yeah…um, I'm sorry." Her head jerks over to me as she looks at me apologetically.

Mr. Franklin is staring at either her tits or her brand and either way, she barely seems fazed. She's not even attempting to cover herself.

"No need to apologize, this was…amusing."

Okay time to break this up. I need his investment and if he keeps looking at her that way I'm going to slam his head against my desk. I snatch her dress off the floor and grab her arm to pull her closer to me and get her into the bathroom.

Smiling at him the whole time, I hold up a finger gesturing for a second to get her out of here. Why today of all days did she decide to show up naked in my office? Any other day would have been perfect, literally any other day. I have fantasized about that even, her sucking my dick under my desk while I'm emailing or on a conference call. I never told her about the meeting so I'm not mad, I just hope she didn't screw this up for me.

She hauls ass and is out and dressed within seconds. I lead her out the door and mouth, *It's okay* before shutting it and discovering my fate.

"I sincerely apologize, sir. She wasn't aware of our meeting."

He actually laughs. "I said no need for an apology, son. That was the best sight I've seen in weeks."

There was never really a doubt in my mind that he would be on board, although, there was a second there where I was getting pretty damn nervous. It pisses me off, because if anything she helped the situation.

---

I climb the steps as I slip off my jacket and find Tavin in her room. She's standing next to her bed in underwear and a baby tee shaking her little ass to an Otep song, which is in no way, shape, or form a dance mix. My cheeks lift with my grin as I tackle her onto the bed. I think the sound of her little giggle fit is the most enchanting thing I've ever heard.

"It had to be today? I've been wanting to plow you on my desk for forever, and you pick today?" I huff.

She scrunches up her nose and I kiss it.

"How did it go?"

"Your little show entertained him, and honestly it helped more than it hurt. You do know I'm not a fan of people seeing you naked though, right? I appreciate the gesture, but damn, girl." She arches her back and laughs. "Hey, I've been meaning to tell you, I have to leave town for a couple of days. If I wasn't going to be working the whole time I would bring you with me."

Her face instantly makes one of the saddest expressions I've ever seen. It's as if I completely shattered her.

"You're leaving?!" Tears gush from her eyes as she sobs

and holds her arms across her chest.

"Whoa, what the hell? What's wrong? It's only for a couple of days."

"When will you be back?" She asks it as a plea and I feel like I broke her heart.

"Jesus, *Lille*, you need to chill. I'll be back Wednesday afternoon."

She composes herself a little and I run my hand through my hair. What the friggin' crap was that? I'm so confused, that isn't like her at all. She climbs up to straddle me and kisses up my neck while she undoes my jeans in a frenzy.

Something's definitely wrong.

I grab her wrists and flip her to her back against the mattress. "What is going on?"

God, she looks so broken. "I just…pass."

"Wow. Really? This has nothing to do with your past. This is about why you're so upset that I'm leaving. You can't 'pass' on the things involving us."

"My life…I don't know what's going to happen."

I feel a pang of fear and release her wrists. "What do you mean?"

She sits up, our noses almost touching. I can feel the little ragged wisps of breath against my lips when she barely whispers, "I *want* you inside of me, Lex. You can't know what that means." Her hand softly rubs my quickly responding cock over the fabric of my pants. "Please, let that be enough."

I'm at a loss. I don't know what to do because I don't know what's going on with her. Kissing me hard, she reaches into my pants. She shows me with her body what she can't say with her words. I just wish I knew exactly what that was.

**Tuesday, June 2nd**

Kissing down her neck and back, I whisper, "Goodbye, *Lille*," to her sleeping body before slipping out of her room and driving to the airport.

My plane lands ahead of schedule allowing me to arrive at the South Scottsdale Vulture location nearly an hour before I thought I would. Thank God, too, because it's the day that never ends on account of the moronic management team.

When I finally arrive at my hotel and get to my room, I fall into the bed and text Tav.

**Hi, Lille. Thinking about that tight little ass. What are you wearing?**

**Jean shorts and a green shirt.**

**You officially suck at sexting.**

**What's sexting?**

**Sex texting. I swear to God, how do you not know what sexting is?**

**How do I do it?**

**Tell me what you want me to do to you.**

**I want you to rip me apart until I'm bloody and full of your come.**

Good Lord.

**Get right to the damn point don't you? We really need to work on your build up, but I can work with that. Send me a pic.**

**Sweet dreams, Lex.**

**Sweet dreams, Tav. Seriously though, send pics.**

*Wednesday, June 3rd*

Pulling onto the interstate, on my way home from the airport, I push the 'call' button for Silas' number.

"Hey, are you back in town?"

"I just got in. Can you get me some pot?"

He snorts, "You still don't have a medical card?"

I can hear the definite sound of sucking.

"Obviously. Do you have any or not?"

"Yeah," he groans and whispers, "that's it, Angel," before telling me, "Head on over."

I hang up and take the north Shadoebox exit to his penthouse. He gives me a half and some papers and he's barely able to keep his hands off the girl he's with, so I'm thankfully able to get in and out.

I'm so excited to see her and the feeling must be mutual because as soon as I walk in my door, I'm instantly wrapped in legs, arms, and kisses.

"Hey, *Lille.*"

Her smile brightens her eyes as she blushes. "Hey, Lex."

She's in panties and an off the shoulder tee, so I can easily slip a finger inside while we make out and I carry her upstairs.

We have a couple days to make up for.

⟜

Her legs are crossed as she sits on my bed, pulling her shirt back on. I throw the baggie and papers in front of her and flash a smile.

"Wanna smoke?"

A huge grin lights up her face giving me the little dimple. "Seriously?"

I nod. "I've never been good with joints. You do it."

She's a pro. She has it ready and lit in a blink. She takes a long drag. "Mmmm, dang. This is good stuff."

"That's how I roll."

She snorts, "Yeah, I bet."

I swear, is she getting hotter?

Sitting next to her, I kiss her neck. "What did you do while I was gone?"

"I was with Tobe."

My body stiffens and her face goes soft as she squeezes my fingers holding her other hand up in a vow.

"I didn't get high I swear."

No blinking. Regardless that I hate she was with him, I feel so proud of her. Her soft hair is silky against my fingers while I kiss her.

We're halfway through our second joint and it's becoming almost impossible to not pounce on her again.

"You're giving me your horny look," she snickers.

"What can I say? Sunny missed you."

She scrunches her nose. "Who the heck is Sunny?"

I point to my dick. "Sunny."

She's gaping at me. "You're seriously one of those guys who names your junk? And you went with Sunny?"

"Yeah, Sunny D."

She loses it, falling back on the bed laughing so hard she's grabbing her stomach, which in turn, causes me to laugh at her laughing. I have no idea if it's actually that funny or if we're just really stoned, regardless, she looks stunning in her hysterics.

"I'll be back, I'm going to get shots." I blow her a kiss.

"What was that?"

"It was an air kiss, silly."

She raises her eyebrows. "An 'air kiss'? I'll have to remember that next time and give you an 'air blowjob.'"

It's my turn to bust out laughing. When I regain my composure, I push her so she's on her back and I climb on top of her. I'm high and the moment gets away from me.

"I love you."

I whisper it so quietly I would wonder if she heard me, if her facial expression didn't tell me otherwise.

Her face drains of every ounce of color as her eyes fill with tears.

She murmurs, "No, no, no you don't. You can't." She hugs herself as she shakes her head. I don't understand. This is more than her being overwhelmed. She's distraught. "I'm not what you love. I'm not what you think I am."

"And what is it *you* think you are? All those horrible things you say about yourself? None of those things are true, *Lille*. You're the only one who thinks that."

She just looks at me as her fingers comb through my hair and over my face. I slip back into her body and tell her all the things that make her special.

We've been lying here falling in and out of sleep so I don't know if it's a dream when I hear a teary whisper, "I'm so sorry, Lex, but you won't love me for long. Still, I… I think maybe I love you, too."

### Thursday, June 4th

Today is definitely a Marshmallow Mateys kind of day. Cara Jo hands me a bowl as Tavin waltzes into the kitchen all hot as hell in her little shorts and bed head. She grabs an apple, climbs up on the island, and starts sketching in one of the notepads I got her. I kiss her head and sit down to pour my cereal when I realize all of the marshmallows are gone.

"What the hell?" I keep looking into the bag as if they will suddenly appear.

Fucking Tavin. This has her name written all over it.

"What did you do to my Mateys, woman?" She tries to conceal her cheeky-ass grin behind her apple. The little shit. I get up and wrap my arms around her waist pulling her off the island while she laughs her ass off. "You never mess with a man's cereal," I growl.

I get her as far as the stairs before I start pulling her shorts down.

"I can still hear you two," Cara Jo calls from the kitchen and Tavin covers her mouth to quiet her laugh.

"Well I'm paying you to ignore it," I yell back with a grin.

Fifty grand says she rolls her eyes.

After work, I walk into the kitchen to find Cara Jo at the stove. She doesn't look up from her cooking as I peck her cheek. "Dinner will be ready in an hour."

"Great, I'm starving. How was your day? Where's Tav?"

She waves her hand toward the stairs. "The day was fine and I haven't seen her since she came down for a bowl a few hours ago."

"A bowl? What for?"

She shrugs. "I haven't the slightest. She's been holed up in her room the whole afternoon."

"Alright, thanks. We'll be back down in a bit."

I take off my jacket as I climb the stairs to find her door is closed. I lightly tap before pushing it open and she's crouching by the closet, obviously messing with something. Her eyes travel up to mine and she jumps about ten feet before closing the closet door and straitening to standing.

"Oh…hi."

Oh dear Jesus, what now? "Hi. What are you doing?"

"Nothing." Her eyelashes flutter away.

Why does she keep lying when she knows I can tell? I rub my forehead. "Tell me what you're doing with the closet, Tavin." I hear a little whining sound coming from inside and I glare at her. "What the hell is that?" She shuts her eyes and sighs. Opening the closet, I find a little tan and black dog sitting there, wagging away with its tail. The poor thing has a hairy, sunken in spot where the left eye should be.

I groan, "Tavin, I don't want a dog pissing in my closet."

Reaching down, I pick the fluffy thing up. It is pretty damn cute. I pull apart the hair on its neck looking for a collar.

"No! Don't kill her!" Tavin springs toward me as she screams.

"What the hell? I'm not going to fucking kill her! I'm just looking for a collar, Jesus." Her shoulders relax as my search becomes futile. "I don't see any identification. Where did you find her? We need to see if she has a chip so we can get her home."

"I saw her sniffing the bushes on the pathway and when I went outside, she came right to me. Besides, Blind Mag likes it here."

I throw back my head with another groan. "You named her?"

And that's what she picks? Blind Mag is her favorite character from 'Repo! The Genetic Opera', however the fact that the dog is actually missing an eye makes it a bit fucked up if you ask me.

"I have to call her something."

The damn dog licks my nose.

"We need to make sure her owners aren't looking for her."

"They let her eye get hurt, and let her get away. They must not care that much." She jerks her head and takes the dog away from me.

"Tavin, if she has a family, we need to find them."

"What if they're mean to her?"

I sigh and rub my forehead. "We have to try."

"So if she doesn't have a family, you will keep her?"

She has never really asked me for anything, so I just pray the dog has escaped from a loving owner's back yard.

"We will talk about that when we get to it."

I'm able to find a vet that is still open and he says the dog is a two year old Yorkshire terrier with no health problems, and of course no chip or anyone missing a dog matching her description.

Great. Looks like I just got a dog.

We make a trip to the pet store to get her a leash, food, a feeding station, shampoo, toys, treats, and even a tee shirt. Please tell me why a dog needs a shirt?

She's on cloud nine with this fuzz ball. She giggles at every lick or bark the creature makes. It's pathetic because I kind of get a little jealous of the thing. That's got to be some kind of new low: getting jealous of a *dog*.


### Friday, June 5th

I glare at Silas as he throws his head back; his laughter booms in my office.

"Damn. You're about pussy whipped to death. I'm a little embarrassed for you." He shakes his head. "You don't even like dogs."

I roll my eyes and pour a drink. "Yeah well, she's obsessed with the stupid thing."

He's still heckling me, the dick. "Have fun with that."

"Don't you have work to do?"

He pushes himself out of the chair and grins. "Yeah, I have a couple runs to make." He backs up toward the door. "Happy birthday by the way, Eric and I can hold down the fort if you want to head out early."

I swallow my drink and place down the empty glass. "And I will take you up on that. Call if you need me."

The traffic is much lighter this early in the day so I arrive home quickly. I pull into the garage, to find Tavin and Blind Mag both covered in paint splatter. Tavin is standing on a step-stool surrounded by five different colors of paint cans as she swipes a paintbrush across a bed sheet attached to the garage wall.

I feel a pang in my chest as I stare in awe. The illustration is extraordinary. One end is a barren forest with twisted and snarled trees, devoid of life or color. The closer it gets to the other side of the piece, the sparser it becomes. Eventually the forest spills over off the edge of the earth, gradually turning into what resembles outer space. There are lights and colors, swirls and designs all floating into an abyss. Amongst it all is a girl with no face. It's the most incredible thing I have ever seen and not just because of who the artist is.

"Wow," is all I can manage at the moment, for some reason it's choking me up. It stirs up dread and sorrow mixed with hope and I don't know why. It's only a painting.

Turning to me, she points inside of the house. "Cara Jo said I could."

That snaps me back and I laugh. "Wow, you ratted her out quick."

Jumping off the stool, she walks to me. "You can buy anything you want. So, I made you this for your birthday. Happy birthday!" She holds her arms out. "It's just a dumb painting and it's so big I don't know what you're going to do with it…maybe take a picture and just toss it? I guess I didn't think this through."

I bring her against me. I'm sure I just ruined my suit and I couldn't care less. "You're crazy if you think I'm throwing this away. It's getting framed and hung in the living room."

She breaks eye contact. "Now you're teasing me."

I take her chin. "No, I'm not. It truly is stunning." I kiss her. "I honestly do love it." And I love you. "Thank you."

After she and the dog get cleaned up, we eat dinner,

have birthday cake for dessert, and fuck in the pool for hours. It's easily my best birthday to date.

I found the lollipop girl and she is more than I could have ever dreamed.

# CHAPTER FIFTEEN
*lies*

**Saturday, June 6th**

*Tavin*

A S SOON AS I OPEN MY EYES, THE ACHE SETTLES IN
and a sharp pain stabs my stomach. This is my last
day with him. Ever. The tears flow no matter how
hard I try to stop them. Even though I knew this wouldn't
be easy, I had no idea it would hurt like this. Is he going to
feel this?

He looks every bit the Sun God he did the night of the
carnival. How did it turn into this? I want to touch his face,
his beautiful face. Why did I do this? Now I know what I'm
missing. Before I was wonderfully clueless, and now I have
tasted a normal life. The idea of going back makes me want
to vomit. I want to taste him as much as possible before I
leave. How am I going to tell him? I slip beneath the sheets
and he's already naked making it easy to put him into my
mouth. The semi hardness quickly turns to extreme hardness as I feel his large hands pull my hair into a pony tail before pushing down the sheets. When I match his green eyes,
I momentarily stop to smile. "I want to swallow your come."

His breathing hitches as his slow thrusting allows me to

give adequate suction. "That's it, *Lille*. Suck my cock."

*Lille*. I can't be her anymore. I savor the taste of him and beg my tongue to always remember. He moans as he pulls my hair and empties himself down my throat.

We get dressed and hold hands as we go downstairs to eat our cereal. It makes me feel good and sad that Cara Jo got me my own bag. I try to act normal when all I want is him inside me and to cry. He keeps giving me weird looks so I smile to give him a false sense of security for as long as I can.

We take a shower, and he goes to his room to get ready. I'm sliding on my underwear when my phone, *the* phone, starts ringing.

My heart falls to my toes. There's only one person who calls that phone. Christopher and Toben always text.

When I pick it up, my fears are confirmed. With a shaky hand I press the talk button.

"Hello, Logan."

His slow voice chills me to my core. "You have made a serious lapse in judgment, plaything."

Shit, shit, shit, shit!

"Yes, Logan."

"I will arrive in two hours. You better be on your fucking knees when I walk through that door."

"Yes, Logan."

Fuck. FUCK! What have I done? What if he finds out about Lex? I know Toben won't tell him, but he just knows things sometimes. He will hurt him. He doesn't care if he was aware of it or not, the fact is, Alexander stole from him. Why didn't I listen to Toben? I text him and he doesn't answer.

I'm going to get sick…

Barreling through the bathroom door, I make it to the toilet before the bile burns up my throat. I'm able to lock the door and get back before another wave hits me and I puke again. I haven't felt like this in years. I never know what

Logan will do. I always think he has done everything he can to me. Haven't I learned?

*It can always get worse.*

There is a knock on the door. "Tavin? Are you okay? Let me in."

"Please, Alexander, leave me alone for a while."

"Tavin—"

"Please!" I cry.

I hear him blow out a harsh breath. "I'll check on you later, okay?"

After a minute his footsteps walk away. I look in the mirror at the filthy, selfish, whore that has uprooted such a good man's life. All he did is try to help me and I'm about to throw it in his face. I hate the girl in the mirror. She's dirty and evil. She's nothing. She's less than nothing! Fuck! I hit the selfish cunt in the face causing my hand to bleed from the shattered glass. I unlock the door to run across the hall and rip a piece of paper from my notebook.

*Alexander,*

*I can't do this anymore. You don't love me. I know you think you do, but you don't. You have no idea what I am. I don't want this. I don't want you.*

The tears hit the paper, smearing the blood from my fingers as I scribble the worst lies I have ever told.

*DO NOT come looking for me. I want you to LEAVE ME ALONE. This was fun. That's all it could ever be.*

*Goodbye, Lex. For what it's worth, I do hope you find happiness.*

*Tavin.*

I leave the note on the dresser. How am I going to get out of here? He's probably in the kitchen so I don't have much time. Grabbing the credit card he gave me, I look to the window. It's my only option. I push on it and I'm able to lift it. This is it.

Tears pour down my cheeks as I turn back to see the place that has made my dreams come true. It's so hard to force myself to push off the window screen. I don't want to leave this life. I don't want to leave him. For a moment I entertain the fantasy of running to him and telling him everything.

*Then he'll see what you really are: a filthy, broken, used up toy.*

I shake away that ridiculous thought. The only thing that would do is put all of us in more danger than we're already in.

Time is up.

I hang my head over the sill and it's far down, but I bet I can make it. I don't have a choice. I climb up on the window seat and throw my legs over the sill and look over my shoulder.

"Goodbye, Lex. Thank you," I whisper.

I flip my body around and lower myself as far as I can before I let go.

Pain shoots up my leg and I bite my tongue to keep in the scream. I think I twisted my ankle because I have to limp as I make my way to the fence. Climbing it is difficult and when I get over the top, I make the mistake of letting go and fall on my back. The oxygen is thrown from my chest as I gasp for air. I give myself a moment to regain my breath before I hurry as fast as I'm able to the end of his street.

I yank out my phone and call a cab. As I wait, my gaze keeps traveling down the street to his house.

The cabby doesn't take long, yet the ride is the longest of

my life. I can't believe I'll never look into those bright emerald eyes again. I'll never feel his touch, or smell his sunshine scent. The burning tears pour down relentlessly and I cannot get to the needle fast enough.

Finally, the driver pulls in front of my house and I hand him Lex's credit card. Storming through the front door, I rip out the kit from below the table. Thank God there's some left. I don't even follow Logan's rules of cleaning the surface and washing my hands. I just sprinkle the white powder into the spoon and add the water. I cook it until it bubbles and throw in the cotton. When the syringe is full, I'm shaking as I tie myself off and find a vein. The prick of the needle sliding in and the appearance of blood sends a chill through my body as I untie the tourniquet.

Down goes the plunger...

*BURST!*

*SWOOSH!*

*I am empty...*

*I am free...*

*I am...*

"LOTUS!"

His voice chokes me even through the high. He's back... Logan... His form leans over me as his angry golden eyes burn into my soul... *SMACK!* That was my face... He never hits my face...

"You think this is going to save you?" He throws the empty syringe at me. "Oh, no, plaything. You cannot fathom the pain coming for you." There's a pressure against my scalp as he yanks me by my hair and smashes my cheek against the scratchy couch cushion. Something wraps around my throat...I can barely breathe... "Once you come down and Toben gets back, we are going to play as we have never played before. That's a promise my little Lotus."

The fabric of my dress hits my shoulders as numbed

bursts of pain spread across my back. Is he hitting me? How long has he been here?

I know the moment he fills me and I grasp for something to hold on to as I give him what's his.

"I'm sorry, Logan…" I cry against the couch.

"Oh, I'll make sure of it, my plaything." He grunts as he takes me, his belt causing my back to pulse with every strike. I push my body against his, thrusting myself as hard as I can.

Dull throbbing runs through my flesh as he hits me again. All my access to air is removed when he wraps something around my neck, tightening with each thrust.

A banging noise forces my eyes open. No matter how hard I try they won't stay closed… Toben? Through slits I see him, and my heart bulges at the seams. It isn't Tobe, It's… Lex.

# Alexander

Light shines into the hallway from the open bathroom door and I follow it to see if she's feeling better. I stick my head inside and she isn't there. My eyes find the bloody, shattered mirror as a queasiness settles in my belly.

Shit. She hurt herself.

"Tavin!"

I call for her as I rush to her room which I also find empty. A fluttering sound draws my attention to the dresser where a bloodied piece of paper flounces across the surface. The breeze blows through the room and I look to find the window open. She actually left out the fucking window. It's not exactly a small drop so I rush over to make sure she isn't lying on the ground with a broken leg, but nothing is there besides the window screen.

I walk back towards the dresser to pick up the piece of paper and the words don't make sense. What the hell happened? She's been off all day. She didn't even touch her leftover birthday cake at breakfast and now she suddenly doesn't want anything to do with me? Does she seriously believe that I'm going to just buy this bullshit note? If she's going to tell me all this, it will be to my face.

I pull out my cell as I run down the hall and call her phone. I hear the music coming from back in her room as I sprint down the stairs to the garage. There's only one place I know of that she would go. My tires screech as I reverse and spin out of my garage and into the street.

I press the button on my dash to call Sasha's number as I slam on the gas and weave in and out of traffic. Her voice fills the car before I cut her off.

"Hey, Alex. What's u—"

"Has Tavin gotten a hold of you?"

"No, why? What's going on?" The annoying tapping of a sewing machine is in the background.

"I have no idea. Keep your phone on and if you hear from her, call me immediately, okay?" I hate how desperate my voice sounds.

"Uh sure... Is everything okay?"

I sigh as I pass the slow-ass in an SUV. "I have no fuck-ing idea."

"Well let me know when you do, alright?"

I hang up without a response as I take the exit. I just know I'm going to find her high. I can feel it. My biggest fear is her overdosing again and I'm too late. My heart slams against my rib cage so hard I feel it in my fingertips.

Pulling in front of her house, I barely allow the engine to turn off before I jump out and sprint across her lawn. Taking the porch steps two at a time, I arrive at her ajar door. I fling it open and burst into her living room only to have my heart ripped from my chest.

Tavin's face is pressed against the couch and she's on all fours as she rocks her body onto the cock of a man around my dad's age. Small noises slip from her lips as she fucks him and he tugs on the belt wrapped around her neck. She takes his every thrust as time seems to collide upon itself.

I look at her face and her eyes stare through me as if she doesn't see me. The yellowish liquid pooled in the bottom of a bent spoon summons my attention from the coffee table before it switches back to the man inside of my girlfriend.

I respond without a thought. My body reacts of its own accord and I'm simply along for the ride. Suddenly my fists crash against his jaw just as his eyes widen in shock. He must have been too focused on fucking to notice me. Well, he knows I'm here now.

A dam breaks internally because I don't stop my assault until he's completely passed out. My clenched fist hits his jaw, his temple, his nose. His consciousness has been long gone when my eyes travel to his forearm. A tattoo of the exact replica of her brand is ingrained in his flesh.

Is this Logan?

Jumping away from him, my gaze switches from his unconscious body to her drugged up one. Her lip is busted and she has lowered her body so she's lying on her stomach with her arm draping over the edge of the sofa.

It pisses me off that I have to force back tears. I feel like I'm going to vomit when I crouch down in front of her. Her eyes land on mine for a moment before staring behind me.

"How could you do this to me?" I choke on the syllables as if they are cotton in my throat.

She mumbles words I can't understand. I can't leave her here and she's going to give me some motherfucking answers.

Picking her up, I storm out of the worst house on the face of the planet and carry her to my car before placing her in the seat.

My fingers yank through my hair and I suddenly feel so hot. My skin is physically burning. I can feel the blood pumping behind my eyes and I drag my hands over my face. Yanking open the car door I get inside and slam it behind me. I'm not done hitting things so I smack my hand against the steering wheel.

"FUCK! Fuck, fuck, fuck!"

How am I going to forgive this? She has to have an explanation, a reason, she has to. I look over at her slumped in the seat as I force back a sob and retrieve my phone to call Sasha. I tell her to get over to my house and hang up before she can respond.

There is a storm of thoughts and emotions swirling around at the moment and I can't pick one to grasp on to. I'm furious that I allowed myself to fall for another girl who deceived and betrayed me. I can't believe that it really just happened, regardless of the image being burned into my retinas, and I'm truly saddened at the loss of what we had. I know that there's no coming back from this, even with the little part of me that prays for a missing piece that will cause all of this to make sense.

She shifts and mumbles as I drive us back to my house. Other than the occasional word, she's unresponsive.

Sasha's car is parked in front of my house when I arrive. Dragging Tavin from the passenger's seat, I lift her from the car and take her into the house. Sasha is standing in the kitchen holding Blind Mag as I carry Tavin across the main floor to the stairs.

"What happened?" She urges behind me.

I can't even begin to say the words aloud at this point, so I say nothing and take Tavin upstairs to her room.

Her room.

She's still coming in and out of it when I lay her on the bed. Sasha stands behind me in the door frame with her arms crossed as I turn to go downstairs for a drink. Or ten.

"Is she okay?"

"She's fucked up. Don't you junkies recognize your own highs?" I bite out.

Her eyes narrow and she straightens her posture. "You're hurting, I can see that, but you better check how you talk to me, brother." I walk past her into the hallway and she follows me back downstairs and into the kitchen as I pull down a glass from the cabinet. "You're clearly way past pissed, I don't know if you should be drinking before you talk to her."

The look I give her must accurately convey how I'm feeling because she shuts her mouth real quick. I grab the bottle to take with me.

"Stay down here with the dog until I come back," I call over my shoulder as I go back upstairs.

Sitting in the chair next to the bed, I wait for her to wake up. It doesn't take long. When she sits up and her eyes adjust to her surroundings, her face falls as she recognizes where she is. Our eyes meet and it's apparent she's still high. Looking away quickly, she pokes at the bed sheet.

"Are you able to hold a conversation?" I bark at her.

She swallows and nods. "Y-yes."

"Who did I just watch you fuck?"

She takes forever to answer and when she does, it's a motherfucking lie. I don't even need to see her eyelashes moving to know that.

"He was just a Clien—"

"DO NOT FUCKING LIE TO ME!" My voice booms in my own ears. She jumps a little, though mostly she just sits there looking hollow. "Why? How could you do this? I've tried to give you another option. A way out, and you still chose that life over me." The desperation in my voice makes me feel weak. I am pleading with her to give me something, anything, and she refuses. She doesn't want redemption. "Talk to me!"

A small shake of her head is her only response. I have tried my best to let her know she can trust me and it's fallen on deaf ears. Was this all a game? Was she toying with me this whole time? I don't know because she refuses to let me in. I give her one last chance.

"Please, Tavin."

Nothing.

I scoff at my own stupidity. I'm not doing this anymore. This is over.

We are over.

"You know what? Fuck this, I'm done." I back away from her. "I thought the most pathetic thing about all of this was that I fell in love with you, but the truly tragic part is that I was delusional enough to actually believe you loved me too."

"I d—"

"Don't you dare, don't you fucking dare say that you love me." I grab my bottle and before I walk out, I turn back to her. "I want you gone."

Allowing my anger to consume my tears, I stomp down the stairs and nearly run into Sasha. I hold up my hand to cut her off before she can ask any questions.

"I want her and her shit out of my house." I down a large drink from the bottle and slam it on the island.

"What happened?!" She yells at my back.

I turn and storm toward her, causing her to take a few steps back. "She fucked someone else, Sasha! She doesn't want help and she doesn't want me. Get her out of my life before I get back. Got it?!"

She goes somber and nods her understanding. I yank up my keys before slamming the door to the garage, behind me.

I don't deal well with emotional anguish. The only thing I know that will help is getting so wasted I don't remember. I think about getting some pussy so Tavin isn't the last thing on my dick, but dismiss it immediately. Sex is the very last thing I want right now.

I don't want to tear the wound deeper by going to The Necco Room, so I choose the first bar I see.

Keeping track is never a thought as I down one after the other. I'm pretty positive the man I saw her with was Logan. I just have no idea who he is other than, most likely, her pimp. The matching tattoo though, that's weird. She doesn't trust me or have the respect for me to give me an explanation, so I'm going to get my own answers. I need to know what happened if I ever have a chance of moving on. She's ingrained herself so deep into my skin that it physically feels as if she's been cut out. I can't believe how easily I let her play me. How much of it was even real? I don't even know who she is and I think I love her? What really pisses me off is I still feel it, I still want there to be a reason. I still want to hope.

Finishing my last drink, I slam some money on the counter and stumble outside.

I should have expected something like this. She's all over the place. There's no order, no patterns. She's hectic and wild, unpredictable and extreme. She's sweet, like antifreeze. She's darkness hidden behind a rainbow, secrets and sex, chaos in a candy coating.

You can't throw a rock without hitting a P.I. office in Shadoebox City and it just so happens that's exactly what I'm looking for. I need someone to help me figure out her story and confirm what her relationship with Logan is. I need to know why she started whoring herself out to married businessmen at fifteen and why she doesn't exist as far as the government is concerned. I need to know why she would do this to me.

I'm only required to walk a few blocks before the blue letters shine like a beacon.

**William Morrison, Private Investigator**

A strand of bells *jingles* as I push open the door. I get a murder-mystery vibe at the way the middle aged, dark haired man sits at a worn, wooden desk at the back of the dimly lit office. I pull off walking straight to him as he raises a brow. Pulling out my wallet, I throw down around five grand and the pictures of Tavin and me from the charity dinner.

He leans back in his chair. "I'm listening."

"Find out everything you can about this girl." My finger taps the photo. "Her name is Tavin Winters." Grabbing a pen off his desk, I rip off a corner of his calendar to write down the address to Hades. "This is her address. You also need to find out what you can about the guy that lives there. His first name is Toben, and I believe the last name is Michaels." I'm surprised I'm not slurring more than I am, but my adrenaline is pumping full force and I'm nowhere near as drunk as I should be. "Do whatever you have to do. Follow them, whatever, I don't care. I'll double it if you make this a priority."

"Consider it done."

I nod and walk back out into the warm night as I pull out my phone to call a car. She flashed into my life, opened me up to something in myself, and made my heart truly beat for the first time, before yanking it all out beneath me. She made me love, and I wish I could hate her for it. I am done with the lies and secrets. I'm getting my own answers and I'm starting with a visit to a California inmate.

# *Tavin*

His face. His gorgeous face was in so much pain and it's because of me. I'm grateful that I'm still a little high because this would be unbearable otherwise. Why didn't he listen? He did the exact opposite of what I told him. I'm kidding myself. I never really believed the note would keep him from coming. I had just hoped against hope that it would.

I don't even know what happened, exactly, I just know he probably made it a million times worse for me. After all these years, Logan might actually do it this time. He might kill me over this. The thought of Toben getting punished fills me with fear. He has always made us pay for each others mistakes. How did I not think this would come down on him too? Logan likes him more than me and it has saved him on plenty of occasions. Toben had nothing to do with this and he went to every one of his playdates. All I can do is pray that's enough.

I did this. Nobody else. This is my fault. I hurt the only two people on this earth that I have ever loved and who have ever loved me.

*Worthless. Dirty. WHORE.*

The bedroom door swings open and for a heart dropping moment I think he returned. Instead it's a livid Sasha.

"What did you do, Tavin? If your goal was to obliterate any chance you have of being with him and to pulverize his heart while you were at it, you fucking succeeded. I'm having a hard time not hitting you right now, you hurt my brother. Bad." She comes closer with her clenched fists at her side. "Who was it?"

She's the sixth person alive to know my story. It was dangerous for me to tell her. I wasn't thinking clearly because I was trashed at the time. She's kept it to herself and I know it eats at her. I deserve her hate too. I sniff and blow my bangs out of my face.

"It was Logan."

Her shoulders sag and her face falls as her eyes get shiny from held back tears. "Oh, Tavin." Her voice is much softer. "You went back?"

"I told you I had to, but you wouldn't listen! Neither of you listened! You think I have a choice." I pick up my bag and begin to gather my things.

"You do!"

"God! You don't get it." I rip my dress down to show her my logo. "I am his property! He will get me back one way or another. He's made that abundantly clear."

She crosses her arms. "Um, no. Sorry. I've kept my mouth shut because I was under the impression you were eventually going to tell Alex and trust him to figure this out. You are sadly mistaken if you think I'm going to just let you go back into that hell. I'll call Drew over here right now and we'll tie your ass up if that's what it comes to. You're apparently into that weird shit anyway."

God she looks so much like him.

"And then what?"

She sighs, "I don't know okay? Right now the only plan I have is to hide you."

"For how long? What about Toben?"

I take off the carousel necklace and lay it on the dresser next to the cell phone.

She wipes her hands over her face. "We need to talk about this later. If Alex comes back and you're still here, things will not be pretty."

Blind Mag is wagging her tail. He will get rid of her. "Blind Mag. What about her?"

She shakes her head and rubs my arm. "You can't bring the dog, Tavin, I'm sorry."

I will never see her again. I pick her up and kiss her goodbye. "I will miss you. I love you, Blind Mag."

I follow Sasha downstairs to her car and as the house that has been my reprieve and my escape disappears in the rear-view, I can feel the high ebbing away while the pain, filth, and fear creep in.

This is a terrible idea. I'm under no illusion that this will work, but I don't know what else to do. Things are already so bad, and if there is one thing I learned from Logan, it's this:

*It can always get worse.*

# *Candy Coated*
## PLAYLIST

1. *Carousel*—Melanie Martinez
2. *Stars*—The XX
3. *The High*—Kat Dahlia
4. *Drugs & Candy*—All Time Low
5. *Good For You*—Selena Gomez
6. *Candyland*—Love and Theft
7. *Hold Me Down*—Halsey
8. *Big Jet Plane*—Angus & Julia Stone
9. *Perfectly Flawed*—Otep
10. *Like Lovers Do*—Hey Violet
11. *The Hunger in Your Haunt*—Crywolf
12. *Beautiful Tragedy*—In This Moment
13. *I Was Made For Lovin' You*—Tori Kelly ft. Ed Shereen
14. *American Candy*—The Maine
15. *Say Something*—A Great Big World ft. Christina Aguilera
16. *Over*—Tove Lo

# Acknowledgments

To my first fans: Salina Donovan, Terry Rains, Kween Corie, Lori Lewis and Katrina Rains. You guys gave me support from the very beginning, which is worth more than you will ever know. Thank you so much for not only being my friends, but for being the first people who believed in me and helped me in achieving my goals.

To my wonderful beta readers: Elaine Kelly, Danielle Krushel, Lia Covington from Lia's Bookish Obsession, Samantha Armstrong, Ali Knight, Samantha Page, and Kim Walker. The brutal honesty and feedback you gave, made this book better than I ever could have done on my own. It wouldn't be what it is now without you. Thank you for taking the time to support me in my debut.

To my fantastic P. A., Elaine Kelly: Thank you so much for everything that you do. I'm so glad you took a chance on me and I appreciate all of your support and help. You are so important to me and my books and I love how you always have my back.

To my editor, Joanne LaRe Thompson: You have been absolutely fabulous. Not only has it been a pleasure to work with you, but you have helped me make some important connections and meet some invaluable people. Thank you for everything you have done for me and this book.

# ABOUT THE
## *Author*

*As an independent author, your ratings and especially reviews mean more than you realize. If you enjoyed the book, please consider lending your support by leaving your thoughts in a review.*

Charity B. lives in Salem Oregon with her husband and ornery little boy. *Candy Coated Chaos* is her debut novel and has more titles preparing for release in 2018. She has always loved to read and write, but began her love affair with dark romance when she read C.J. Robert's *The Dark Duet*. She has a passion for the dark and taboo and wants nothing more than to give her readers the ultimate book hangover. In her spare time when she's not chasing her son, she enjoys reading, the occasional TV show binge, and is deeply inspired by music and photography.

For news on upcoming releases go to charitybauthor.com

69748178R00202

Made in the USA
San Bernardino, CA
21 February 2018